A PLUME BOOK

WRITTEN ON MY HEART

MORGAN CALLAN ROGERS lived along the banks of the mighty Kennebec River in Bath, Maine, for all of the years of her childhood. With the exception of five years spent in beautiful western South Dakota, bodies of water have always been her compass. She began writing fiction when she was eight, sitting at an old camp table on a screened-in porch in a cottage located near the New Meadows River in West Bath, Maine. She has traveled many paths during her lifetime as an editor, journalist, librarian, actress, grocery clerk, secretary, teacher, and singer. Writing has been the thread running through it all. She has published several short stories and countless articles for regional newspapers and magazines. Morgan holds an MFA from the University of Southern Maine's Stonecoast Creative Writing program. She is the author of the international bestseller *Red Ruby Heart in a Cold Blue Sea*, published by Viking in 2012. She lives in Portland, Maine, with her cat, Petula Mae.

Praise for *Red Ruby Heart in a Cold Blue Sea*

"Rendered first-person in confiding, colloquial prose. . . . [Like] the bittersweet coming-of-age movies (see: *Stand by Me*, *The Last Picture Show*) that don't get made much anymore." —*Entertainment Weekly*

"Deeply moving. . . . Callan Rogers writes with a superb sense of place and period, delving deftly into true-to-life responses to unexplained loss. . . . A realistic and resonant coming-of-age novel." —*Kirkus Reviews*

"Callan Rogers's astonishing debut brilliantly illuminates deep loss, impossible longing, and our yearning to hold on to love no matter what, all told in the lake-clear voice of one remarkable young heroine. So rapturously moving, page."

"Rich in landscape and character, with regional dialect and phrases that will tip many mouths into grins."　　　　　　　　*—Booklist*

"Refreshing. . . . A piercingly knowing portrait of the complicated thoughts and actions of a maturing teenage girl. . . . With a one-of-a-kind setting and dialect straight from the shore."　　*—Portland Monthly*

"Incredibly detailed, rich, and real. . . . You will find yourself drawn into this book quickly and fiercely."　　　　　　*—The Maine Edge*

"The young, prickly, and thoroughly endearing narrator of *Red Ruby Heart in a Cold Blue Sea* got to me in a big way. I loved spending time with Florine, and I'm still thinking about her. She will break your heart and make you glad she did."
　　　　　　—Monica Wood, author of *Any Bitter Thing*

"At once very personal and very broad in theme and atmosphere, *Red Ruby Heart* is a lovely novel, long on heart. Morgan Callan Rogers has a confident, almost playful prose style, and she bears down on this story from the first paragraph, never faltering in her mission to convey her characters and their painful paths with honesty, compassion, and humor."　　　　　　—Susanna Daniel, author of *Stiltsville*

"*Red Ruby Heart in a Cold Blue Sea* spun me deep inside its feisty, honest heroine, Florine. A classic story of paradise lost, this is a beautiful and wise coming-of-age story set on the Maine coast, where grief—harsh as the granite shoreline—is suffered, solaced, and survived. I love this book, with its fresh-baked bread, stars and waves, wind-worn houses, mysteries and truths. A wonderful first novel."
　　　　　　—Beth Powning, author of *The Sea Captain's Wife*

"A heartwarming 'coming-of-age-story' set in what is arguably the continent's most beautiful location."　　　　*—Hudson Valley News*

"Readers who enjoy coming-of-age tales and small-town stories will appreciate this well-crafted debut novel that tugs at the heart without falling into sentimentality."　　　　　　　*—Library Journal*

Also by Morgan Callan Rogers

Red Ruby Heart in a Cold Blue Sea

Written on My Heart

A NOVEL

Morgan Callan Rogers

A PLUME BOOK

PLUME

An imprint of Penguin Random House LLC
375 Hudson Street
New York, New York 10014
penguin.com

 REGISTERED TRADEMARK—MARCA REGISTRADA

LIBRARY OF CONGRESS CATALOGING-IN-PUBLICATION DATA

Rogers, Morgan Callan.
   Written on my heart : a novel / Morgan Callan Rogers.—First edition.
     pages ; cm
   ISBN 978-0-14-751704-3 (softcover)—ISBN 978-0-698-19861-6 (ebook)   1. Newlyweds—
Fiction.   2. Mothers and daughters—Fiction.   3. Missing persons—Investigation—
Fiction.   4. Domestic fiction.   I. Title.
   PS3618.O4656W75 2016
   813'.6—dc23   2015036700

Printed in the United States of America
10 9 8 7 6 5 4 3 2 1

Set in Granjon LT Std
Designed by Eve L. Kirch

For Beth, Joe, and Alessandro.

Love is all that matters.

1

The night before my wedding, my best friend, Dottie Butts, and I sat on my side lawn staring up at the sky. The soft blue of twilight mingled with the dark. All was quiet, save for the sound of Dottie sucking down Narragansett beer from a sixteen-ounce can. Beer and I had never gotten along, so I wasn't drinking. Besides, I was pregnant. The next morning, Saturday, June 12, 1971, I would get up, dress in a wedding gown once worn by my grandmother, and walk the short length of this very lawn to meet my husband-to-be, Bud Warner, the love of my life and the father of the baby soon to be born. Bud and I were both twenty years old.

Dottie said, "Not many people have a baby shower the night before they get married. You made out pretty good."

Until just a few hours earlier, the inside of my house had been strewn from hither to yon with baby presents and wrapping paper and ribbon. For almost nine months, I had been collecting what I would need for a girl baby, because I had a strong feeling that she would be a girl and I was going on faith. But the night's haul had given me enough for three babies of either sex. We were set, no matter what.

"Thanks for getting everyone together and doing that," I said.

"Just doing my maid-of-honor duty," Dottie said. "Ma's been keeping me straight on all the things I'm supposed to do. Don't come natural to me, being a maid of honor. Not much maid to be had in me."

"You're doing fine," I said. "No reason why you wouldn't. Besides, you're my best friend. Matter of fact, you're my only friend."

"You need to get out more, then."

"I won't be socializing much in a couple of weeks."

"Guess not," Dottie said. "You know, I got to thinking. Last time I wore a dress was in high school. Hasn't come up all through college. Can't say as I've missed it."

"You said you liked the dress," I said. "Your exact words in the store were that you thought it was 'some pretty.' You look nice in it." Suddenly, a lazy movement inside of me touched my heart and brought tears to my eyes. I said to Dottie, "Don't you want to be my maid of honor? You didn't have to say yes."

Dottie set her beer can on the lawn and sat up on the edge of the chair. "Florine Gilham, you crying?" she said. "Really? You crying?"

"No." I sniffed.

"Oh, for heaven's sake, of course I wanted to do this," she said. "Thick and thin. That's you and me. I'm thick and you're thin. You're the only person can get me to put the dress on, so cut it out."

"You think it's pretty, right? Because it is pretty."

"It's the prettiest dress ever made, anywhere, in the history of dresses," Dottie said. "It ain't its fault I don't wear dresses. Don't get so worked up."

We went back to studying the sky.

Darkness had settled in as we'd been talking, but millions of stars had leaked through it. Three of them contained the souls of my parents and of my grandmother, Grand. One twinkling star contained the spirit of my joyful, lively mother, Carlie, who had vanished when I was twelve. I didn't know if she was dead or alive, but placing her in the sky with Daddy and Grand made sense to me, as she was as gone to me as they were. Daddy's star was one of the larger ones, because he had been a big man with a stubborn heart, set in his ways. Grand's star radiated rays of light. A practical woman, her faith in those on Earth and in heaven had been unshakeable. How I missed those three dear souls.

"They see you," Dottie said. How she knew what I was thinking was beyond me, but her ability to do that bound her to me. She and I, born one day apart, were more like sisters than friends. Thick and thin, she'd said. She was right.

My eyes filled again. "I don't want to cry," I said. "It's the baby making me do it."

Dottie laughed. "Mean baby."

I said, "I just wish so much they were here for everything."

"Well, you and that baby got them inside of you. 'Course, it ain't the same as having 'em here, I know that, but it'll have to do."

I smiled. "You sound like Grand," I said.

"Could do worse," Dottie said. She hoisted herself out of the chair and reached for my hands. "I got to get my beauty sleep," she said. I grabbed onto her and she groaned as she pulled me up.

"I'm not that big," I grumbled.

"Oh, yes, you are." Dottie laughed. "That baby is going to weigh more than my bowling ball. That's a good twenty pounds, right there."

"Oh, stop," I said, "most of it is water weight."

"Water weight, my ass," she said.

"Give me the beer can," I said, "I'll toss it out for you. Don't want the path to Pastor Billy strewn with empties instead of rose petals."

"Guess not." We stood there for a minute. My marriage would mark a distance between us. We would always be best friends, but my relationships with Bud and the baby would bump her a couple of notches in my heart. Dottie and I had been through everything together. But our paths, while still joined in friendship, would branch off to include other people and places. I wanted to say, *How could I have gotten through the last few years without you? Do you know how much you mean to me?* But that wasn't like us, so instead I said, "Well, thanks. See you tomorrow."

Dottie waved good night as she turned to go. "Don't thank me yet," she said. "We got to get you two married, first."

"That's going to happen. Come hell or high water," I called as she walked off into the dark. I listened to the steadiness in her footsteps as she covered the short distance down the hill to her parents' house. The screen door squealed open, and then shut with a bang. Someone in the house spoke to her and she answered, but I couldn't hear the conversation.

My ears pitched themselves toward the sounds in the harbor. The water exhaled in a continuous sigh as it traveled out with the tide. Small waves shushed themselves against the rocky beach. I closed my eyes and let the sounds come into me before I looked up at the stars again. "You hear me?" I said to the three that were listening. "Come hell or high water, tomorrow, I'm marrying Bud. Put a good word in for us."

When I looked down, I got dizzy. I pulled on the handle of the screen door that opened into the hallway of what had once been Grand's house. It was mine, now—mine and Bud's, and soon, our baby's house too.

The women and girls who had attended the baby shower had cleaned and stacked everything so that I wouldn't have to deal with any of that. It made me grateful for the way we took care of one another. I hauled myself up the stairs to the bathroom and had a long pee.

Afterward, I looked at my face in the mirror over the sink. Usually, my features were sharp, all bones and shade, but my weight gain from carrying the baby had filled in the angles. I looked young and soft, something I'd never thought about myself. I smiled, and the tired, violet half-moons under my hazel eyes disappeared. A pinpoint of light glowed in the center of my pupils.

"Mrs. James Walter Warner," I whispered. "Mrs. Bud Warner. Florine Warner."

As if he had heard me, Bud walked through the front door and whistled his way up the stairs.

I met him in the hall and blocked him so that he had to pause on the top riser. We stood face-to-face. The residue of beer and cigarettes from his bachelor party clung to his clothing. His eyes shone from the booze. A crooked smile inched up the right side of his face and he gave me a slow wink.

"Hey," he whispered.

"Hey," I whispered back.

Bud put his hands on my belly, leaned forward, and gave me a soft kiss. Then he said, "Back up so's I can get to the bathroom. 'Gansett's gone right through me."

I stepped back to let him pass and I went into the bedroom. I pulled the two window shades down against the night crowding in. I almost split myself apart with a belly-deep yawn and suddenly I was so tired I couldn't move my arms to take off my clothes.

Bud came into the bedroom.

"Will you undress me?" I said.

Bud grinned. "That's my girl," he said.

He used his gentle, warm hands to tug and pull, unfasten and unhook, as I stood there, drunk with exhaustion and with the way he was touching me. Soon, I was naked but for my panties, which rested in a soft cotton puddle on top of my feet.

Bud stepped back and took me in, top to bottom.

"What?" I said.

"Just checking out my work," he said. He stripped down and I got to admire his thin body. When he saw me taking him in, he shyly looked at the floor. "So much for not seeing the bride the night before her wedding," he mumbled, trying to turn my attention somewhere else. He thought he was too skinny.

"I like it this way," I whispered. I took his hands in mine and we looked into each other's eyes. A rare blush of tenderness wrapped itself around us. No jokes, no rushing to bed, no wisecracks. Bud raised a hand and ran it down my full-moon face. "I love you, Florine," he said. "Whatever happens, I love you."

"I love you too. We're in this, together."

As far as I was concerned, that was our wedding ceremony. The next day would bring the formal vows with everyone cheering us on, particularly my soon-to-be mother-in-law, Ida, who was overjoyed that Bud and I were going legal. But in that moment, I had heard everything I needed to know.

Bud slipped into bed and I slid in after him. He spooned me and, like that, he fell asleep. The tickle of his breath against my neck was as comforting as a cat's purr, but as was so often the case these days, I went from sleepy to awake.

I made the best of the hour I was up by thinking about Bud and me and how we had arrived at this place in our lives. I had loved him before I had even known what that meant. I had grown up on the hill above his place.

Four houses stood on The Point, houses built on slabs of granite by generations of fishermen almost as tough as that rock. Grand's house had been the first one built. Daddy's house stood across the road from it. Dottie's house set across the road and below Grand's house, halfway down the hill. Bud's house hunkered down on a wide level ledge directly above the wharf and beach.

The Point was one of several fingers of rocky land carved by glaciers and the ceaseless pounding of the North Atlantic. Little harbors, such as the one in The Point, held boats relatively safe from most of the action. Independent types who loved the sea had settled this place. They could have lived in the town of Long Reach, about ten miles up the coast. Life might have been easier that way. But something in their natures chose the elements, and the freedom and challenge of hard work. Daddy, Dottie's father, Bud's father, and their ancestors had driven the prows of those boats into the roughshod sea day after day. If nothing else, we were resilient.

Bud was about six months older than Dottie and me. He lived through part of a fall and a whole winter before I barged onto the scene. "As soon as you could run," his mother, Ida, had told me a short time before the baby shower, "your little legs carried you down the road to our house. You used to play in the driveway with Bud until one of you made the other one mad, and then we would walk you back up the hill."

"Did I just run loose? Where was Carlie?" I asked Ida. I called my mother Carlie because she had wanted to be called by her first name. "Mama sounds weird to me," she told me when I asked. I didn't care what she wanted to be called. I knew who she was to me.

"Your mother was right with you," Ida said. "You think she'd let you run down the road alone?"

"I don't remember," I said. Carlie had taken with her any stories she might have told me. "But I remember playing with Bud."

Something about him, even then, made me feel strong and protected. He was a calm little boy who had grown into a quiet and easygoing man, unless something really riled him up.

He was the leader of the four of us. Besides Dottie, Bud, and me, our little gang included Glen Clemmons, who was also our age. Glen's father, Ray, ran the general store, close to the road that led to Long Reach. When we got together as a foursome, each of us contributed to whatever mischief we might decide to get into. Glen had the bad ideas, Dottie complained but went along, I thought Glen's ideas were fun, and Bud was the voice of reason that no one ever listened to until it was too late.

I might not have tuned in on his advice, but I heard his heart in my heart, always. His presence took root in me. I looked for him, even when we were with other people. Four years after Carlie went missing, I lost Grand to a stroke. My life took a header even as Glen, Dottie, and Bud found ways to get along in the world. Bud hooked up with a pretty, popular girl named Susan. I quit high school and took up with Andy Barrington, the son of rich summer people. At seventeen, I gave my virginity to him and learned how to smoke pot. I also almost died when Andy and I got into a bad car accident.

Bud's was a welcome presence as I healed. Armed at this point with a real understanding of how short life could be and how fast things could change, I fought for his love, and his own restless heart chose mine.

When I was eighteen, my father died of a heart attack on his lobster boat, the *Florine*, on a beautiful July day. Bud moved in with me a few days after his funeral. He took a job as a mechanic at Fred's garage, up on the road to Long Reach. He wasn't a great cook and he left his dirty clothes on the bedroom floor, but he saved my sanity. He held me close when the dark tried to slink into my soul through the cracks in my heart, and he brought me back into the land of the living.

We lived together for a year. We loved sex, so we shouldn't have been surprised when we made a baby in the early fall of 1970. When I told him, Bud blinked a few times, shrugged, and said, "Well, we'll manage."

We were both only nineteen at the time, but we were made of sturdy stock. It helped that Grand's house was paid for. Bud and I managed to take care of the taxes and, so far, the day-to-monthly bills, but a new baby would up our spending in a big way. To help with finances, I struck a deal with Ray at the general store and he started to carry more of the bread that I baked from Grand's recipes. Ray also took orders for my knitting and crocheting, and for Christmas wreaths. Only a few years back, I'd considered all of this a chore. Grand had been determined to make me useful, and I had found it a pain in the butt. But after her death, I began to appreciate what she had taken the time to teach me. Doing these things reminded me of her. I came to love creating something warm, beautiful, and lasting, or something that tasted of comfort, or helping The Point women put together wreaths for the annual Christmas season craft fairs.

As the baby claimed its space inside of me, I thought about whether Bud would ask me to marry him. As long as I had loved him, I had dreamed of being married to him, but after all that had happened, it was enough just to have him with me. I was content with that. But in May, maybe at the urging of his mother, who said nothing with her mouth but everything with her eyes, he had asked me to marry him one night at suppertime.

"Wondering," he'd said, as I was easing a forkful of peas over my big belly.

"What?" I said.

"Want to get married before the baby comes?"

Several peas jumped ship and tumbled down the slope of my stomach.

Bud scraped his chair back and walked around the table to me. He knelt down beside me and folded my left hand between his own hands. "Florine Gilham," he said, his dark eyes just as dead serious as I'd ever seen them, "you're a keeper. I can't think about my life without you. Will you marry me?"

Could he feel the pulse of the hand cradled between his own? My heartbeat picked up so, the baby turned over. "Of course I will," I said.

We kissed for a little while and then he broke it off. "Don't have a ring," he said.

"Wait," I said. Bud hoisted me to a standing position and I waddled upstairs to our bedroom.

I headed to the bureau, to Grand's wooden jewelry box. Her husband, Franklin, my grandfather, had made it for her and carved her name, Florence, into the top. The hinges creaked as I lifted it up and looked inside. Grand never had much use for frippery, as she called it, but a few choice things were tucked inside. I plucked her diamond ring out of its velvet holder, pushed it over my swollen finger to see if it fit, took it off, and then squeezed it tight in the palm of my hand. Once downstairs, I handed it to Bud and he slipped it back onto my finger. Then Bud went back around the table to finish his supper.

In less than twenty-four hours, we would be married.

My husband-to-be turned over in bed and faced the wall, wriggling his back and butt toward me so that we touched. With the effort a whale must make to breach so it can breathe, I shifted my bulk so I was on my back. I draped my right arm over his hip and drifted off to sleep.

2

Our wedding day started with a visit from my late father's girl-friend, Stella Drowns. No one locked their doors on The Point. She barely knocked before she charged in, hollering, "Yoo-hoo!"

Bud shot straight up in bed. "You fucking hoo?" he said to me. "Is she for real?"

"We're in bed, Stella," I yelled at the top of my lungs. "Come back later."

"Oh, I'm sorry," she called from the bottom of the stairs. "I'm just so excited about today. I brought you a coffee cake. Figured you could use the sugar and the energy."

"Could have used the sleep too," Bud shouted.

"Hope you're not that cranky all day," Stella hollered. "Happy wedding day!" She slammed the front door on her way out.

"What did Leeman ever see in her?" Bud said. "She's out of her mind."

"Coffee cake," I said. "He liked her, um, cake."

Bud rubbed his hands over his face. "You want cake and tea?"

"That's a great idea."

He climbed over me and stood naked in the early morning light. He scratched his butt and went across the hall to the bathroom. The baby did the twist in my belly. I put my hand on her to calm her down, but she kept it up, as if the prospect of coffee cake for breakfast and a wedding for lunch excited her as much as it did me.

The front door downstairs opened just as Bud flushed the toilet. I tried to catch him before he headed downstairs, but I was too late.

"Jesus, Mary, and Joseph," he yelled.

"That your wedding suit?" I heard Dottie say.

"If people don't stop barging in, it might be," Bud said.

"Where you going to put the rings?"

"Glen's supposed to have them."

"I say, wear what you got on, then. Supposed to be hot this afternoon."

"Come on up, Dottie," I called.

"Why? The entertainment is down here," she said.

"Wait here," Bud said to Dottie, and he took every other stair to the bedroom. His face was scarlet. "We're going to start locking the damn door," he said. "Right after Dottie leaves."

I grinned. "What's done is done. Now she knows why I'm marrying you."

Bud pulled on a pair of jeans and hauled a white, holey T-shirt over his head. He was still sputtering when he left the bedroom and bounded down the stairs. "That coffee cake is for us," I heard him growl at Dottie, who was more than familiar with our kitchen and could smell a baked good from miles away.

"Just testing it out," she answered him. "I approve. Here, I cut a piece for you."

"Going down to the folks' house," Bud called up to me. "See you at the wedding," and he was gone. I hauled myself and the baby out of bed, shuffled to the window, and pulled up the shade. Dust motes sifted through shafts of sunlight.

"Coming up," Dottie said from the bottom of the stairs.

"Bring me some coffee cake and some tea. With milk," I said.

"Hope you're not going to be this bossy all day," she grumbled.

"Not promising anything," I said. I waddled over to the rocking chair and grabbed an old green sweatshirt hanging off the back of it. It had been my father's once, and he had been a big man. I plunked down on the rocker and tugged my pregnant-lady shorts to just underneath my breasts.

By the time Dottie got upstairs, I was standing in front of the mirror, looking at the blond, red, and brown frizzled curly mop I called hair.

"What the hell am I going to do with this?" I asked her.

She set my tea and a plate mounded with Stella's coffee cake on the bureau. She stood alongside me at the mirror and ran her hands through her brown pixie cut. "Cut if off," she said. "That'll take care of that problem."

"It's a serious question," I said. "What do you think I should do? Up? Down?"

"You're asking the wrong person. Evie knows about that shit. She'll fix you up."

Evie was Dottie's younger sister. At fourteen, she was a handful. "Evie wants what she wants when she wants it," Dottie had said more than once, "and the only time she doesn't want for something, she's asleep." What mattered about Evie that day was that she would have good ideas. I changed the subject.

"Stella dropped by with the cake and woke up Bud. He wasn't awful pleased."

"She probably just wants to be part of the wedding," Dottie said.

I sighed. "Oh, I know," I said. "But I don't want her fussing around while I get ready. She'll get weepy about Daddy not being here, and then I'll get weepier than I already am, and I don't need that today."

"I guess not," Dottie said. "Anyways, Evie'll be over soon, with Madeline. You don't want to see either of them before they have their coffee."

Madeline was Dottie's mother. For money, she worked at the post office up the road. For joy, she painted seashore and ocean scenes in watercolor. Some of them brightened the walls of our house. Once in a while, she'd sell a painting to a tourist Ray sent down to the house. I loved Madeline. Every time I'd gone to Dottie's house—and I'd gone there thousands of times—she acted as if I were a long-lost friend who'd just come back from somewhere far away. On my wedding day, she was going to pick flowers from Grand's side garden to decorate the food and drink tables, and then fashion a bouquet out of peonies and beach roses for me to carry.

"I'm so lucky to have you all," I said to Dottie. "Hey, leave me at least a piece of that cake, please."

"It's all yours," she said, grabbing a last nibble.

I slipped the remaining piece of coffee cake into my mouth and took a sip of hot tea that coated my tongue with melted, brown sugar–crumb topping. "Mmmmm," I said. Stella really could cook. She had reeled Daddy in by bringing him a coffee cake and making him a couple of dinners. She drove me crazy, but sometimes she touched my heart and on this day, I loved everyone.

Dottie and I puttered around for a couple of hours, making sure the house was to rights and then suddenly, it was ten o'clock, only three hours away from the wedding. I rushed upstairs for a bath. When Madeline and Evie showed up, I was standing in the bedroom combing the tangles out of my wet hair. Right away, Evie took over.

"Let me do that," she said. "Wait. Let's sit you down first. No, not the rocking chair—I need to work on your hair from the back and sides. *Dottie!*" she hollered downstairs. "Bring up a kitchen chair." I braced myself against the possibility that Dottie would holler back that Evie could just fetch it herself or else go to hell, but to my surprise, she carried a chair upstairs and set it in front of the mirror, exactly where her sister told her to put it.

"Anything else, Your Highness?" Dottie said.

"Nope," Evie said. "Go away."

"I'm the maid of honor. I got rank over you." Dottie set her solid self down on the mattress and settled in to watch over me as only a best friend can.

I said, "I got rank over both of you. Dottie can stay."

Evie shrugged. "Well, whoever stays, you got to take off that sweatshirt first. It'll mess up your hair and we're only fixing it once."

I whipped off the shirt and we all admired my swollen boobs and bloated belly, along with the strange line of reddish-brown hair that had sprouted down the center of my stomach during my pregnancy. Dottie took my fancy lacy bra from the wedding-wear hanger and hooked the back for me while Evie scared up some towels from the bathroom. I sat down, and she began wrestling with my hair. I closed my eyes while she worked. I loved the light feel of her quick hands as she gently pulled, brushed, braided, and twisted my hair into shape. She hummed some tune I didn't recognize in her husky voice as she worked.

Down in the side yard, I heard Bert Butts, Dottie's father, working with Glen as they set up tables and chairs in the backyard. Madeline's voice entered the mix, along with the clatter of Grand's silverware, plates, glasses, and cups. I'd suggested paper plates and cups to her, but she said, "We can break out the good stuff for this day, Florine. Your wedding day is worth it."

After a while Dottie got restless and wandered downstairs and outside into the side yard to "see if there was something I can do."

I half dozed in the chair. I jumped when Evie said, "There."

"You done?" I said, opening my eyes. She stood in front of me and I looked up and into her beautiful blue eyes. A forest of dark lashes surrounded them.

"Looks good," she said. "But you're not going to peek until we make you up."

"I don't know as I need much," I said, and Evie rolled her eyes.

"Let's bury the freckles," she said.

"I like my freckles."

"Just for the day," Evie said. She tilted her head and studied my face. "Humph," she said, and reached for a bag filled with enough makeup to beautify the seven women living on The Point for a year.

She smiled at me. "You got bones to die for," she said. "Let's bring them out."

"Aren't they okay where they are?"

She rolled her eyes again. "Blush," she said. "We're putting blush on them. You should take this seriously. I'm good."

"If you say so," I said.

She grinned. "I do," she said. Her curly black hair framed her pale, heart-shaped face. Her nails were pearly pink and her mouth, made for kissing, matched the color of her nails.

"She knows she's pretty," Dottie had said to me, more than once. "Well, she may have the looks, but I got the brains and the personality." Sometimes, I wondered if Dottie might be a little jealous of Evie, but I never brought that up. Evie was the pretty one, but Dottie had my heart.

Finally, Evie was done, and just as the sun hit the far wall of my bedroom I stood up and stared at an unfamiliar creature who looked back at me.

My hair was a mass of sprayed-stiff, strawberry-blond whipped cream, winding in and out of its own coils as if playing hide-and-seek. The freckles on my face had been blotted out by a blizzard of powder and blush. My startled greenish eyes peered out at me from behind shutters of thick, brown mascara. My long mouth sparkled with a smear of glitter slashed across the top of a spicy pink-brown lipstick.

"Well, what do you think?" Evie said.

"I'm afraid if I talk, my face will break."

Evie frowned.

"Just give me a few seconds," I said. "I have to get used to it. I think I look pretty, but I don't really know what that means yet."

"You look beautiful. You are anyway. I just brought it out," Evie said.

Someone walked through the house and stood at the bottom of the stairs. "Can I come up?" Maureen called in her sweet voice. My heart smiled. I loved Bud's younger sister.

"Maureen, come check out Florine!" Evie yelled, and Maureen rushed up the stairs and stopped in the doorway of the bedroom. Her light-brown eyes widened and her mouth formed a perfect O.

"What do you think?" Evie asked.

"Florine!" Maureen said. "You look so pretty. Wow!"

Maureen was thirteen, a year younger than Evie. Whereas Evie looked like a grown woman, Maureen was a gangly work in progress. Straight light-brown hair flipped and flopped over her shoulders and down her back. Her legs and arms were a tangle of knobby joints and long, thin bones. Her eyes took up most of her face, her nose was long and narrow, and she had yet to grow into her mouth.

She and Evie were not friends like Dottie and me. They liked each other, but they didn't have much in common. Maureen, like her mother, loved all things that had to do with church, while Evie tended in the opposite direction. Evie was a force, while Maureen radiated light from someplace inside herself.

"I don't know where she came from," Bud said about his sister once, after I had commented about her "glow." "The rest of us are gloomy as hell."

"Ma said to give you this," Maureen said to me. She held out a clothing-size box wrapped in silver paper and tied with a white ribbon.

I took the box from her and placed it on the bed. "Thanks," I said.

"No, you have to open it now," Maureen said. "It goes with your wedding gown."

"Maureen, you do it," Evie said. "Florine might chip a nail."

Maureen looked at me for further instructions.

"Go ahead," I said. She tore the ribbon and wrapping paper off the box. Before she lifted the lid, she said, "Ready?" I nodded and she lifted the top and parted the crinkly white tissue paper. I caught glimpses of silk material before she gently raised the garment from its resting place.

"Oh my god," I said, and gasped.

Ida, who made beautiful quilts, had already performed a miracle by taking Grand's old wedding gown and stitching in a lace and flowered panel that gave the baby room and made me feel almost pretty. But this new thing was beyond beautiful to me, and yes, precious. The patchwork petticoat was totally made from bits and scraps of my parents' clothes.

"Don't cry!" Evie shouted. "Your mascara will run."

But cry I did. "Who made this?" I said.

"Ma," Maureen said. "She said it would give you something old, borrowed, blue, and new, all at once."

"Oh my god," I said again, and my trembling hands reached for the thing she was holding. "It's precious. Just precious."

"Bud snuck Ma into the house while you and Dottie were shopping for Dottie's dress," Maureen said. "She went through the storage boxes you have. Stella gave her some of your father's things."

I saw bits of Daddy's hankies and parts from one of his summer shirts quilted throughout the petticoat. I fingered each star-shaped patch, which were the colors of summer and memories.

"It's beautiful." I sniffed. "Oh, Ida."

Maureen said in a quiet voice, "So, you like it?"

"She's ruined her face." Evie sighed. "I'd say she does."

"See the blue patch toward the bottom?" Maureen said. "Ma sewed your names and the date in it. See? It says, *Florine and Bud, June 12, 1971.*"

"I wish she was here so I could hug her. Where is she?" I asked.

Maureen laughed. "She's got Bud and Dad to deal with," she said.

"They're a handful, I guess," I said. "How's Sam this morning?"

"He's okay," Maureen said. "He's ready." Bud's father was a lifelong alcoholic, and near the last stages of cirrhosis of the liver. But that hadn't stopped him from drinking.

I wondered how sober Sam was that morning. He was standing in for my father, and I hoped he would be able to walk me down the aisle.

"We have to fix your makeup," Evie said. "Thanks for nothing, Maureen."

Maureen ignored her. "Bye," she said. She hugged me and clattered down the stairs, meeting Dottie on her way up.

"Jesus, what did you do to her?" she asked as she sashayed into the room. I shot her such a look she said, "You look nice, Florine," and shut up.

After Evie repaired the damage, we got ready. Dottie hauled the blue dress over her head, and then helped me step into the beautiful petticoat, which swished against my bare legs. She called Madeline upstairs to help lower the tent of a wedding dress over my hair and face without touching either of them. As a last touch, Madeline perched a circlet of daisies and clover on my hair. The three Butts women stood back and checked me over.

"Probably the best you'll ever look," Evie said to me. "Do not cry. I mean it."

Madeline's smile wobbled as she said, "You take my breath away, Florine."

Dottie pursed her lips and said, "You'll do," and then she walked over to the window and looked down onto the side yard.

White lace swirled around me as I turned toward the mirror, but I didn't see me in the reflection. Instead, I saw someone who looked much like her grandmother must have looked at twenty. Carlie had blessed me with ginger highlights in my hair and in the freckles on my face, and Daddy had blessed me with his height, but it was Grand who showed up in the mirror. She was right there with me. I heard her say, *Heaven's sake, you didn't turn out so bad. Now, you go get yourself married to Buddy so's you can have that baby.*

"I will," I whispered, my eyes shiny.

"Well?" Evie said. I looked at her and nodded.

"You did good, Evie," I said. "Thank you."

"You're welcome," she said.

We got ourselves downstairs and Madeline handed Dottie and me our bouquets, and then she and Evie joined the small crowd on the lawn. Dottie and I went out the kitchen door, away from the onlookers, to join Sam, who stood waiting for us. I kissed him on the cheek, trying not to be shocked at the yellow tint of his skin and by the fact that his eyeballs were yellow too.

"Christ almighty, you look just like Florence did," he said, seeing Grand, just as I had seen her. "Don't she look like her grandmother?" he asked Dottie.

"I guess," Dottie said, too busy tugging on her dress to pay much attention to me.

I buried my nose in one of the giant peonies in my bouquet. The smell of June filled my heart as the warm sun spun melted honey over my head. A seagull laughed and I turned my head to see the water in the harbor winking diamonds at me.

Someone on the lawn lowered a needle onto my old record player. The first notes of "Here Comes the Bride" sounded, and I hooked my arm through Sam's. He kissed my cheek. "Glad to have you aboard," he said. "You and Bud be good to each other, now, you hear me?" I nodded. Whiskey perfumed his breath, but we held each other steady as we began our march toward Bud and Pastor Billy Krum.

Since we were holding the wedding on the lawn, I had decided to go barefoot, and the grass was smooth and cool beneath my feet. The baby rolled over just as my eyes lighted on Bud, and I smiled. He answered my smile with one of his own as he told me he loved me with his eyes. As Sam and I closed in on him and Pastor Billy, I saw that he was shaking.

I may have been walking past people who had known Bud and me our whole lives, but that didn't calm my nerves. The lawn seemed twice as long as it was, but finally, Bud and I stood face-to-face in front of the dusty pink fireworks display of peonies in bloom. I handed Dottie my bouquet, careful not to meet her brown eyes, as I was afraid I might cry or burst out laughing for nervousness.

Bud's dark eyes danced with tears. "You look beautiful," he whispered.

"It's okay," Pastor Billy murmured, "it'll be over in a minute." His blue eyes twinkled and he winked. "Dearly beloved," he began in his deep pastor voice. When asked, Sam gave his permission for me to marry his son, and then he walked over to where Ida waited for him.

Pastor Billy heard our vows to love, honor, and cherish each other until death did us part. Glen fished two gold rings out of the pocket of a gray suit that fit like he'd probably borrowed it from someone. Bud's trembling hand shoved the smaller ring over the knuckle of my swollen left ring finger. I did the same for him with the bigger ring. We kissed soon after that, a dry kiss that sealed our vows, and we were pronounced man and wife. We turned to face our families and friends.

"May I present Mr. and Mrs. James Warner," Pastor Billy announced, and everyone clapped and whistled. "Now, let's party," Billy added, and everyone clapped and whistled some more.

The reception was held about two yards from our wedding. Everyone grabbed something to eat or drink, and the party commenced.

Dottie's father came over and hugged me. He grinned and said, "So, when you two thinking about having kids?" I smacked him and he grinned and guzzled some beer. Stella, who had followed him over, grabbed both of my arms and said, "Oh, honey, you look so pretty. Your father would have loved to be here, and I'm sure Leeman wouldn't have minded that you're so far along."

She didn't let me go right away. As always, I couldn't help but stare at the scar that ran most of the length of her right cheek, the result of a car accident when she had been a teenager. She squeezed my arms and I locked onto her gray eyes. "We miss him, don't we?" she said. Gin tickled my nostrils. Since my father's death almost two years earlier, Stella had gone on several drunken benders. I nodded a little before pulling away from her as gently as I could. I missed my father like crazy, but it was my wedding day.

Dottie did her maid-of-honor duty and stepped between us. "Now, Stella," she said, "don't insult the pregnant bride on her wedding day. Let's go toast all the virgins we know. I'm thinking it will be a half a shot-glass-full, at least." She threw her right arm over Stella's thin shoulder and walked her over to a makeshift bar set up on a folding table in front of a couple of sturdy forsythia bushes.

"Hello, daughter-in-law," Ida said from behind me.

"Oh, Ida!" I cried as I spun around. "The petticoat. The petticoat is . . . it's . . ."

Evie sauntered by. "Don't cry," she muttered.

Ida smiled. "I'm glad you like it," she said. "You look absolutely lovely. It's time for your first dance. Are you feeling up to it?"

I nodded. "Might as well get it over with." Neither Bud nor I was a dancer in private, let alone in public. We'd practiced a few times, but the size of my belly, and our own clumsiness and giggle fits, had blocked our progress.

Maureen ran up to Ida and me. "All set," she said. "You nod, and I'll put on the record for you."

"Thanks," I said, feeling a rush of goofy love for all of Bud's family. Maureen tried to wrap me in a hug. When the baby kicked between us, she jumped back. "Whoa!" she said.

"Saying hi, Aunt Maureen," I said. Maureen dashed over to the record player.

My eyes swept the side lawn for my husband and found him downing beer with Glen over by the beach-rose bushes. I nodded his way and he joined us.

"Ready?" I asked him.

"Ready or not," he said.

We both jumped when Maureen shouted, "And now, the bride and groom are going to dance their first dance."

Bud blushed, the twenty-odd people in the yard clapped, and Maureen set the needle on the old 45 rpm record. It scratched and popped its way onto "Love Me Tender," by Elvis Presley. Bud took my right hand with his left and threaded his right arm around my bulk. The minute Elvis started to sing, I was gone. "I shouldn't have picked this song. It was my parents' song," I choked out between sobs.

"Hush," Bud said, "it can be our song, okay?" He wiped away my tears with his fingers. "It says what I think about you. I'm happy you picked it."

I blinked the tears back into the box of sorrowful keepsakes I kept inside my heart. "I remember Carlie and Leeman waltzing in the kitchen to it. I miss them so much, Bud."

"I know you do," Bud said. "But you got me and Junior. No one's going to take us away from you."

"Okay if I cut in?" Glen asked.

"I don't know as you're supposed to cut in during the first song. But you timed it just right. Glad you're here," I said. He had a knack for doing and saying the wrong thing at the right time.

Glen was about four inches taller than Bud, who was my height. It
felt nice to look up into his snapping black eyes. He was only a couple of
months younger than Dottie and me. He and Bud were like mis-
matched twins, so different, but as close to each other as Dottie and me.

"Glad I'm here too," Glen said. "Wish I could stay longer." Right
after high school graduation he had joined the army and had gone
through basic training. In less than a month, he would head for the war
in Vietnam.

Bud wasn't going near Vietnam or anywhere else, for that matter.
His number had come up in the draft lottery and he had gone for his
physical, but he had been declared unfit for service. As a baby, he had
developed near-fatal pneumonia and his lungs were scarred. He also suffered from asthma from time to time.

Although he had dreaded being picked for the draft, his 4-F status
had bothered him. "Thought that might happen," he told me. "Didn't
want to go anyways. Stupid to go fight someplace I have to look up on
a map." After saying that, he had taken a long walk, which was something he did when he had to think.

"You like the army?" I asked Glen as we shuffled through our
clumsy dance.

Glen shrugged. "It'll keep me off the streets," he said. "When I come
back, I'm going fishing. You hold Leeman's boat for me, maybe?"

"We'll keep her for you," I said, hopeful that my father's lobster boat,
the *Florine*, might get to do what she'd been built for, once again. As of
now, she sat in her cradle on dry ground in Daddy's yard across the street.

When the song ended, Glen bent and kissed me on the forehead.
"You send me pictures of the baby? It's almost like it was mine."

"How do you mean that?" I asked with a grin.

He blushed. "I mean . . . Well, you know what I mean. All of us have
been so close."

"I know," I said. "I'm teasing you. I'm glad you're going to be in this
baby's life." A touch of nausea made me dizzy and I grabbed Glen's
arm. "Sit me down, would you?" I said to him.

He led me over to a line of metal folding chairs set before the peonies and I plunked down onto the warm metal surface of one of them. Bees buzzed and wove their way through the garden. A flower brushed my cheek and I buried my nose in its silky folds. The baby kicked me a couple of times and then settled. Maureen put "Going to the Chapel" onto the record player and almost everyone started to dance, except Dottie, who stomped her way across the lawn, tugging at her dress as she came toward me.

She sat down beside me and we watched the dancers for a few minutes. Pastor Billy hopped and bopped with Maureen, twirling her in circles as she giggled and tried not to get jumbled up in her legs.

"Ain't that cute," Dottie said. We turned our attention to Evie, who was dancing with Glen. The red dress she wore was so tight it might as well have been body dye. Her little butt wriggled its way up to the tips of her fingers and down to her toes. "Looks like she's been practicing," I said.

"For what, I'm not sure," Dottie said. "Whatever it is, it's packed with trouble."

"Think Glen notices?" I said. He grinned like a fool as Evie spun around him like a curvy tornado, laughing with her mouth open wide.

"Have to be blind not to," Dottie said.

"Speaking of Evie, how's my makeup?" I asked.

Dottie produced a crumpled Kleenex from the pocket of her dress. She dabbed it here and there on my face, pocketed the tissue, and squirmed in her chair.

"Take off the dress if you want," I said.

"Nah. I'll wear it for a little longer. Someday, you'll owe me a favor, and I can use this to remind you of all I've done for you in my life."

"I do appreciate everything you've done," I said. "By the way, I might need you to babysit sometimes."

"That's something else I get to do for you," Dottie said. "What you doing for me?"

"Making you an unofficial aunt," I said. "Something happens to me, you take the baby? You okay with that?" When she didn't say anything, I looked at her. "You crying?" I said. "Are you crying?"

"Jeezly flowers stink to high heavens."

"So, if something happens . . ."

"Well, yes, but it better not," she said. She suddenly stood up. "I can't stand this dress no more," she said. She walked quickly toward Grand's house, head down.

The wedding guests danced and drank. We all ate hamburgers, hot dogs, and some of the platters Ray had put together for the day. "Free of charge," he'd told me, which let me know he held me in high esteem. Ray was famous for pinching the green out of a dollar.

Sometime during the afternoon, Glen remembered that he was best man and he decided to toast us. He cleared his throat and raised a Champagne glass. "These two people are my best friends," he started out.

"Hey!" Dottie shouted.

"Dottie too," Glen added. Then he frowned. "Now you made me forget," he said. He looked at the sky as if the words might be written somewhere up there. After a minute, his face lit up and he said, "Oh, yeah! I wish them and the baby all the happiness in the world and I hope they'll remember to keep a beer in the fridge for me. Glad to see that Bud got smart. He couldn't do no better than Florine." Everyone clapped and Glen looked so relieved that I laughed.

Bud pulled the garter from my leg without much ceremony, much like the way he undressed me at night. The three single men at the wedding all looked content to stay that way. Ray looked down at the grass just as Bud threw the garter. Glen ducked behind Pastor Billy, so Billy had to catch it. "Not fair," he said with a laugh.

Dottie wouldn't even stand with the single girls. Evie couldn't reach up with her dress as tight as it was, so Maureen snagged my side-garden flower bouquet. "I'm so happy I caught this," she whispered into my ear. "I'm going to marry Billy someday."

I grinned at her. "You are?" I tried to do the math in my head, but the Champagne from the toast had made me woozy. Billy had to be at least fifteen years older than Maureen, though I didn't know his real age.

"It's a secret," Maureen said.

"I won't tell," I said.

She sat down on a folding chair in the middle of the lawn as Billy knelt before her with the garter. His face went pink as he pushed it above her bony knee. Maureen's blush matched his own.

The day melted into a pale orange sunset and the tide in the harbor turned, showing us its other side as it flowed along. Glen spun records, drank beer, and sang out of tune to almost every song he lowered onto the turntable. The girls and women danced together, or with Billy and Bert. Ray sat off to the side with Sam, who refused to go home, although he looked as if he could knock on death's door and be welcomed in anytime.

I did my best to keep up with my own wedding. I danced a couple of times, ate some wedding cake, and drank a little more Champagne. But finally, my body and my baby were ready to call it quits. Dottie and I stood together on the lawn as I looked around for Bud. I finally spied him walking a tipsy Stella across Daddy's driveway toward the house.

"I owe you more favors," I said to Dottie, who now sported shorts, flip-flops, and a T-shirt that read, BOWLERS NEVER STRIKE OUT.

"How come?"

"You rescued me from Stella," I said. "Thanks."

"She wasn't that bad. Talked about Leeman most of the day to anyone who might listen. 'Bout how she wished they'd gotten married. Seems to me she ought to get some kind of hobby, so she could think about something else and not be so sad."

"She doesn't want to think about anything else," I said.

I watched Bud walk back to me, admiring the way the westerly sun hit the side of his face. It shone on his dark hair and sparked his eyes into lit pieces of coal. As he reached me, he took my hands and said, "Well, Mrs. Warner, it's about time for our honeymoon."

Dottie said, "This shouldn't have nothing to do with me. If it does, there's something wrong." She walked off toward her mother, who was beginning to clean up, alongside Ida. Madeline handed Dottie a tray of dirty dishes. "Don't you dare drop any of this," I heard her say as Dottie walked toward the house.

"Our honeymoon suite is right over party central," I said to Bud. "What kind of time are we going to have with the tunes and the talk going on all night?"

"We're not staying here tonight," he said. "Ma and Dad booked us a room at the Stray-Away Inn down the road." The look I gave him made him grin. "Your bag is packed," he said. "Let's go."

"I'm going to change first," I said.

"Hurry up," Bud said, and headed for the bar.

"Such a nice day," Madeline said as she helped me out of the dress. "Bud looked so handsome and you, well, you . . ."

"I had a lot of help," I said. "Thanks to you."

"My pleasure. May be the only wedding I ever get to help with. Don't know what either of my girls will end up doing. I can't see Dottie marrying anyone, and I'm just hoping Evie doesn't get pregnant before she's out of high school."

I didn't know what to say about that, so I hugged her, holding on maybe a few seconds too long, but Madeline didn't seem to mind. When she left me, I dressed in a honeymoon ensemble consisting of a pair of shorts and a huge T-shirt. Then I went into the bathroom and washed what makeup would come off from my face. I hoped the Stray-Away had a shower so I could wash the gunk from my hair. I lumbered down the stairs. In the kitchen, Madeline, Dottie, Evie, Maureen, and Ida were busy coming and going with glasses, plates, silver, and food. "I feel funny not helping you out in my own kitchen," I said. "Do you want me to—"

"We want you to go honeymoon," Ida said. "We'll get this." With that, she turned her back and ignored me. So did the rest of them.

I looked out onto the porch, where several rocking chairs sat facing two wide windows that looked over the harbor. Glen sat in one of the rockers, taking in the quiet movement of water and the aftermath of sunset.

I walked through the kitchen, onto the porch, and sat down in the rocker beside Glen. When he looked at me, I saw new lines around his eyes and setting on either side of his mouth. I hadn't noticed them while we were dancing. He was only twenty, like the rest of us, way too young for those lines.

"You okay?" I asked him. He turned back to the water.

"Yup," he said. "I'm good. Trying to remember how this looks so's I can picture it when I'm over in Vietnam."

We rocked for about ten seconds, and then he said, "I don't want to go over there. I don't want to be in the army. I don't know what the hell I was thinking about when I did it."

A lone seagull flew across the harbor and toward the ocean, drawn toward a nightly resting place known only to itself and a few thousand others.

"I'm sorry," Glen said. "Christ, it's your wedding day."

"That's okay," I said. "I can sit for a minute." We rocked in unison. "I wish I had something that would make you feel better," I said. "I guess I could say that everything will be okay, but you're the one has to do it."

"Dumbass thing to do," he said.

"You sound like Ray," I said.

"Hah. Funny thing is, I think I did it so's he won't think I'm such a bonehead."

"You're not . . ."

"Hell I'm not," he said. "Big, dumb Glen."

"He related to stupid-ass Florine?"

Glen smiled.

Another seagull glided past the windows toward the sea and sleep. I pictured it settled down, yellow eyes closed, head tucked under its smooth gray wing.

"Love this time of day," Glen said. "So damn quiet."

"They have this time in Vietnam," I said. "Got the same moon and the same sun too. And stars."

"Might have different stars."

"Same sky."

"Different sky."

"Same sky. Different place."

Behind me, I heard Bud ask his mother if she'd seen me.

"We're out here," I hollered to him.

"You ready?" he said behind me. "Oh, hell, here you are with another man already. We ain't even had a honeymoon yet."

Glen stood up. "You better get going, before you have that baby," he said. He helped me out of the chair and I reached up for a hug. "You'll be all right," I whispered into his ear.

"Yup. She's a good one," he said to Bud. "Not too many of them around."

"Oh, there's plenty," I said. "You'll find the right one when you got the time."

"Doubt that," he said.

"Cheer up or I'll kick your ass," I said.

"She will," Bud said. He and Glen did that clumsy back-slapping hug that men do, and then he took my hand and we walked through the kitchen, turned left, and walked down the hall and out the door.

If I were to write about my one-night honeymoon for the local newspaper's society pages, it would read something like this:

> Mr. and Mrs. James Walter "Bud" Warner left for their trip down the coast to the Stray-Away Inn, where they dined on lobster and steak—Champagne compliments of the house—and watched the stars from the balcony connected to their suite.
>
> Mrs. Warner presented Mr. Warner with the keys to her mother's 1947 coupe, Petunia, which caused Mr. Warner to gasp and hold his bride of less than 24 hours and swear that he would love her for the rest of his life. Mr. Warner presented Mrs. Warner with a ring containing a tiny emerald in the center of it to replace the one she had tossed overboard during her father's burial at sea. Mrs. Warner cried and kissed him so hard they both

almost passed out. They attempted to consummate their marriage, which was tough because the baby took up most of the room needed to do that in any proper way. They smiled themselves into sleep.

❧

What I wouldn't write is what happened sometime in the night when I woke up in a sweat, fear spreading its fingers outward from the center of my heart. Something was wrong. Or was it? Bud slept heavy beside me. My hand slipped to my belly. All was calm there. Still, I couldn't throw off the feeling and I needed to move. I hoisted myself out of bed, slipped through the balcony doors, and looked out over the clear June night.

The seagulls had long gone home and the dark was thick with silence. Night spread a soft glove over the water. The horizons blended so well, I couldn't see where ocean ended and sky began. My heart slowed down as I sucked in the sea air. My shaking lessened eventually. The baby kicked out and turned.

Oh, how much of my soul did I owe to that sea! What ever would I have done without the water nearby to soothe night terrors? How many times had I walked down to the lobster wharf, or picked my way along the path to the little beach to immerse my feet in the cold salt water for comfort? Just looking out at the never-ending tide untangled the knot of grief and confusion I held inside, smoothed it out with liquid fingers, and floated it downstream.

Bud knew I was afraid I would lose him. Knew I was afraid that, at any given moment, I could lose anything. That's the way things had gone for almost eight years, ever since Carlie's disappearance. What was to stop time and circumstance from taking away this baby or my husband?

I heard the bed creak back inside our honeymoon suite and then Bud was behind me on the balcony. "You're all right," he said, wrapping his arms around me from the back. "We're all right. Junior is doing okay too. Nothing will happen to us."

"How do you know?" I said.

"I don't. But the odds are on our side. Pretty soon, you ain't going to have time to worry about things that probably won't happen."

We swayed in the darkness on the balcony, listening to a school of fish jump until my eyelids drooped and I whispered, "Let's go in." Bud and I lay on our backs in bed, held hands in the dark, and slept.

3

My fear of something awful happening started when I was twelve, during the summer of 1963.

Carlie loved to travel but Daddy didn't like to leave The Point. To satisfy her need to see something new, every year Carlie and her friend Patty, a waitress at the Lobster Shack where they both worked, traveled three hours north up the coast to a motel in Crow's Nest Harbor. That summer, while they were there, Carlie walked into town one day and was never seen anywhere, by anyone, again.

Not knowing what happened to someone is hell on Earth. Countless catastrophes can befall a person. Believe me, I went through most of them in my mind. I even had visions, real visions, about how my mother may have met her end, each scene more horrible than the last. Nightmares grabbed hold of my heart and shook it until confusion and fear almost broke me in two.

My head also veered in another direction regarding my mother's fate. This path was as dark, in another way. Sometimes, I believed she had actually left me for another life. That possibility caused me to constantly look for her wherever I went. A crop of red hair threw me into a tizzy, particularly red hair on a woman walking with a little bounce in her step. I stopped going anywhere because I was always on alert, which tuckered me out. But I had to hope in my worn-out heart that she was alive somewhere. It was better than her being dead.

Carlie was a joy to be around, full of life and laughter and mischief. She was always pulling something. She and Patty loved to shake things up. The last trick they pulled together was this: Patty and Carlie got drunk after a shift at the Lobster Shack and they dyed their hair. Patty went to Carlie's red, while Carlie took on Patty's blond. This unannounced change upset my father, but she charmed him into liking it. Not too long after that, Carlie and Patty left for Crow's Nest Harbor.

Daddy looked and searched and called everyone who could possibly help find Carlie. When no one could, he took to the bottle and left me to fend for myself for the most part. Mornings, if he got up in time, he was still drunk. He'd throw together some kind of lunch for me and then growl if I questioned anything. I had always been a good student, but I hated going to school because, besides being flat, tall, and skinny, I was the girl whose mother had vanished. I could sense the other kids' eyes on me and hear their whispers. But no sense talking to Daddy about it. He told me to "get on with it." But neither of us got on with much of anything. Without Carlie, the heart and soul of our family, things fell apart.

Stella showed up around Christmas that year, only four months after Carlie's disappearance. I hadn't liked her before she showed up, and after she showed up I hated her. Stella had dated Daddy in high school, and then waited around for him to ask her to marry him. She left town in a huff, hoping he would chase her and beg her to come back. Instead, Carlie met Daddy and Daddy married her. Stella came back, started working at Ray's, and took every chance she could to be mean to both Carlie and me. When she showed up at Daddy's house *and* pretended to like me, it was a bit too much to take. I made no bones about my disgust for her, but Daddy needed little persuasion to let her take care of him. He didn't care how I felt. After a season of their nonsense, I decided to run away, but Grand stopped me at the end of Daddy's driveway and took me into her house.

Grand was Daddy's mother. She was a big-boned, big-hearted Yankee, loving and practical. As I mentioned, she taught me things, made me

toe the line, and could not have been a better influence on a lonely, confused, grieving girl. Grand had a love affair with Jesus, a sure, pure devotion. She didn't force me into a relationship with him and she didn't judge
me, the way I felt Ida did at times. She just lived her life according to the
way she thought Jesus would want her to, with tolerance, patience, and
humor that she used as examples to keep me from flying off the deep end.
I lived with her for four years before I lost her to the stroke. I was seventeen. That's when I quit school and took up with Andy Barrington, who
was as fucked-up as me. He was driving when we had the car accident.

The accident was triggered when Andy's father, Edward Barrington,
surprised us by traveling up to the cottage and disturbing our winter love
nest. I remember what happened up until the accident. Edward had
come to take Andy back home to Massachusetts with him. He told me
that Andy had been thrown out of many schools for smoking dope,
which surprised me because Andy had told me he was up at the cottage
to "take a break." Andy told his father we weren't coming with him, but
Edward told him the sheriff was on his way. We walked outside, heading for Andy's truck so we could leave. Edward followed us, slipped on
the back steps of the cottage, and knocked himself unconscious. Andy
ignored me when I suggested we help him. Andy took Edward's car
instead of his truck because he said it was faster. We took off at a high
rate of speed. The last thing I remember was flying into a grove of trees
made to look fragile by the car's headlights. We should have died, I guess,
but we ended up in separate hospitals in separate states, both badly hurt.
I recovered at Daddy's house. Edward survived and sent Andy to military school. I never heard from him again.

Daddy and I grew closer while I got better, although I gave Stella a
hard time. When I was able, I made a break for it over to Grand's house,
with Bud's help.

Daddy died the summer I was eighteen. Sometimes, it feels like it
never happened, even though I was with him on the boat at the time,
and when we buried him at sea. But Stella, who really did love him, will
always remind me that he's gone.

Throughout all of this, I grew to appreciate the little community I lived in. The Butts family, the Warner family, and Ray kept an eye on me, fed me, took me in for overnights and parties, and made me part of their families. Now that I was older and things were normal, I hoped to give them some of the support they'd given me as Bud and I, and the baby, settled into our lives as a married couple.

I gave a lot of thought to the kind of mother I wanted to be. I couldn't wait for the baby to call me "Mama." Me calling my mother Carlie was okay with me, but I admit that sometimes I felt more like her friend or little sister. Grand took charge, gave me orders, told me what my responsibilities were, and let me be a kid. That's what I wanted for my kids. It was my job to take on the big stuff. It was their job to not have to worry about that.

I wanted calm. I wanted peace. I wanted nothing more than to be a wife and a mother and to make beautiful things and bake wonderful bread. I wanted to wake up and look out and be grateful for the place I lived and the day just ahead. But I had been through too much to expect that life would be simple. Thus far in my life, Fate had a habit of flinging me ass over teakettle into yet another unasked-for adventure. I hoped that my settling down would bore Fate.

But, as Grand liked to say when I was impatient, *"Wait and see, Florine."*

4

We came home after our honeymoon night to a house decorated with ribbons and a refrigerator full of wedding food. We ate leftovers for a few days, and after that, Ida brought supper to us almost every night. I was thankful, because the downward pull of the baby pressed against my weakened back. The car accident had twisted it badly, and I would always have pain. Sometimes I cursed out Andy as I beached on the sofa, knitting baby blankets and sweaters sized from birth to one year old. I pondered what to name a girl. Bud had taken charge of naming any sons we would have.

"Why can't I think about boy names?" I said.

Bud shrugged. "I like the idea of you naming our girl."

"How many kids you think we'll have?" I asked.

"About ten, I think."

"That's a lot of names. We'd better get cracking."

"Later. It's wicked hard to be on top of you these days. I'm scared of heights."

We were joking about the number of babies. I knew that my body wouldn't be able to do this ten times. My doctor had been surprised that I had gotten this far without the pain that was just setting in.

"Stupid," I said, aloud, one afternoon. "Stupid me."

"What's stupid?" Ida said from the front hallway. Sometimes, I swore my mother-in-law balled up noise and tucked it into her pocket to nap.

"Someday, I'm going to hear you before I see you," I said. Ida smiled and headed for the kitchen with a covered dish for supper.

"Want some tea?" she called.

"No," I said, "but I want to have this baby."

"I'll bet you do."

"The next time I get pregnant, I'm going to shoot for the other three seasons and leave summer out of it. It's hot!"

"Certainly is," Ida agreed. She came into the living room carrying two glasses of iced tea. "I thought you'd like the ice," she said, sitting down in the overstuffed chair next to the sofa. "You know, you could stay upstairs in bed."

"And miss all the action?" I said. "I'd rather be here during the day. Breaks it up."

"It's June twenty-eighth," Ida said. "Your due date. I thought we could toast the day." She handed me a glass and we clinked them together. I moved several skeins of yarn so I could set the glass on a coaster on the coffee table in front of me.

"I don't think much will happen today," I said. "No earthquakes down below."

Ida smiled. "Maybe not, but soon," she said. "And I have a favor to ask you."

"Ask away," I said.

"Will you let me take the baby to church?"

Ida's request wasn't a surprise, but it made me squirm all the same. She loved Jesus as much as Grand had, but Ida liked to push him toward those, like me, she felt might be in desperate need of his services. I envied both Grand and Ida's faith but I didn't share it. Bud's need was less than mine. We had gone to church and listened to Pastor Billy preach for the years we were forced to go, and as soon as we could, we quit going. Our Sundays were spent believing in each other.

I sighed. "Ida, I don't know. Maybe we'll wait until she's older."

"What would be the harm?"

I shrugged. "No harm. I'm not sure I want her going to church right off. Let me talk it over with Bud." I twisted to relieve my numbed right butt cheek.

Ida nodded as if what I had just said was what she had expected to hear. "Please don't be upset," I said.

"The baby might like it," Ida said. "Jesus works in mysterious ways."

"I know that, for sure," I said. "But let us come to that on our own, if you don't mind. That way, it would be our idea."

Ida swallowed the rest of her tea and got up to leave. "I guess," she said. "But maybe you and Bud should have a talk with Billy about it."

"Maybe," I said.

Before she could turn to walk toward the hall I said, "Wait!"

And a streak of lightning tore through my belly.

I talked to Jesus a lot the rest of that day, night, and the morning of the next day. I hissed his name through gritted teeth and shouted it into the ceiling of the delivery room. Bud, pale as skim milk, stood beside me and told me to take deep breaths and just relax, relax, until I swore at him and told him to get out, that I didn't need him, I'd never needed him, I didn't need anyone, and why didn't he leave me alone. But he didn't leave, and finally, the baby found the tiny escape tunnel and I began to push, push, push and then, there she came, all seven pounds six ounces of her, screaming at me and at anyone within a half mile of her voice.

I named her Arlee June before she could go from blue to pink. They took her from me for a minute or two, and then placed her on my chest. Bud and I cried, and I pledged to her that should anyone dare touch one copper hair on her head, they would suffer great harm. She blinked and cooed and my heart was swallowed up by love so intense I shook with it.

"Tuesday's child is full of grace," Madeline Butts said to me, sometime after Arlee and I had been cleaned up and they brought her to me. She and Dottie sat in matching tan visitor chairs by the bed.

"She's a looker," Dottie said.

"Can't you see it?" I said. I could, plain as the minute nose on Arlee's perfect face. "She looks exactly like Carlie."

"I guess she does," Madeline said. "She has her red hair, sure enough."

"Why did you name her Arlee June?" Dottie asked.

"Rhymes with Carlie, but the l-e-e is for Leeman," I said. "The June is because she was born in June."

"Makes sense," Dottie said. "Arlee Dot would have been nice, though."

Arlee and I slept away much of our first afternoon together, until about six o'clock, when Bud came back and we wondered at our baby, who was the most beautiful child ever created.

"Time to have another one," I said to Bud as he held our daughter. He looked up at me, his eyes stupid with love.

"Let's spoil this one for a while," he said. "And before we do have another one, we should think about where we're going to live and get settled."

My heart sank. Bud was restless and I knew that. He talked about seeing new places, all the time. For the time being, he worked at Fred's, but Fred had told him that his brother, Cecil, who had a garage down to Stoughton Falls, might be looking for help in the near future. Bud had gotten all fired up at the thought of an adventure, so we had driven south for about two hours to check out the area. The autumn leaves along the drive had been pretty, but Stoughton Falls was tiny, and it lacked the backdrop of an ocean. None of that had fazed Bud, though, and he hadn't stopped thinking about working there since.

For me, moving to Stoughton Falls meant no sassy whitecaps whipped up by flirty winds. No watching the sunrise yawn its way up over the east and stretch out into day over The Point and the harbor. No double-yolked sunsets dipping behind the pines at night. No sweet, familiar house. No people that I knew. I went quiet whenever he mentioned it. This time was no exception.

As he nuzzled Arlee's fuzzy head, he said, "Florine . . ."

"I know," I said. "I'm still getting used to the idea."

A shadow fell over his face.

"What's wrong?" I asked.

"Dad's not doing good. I should go and see him."

About two hours after Bud had driven me to the hospital, Ida had called an ambulance down to The Point for Sam, who had taken a turn for the worse. He was waiting out the last stages of his life, only one floor below us.

"Tell him we love him," I said to Bud. He nodded. I wanted to take the sadness from his eyes. I said, "Bud, when the time comes, we'll move for sure, and I'll be glad to do it."

He kissed us and left to go visit Sam. Arlee fussed and my breasts went heavy. She bumped and bobbed for a minute or so and then she grabbed onto a nipple. "Yowza!" I said. "If you're this strong now, what's this going to feel like when you're older?" Arlee drifted into a milk-drenched stupor about ten minutes later. A nurse moved her to the little crib beside me, and I fell asleep beside her.

Some time later, I heard an "Oh my god." My eyes shot open and I sat up before I was even awake.

Stella stood over Arlee's crib. I could smell booze from across the room.

"Are you drunk?" I asked.

She shook her head. "Well, what a nice greeting," she said. "No, I'm not drunk. I don't drink nearly as much as you think I do. I wanted to see Leeman's grandchild. I was hoping that she might look like him. But I can see you've got your mother back."

"She looks like herself, mostly," I said.

"Well, of course she does," Stella said. "But she's definitely Carlie's granddaughter."

"And she's my daughter," I said, "and we're both tired, Stella."

Stella put her hand down to touch Arlee's cheek. I held my breath.

"Soft," Stella murmured. "Well, I won't take up any more time. I just wanted to see the baby. Are you feeling okay?"

"Ripped from stem to stern. But otherwise, fine."

Stella raised an eyebrow. "You'll heal. You always do," she said, and she left.

Stella and I had such a strained relationship. We would never be friends, but there were things to be admired about her. The way she loved Daddy, for instance. The way she went after what she wanted. The way she kept a secret between us, instead of telling him.

When I was fourteen, I'd snuck into Daddy's house one day while he and Stella were out. I hadn't been there for a long time. When I saw that Stella had completely redecorated it, I went into a rage. I broke glass and threw things around before I ran off. When my conscience got the best of me, I hurried back to fix it before they got home. But Stella was there, and she caught me. She told me to get out, but she never told Daddy what I had done. He never knew. For that, I was grateful. Still, our relationship was built on unsteady ground, and things could go wrong with a misread look, or the tone of a voice. I was temperamental and she drank too much.

That night, Bud wheeled me and Arlee down to Sam's room. His skin was the color of a buttered moon, and his breath rattled in his throat, but he smiled when he saw his granddaughter.

"Beautiful," he whispered. Bud held Arlee so Sam could stroke her hair and her face. We stayed only five minutes, and then Bud pushed us back to the elevator and pressed the up button. We rose to a higher floor filled with light and new babies.

5

No time for my aching back. No time for knitting, reading, baking bread, or goofing off. No time to finish dishes, housekeeping, laundry, cooking, or going to the bathroom. No time to brood and mourn over those no longer in my world. My tiny infant girl held the clock hostage with demands that ranged from feedings to diaper changes to sleeping and back again. And although she had been quiet in the hospital, almost from the minute we stepped over the threshold that separated the outdoors from Grand's front hall, Arlee discovered her lungs.

Bud and I settled into a routine, understanding all too soon that our efforts to keep our lives on track could be blown to bits by Arlee's crying for no reason or for a real reason. Both of us carried her as if she were made of glass for the first few days. Ida and Maureen helped, but they could also leave. We could not.

"You realize this is for about eighteen years," Bud whispered one night in bed as we lay there, half asleep on our covers. July was keeping her midsummer breezes to herself that night. She'd been playing them close to her chest for the two weeks we'd been home. I was so hot. My breasts hurt, my stomach felt like jelly, and my crotch ached.

"I was thinking we could send her off at about six. Or two, if she's smart," I grumbled. He moved his hand toward me. "Don't touch me. I hurt everywhere. I'm tired everywhere."

"You're not the only one," Bud said, and turned over as I continued to rag about how much more I had to do than him, even though I couldn't complain, as he was a big help.

We'd switched our bedroom around so we could get out of bed on both of our sides, instead of Bud climbing over me to get to Arlee when she woke up at night. He took the midnight shift, which I appreciated, but I was the milk machine so he brought her to me. When he got home at night after work, he was tired, but he was good about taking her. I was happy for the sitting porch next to the kitchen, with its line of rockers and room for a bassinet. It became a mini nursery. Since it was summer, we could open the windows and let in the harbor breezes and noises.

"I'm so tired," I bitched to Ida one day. I should have known better.

"Did you expect not to be?" she asked.

"I don't think I knew what the word meant," I said.

Ida smiled. "Get used to it," she said, and then she took Arlee for a couple of hours.

Bud didn't get many naps. He got up to go to work, even though he might have been up half the night. Then he came home and ate supper. Most nights, he drove up to Long Reach to visit his father in the hospital. Later, he nodded off in front of the television set.

"Remember those ten kids we talked about having?" I shouted to him one late afternoon as he sat in the kitchen, jiggling our screaming baby and waiting for supper.

He rolled his eyes and carried Arlee outside. I watched him walk down the ramp to the wharf, where he lowered himself into a weather-bleached Adirondack chair. As the harbor water rocked the wharf with gentle green hands, our daughter's cries softened and stopped.

I loaded up a plate with shepherd's pie and took it down to him. I took Arlee from him while he ate. I sat on the arm of the chair and listened to water *bloop* against the wet pilings beneath us. Bud's fork tinged like a bell against the plate.

"This is peaceful," I said. "Maybe we should eat here every night."

"Might as well," Bud said. "We're not going to move anytime soon."

Arlee muttered against my shirt, then stilled.

"Why not?" I said.

"Cecil don't need anyone right now. I asked Fred today."

"That's too bad."

"Is it?"

"I know it's what you want."

"So? Doesn't really matter."

"Yes, it does."

"I got to get to the hospital to see Dad," he said. He clattered the fork against the plate and Arlee jumped in my arms. We walked up the ramp to the house.

"Do you want us to come with you?" I asked him as we reached the yard.

"No. Calms me down to think of you here." He set the plate and fork on the lawn, and wrapped his arms around us. He kissed me with salty, potato-flavored lips.

"I'll call if something happens," he said. He started up his Ford Fairlane and chugged up the road and out of sight.

I cupped my daughter against me and nuzzled her sweet head. "I need to be there for your daddy," I confessed to her.

ᥱᵒ

I put Arlee down at about eight o'clock in her bassinet on the porch. When the phone rang, I picked it up as fast as I could. But as I said "Hello," Arlee began to cry.

"Damn. Did I wake her up?" Bud sighed.

"Dust bunnies hopping across the floor wake her up," I said.

"The doctor thinks Sam will go tonight. We're going to stay with him."

"I'm here," I said. "We're here."

We hung up a couple of minutes later and I fetched my girl. It took a changing and another feeding to convince her that sleep was probably her best choice. I took her upstairs and set her on her back, in the crib. Afterward, I wandered out into the side yard and sat down in a lawn chair. My legs throbbed as I thought about how two weeks ago we hadn't had a crying baby to care for. Just sixteen days ago, Sam had been that much further from dying.

I didn't know much about my father-in-law, really. Like Bert Butts and Daddy, Sam was a lobsterman. Height-wise, he was the smallest of The Point men, but drink-wise, he kept up with the best of them. He could be touchy, the depths of which Bud told me about during nights we revealed the secret lives we had led growing up.

One night when Bud was about ten, he told me, Sam had roused him by hauling him out of bed and pushing him into the living room. He proceeded to throw everything in Bud's closet out onto the floor, flipped the mattress off the bed, and said, "There, dammit. Maybe you're better off in a pig's sty."

"What was he talking about?" I asked Bud. "What had you done?"

"I hadn't hung up my jacket. I'd left it on the back of the kitchen chair."

"Wow."

"I had school the next day, and I didn't have time to pick anything up before leaving that morning. That night I overheard Ma tell Dad that she had put the room to rights and that he might consider giving up some of the liquor that made him so crazy and start praying to the lord for help."

"Ida said that?"

"Ma believes that the meek shall inherit the Earth, and she goes about proving it every chance she gets."

I said a prayer for Sam and sent it up to the moon and the stars as night spun out its story. I went to bed at eleven and fell into a mother's waking sleep. Only an hour later, something woke me up.

I hopped out of bed and hustled toward Arlee's room just as a

high-pitched shriek punched through the open window in my bedroom. I froze. Arlee whimpered. The shriek came again, followed by
words.

"You killed him. You did. He was mine, and you killed him, you
selfish bitch." It sounded like Stella, but not like Stella. The hair on
the back of my neck rose as I left Arlee's room and crept to my bedroom window. Sure enough, it was Stella, tripping through the pan-
sies and petunias in the side garden. The glass from a bottle she was
holding glittered as it caught the half-moon. She fell into a cluster of
budding daisies and I winced as she crushed them. She struggled up
and stepped on Bud's supper plate, which was still setting in the side
yard by the lawn chair. It cracked under her bare feet.

"You bitch," she screamed again. "You took away the only thing I
ever wanted. You think you hate me, I hate you worse. I hate you for
killing your father. You killed him!" This last sentence was filled with
drunken rage like to have ripped her little body in half. She smashed
the bottle against the side of the house. The force caused her to fall
backward into the beach roses and she cursed the thorns as she tried
to right herself.

I slipped on a pair of jeans and a T-shirt and walked across the hall.
Miracle of miracles, Arlee still slept. I closed her door quietly and went
back over to the bedroom window. Stella was picking roses and thorns
from her clothing. "Your fault," she whimpered. "All your fault."

I'd never seen her like this and I wasn't sure I could handle this
alone. I decided to call Sheriff Parker Clemmons and Bert and Madeline Butts. They would be able to calm her down.

I creaked my way down the stairs, through the living room, past
the front hall, and into the kitchen, toward the wall phone. Before I
could pick it up, Stella banged on the kitchen window and hollered, "I
see you! Come out here and tell me why you killed your father. Do it,
or I'll break this window. Don't you go near that phone."

I picked up the phone. Stella bent down, seized up one of the big
rose quartz rocks Grand had gathered to decorate the borders of the

house, and heaved it through one of the kitchen windows. Glass shattered. I ran outside.

"What the hell is wrong with you?" I screamed. I faced Stella, who still stood in front of the shattered window, looking as if she couldn't believe she had done it. She turned and said, through her gritted teeth, "It's almost the second anniversary of when you killed your father. Doesn't surprise me that you don't remember it."

"I know damn well what day it is, Stella. He died of a heart attack. I didn't kill him. And you are some holy-o drunk," I said. "I'm not arguing with whatever craziness you've swallowed. Go home and sober up."

"You'd like that, wouldn't you?" Stella said. "And you know what? Your mother was a whore. She wasn't the saint you think she was."

Arlee finally began to cry. "Go home," I said. "You've waked up the baby."

"Oh, I've waked up the baby. Well, that's too goddamn bad."

Someone, most likely Grand from her rocking chair in heaven, touched my soul, and for a few seconds I understood the pain clawing at Stella's heart. Soft as I could I said, "I'm sorry you miss Daddy so much. I miss him too. But shouting at me and getting mad at me won't bring him back. You need to go home and sleep this off."

Stella responded by bending down and picking up the fork Bud had used for supper. She ran at me, and before I could grab it away from her, she scored my cheek with the prongs. The pain, and Arlee's cries, made me crazy, but before I could wrap my hands around Stella's twiggy neck, Bert Butts pulled us apart.

"Grab *her*, goddammit," Stella screamed. "She's a killer!"

Bert put his big lobsterman's arms around Stella's slight body and held her to him as she struggled.

Dottie and Madeline had followed Bert. Dottie's eyes were dazed, but Madeline, who appeared to be more on top of things, said, "What the hell is going on?"

I held my hand up to my bloody cheek and moved to go into the house to get to Arlee. Dottie stopped me. "I'll fetch her," she said. Madeline took me into the kitchen as Parker rocketed down the dirt road in his car, lights flashing.

"I called him," Madeline said. "Thought you were being murdered." She gaped at the broken window. "My god," she said, "did Stella do that?"

I sat down hard at the table. Madeline wet a cloth at the sink and dabbed at my cheek. "She got you good," she said. "You had a tetanus shot lately?"

"Doesn't sound familiar," I said.

We listened to Stella cry and protest as Parker and Bert talked to her outside.

Dottie came downstairs toting my red-faced baby and I took her and tried to settle her down. I told Madeline and Dottie that I had been waked by Stella's screams, that I had tried to talk to her. "Things bottomed out fast," I said.

"She's drunk," Madeline said.

"No shit. That's nothing new," I said. "But she's never attacked me."

"She's been alone in that house too much," Madeline said. "Ida and I have both tried to get her out, but she's been stubborn about leaving. I guess everything got to her tonight, somehow."

Sadness washed over me. "The hell of it is, she's right," I said. "I probably did kill Daddy."

Madeline said, "Your father had a bad heart for years, Florine."

"Yes, but I was hard on him."

"You was hard on everyone after Carlie went missing and Stella showed up," Dottie said. "None of the rest of us died from it."

Madeline rolled her eyes. "Dorothea, you have such a way with words."

"Just telling it so Florine can understand that she didn't do nothing wrong. She wasn't awful nice, but she had some reasons. She sure as hell ain't no killer."

I gave Arlee an idle boob to suck on. "I hope my milk isn't sour," I said.

Madeline asked me where we kept the first-aid kit, and set off for it.

Sheriff Parker Clemmons came into the kitchen, saw me nursing Arlee, turned on his heel, and started to leave.

"It's okay, Parker," I said. "Dottie, get me a dish towel." She fetched it, and I put it gently over Arlee's head and my boob. "All covered up," I said. "You can look."

Parker turned around and came back, but he didn't take his eyes from my face or from the notebook he pulled from his shirt pocket. Parker was Ray Clemmons's younger brother, but they looked completely different. Parker was tall, while Ray reminded me of a barrel with legs. Both spoke in short, to-the-point sentences. Parker asked me to describe the evening's events. I explained what had happened. He asked me if I wanted to charge Stella with trespassing, vandalism, and assault. Part of me wanted to hit her with the book. But part of me remembered her keeping my teenage vandalism a secret from Daddy, and so I said, "No. Let her sleep it off."

"You sure?" Parker said.

"No, but what the hell."

Madeline returned with Band-Aids, hydrogen peroxide, cotton balls, and an old bottle of iodine. She said, "Really, Florine? She broke your window and bloodied your face. You sure about this?"

"No," I said. "But I owe her a favor, and Daddy loved her." To Parker, I said, "But I sure as hell don't want her near me, or the baby. Can we make sure that doesn't happen?"

Parker said, "We can get it down on paper."

Madeline disinfected my cheek and we decided that the scratches weren't deep enough for stitches. We left them open to the air so the wound could breathe. Parker finished up and walked Stella home. We decided it was a good idea for Dottie to sleep on our sofa for the rest of the night. I put Arlee back to bed and went downstairs to sit with her for a while.

Dottie said, "What did you mean when you said that you owed Stella a favor?"

I shrugged. "I'll tell you someday, but not now. I'm too tired."

Dottie let it drop and we watched television until I went to bed.

My face throbbed and it was hard to get comfortable. I finally wrapped Bud's pillow in my arms and that did the trick. Dottie and I shared an early breakfast with Arlee. Bud called me at about eight o'clock. Sam was gone, he said.

I said, "Come home."

6

Besides being pastor, Billy Krum was a lobsterman and a handyman. The next day after Stella's attack, he served double duty at the Warner households. He showed up at about ten in the morning and walked down to Ida's house to talk to her about Sam's service, and then he helped Bud fix our kitchen window.

He was a good-looking fella, as Grand had noted to me, trusting that I wouldn't pass that on lest it seem disrespectful. She was right, though; he *was* a good-looking fella. He reminded me of Daddy. His eyes took on the color blue in a serious way, and his skin was ruddy for life. His age was up for debate, but Maureen Warner said she thought that he was about twenty-nine or thirty. "There's barely seventeen years of difference between him and me. If we get married when I'm eighteen, he'll only be thirty-five or so. That's not so old," she told me one day.

"That's pretty old," I said.

She lifted her stubborn chin and shook her head. "Not really."

"Well," I said, "my parents were twelve years apart. That worked out until Carlie went missing. But they were happy before that, as far as I know."

Whenever I saw Billy, I thought about Maureen's crush on him.

As he and Bud removed the busted window from its frame in the kitchen, the summer breeze sifting off the water laid its warm fingers on every person and item in the house. I brought Arlee downstairs and put her in her bassinet and in a rare moment of idleness, I watched the men work.

Bud looked awful, as was to be expected. He hadn't slept all night. When he had seen the cuts on my cheek earlier in the morning, I had to talk him out of letting Stella have it.

"We'll deal with it later," I said. "We have enough going on today."

"Well, that's bullshit," he said, but he left it alone. As I watched, he turned away from Billy and me and wandered down toward his mother's house.

"He's in a state today," I said.

Billy nodded. "That's to be expected."

"Yes," I said. I wanted to follow him and take him walking. I would hook my arm through his elbow and we would find ourselves beneath two rows of tipsy pines that had nothing to do but shade us as we strolled underneath them.

"I bet Sam would want to be buried at sea," I said to Billy. "Like Daddy."

Daddy's remains were drifting along the floor of the ocean somewhere, although he had a grave in the cemetery up on the hill near the white church where Billy preached. The men, including Billy, had spirited his body away at some point during the day of his funeral. They had roused me at midnight and we had taken him home to his beloved sea, said goodbye to him, and dropped him overboard. We had told no one. As far as I knew, Stella thought Daddy was buried in the cemetery. His plot was the most flowered and watered one in the whole place.

Billy didn't answer me. Instead, he walked through the empty window frame into the kitchen and went to the bassinet on the porch. He looked down at a sleeping Arlee, a smile around his eyes. "I remember your mother well," he said. "This little girl looks like her."

"Carlie had more hair and she was bigger," I said. Billy smiled.

"You're God's little wiseass," he said. "That's for sure." He frowned at my cheek. "You probably should have that checked out."

"It'll heal," I said.

"I'm going to see Stella after I leave here," Billy said.

I moved over to the missing window and looked over at the house across the driveway. No sound. No movement. I shivered.

"She was so crazy last night," I said. "Not sure what set her off."

"Loneliness. Grief. Watching you continue on with your new family. Missing Leeman something awful, I imagine."

"I know all that. I just don't know why now."

"No reason that makes any sense to any of us, or maybe to her. She's been to see me a couple of times, just to set and talk. That's something you could do, if you had a mind to do it."

"That's right," I said. "I could. If I had a mind."

Billy smiled and shook his head. He walked back through the open window and returned to work. "Grand used to say about you that Jesus needed someone to keep him on his toes."

"Well, Jesus can relax for a while. I'm plenty kept on my own toes with this baby."

And as if on cue, Arlee made a sound, and I went to her. I picked her up and we walked down to Ida's house. Our joint appearance would help keep the sadness in the shadows and help us all through the next few days. On the way down the hill, we met Bud heading up to help Billy. He took Arlee in his arms and held her to him for a few seconds, then he kissed me and handed our baby back to me and we continued on our separate ways.

We decided to hold the funeral lunch for Sam at Grand's house, because it was bigger than the Warner house. As soon as I knew that, I began to clean while Ida and Maureen kept Arlee. All day long, in between feeding Arlee and then dusting and sweeping and polishing up, I kept my eye on Stella's house. But it remained quiet. No one came out. No one went in. Her car was still parked there when we left for the wake.

Once inside the funeral home, we spoke in quiet tones as we stood in front of the closed, dark coffin containing Sam's remains.

"I would have left the lid up," Ida said. "He didn't look so bad and they can do wonders with makeup these days. But he didn't want that. He didn't want anyone saying how good he looked. 'I'll be dead,' he said. 'How good could I look?'"

Sam had a lot of friends, most of whom he had grown up with and had known him most of his life. We all knew them too, in one way or another. If I didn't recognize them by name, I knew them by their boat names. The tall bald man ran the *Boden*. The gray-bearded man with hands the size of big flounders was captain of the *Celeste*. Most of them were quiet, but the sight of the baby in my arms made everyone relax a little more. It was good to chat with mothers and grandmothers and to people who had known my parents and saw them in Arlee. A few folks asked about the scratches on my face. I didn't want to go into the whole fight with Stella, but I got tired of mumbling this and that about it. Finally, I said, to Tillie Clemmons when she asked, "It was rough sex." Tillie, who was as talkative as her husband, Parker, was quiet, spread the word. I got a few shocked stares, but no one else asked me any more questions.

As the evening wore on, we wandered through the carpeted rooms with the long, thick drapes, nodding at one another with shy eyes or whispering bits of comfort. Finally, Ray Clemmons said to Dottie and me, "Why are we so goddamn quiet? He's dead, for chrissake. He can't hear nothing." Dottie and I giggled at that, and then giggled even harder when several people shot us cross looks. We ended up standing outside on the lawn with Madeline, watching Long Reach cars whoosh by. Arlee's fussing made my breasts heavy and I told Bud goodbye. Dottie drove Arlee and me back down to The Point.

The service was held almost two years to the day of Daddy's funeral. At the church, a tearful congregation sniffed and listened as Billy gave a solemn and personal remembrance of a man who wouldn't have set foot in church but for his determined wife. Ida wept in the front row alongside a hiccupping Maureen. Bud remained tearless beside me in the pew, but his hand never parted from mine.

At the graveyard on the hill, the sun and a summer wind held sway. Hair blew back from sad faces, dresses danced and settled as if they were on a clothesline, black pant legs whipped back to outline bony knees and legs. The coffin was lowered into the earth, flowers were strewn over the top of it, and we filed away from the grave to continue on with the day.

Dottie, Evie, and Madeline were at Grand's house when I showed up. Most of what we had to offer had been put out on a long table set up against the rose bushes in the side garden to block the wind. Dottie and Evie were on the porch swapping off a fussy Arlee as Madeline finished up coffee and tea.

"She likes me better," Evie said to Dottie.

"Well, that would be a miracle, now wouldn't it?" Dottie shot back.

I took Arlee from the squabbling sisters and went upstairs to feed her. I listened to the slamming of car doors and the murmurs of mourners as they filed into the side garden and into Grand's house. Arlee sucked and purred for a while before she fell asleep, her open mouth still on my nipple. I put her to nap in her crib and paced back to our bedroom, not ready to go downstairs and face my guests.

I looked out of our bedroom window toward Daddy's house and saw a car parked in back of Stella's car. It looked familiar. Then I remembered Stella's sister, Grace, who had come to take Stella away shortly after Daddy died. Was she back to take her away, again?

"Florine, do you have more cream for the coffee?" Madeline called.

"Yes," I called back, and I joined the people celebrating Sam's life.

Most people left within an hour, but the captains of the *Boden* and the *Celeste*, along with Bert, Bud, and Billy, sat in the side yard and drank up all the beer so we wouldn't have to do it later.

At midnight, my exhausted and half-drunk husband left our bed. Through half-raised lids, I watched him pull on his jeans.

"You going for a walk?" I said. "You all right? Want me to get up?"

"No. Go back to sleep. We're going out to sea," he said. "We won't be long."

"Does Ida know?" I whispered.

"She's coming along," Bud said. "Bert's taking the family out."

"Why didn't you tell me?"

"I figured you'd be better off here with the baby."

It made me grumpy that he had left me out, but I let that go, and when he bent down to me, I put my hands on either side of his face and gave him a long, deep kiss. He snuck downstairs and out the door. I drowsed and listened until I heard the *Maddie Dee*'s motor start up. Bert put her into gear and she chugged toward the ocean.

"Goodbye, Sam," I whispered, and I went back to sleep.

Sometime later that night, I woke up. My breasts were full, but my baby hadn't cried. Crap, I thought, I'll have to wake her up. I settled back into the mattress for a sleepy minute. As I lay there, I heard a man singing. I got up and went into Arlee's room. No baby. My heart thumped as I stood at the top of the stairs and took in the voice downstairs. It sounded like Bud, although I'd never heard him sing. I tiptoed down the stairs and through the house. As I moved closer to the porch, where he sat rocking, I caught the words to the tune he was singing to his daughter.

> *"Who's that knocking at my door?*
> *Who's that knocking at my door?"*
> *Said the fair young maiden.*
> *"It's only me from over the sea,"*
> *Says Barnacle Bill the Sailor . . .*
> *"My ass is tight, my temper's raw,"*
> *Says Barnacle Bill the Sailor.*
> *"I'm so wound up I'm afraid to stop,*
> *I'm looking for meat or I'm going to pop,*
> *A rag, a bone with a cherry on top,"*
> *Says Barnacle Bill the sailor.*

I peeped over the rocker to see that Arlee was wide-eyed and awake, watching him. I put my hand on his left shoulder.

"Nice song," I said.

"It's my lullaby," Bud said. "Sam used to sing it to me." I settled in my rocker while Bud went through every verse of "Barnacle Bill the Sailor" before handing Arlee to me.

"I think her hair is curlier, after that," I said, lifting my T-shirt to feed her.

He shrugged. "Nothing wrong with that," he said. "Nothing at all."

The next morning I noticed that the car in Stella's driveway hadn't moved. Grace, if it was Grace, was still there. I lifted my hand to my face and ran it over the scratches. They were hardening to scab, and my cheek itched.

"Don't scratch," Bud said.

"Hard not to," I said.

"Stella is a friggin' wack job," Bud said. And with that, he left for work.

I got busy with baby and house during the morning. At noon, I decided to take her up the road to Ray's to pick up some groceries. I snuggled her into my old buggy. The carriage rocked as the wheels took the shocks from the bumps in the road.

"Wait up!" someone called. I turned to see Maureen flying up the road wearing a thin cotton dress and no shoes. When she reached us, she skidded to a stop.

"Where are you going?" she asked. "Can I steer?"

"Up to Ray's," I said. She curled her long fingers around the buggy handle and we began our little walk. Before we could start a conversation, a door slammed off to our right. I looked over to see a stout woman tromping down Daddy's driveway. It was Grace. I recalled the scowl on her face.

"Why don't you keep walking," I said to Maureen. "I'll meet you at Ray's in a minute." Maureen plugged on up the hill as I planted my feet and waited.

Grace stopped about three feet away. I noted the resemblance between the sisters, except that, judging by her build, Grace had claimed a good portion of whatever they'd eaten during their childhoods.

"Stella's gone away for a while," Grace said. "I'm here now."

"Good for you," I said. My cheek itched and I reached to scratch it.

Grace smiled. "She got you good, didn't she? Boy, don't she hate you." She turned and walked away. I sputtered like a seized engine as I hurried to catch up with Maureen.

"Is Grace staying long?" I asked Ray Clemmons as he bagged our groceries.

"Don't know," he said.

"Where did Stella go?"

"Grace ain't giving out the address," he said. "No idea of where she went, but here's hoping she stays gone for a while. She needs to find what mind she's lost."

"Has Glen written you a letter yet?" Maureen asked.

"Nope. His mother got a note from him. Said he was doing okay. Said it was hot. Not much else."

Maureen said, "Can I have his address?" which surprised us both. Ray gave it to her and we rattled back down the hill.

"You going to write to Glen?" I asked.

She shrugged. "Probably could use all the mail he can get," she said, which shamed me, because I hadn't written to him since he'd been gone, nor had I sent a photo of the baby. I vowed to do that soon. It didn't seem real to me that Glen, who bungled just about everything, was tracking down some enemy with a weapon in his hand. "Copy the address for me," I said to Maureen. "I'll send him some pictures of Arlee."

Dottie came over later that day and I told her about the encounter I'd had with Grace.

"It was so strange," I said. "Not 'Sorry she ripped up your face,' just, 'Boy, don't she hate you.'"

"Well, she's to the point," Dottie said. "How long she staying there?"

"I don't know," I said.

Daddy had willed his house to Stella, so I supposed that members of her family could stay there. But did Grace plan to live here permanently? Would the whole Stella clan move in? Oh, sweet Jesus, I hoped not.

"Maybe she's having an off day," Dottie said. "I'll keep my eye on her. Maybe she bowls. Looks like she's built for it. Maybe I can keep her busy. We're a man down on the team. She might be the answer to our prayers."

"Might as well make use of her while she's here," I said.

Dottie was a big-ball bowling champion with several trophies to prove it. She had started rolling strikes in high school. She tried to teach me once, and then told me that it was a good thing I had other talents to rely on to make my way in the world. She had played all over the state and was thinking about turning pro. But her roots were strong and Bowla Rolla, the alley where she had started her journey, was her favorite. Just a month ago, she had won her latest trophy there. Dottie, a woman not given to pride, beamed when she told me. "Five highest scores for a woman in that alley, ever," she said.

She tried to talk to Grace about bowling, but it turned out she was immune to even Dottie's charm. "She's about as wacky as they come," Dottie concluded.

7

Summer boiled over into fall's territory. Arlee got more interesting and took up more time than seemed possible. The anniversary of my mother's disappearance in mid-August almost went by without me noticing that she was still gone.

But I did remember. I walked down to Ida's house and asked her to take Arlee for a few minutes. I made my way to the stony beach and sat down on a familiar barnacled rock to think about her. I shut my eyes and tried to remember her face. I saw different features clearly, but not at the same time. I could not wish her whole face into my memory and my heart beat faster as I realized she was fading away.

I stood up and paced back and forth for a minute or two. I looked out to sea for comfort and had a sudden urge to swim out to Bert Butts's white ball mooring. The day was warm and no one was around, so I stripped down to my bra and panties, waded into the chilly water, and struck out on my own, counting my strokes as I swam. I thought about the time Bud and I had raced each other to this mooring. I couldn't remember who won, but what I did remember was us holding hands and diving down and down, coming up only when our lungs begged for air. It had been a beautiful day, one that may have meant the beginning of love for both of us. But Carlie had vanished on the same day, possibly as Bud and I swam and flirted. The fact of that changed everything.

As I reached the mooring on this sad anniversary, I felt only the dregs of loss and I didn't linger. I started for the shore again using a breast-stroke, watching the way my white arms and wavy fingers pushed the water aside. I was almost to the beach when Ida appeared with Arlee in her arms. I wondered if she would mention my swimming attire, but after giving me a quick once-over, she smiled.

For some crazy reason before Arlee was born, I pictured being able to click along doing what needed to be done while Arlee napped. But it didn't quite work that way. For one thing, all the clicking and cleaning in the world wasn't possible in the time she was down. And sometimes, I took naps too, leaving dirty floors, undusted furniture, and piles of wrinkled clothes to breed and multiply. When Arlee was up, it was all about her. I began to get behind on the chores, which wore on me, because I hated clutter. One morning Bud had the courage to ask for a clean work shirt.

"This baby takes up all of my time," I said. "I don't have time to wash your damn shirts. I don't have time to iron. You're going to have to learn how to do it." I cried and ran upstairs to our bedroom. I lay on the bed sobbing, feeling stupid with tiredness, wondering how anyone ever did this. The stairs creaked and Bud stood in the doorway with Arlee in his arms.

"You okay?" he asked.

I wiped tears off my face, sat up, nodded, and smoothed down my grubby T-shirt and my baby-food-stained jeans. I took Arlee from Bud and we all trooped downstairs.

"I'll wear the shirt I wore yesterday," Bud said on the way down. "What the hell. It'll just get that much greasier. I'll try to get home ear-lier, help out."

We reached the bottom of the stairs and I turned and kissed him. "I'll wash shirts today. I can do it. I know I can. I know you're tired too."

But Arlee began to fuss the minute he went out the door and things continued along in that vein for most of the morning. I fed, changed, and burped her, walked from the stairs to the porch, rocked, fed, changed, burped, and so on until early afternoon. I finally ended up in our bed, holding her while she fell asleep after a feeding. I managed to plant her in her crib for her nap. I hurried downstairs and soaked Bud's dirty shirts in ammonia in the kitchen sink before I stuffed them into Grand's good old washing machine.

After that, I stood in the middle of a kitchen floor so dirty that I was walking on gravel and sand instead of linoleum. But before I could take a step toward sweeping and washing the floor, someone hammered on the front door. Arlee shrieked from her crib upstairs as I ran into the hall and threw the door open. Grace Drowns stood there.

"Oh my god. What?" I cried.

"Move the boat out of the yard. Takes up too much room."

My jaw dropped. "What?"

"Move it, or I'll sell it," she said, and she turned and walked away.

I thought about running into the kitchen to grab a knife, but I figured she'd be too far away to hurl it into her spine by the time I got back.

As I took the stairs two at a time to get to Arlee, I shook, I was so mad. I stopped outside of her room and turned into my bedroom to calm down. While she cried, I looked at the *Florine* sitting in the side yard of Daddy's house. Stella hadn't minded that she was there. The boat had belonged to Daddy, she said, and anything that reminded her of Daddy comforted her. In fact, at some point last fall, Stella had laid a ladder against the *Florine*'s broad hull, probably so she could climb up and hang around in the cabin, drink, and remember him.

I took a deep breath, walked across the hall, and held Arlee against my pounding heart until her cries sank into me and drove out all thoughts of crazy Grace.

I talked to Bud about Grace almost as soon as he came through the door after work. He was wild when I told him what she had said to me. "We don't have to move the boat," he said. "She ain't got any business asking us to do that. Who the hell does she think she is? I'm going to talk to her." He left our house and walked toward Stella's.

Grace came toward him before he could get to the front door. She planted herself like a stubborn cow and they faced off. At first Bud's voice was low and reasonable, but soon he was waving his arms and shouting. Finally, he stalked back toward me, and Grace went back into the house. Before he reached me, he swerved and headed for the Buttses' house.

"Gonna talk to Bert," he growled as he went past. I went back into the house to tackle supper. He was gone for about twenty minutes, and then he slammed through the screen door before I could say, "The baby . . ." Right away, she began to cry. I picked her up from the bassinet and we joined him in the kitchen as he paced and raved.

"She says that because it's on her sister's land, she has the right to sell it," Bud said. "She didn't even hear anything I had to say. It's like talking to a rock."

"What did Bert say?" I asked.

"He says she can't sell it, because it's not hers to sell, and since it's Stella's house and Stella wants it there, she's full of crap about what she can and can't do. Says not to worry about it, she's just blowing smoke out her ass."

Bert and Bud spread the word to everyone they knew that, contrary to what they might hear, Leeman Gilham's boat, the *Florine*, wasn't for sale. As days passed, I tucked the whole thing away and relaxed about it and, of course, that was when someone knocked at my door.

I'd never seen him. He was a nice-enough guy, youngish, black beard and blue eyes. Tan face and rough hands like a fisherman. Medium build. He smiled. I smiled. I must have looked like an idiot, standing there with spit-up milk on my shirt, hair looking like a truckload of mice had held a wrestling match in it.

"Yes?" I said, and after that, all pleasantries were off. After I recovered from the perfectly innocent question he put to me about the boat's sale price, I ranted that the *Florine* was mine and would stay mine, contrary to what that bitch across the road thought, and he might as well go fry eggs on hell's roof as to think I would ever let it go and I was sorry that he'd been led down God's garden path but no. No. And no.

He left in a huff and I just spun with rage in the hallway for a minute. Then I sat on the porch and rocked until I calmed down. When I could breathe without exhaling fire, I went upstairs and picked up Arlee, who was deep into her nap, and we walked down the hill to Ida's house. The sight of the harbor calmed me, as it always did. The tide bustled by, whitecaps twirling back on themselves like curls of meringue.

Ida's face beamed when she saw us. She took Arlee from me as carefully as she would handle flower stems made of threaded glass. I made us cups of tea and we sat down in the living room.

"A guy came by, asked how much the *Florine* was," I said, recounting the story.

As I talked, Ida looked out of her picture window toward the harbor, nuzzling Arlee. When I finished, she said, "Why don't you just move the boat?"

"What?" I said.

She shrugged. "Move the boat. Have Bert trailer it down and back it into our yard. That way, Grace will be out of your hair."

"Well, that's not the point," I said.

She sighed. "What is the point?" she said. "It's the easiest thing. Then you can give all your attention to this sweetie pie." She shuffled into her kitchen, humming a hymn to Arlee as I sat there and wondered how the day had taken such a twist.

That night, I said to Bud, "I think I just met the woman who got your father to church every Sunday."

"What did she want?" Bud asked. "Whatever it is, just do it."

We moved the boat. We parked her beside Ida's house, where the *Florine* could reflect on the tides and look forward to Glen's return.

When Grace demanded that we move Bud's 1947 coupe, Petunia, out of the shed that Daddy had built for her when she had belonged to Carlie, we did that too. Bud drove her up to Fred's garage and parked her in a shed on Fred's property.

It was time to move on. Ida had been right. It was the easiest thing to do.

8

Fall was mild that year. The leaves were slow to change and what storms we had lacked spirit. October moseyed in with a lazy yawn and absently brushed September aside like a tattered cobweb.

October 13 would have been Carlie's thirty-ninth birthday. I spent much of that day wishing that she could have played grandmother. Ida was wonderful, but Carlie would have perked things up, had she been around to do it.

"Someday," I told Bud at supper that night, "I'll find out what happened to her."

"Someday, you will," Bud said.

Arlee went down early that day, just as an almost-full moon rose. Bud and I stood in the side garden and watched it come up over the trees, silvering The Point from tip to root. Bud said, "Good night for a walk. You feel like it?"

He fetched Maureen to sit with Arlee. We decided to walk through the woods to the state park, but to do that, we had to cross Daddy's yard and climb over The Cheeks, a cracked boulder that led to a trail that would take us to the park proper. The kitchen light was on in Daddy's house and we stopped to consider Grace's wackiness on our way through the yard.

"Think she'll shoot us?" Bud whispered.

"Let her try," I growled.

"If it comes to it, I'll talk her down," he said.

"Yes, that's worked well so far," I said, and he nudged me.

We snuck across the lawn, stepping onto the fallen leaves heel to toe so that they wouldn't crackle and pop under our feet. We scrambled up over The Cheeks and Bud turned on his flashlight. The childhood path was not as worn as it had been once, when we had used it on a regular basis. When we reached the park, Bud switched off the light and we became part of the moon's blue-tinted mystery as we stood underneath the trees.

"Which way do you want to go?" Bud asked.

"Let's go down to the ledges and sit on the bench," I said. We held hands and listened to the night's tiny whispers as our lungs filled with the nighttime scent of the sea. In just a short time, we made out the outline of a bench overlooking the ocean.

The bench had been put there by Andy's father, Edward Barrington, along with a plaque that read: *On life's vast ocean diversely we sail, Reason the card, but passion is the gale*. Once I had thought the man who had written it, Alexander Pope, had been a relative of Edward's, but Dottie, now college educated, had told me he was a poet.

I couldn't think of Edward without memories of Andy. Thinking of either of them made me uncomfortable, made my injured back twitch, made me recall terrifying things. I wished they didn't live anywhere near The Point, but their family had settled close by ages ago, and if I had to be fair, they had a right to be there, even as we had claimed our pieces of land.

We were fishermen's kids and we came from different worlds. We should never have had anything to do with them. We got involved in their lives because of one of Glen's grand schemes. We were twelve, we were bored, it was summer, and Glen had piles of firecrackers from his father's back storeroom in his possession. When Glen suggested a fire-cracker raid on the cottages, Bud tried to warn us off, but the rest of us longed for adventure. One night we four snuck through the park to the

Barringtons' cottage, where Andy caught us and offered to help. While the Barringtons and their friends partied above us on their big porch, we piled up firecracker hills, lit fuses, and bolted. But the porch caught on fire and we got caught. All of us had to go up to the Barringtons' the next day to say we were sorry. Andy stood in back of his father, not looking us in the eyes as Edward made us apologize, acting high-and-mighty in front of our sets of parents. Dottie had said it best. *"He passed down the line of us like we was fresh recruits."*

"I wish we'd never met them," I said out loud.

"Who?" Bud asked.

"Edward and Andy Barrington."

"Let's not spoil a nice time."

We reached the bench, sat down, and looked out over the moon-struck water. Bud kissed my cheek. "You okay?" he asked.

"I'm so glad you picked me," I said.

"Well, I'm glad you picked me."

We grinned at each other and kissed, and as we did we heard a thump in back of us. We broke apart and turned in time to see the figure of a man hurry back up the path. Bud jumped up, but I grabbed his wrist. "No," I said. "Whoever that is, let him go."

"Let's go back anyway," Bud said. "The mood and the moon aren't getting along." He hustled me up the path and we glanced to the left and to the right, hoping not to glimpse the running man.

That night, I dreamed of Carlie. She paced back and forth from one side of my brain to the other, like a caged animal. She was wearing a black leather coat that came down to the tops of her thighs. High, black boots covered her knees.

"Carlie?" I said to her.

She stopped pacing and looked at me.

"Where did you get those clothes?" I asked her. "I've never seen those clothes."

"We're not what we are," she said. "And we're exactly what we are."

"Okay," I said. "But what about your clothes?"

"I'm just telling you." She started to pace again.

"The way out is through my eyes," I said. She turned, walked toward me, and when I opened my eyes, she disappeared. I got up and went into Arlee's room, where I sat in a small rocker next to her crib and watched the moon kiss her pure, smooth face.

℘

At the general store the next day, Ray told me that Stella had gone somewhere to dry out. "'Least, that's what Grace told me."

"She tell you where?"

"You going to visit her?" Ray looked up at me over his half-glasses. The bristles of his gray crew cut glinted in the overhead light over the cash register.

"No," I said. "But she attacked me one day, and she was gone the next. It's kind of like Grace killed her, buried her somewhere where no one will find her, and then took over her house and her life."

"I guess you got a right to have that much imagination," Ray said. "I got a letter from Glen the other day. Says the food is crap and he's got bug bites from the top of his head to the bottoms of his feet. Says he has to keep his boots on to keep things from crawling inside of 'em. Says it isn't like he thought it would be. Don't know what he thought. The army ain't a vacation. Got to work during a war."

"Guess he thought he was doing the right thing," I said.

"He don't know the right thing from the left thing," Ray said.

9

The snarling, hateful winter we had in 1972 shredded autumn. Incoming and outgoing tides bulldozed ice cakes into the harbor and piled them on shore like the teeth of broken sea monsters. Cold slathered a sheet of sheer ice along the dirt road leading to and from The Point.

The sound of spinning, smoking tires became part of January and February's song. We spread salt and sand outside, but finally Bud and everyone else, except for Grace, who didn't seem to need to go anywhere, parked their cars and trucks up the hill by Ray's. Every time we went outside, an unforgiving wind pounced on us with bitter, sharp claws. No one went out unless they had to work, go to church, or buy groceries.

On rare days when winter pulled back to regroup and allowed an exhausted sun to burn through the low-down clouds, I bundled up Arlee until she couldn't move, strapped her to my chest with a thick, shawl-like sling I had knitted for her, and minced my way in toddler-style steps up to Ray's or down to Ida's.

Once, we ended up staying overnight at Ida's house when a hideous blizzard swooped in during a late-afternoon visit and made it clear that even walking back up the hill to Grand's house wasn't going to happen in a way that would be safe for us.

"I read once about farmers tying ropes between their houses and barns so they wouldn't get lost going back and forth during storms," I said to Ida as we sat in her kitchen after supper, watching snow skirls spin around like hula hoops on tricky hips.

"I believe it," Ida said.

"No school tomorrow," Maureen sang.

Ida winked at me and said to her daughter, "Good. Bible study."

Maureen's smile faded just a little and I had to laugh.

"You too," Ida said. "Do you good."

"Most likely," I said.

"Hah," Maureen said. "Now you're trapped."

"Not if I walk up the hill before breakfast tomorrow morning," I said.

"*The wicked flee though no one pursues, but the righteous are bold as a lion,*" Ida quoted. "Where is that from?" she asked Maureen.

"Proverbs 28:1," Maureen said.

"Name that tune," I said. Maureen's eyes lit from within but she didn't dare to smile. Ida shook her head at the both of us, and thankfully, Arlee began to cry from her crib in Bud's old room. "Well," I said, "no rest for the wicked," and I went to fetch her. I settled us in the rocker next to the crib and as I fed her, Bud stamped his way in through the front door. "Holy shit, it's bad out there," I heard him say. I snorted, imagining the look on his mother's face. I heard his step as he walked through the living room and into his bedroom. He bent down and kissed my cheek.

I gasped at the cold.

"Yeah," he said. "No work tomorrow. Fred threw out his back when he fell in the parking lot. Told us all to go to hell, then he told us to stay home tomorrow."

"We may have Bible study if we don't get out of here tomorrow morning," I said.

"Well, we'll have to do some sinning tonight, then," Bud said, "and pray for sun in the morning."

"How did you get out of it?" I asked. "Growing up?"

Bud grinned. "Sam, believe it or not. Told Ida that church on Sunday was enough and that he needed me on the boat. So, I went on the boat. How'd you get out of it?"

A trickle of regret slipped through me. "Grand asked me once if I wanted to come down here with her. I was kind of an asshole about it. I think I rolled my eyes and told her that I wasn't going to sit with her and Ida and talk about begetting and smiting. I had better stuff to do."

"Wow," Bud said. "She didn't get mad? How come you're still alive?"

I switched Arlee over to my right boob. "Grand was disappointed," I said. "She said something like, 'Well, Jesus loves you, anyway. And so do I.'" I sighed. "Would it have been so much to do? I was so horrible to her, a lot."

"Well, now you got someone to do that to you when she gets old enough," Bud said. "I imagine Grand's up in heaven, happy as hell because you'll get to see what it's like. So it all evens out in the end."

We did commit some hushed-up sinning in Bud's narrow bed that night. Afterward, as we slept, the latest blizzard beelined it out to sea to beat the waves up into twenty-foot rollers hissing froth and fury. On land, the sun shook itself awake in time to light the day. Bud and I tried to make a quick getaway the next morning. Ida beat us to it, but she didn't mention Bible study and neither did we and after cornflakes and tea, I gave her a big hug and my little family struggled up the hill to home.

It was chilly inside, as if the absence of us gave it no reason to keep up the warmth. Bud turned up the heat and I put Arlee into her playpen in the living room.

"You watch her while I take a bath?" I asked Bud.

"Got to shovel, but the snow will be there when I'm ready," Bud said.

"I noticed you got some new muscles last night."

"Bullshit." Bud laughed. "You buttering me up?"

"I mean it."

"Not to change the subject, but to change the subject, I got the mail at Ray's last night before I come down to Ida's. It's on the kitchen table."

I picked up the envelopes and started upstairs. Four of them were white and long and probably had bills tucked inside of them. The fifth one was small and cream colored, like special stationery, with a little note tucked inside. My name was on the front, printed, all capital letters. Freeport postmark. I stopped on the landing, worked my thumb under the flap, and ripped it open. I pulled out a folded white piece of paper, not the matching cream color, as I had expected. I shook it open and read the following words: *I will love you forever.*

"Hey," I said. "Hey. I love you forever too."

"What?" Bud called from the sofa, where he was watching the *Today* show, bouncing Arlee on his knees.

"I said, 'I'll love you forever too.'"

He turned and looked up at me on the stairs. "That's nice. I'll love you forever, back."

I walked down the stairs. "Who's bullshitting who now?" I said, and I handed him the letter. "I got your note," I said. "What's the occasion?"

Bud frowned. "I didn't send this," he said.

"Oh, come on," I said. "If you didn't do it, who did?"

Bud shook his head and looked at me, his black eyes serious as could be.

"I didn't send this," he said. "I'm not kidding. I don't write like that."

I studied the words again. "It's printed," I said. "Could be anyone's writing. I thought it was yours. Who else would have written this to me?"

Bud shrugged.

"You really didn't?"

"No," Bud said. He handed Arlee to me and looked at the letter again. He looked up at me. "Is this from Barrington?" he snapped.

"What?"

"Andy Barrington. He's around, you know."

"I didn't know that," I said. "He's not stupid enough to mess with me, or with you. Why would he do that?"

"Well, who the hell would have sent it?"

"Bud, I really don't know. I'm as freaked-out as you are."

"Fuck," Bud said. "I got to shovel."

"You don't believe me?" I said.

"Well, someone goddamn sent it," Bud said, his eyes blazing. He punched his arms through the sleeves of his plaid flannel jacket.

"Calm down," I said. "I don't know who sent this. I thought you did. You didn't. So, as far as I'm concerned, I don't give a damn who did it."

"Well, it's fucking weird."

"Yes, it is," I said. "I'll ask around as soon as I get a few minutes or when the ice melts. Is that okay with you?"

"I'm going outside," he said, and he left.

Arlee grabbed a piece of my hair and pulled. The pain brought me back to the present. As I unwound my curls from her little hand, I said to her, "Maybe we should have stayed for Bible study."

Bud was outside for about an hour. He was still steaming when he came inside. I pointed to Arlee in her bassinet on the porch.

"Okay," he said as we sat down on the sofa, "we got to figure this out."

And we tried. We thought about all possibilities. I called Dottie at school. We wondered if Glen might have done it. I even thought about Stella or Grace. Bud brought Andy Barrington up again, saying he was going to take the letter up to the cottage and ask him about it. The next day he did just that, but no one was there. "He's cleared out," Bud said, and even though I hadn't known he was there, I felt relieved. "I'll talk to him when he gets back. He's like bad news. He always comes back."

"How do you know?"

"I keep an eye on him," he said, and the subject of Andy shut tight with a bang.

The mysterious note bothered us for a little while, but sometime around March, I tucked it away in the bottom of my underwear drawer and forgot about it as days dipped and rose according to the whims of my baby.

March was lost to winter, but spring fought back in April. In May, the war was over, and spring took its rightful place. I had my twenty-first birthday on May 18, and when Dottie came home from school we celebrated her birthday too. What time and love Arlee didn't take up belonged to the man who would love me forever. Bud didn't need to send me a letter to let me know that. It was written on my heart.

10

About a week after my birthday, Arlee began to master walking, when it became clear to her that getting from one place to another would happen faster if she used the funny-looking things on the ends of her legs. She hung on to edges and curves to make her way from here to there, and Bud and I held her between us for hours, walking from the kitchen to the living room and back and taking her outside when the weather was nice.

On June 12, 1972, our first wedding anniversary, Bud, Dottie, and I sat in lawn chairs and watched Arlee play with pieces of grass and clover on the lawn. Suddenly she stopped, frowned, placed her palms on the grass, pulled herself to her feet ass-end first, and began to walk. Three steps. Plop. Up again. Three steps. Plop. Four steps, teeter, recover, then five steps. The three of us laughed and clapped for her as she made her way to us, her face lit by joy and the June sun.

"Oh, boy," Dottie said. "You're in for it now."

Arlee headed for Bud and he stood and caught her, throwing her into the air with a look on his face that made me say "I do" again, out loud.

"Do what?" Dottie said.

"Marry Bud," I said. Dottie raised her eyebrows and shrugged.

Bud put Arlee down and they moved across the lawn. He seldom grinned, but as he walked with his daughter his face cracked open with happiness. As I watched them, I mourned the part of Arlee's life where she had needed me for everything. Now she would be under her own steam while I trailed after her, trying to keep her from breaking her head, and her heart, on hard, pointy surfaces.

"Well," I said, "guess it's time to have another one."

"Let's wait until we move," Bud said.

"You moving?" Dottie said. I hadn't told her yet. Cecil needed help, at last.

"Yep," I said.

"Got a job in Stoughton Falls," Bud told Dottie. He caught my look and his smile grew smaller. I could ruin his good day by being cranky or I could ball up that feeling and toss it away. I took a deep breath and let it out. I thought about something I had overheard Carlie say to Patty on the phone once. "Being married means never having your own way again," she had said with a sigh. She had been right.

"Got to find a place to rent for fall," I said to Dottie. "Want to go on a road trip?"

"Sure," Dottie said. "Who knows? Might look around myself. More bowling alleys near the city. Could get a job there in some school after I graduate."

It cheered me up to think that Dottie might be teaching gym to schoolkids in Portland, Maine's biggest city, or somewhere else near Stoughton Falls, so that she could drop in anytime. I settled that it would happen in my mind, and with that, she and I got up and chased Arlee around the yard until we wore her out.

❧

Three weeks later, on a warm July day, Glen came home.

Arlee might have known that something about the day was different. I had opened up the storm door to let a summer breeze drift through the locked screen door, and of course Arlee was attracted to it. She loved hitting the screen and shouting, "BAM! BAM! BAM!" I chased after her and brought her back to the kitchen, time and again.

In between bouts of chasing Arlee, I was baking bread to sell at Ray's. I had upped my bread making because Ray had gotten a lot of requests for it. I was making all the bread he would take, because it gave us extra money to move and set up in Stoughton Falls.

When fall came, we planned to leave Grand's house empty. The house would have plenty of minders, though, in the persons of Ida, Maureen, Bert, and Madeline. If it worked out, we would stay in Stoughton Falls for the fall, winter, and spring, after which Arlee and I would come back to The Point and reopen the house for summer.

"Slow down," I called to Arlee, who had dashed for the door again. I was worn out and it wasn't even noon. It had crossed my mind to take her down to Ida's house so I could finish with the bread, but I needed to be more independent. After all, Arlee and I would be alone in Stoughton Falls. We would be partners in crime, she and I. I ran into the hall to grab my daughter. But I stopped suddenly. A tall figure stood just outside the screen door, blocking the light. I hurried toward Arlee, who had been shocked into standing still. "Come here, honey," I said. I picked her up and backed toward the kitchen, where I supposed I could grab a knife or something to defend us.

"Florine, it's just me," a familiar voice said.

"You scared the shit out of me," I said. I flipped the lock up on the screen door and let Glen into the hallway. "I'm so glad you're back," I added. I reached up to hug him with Arlee squeezed between us. My nose, pressed against his uniformed shoulder, picked up sweat and the smell of something burnt. He wrapped his big arms around the both of us and held on until I finally said, "You can let go. We won't run away." He did, but slowly, and we stepped back from each other.

I saw Bud every day, so noticing any changes in him came slow to me. But I hadn't seen Glen for a year. This was no pudgy high school graduate standing in front of Arlee and me. This was six feet two inches of man. He wasn't thin—he would never be thin—but the army had sanded down his softness and varnished his body with muscles. He stood straight and looked down at us with sharp eyes that had seen what there was to see far outside of our little world and beyond that. He looked strange to me until he opened his mouth and the Glen I knew came out.

"She what become of you and Bud foolin' around?" he asked, reaching for Arlee, who reached back.

"Here," I said, and handed her over. "I meant to send pictures . . ."

Glen shook his head. "It's okay," he said. He bent his right arm and made a seat for Arlee. She reached for his chin and patted his shaved face and he laughed.

"She likes you. Arlee doesn't take to just anyone," I said.

"Well, she heard her uncle Glen talk while she was baking in your oven," he said. "'Course she knows me."

"You want to come in?" I said. I had a million questions but I couldn't think of what to say first. We headed for the rockers on the porch. "How long you home?" I asked.

"I got about a month," Glen said. "Then I go back for six more months." He sat down with Arlee still in his arms.

"Want a beer?" I said.

"Sure," he said. I flipped the top on one of Bud's Schlitz cans and handed it to him. He sipped at it and lowered it to the floor next to the chair. Arlee watched every move he made without a sound.

"Can we talk while I finish making this bread?" I said. "I'm supposed to have it up to Ray's sometime this afternoon."

"Sure," Glen said. "Or not talk. I could just as soon sit here with this princess and watch that beautiful water move."

"Good," I said. I went back to the bread, kneading it down and tearing it into two rounds. I plopped them into bowls and set them on the wide windowsill Billy had added on when he'd replaced the window Stella had broken. The sun shone down on the damp dish towels. The heat from it would fire up the dough beneath the towels. I washed and dried my hands and wandered back onto the porch. I opened my mouth to say something, then shut it as I took in Glen, sound asleep in the rocking chair, my little girl snoozing against his chest.

The bread was baked and finished by the time Arlee woke up. I took her from her still-sleeping buddy and she fussed for a little bit as she came back to Earth. I took her into the yard and fed her a late picnic lunch, but she was more interested in getting back to Glen and she headed for the house.

"Glen's asleep," I said. "Let's walk up to Ray's with the bread." I picked her up, crept into the kitchen, and tucked the four warm, wrapped loaves of bread under my arm. We snuck out again to the sound of Glen's soft snores.

On the way up to the store, Arlee wandered off to pick up a blade of grass or to bring me a rock. I would take each thing home and put it into an old cigar box that had belonged to my grandfather, Franklin, for safekeeping. I pocketed a gray rock, a tired blue jay feather, and a dusty daisy. It took us a half hour to take the five-minute walk up the hill. Ray's face lit up when he saw her. He pulled a crinkled paper bag from underneath his counter, reached in, and took out a gumdrop. He held it in the palm of his hand and Arlee grabbed it.

"What do you say, missy?" he said.

"Sa," she said.

I handed over my bread.

"Glen's at my house," I said. Ray's eyes widened.

"Glen's home?" he said.

"You didn't know that?"

"He don't tell me nothing," he said. He handed Arlee another gumdrop, rolled down the top of the bag, and stashed it beneath the counter.

"I would've thought you'd know," I said.

"Christ, no," Ray said. He turned away and stuffed packs of cigarettes into their slots.

"I'll tell him to—"

"Don't bother," Ray said. "Don't bother." He didn't turn back around, even when Arlee said, "Bye." We left the store just in time to catch a ride down to the house with Bud. "Glen's asleep on the porch," I said.

"He's here?" Bud said.

"Either him or his ghost."

"Cecil called today. Wants to know if I can start earlier."

"When?"

"Middle of August," he said. "He's going to put me up in a little shed down by the water on his property."

"Great. Does it have water and a bathroom?"

Bud shrugged. "I can deal."

We pulled up in front of the house and he got out. Arlee scrabbled off my lap and crawled over to the driver's seat. Bud lifted her out while I sat in the car counting whitecaps on the water. Bud came around and opened the passenger door, leaned down, and said, "You sitting there all night?"

"Do I have a say in whether you go or not?"

"You do, but I'm going. I got to get started, Florine."

That settled, we went into the house, where Glen was fixing us some kind of hash from stuff he'd dug out of the refrigerator.

"Rations," he said. "Thought I'd best move my lazy ass."

"Why?" Bud said. "You never cared about moving your lazy ass before."

"True," Glen said. "Good to see you too."

I left them all in the kitchen and went outside. I walked down to the wharf, sat down on the edge of it, slipped my sneakers off, and stuck my feet into the water. It was cold until my feet got used to the temperature. I looked down at my toes, the nails unpainted since I'd given birth. "You look like hell. What do you have to say for yourselves?" I asked them. One foot rubbed itself over the other, as if it were embarrassed.

The ramp shook as someone else walked down to the wharf. I thought it might be Bud coming to tell me that he loved me more than life itself and so he would wait until the fall as we had planned, but it was Dottie.

"Bud's going to Stoughton Falls soon to start work," I said.

"Hello, Dottie, how was your day? Fine, thank you," she said.

"How was your day, Dottie?"

"Good enough. Water warm?"

"Takes a few seconds." She rolled up her summer-job state-park uniform pants, took off her shoes and socks, and eased herself down beside me. We both looked at our feet in the water. "Feels good," she said. "Look at how fat my toes are."

"Mine look like worms," I said.

A cormorant poked its sleek head above the water's surface, spied us sitting there, and ducked back down.

"I guess Bud's got to work," Dottie said. "Wants to do his best. No harm in that."

"You're supposed to say, 'Oh, Florine, my best friend in the world, you poor thing. How can I help? What can I do? How can I ease your pain?'"

"Screw that," Dottie said. She shifted beside me. "Did we ever meet Andy Barrington's mother?"

My toes curled at the sound of "Barrington." "Never met the woman," I said.

"She fell off the rocks by that bench Mr. Barrington put up."

"No shit," I said. "When?"

"This afternoon. She was higher than a kite. Came through the woods and sat down with some family having a picnic. Tried to talk to them but she wasn't making much sense. Left them and went off down the path. The mother come to me, said she seemed out of it. I walked the way the mother told me she went. Got to the bench. That metal plaque with the saying on it was lying on the ground next to a screwdriver. The bench was scratched up where she'd pried it off. Heard someone yell and found her catty-corner on the rocks, cut up and bloody, hollering away."

"Hollering what?"

"Couldn't make sense of it. I called for some help and we hefted her back up onto the path and got her on her feet. We tried to clean her up, but she got riled and said she wanted to get out of there and get home, so I walked her back up the path to the house—place still gives me the willies—and waited until the maid come to the door."

"Louisa?"

"That her name? Anyways, Louisa hauled her inside, said thank you, and pretty much shut the door in my face."

"Every one of them is a pain in the ass," I said. "I wish they'd just go away."

"You think they do it on purpose? You don't even know her."

"She's a Barrington. That's enough," I said. "Speaking of pains in the ass, Glen's at the house with Bud. Come have supper with us."

It was good to have the four of us together again. We talked that night about what we had done and who we had been, not who we were and what we were going to do. We drank beer and took a trip back down memory lane, remembering times that would never come around again.

11

Glen didn't talk about the war much, except to Bud. He didn't flirt with Evie Butts, who fidgeted and wriggled around him like a dog in heat. He thanked Maureen for writing to him, but told her it was okay if she didn't do that. He didn't go uptown to Long Reach to visit his high school buddies. In fact, he didn't do much of anything.

Most of the time, he slept on Grand's porch, in her old rocker. I fed him and went about my day while he rocked and slept and rocked. Bud joined him there when he got home from work. After supper, they drank beer and talked until the night switched places with dawn. One night, cranky, cold, and lonely, I came downstairs at about midnight. I said to them, "Time to go night-night," and I huffed back upstairs. Bud followed me right away, leaving Glen on the porch. "Thank you," he said as we got into bed, and he was asleep two seconds later.

The next morning at the kitchen table, after I'd coaxed Glen into the kitchen with six scrambled eggs and half a pound of bacon, I said to him, "What is up between you and Ray? I told him you were home and he didn't know. I felt bad for him."

Glen snorted. "Don't go feeling too awful sorry for him," he said.

"Why not?"

"He told me the army might be the best thing for me. Give me a good start in life. Christ, Florine, it's hell. You don't know. You just don't know." And with that, he wiped his face with the paper napkin I'd provided, got up, kissed the top of my head, gave Arlee a big hug, and left the house.

"Glen's gone back," Bud told me that night. "Called Fred's and told me goodbye."

"I hope it wasn't because of me," I said. "All I did was ask him about Ray, and he stomped out of the house."

"Leave was over anyway," Bud said.

"He's not who he was," I said.

"None of us is," Bud said.

"Do you ever wish you had gone into the army?"

"No," Bud said. "I don't think I could've stood being told what to do, more so if what they was telling me to do was crazy."

☙

The next morning when someone knocked at the screen door, I hoped it might be Glen, come back to us. But this shadow form was tiny and most unwelcome.

"Go away," I shouted, and I snatched Arlee away from the door and stepped back, ready to run.

"Florine," Stella said through the screen, "don't be afraid. I came to say I'm sorry."

"Go away before I call the sheriff," I said. "Parker told me to call him if I needed to, anytime. I don't want you anywhere near us."

"I don't blame you," she said. "I was kind of crazy."

"Kind of?"

She sighed. "Okay," she said, "I'm calling in my chips from that time you wrecked my bedroom," she said. "I just want a little of your time. That's all I want from you."

"I would think you scratching up my face evened things out. I don't owe you anything."

"Well, I'm sober and I want to apologize."

"You can do it from there," I said.

Another sigh. "I guess we're just destined to tolerate each other. Okay.

I'm sorry for every miserable thing I've ever done to you. I'm sorry for how I made you feel when I slept with your father, even though I loved him more than life. I'm sorry for being drunk all the time after he died. And I am very, very sorry for attacking you. Thank you for not pressing charges. I will not bother you, or your family, again." She turned to go.

Goddammit, Grand, I said to my grandmother, who pushed me toward Stella's apology. I walked to the door and said, "Wait."

Stella stopped. I noticed that she wore no makeup and that she looked older. Tired. "That baby isn't such a baby anymore," she said, taking in Arlee's rosy cheeks and redder-than-ever hair. "And she is the picture of her grandmother."

"Yes, she is," I said. "Are you moving away or are you back?"

"I'm back," Stella said. "It's my home."

"Grace leaving? She's a real hoot."

"When Grace focuses on something, she nibbles on it like a squirrel with an acorn. Anyway, she's staying with me for company for a while. I'm sorry she made you move the boat. I love that boat too. As far as I'm concerned, you can move the *Florine* back onto the lawn."

"We'll leave her where she is," I said. Arlee whimpered and put her head on my shoulder. I stroked her hair. "Stella," I said, "I'm tired of this crap. I have a baby now. We'll never get along. Let's just start and stop right here."

Stella nodded. "All right," she said. "I'd like to hear the word 'forgive' from you, but I can wait."

I couldn't say the word. Instead, I said, "I hope you're able to stay out of the sauce."

Stella nodded. "Me too," she said. "I'll see you."

I didn't tell her that we were moving.

❧

The night before Bud left for Stoughton Falls, I took Arlee down to her grandmother's house for her first overnight. I tried to be calm, but I failed.

"She'll probably wake up in the middle of the night," I babbled to Ida.

"She'll want a hug, and a bottle. She doesn't stay up long; it's more like she wants to know someone is there. She wakes up really early. Usually, Bud takes care of her in the morning so she might be strange about that. But I'll be down for her before breakfast."

Maureen took Arlee's hand and led her into the living room and out of my sight.

"Florine, she'll have a wonderful time," Ida said.

To my shame, I began to cry. "I know," I said.

"Bud will be okay too. You knew what you were getting into when you married him, Florine," Ida said, her voice gentle.

"I know," I said. "He's always wanted to leave."

"You need to let him try things out," Ida said. "He's had sparks in his shoes ever since he was a little boy."

"I told him I would go anywhere with him," I said, "but that was before we were actually leaving."

Ida said, "Go and be with Bud. Have a wonderful night and don't let him know how you really feel. Send him off with a smile and he'll be happy to come back."

I left my little girl with her aunt and her grandmother. With every step up the hill, my legs and feet felt as if they were being torn from their roots.

Bud and I had a light supper. We didn't talk much, partly because we were used to being interrupted, and partly because I had to concentrate on not running full tilt down to Ida's to grab my baby back. We packed everything that Bud needed to live in Cecil's shed, so that he could just hop into the car and take off in the morning.

After that, we went to bed. It was strange to be able to make love noises without being afraid of waking Arlee, but Bud's body and the way it moved with mine brought back things I had almost forgotten about during my first year as a mother. We loved each other into deep sleep at about midnight, but soon after that, I woke and was up before I knew what I was doing. My feet automatically started for Arlee's room. I stopped in the hall and turned around. I walked across our bedroom to the window and looked down over Ida's house. All was dark and, although I strained my ears, I couldn't hear a sound, which I hoped meant that Arlee was asleep.

Bud whispered, "Come back to bed, baby. She's safe." I went to him and we found each other again.

He left as the sun rose over The Point, but before he did, he pulled me close and whispered, "I told you when we got together our very first night, Florine, I ain't leaving you. I'll always be back. Count on it."

"And I will never leave you," I said.

I stood on the road and let the rising sun warm my face. Then I ran down to Ida's house.

12

"When you going to get a license?" Dottie asked me. "When I get a minute," I said. "I've been kind of busy." "Doing what?"

She ignored my look. We'd been in the car for about two hours. She was driving me to Stoughton Falls to look at a house trailer that belonged to one of Cecil's friends. Over the phone, Bud had told me that he'd checked it out and that he thought it might do for us for a start.

He called me every day from a phone at the back of Cecil's garage. Auto-repair noises took up a lot of ear space at first, but I learned to tune them out in favor of my husband's quiet, deep voice.

Life in the shed was interesting, he told me. He shared it with a bat that came out every night. Said he just ducked into his sleeping bag while the bat cruised the shed, snapping up bugs before flying out for the night. "Never have a mosquito in the place," he told me, like it was a point of pride. He soaped up and shampooed in a nearby pond, he said, and an old double-seater outhouse sitting near the shed took care of his other needs.

"Why?" I said.

"Why what?"

"Why two seats? How would that happen? Do people wait for each other so they can go to the bathroom together? Don't you think that's weird?"

"Hadn't thought about it."

"Do you switch off seats?"

"No, I use one."

"Which one?"

"The one on the left. This what we're going to talk about?"

"Arlee said 'Ida' today. Only it was more like 'Ia.'"

"That's my girl."

"How's work?"

"Lots to do up here. Cecil's got a good thing going. Busy from morning to night."

"Me too. Baking lots of bread."

Long pause.

"Bud?"

"Shit," he said. His voice quivered. "I miss you so much."

My throat closed, but I managed to squeak out, "Me too."

We heaved and sighed over the phone for about ten seconds.

"I need you here," he said.

"I need you," I said. "Period."

I looked out the window at the way the generous August sun cast a pale gold sheen over The Point. A cicada's zzzzz high up in a nearby tree signaled dog days. It was hot. It was sunny. It was perfect, except for no Bud. Arlee looked for him every day and she fussed when he didn't show up, but I didn't tell him that over the phone because I didn't want to break his heart. I didn't tell him that she stood in front of the screen door and waited for the sound of his car. I didn't tell him that I cried as I watched her wait for him and that I had to distract her to get her away from the door.

One day, early in the morning, Bud called. "Cecil may have a line on a place for us to live," he said, not even trying to contain the excitement in his voice.

"That was fast," I said, while I thought, Well, crap, it's real now.

Bud was due home the next day, Friday, but we decided that he should stay there through the weekend so Dottie and I could ride up on

Saturday and check out the trailer. So, my best friend and I, along with Arlee, found ourselves driving toward Stoughton Falls and Cecil's garage, where we would pick up Bud and go on to see the place together. Arlee sang a song only she understood from her car seat in the back.

"Don't think I want to live in a trailer," I said to Dottie.

"Now, you don't know until you see it," Dottie said.

"What if I hate it?"

"Why you worried about something hasn't happened yet?"

"Just getting ready for the worst."

"You got to change your attitude."

"When you going back to college?"

"Not soon enough for you, I guess."

"I always miss you when you go."

Dottie slowed down as we reached a stop sign. We had reached Route 100 in Stoughton Falls.

"Left or right?" she said.

"Right," I said. "Cecil's is down the road."

Cecil closed on weekends, so we found only Bud slouched on a bench beside four giant green doors hiding the greasy cave where he tinkered with other people's cars and trucks. My mouth slid up to a grin when I saw him. Dottie played chicken, driving as close to him as she dared before his smirk made her stop. She hadn't even shifted into park before I jumped out and filled my empty arms with my husband. I drank in his scent of automobile oil and car paint as if it were Champagne. I found his lips just as he found mine, but before we could get much further, Arlee whined from the backseat and Bud let go of me and bent to take her from her car seat.

Dottie got out of the car and stretched. "I ain't kissing you," she said to Bud. "But I got to pee, that's for sure."

I did too, so Bud let us into the office and waiting room beside the garage and gave us a tour. The garage, with its four lifts, was twice as big as Fred's shop.

Dottie raided the candy machines in the office and stuffed her pockets with M&M's, gumballs, and peanuts. "Well, we going to see the trailer or what?" she said.

We got back into the car. Bud climbed into the backseat beside Arlee, and we turned around and drove back toward the intersection. We went through it, and about a half a mile farther Bud said, "Turn in here," and Dottie took a right into a dirt driveway.

The trailer sat to the left of the driveway. "It's pretty big," Bud said. "See, they got a picture window and a fence around the yard so Arlee's got a place to run."

Dottie stopped the car in front of a small, dark-brown shed with a wide door. "I'm thinking of storing Petunia in here," Bud said. "Or we can use it however you want." He hopped out of the car. "Backyard too, with a picnic table."

I sighed as I forced myself out of the passenger seat.

"Give it a chance," Dottie said under her breath. "It don't look so bad."

I held Arlee as we followed Bud into a small backyard with the picnic table he had mentioned. A garden shed stood to the right of the yard. The lawn had been mowed a few days earlier. The blue siding on the back of the trailer looked cared-for. Propane tanks, closed in by a high, dark fence, stood close to the right side of the back of the trailer. A line of stunted firs and pines crowded the edge of the back lawn.

"We can clean them out, make some paths through the woods," Bud said.

"Ain't that illegal?" Dottie said, but Bud ignored her as he walked toward the front of the trailer.

The good-size front yard was surrounded by chain-link fence. "You can make a garden in the yard," Bud said. "Plant flowers, maybe?" A small gate in the fence led up a set of steps to the front door. Bud unlocked the door and we followed him inside.

I put Arlee down and she ran to the picture window that looked out into the front yard. She put her small hands on the glass surface. Little prints remained when she took them away. She ran down the hall, Bud chasing her.

"It's not horrible," I said to Dottie. The space inside surprised me. The kitchen took up the right end of the trailer, with cupboards and counter space. Off of that was a little room with space for a washer and dryer.

A small bar separated the kitchen from the widest part of the trailer. On the right, I could fit a dining-room table and chairs. To the left, where the picture window was, we could squeeze in a sofa, a chair or two, a coffee table, and a television set. Dottie and I followed Bud and Arlee down the hall. A large room at the end of the trailer would be our bedroom, should we decide to live there. To the right was a bathroom bigger than the one at Grand's house, and next to it, two small bedrooms sat side by side.

"One can be a bedroom for Arlee," Bud said. "Maybe you could use the other room to do some knitting or whatever you want."

"Or a guest room," I said. "For Dottie, when she wants to drop in."

"Sounds good to me," Dottie said. "I ain't sleeping on the sofa."

The tour over, we ended up back in the living room. I looked outside at the yard, and beyond that, at Route 100, which, on a Sunday, wasn't as busy as it would be on a weekday. I would find that out later, along with details I couldn't take in on that day.

"Well," Bud said. "What do you think?"

"It's okay," I said.

Dottie took Arlee out into the yard while Bud and I stayed inside the trailer and broke in the floor of our bedroom. We were harsh in our eagerness to attach ourselves to each other again, if only for a few minutes. Our bones ground together as we tumbled from corner to corner and back to the middle of the room.

"Thanks for the privacy," I said to Dottie on the way home.

"I aim to please," she said. "Is it always that quick?"

13

Every car and truckload that went up the hill from The Point toward Stoughton Falls broke my heart. We took some of the furniture from the house, but left most of it there, where it would wait in the silent dark of wintertime for our return in late May. We mothballed furniture, covered everything with old sheets, and tied our heartstrings to a post on the headboard of our bed.

Finally everything was done. I stood in the doorway that September twilight, unwilling to turn out the hall light while Bud sat in the car with our cranky baby. Finally, my finger pushed the light switch, I heard a tiny click, and Grand's house went to sleep as we bumped up the hill and away. I didn't look back and I fought not to cry.

About halfway to Stoughton Falls, I looked at the side of Bud's dashboard-lit face. "We're summer people now," I said to him.

He grunted. "Who'd a thunk it?" he said.

I kept myself busy the first few days by arranging furniture and putting things away. Arlee and I went outside often. She played while I cut the grass with a little rolling mower we bought at the Elephant Mart down the road. We watered the one sorry rosebush sprouting under the picture window. Traffic was heavy on Route 100, especially during morning and evening commutes into Portland, about twenty minutes away. I found that if I shut my eyes and tried hard enough, I could imagine the *whoosh* that the cars made sort of matched the sound the harbor tides made as they washed in and out. Homesickness came in roiling waves, but I didn't dare call Dottie or Ida. I didn't want them to think I was a sissy. I told myself to get with the program a hundred times a day. I thought about Bud. "This is fun. This is an adventure," I said to Arlee, often.

"Fuh," she replied.

"Fun," I agreed.

I cleaned the trailer and sometimes I made bread and when I had gone through my little routine, I willed Bud to come home early. He was done for, most nights, but after he washed away the daily grime he kept Arlee out of trouble while I made supper. He put her to bed and read her stories, after which he joined me in the living room and later, in bed. When he was home, it was a good and quiet time.

"It's almost like a vacation," I said. "Just us. No Stella or Grace. No Ray, no . . ."

"Bible-thumping mother?" Bud said.

"I love Ida," I said.

"Me too, but just us is fine with me."

All that couldn't last, of course.

One October morning, I told Arlee to stay out of trouble while I ran to the bathroom to throw up. Dr. Anna Pulsifer told me that the baby I was carrying was due on May 8th. The nausea would pass, she said. But she was wrong.

Being the queasy, pregnant mother of a toddler was a pain in the ass for both Arlee and me, but we made a game out of it. When the urge struck I stuck her in her playpen, held up my finger, said, "Wait," and ran for it. She learned to stay put until I returned to her and we went into the kitchen where, with me shaky and sick, we shared crackers.

"I don't understand this," I said to Ida, over the phone. "I was never sick with Arlee."

"Each one is different," Ida said. "I was the opposite. Couldn't keep anything down with Bud, but Maureen was another story. No rhyme or reason to it. Ginger ale and saltines worked for me."

It didn't do the trick for me, and one night, after a busy day of running for the toilet and chasing Arlee, I said to Bud, "I'd like to have this baby now, please."

"You need some help? Ma will come help."

"I know," I said. "But I don't want to bother her. What if she wants to have Bible study? She's so much better than I'll ever be. It makes me nervous that she thinks I'm going to hell after I die."

"She loves you anyway," Bud said.

"So you agree I'm going to hell after I die?"

"Walked right into that one, didn't I?" Bud said.

"Hard to walk around it," I said. "I don't need help. I can handle this."

But it got worse. A couple of days after a half-assed Thanksgiving for the three of us, Bud left work to rush me to Portland to Maine Medical Center's emergency room. After they stuck a needle in my arm to pump fluids into my dried-up body, and told me I had something called hyperemesis gravidarum (a fancy name for Puke-itis), Bud called it.

"Arlee needs someone who can keep up with her," he said. "And you need to rest."

Ida showed up two days later and put me to bed with soup and crackers.

"I know you're not hungry," she said, "but you have to keep trying."

"Where's Maureen?" I asked her as she sat on the bed and watched me eat.

"Madeline's keeping an eye on her. When you lived alone in Grand's house, we watched over you more than you knew. She'll be fine. And so will you."

"Doesn't feel that way right now," I said.

"The baby's healthy, I'm here to watch Arlee and I'm glad to do it, and Bud can go to work. That takes pressure off all of you."

"I appreciate it, Ida, but I'm still sick as he——. I mean a dog."

Ida smiled. "Florine, you can swear in front of me. Jesus won't take off points for a good swear, now and then."

"I miss Arlee," I said. "I know she's in the living room with Bud, but I'm losing so much good time with her."

"She seems to be just fine. Babies are resilient. She knows you don't feel well. They pick up on a lot. She's got her daddy out there with her."

"I know," I said, trying not to get irritated. "I know she's tough as nails. I'm saying *I* miss spending time with her."

"You'll get that time back when you're better. She's loved, she's happy, and she knows you're nearby. You need to stop worrying and concentrate on getting better."

What I really wanted was someone who would listen to me whine and feel sorry for myself. Ida was no fun. Everything she said made sense. I sighed and plugged away at the soup and crackers. Nausea met them halfway down, but I was determined to keep the food in my stomach. I was more afraid of disappointing Ida than I was of losing precious fluids.

Arlee's second Christmas passed with Ida, Maureen, Bud, and sometimes me gathered around a tiny tree. Bud had driven to The Point to bring Maureen to Stoughton Falls and they had gone out into the woods together to cut it down. They put the tree up and we decorated it with ornaments and lights Ida bought from Elephant Mart. I stayed in bed for most of the holiday, but we did the best we could. Maureen went home after a couple of days, and Ida stayed on until the second week in January 1973, when a boatload of flu snagged against the shore of the new year and caught Maureen off guard.

The day after Ida left, Bud said, "You going to be all right?"

"I'll do my best," I said.

We struggled through to the middle of March. Bud took me in for fluids twice a week. He and Arlee found something to do while they pumped and plumped me up. Some days were useless as far as my being able to help, but somehow, as Ida had noted, Arlee sensed how I felt. We took long naps on my bed. Bud went to the Stoughton Falls library and got a library card. He toted home piles of children's books recommended to him by the librarians. I read to Arlee in bed or on the sofa, or we watched *Sesame Street* and *Mister Rogers' Neighborhood*. At night, Bud completely took over.

I still felt sorry for myself, but Bud was getting impatient and tired, and his mother's matter-of-factness crept into his conversation more and more. One night when I whined, "Do you still love me?" he snapped, "Don't be so foolish, of course I do. But I'll tell you right now, I'll be goddamn glad to see this one come out."

In late March, the nausea came back full tilt, and my back began to act up, to the point where I could barely walk, let alone run after Arlee. I was too sick to care for her, and Bud reached his wits' end.

The morning I couldn't get up, he said, "Florine . . ."

I said, "I know," tears streaming down my face.

We packed Arlee's clothes and her toys and Bud took her down to The Point. She left me with a smile on her face, snuggled in her Daddy's arms, carrying Dodo the donkey. Rivers of water ran down my face from the time I heard Bud pull out of the driveway until the time he returned to hold me in his arms and tell me that she was playing a game and eating a cupcake when he'd left her.

I took the sheets off her crib mattress so that I could hold them to me and smell her. At night, I imagined her squeaky voice calling out for one of us.

"Goddamn quiet," Bud said one night in bed.

"I hear her talking and running through the trailer," I said.

"I do too," he said. "Drives me crazy."

"Do you think we can drive down to see her?"

"You really want to do that? Even if you could, it would rip you up to leave again."

He was right, but that didn't make it any easier.

Once, Ida let me talk to Arlee on the phone, but it confused her.

"Mama?" she said. "Mama?"

"Here, honey," I said. "Mama's right here."

"Mama. Mama. Dow." When Ida let her go, she ran through the house calling my name, which killed me.

Not having to care for both Arlee and me eased things for Bud, but he still had to come home to my grumpiness. It was hard to carry on a conversation when all I wanted to do was throw up. Every day I got up after Bud had gone to work to try to make some kind of supper for him, but that was a lost cause. The baby had gotten big, and my dizziness made it almost dangerous for me to try to do anything. Bud had to make his own meals, plus bowls of soup, ginger ale, and crackers for me.

And then, of course, my fear of losing Arlee forever in some way surfaced because she wasn't right there in front of me. I knew her grandmother and her aunt would protect her with all of their fierceness and love, but accidents happened. I had nightmares where I couldn't get to her, and others where I couldn't find her. I had nightmares where I saw Carlie walking off with her, and I couldn't catch them.

Apparently, how I acted out during those dreams affected Bud's sleep, because one night he woke me up and got tough with me. "Cut this out," he said. "I miss her too. Let me sleep. You sleep. Let's all sleep, for chrissake." He brought me a glass of water and said, "Now, go to sleep," and I did.

One Saturday morning, after he brought me a bowl of oatmeal and then sat on the bed beside me, I said, "You didn't sign up for this, Bud. I'm sorry."

A quick flash across his face told me that he thought so too.

"Of course, I didn't sign up for it either," I said, my temper at the ready.

"I know," he said. "It's been a tough time for you."

"I guess this is what life is," I said.

"Christ," he blurted out, "I hope it gets better than this."

That made me mad. "Well," I said, "if you don't like it, feel free to go."

He looked at me as if I was crazy. "Sometimes," he said, "I get to say what I'm thinking without being yelled at. It's been tough for all of us. I was just getting it out by saying that. No sense in sugarcoating it. Give me a fucking break."

"Why don't you take a fucking break," I yelled, and he did. He slammed out of the trailer and didn't come back until the afternoon. He walked into the bedroom and mumbled, "I'm sorry."

"I am too," I said, but we were still both tender to the touch and we weren't ready to make up. He went into the living room, leaving faint traces of something that smelled like whiskey behind. By nighttime, we were over it. We held each other and I told him I was sorry.

I decided that thinking good thoughts no matter how I felt would be better for my baby. I put my trust in Ida and Maureen and focused on Arlee's brother- or sister-to-be. I closed my eyes and rubbed my belly, which made the baby kick and move. I turned on the radio and let it hear the latest songs. Baby liked the Carpenters, Elton John, and John Denver the most, or at least I did. I sang Elvis and the Beatles to it in a rusty voice while I stretched out on the sofa or in bed.

On Tuesday, May 1, at about nine in the morning, they cut me open and took all six pounds of my baby boy from me. Bud named him Travis because he had heard it somewhere and liked it. We added Daddy's first name, Leeman, for his middle name. I wanted to add Sam's name too, but Bud shook his head.

"Are you sure?" I asked. "We won't have any more." We had decided to tie my tubes. I would not go through this again. Neither would Bud.

"I'm sure," Bud said. "We got Dad in our blood. That's enough."

14

On my twenty-second birthday, Bud and I took Travis home to The Point. As we passed Ray's, my heart sped up, and I don't think that it was just my mind telling me that Bud's foot pressed down a little harder on the gas pedal. The pure blueness of the harbor snatched my breath away. We bucketed down the hill to Grand's house.

Madeline Butts came out of her house and waved at us from her green lawn. "Welcome back!" she hollered. As Bud stopped the car in front of the house, Ida, Maureen, and a little girl I almost didn't recognize walked up the hill to meet us.

"Please take the baby," I said to Bud, and handed Travis over. My legs shook as I got out of the car. God, would she remember me? Oh, yes. Before I could call her name, the little girl broke away from Maureen's hand and headed for me in a jerky run, her small face lit by a big smile. "Mama!" she cried, and then she was in my arms. I held her tight, trying to take her all in at once.

"I missed you, so much, sweet girl," I whispered. Arlee muckled onto my ribs with her now-long legs clinging like a starfish to a rock.

"Told you she wouldn't forget you," Bud said. Arlee reached for him and we switched kids off so that he could hug his daughter.

"She's been so excited," Maureen said. "I told her Mama and Daddy were coming home and she woke me up at sunrise, holding her best dress out, ready to go. She's been wild ever since."

"She's heavier, that's for sure," I said. "And taller. What have you been feeding her?"

Ida was transfixed by Travis and didn't hear me. It was hard not to fall under his spell. He was a beautiful baby, and I say this with the understanding that many babies are less than pretty. It isn't their fault. They grow into themselves. But Travis was a handsome boy from the start.

"He looks like Leeman," Madeline said. "He's just so sweet."

He did look like my father. His hair was pale and curled in waves over his head, and Daddy had passed his sky-blue eyes on to his grandson. His hands and feet were big for a newborn. And he *was* sweet, for the most part, except when he wasn't, and then his mood rumbled in like a sudden summer thunderstorm before leaving as if it had never been there in the first place.

"How are you feeling?" Madeline said. "You had quite a time."

"Good," I said. "A little sore. It's weird to remember how sick I was."

"Happy birthday, by the way. Dottie comes home next week," she said.

We stood outside for a few more minutes, holding babies, catching up, and then the house in back of me spoke out and said, *I'm waiting. I've missed you. You ever coming inside?* Madeline kissed me on the cheek and trotted off. Ida and Maureen headed down to their house. For a few seconds, Arlee was confused, but when I said, "Come on," she frisked around us like a lamb and followed us into the house. I walked right into the kitchen, where the sun hit the table, and I let out the breath I had held for over nine months. "We're here," I said. "We're home."

Someone, or more than one someone, had dusted and swept out winter for us, and turned on the water and the electricity. Bud checked the refrigerator. "Milk. Bread. Butter. A dish of something for supper," he said. "Ha! And a six-pack of Schlitz. All set."

I headed for the living room and stopped in front of Grand's red ruby glass cabinet on the way. Every piece of glass sparkled and the cabinet had been wiped free of dust, its shelves polished and shining. I tried not to look at the empty space in the center of the top shelf, where Grand's red ruby heart had set until New Year's Day, 1964, when, enraged by Stella's growing relationship with Daddy, I had grabbed the heart, run to the ledges in the state park, and thrown it into the sea, begging for some sort of trade that might bring my mother home. Carlie hadn't come back, but Grand had been quick to forgive me for my temper and my impulsiveness. The empty spot reminded me of her goodness.

History filled this house, but I didn't have time to dwell on it. Travis brought me back to the present with a tiny whimper. "He needs a bottle," I called to Bud.

"So do I," he said as he went out to the car, Arlee skipping behind him.

"Thanks," I muttered. I went into the kitchen and warmed it up myself. Every noise I made, the clanking of the metal pan, the *shish* of running tap water, the click of the stove knob, was music to me. The sound of the gulls bitching at one another outside, the wind chasing its tail off the water, the smell of the clean May sky, all of it was glory on Earth.

With the bottle warmed, I took my son out onto the porch for his first sit-down in one of Grand's rocking chairs. I settled my butt onto the woven bamboo slats, placed him in the crook of my arm, and put the bottle into his greedy mouth. Behind me, I heard the pitter-patter of little girl feet as Arlee traipsed into the kitchen. "Mama, where you?" she called. *Where you?* How many times had I said that in my mind after Carlie had gone away? And how many times had I wanted to hear what I was about to say. "I'm right here, honey. Right here."

When Arlee reached us, she stared at the fuzz on top of Travis's head. Then she saw the bottle in my hand. "Me," she said.

"How about you feed Travis?" I said. She scrambled up into the chair next to me.

"You're the boss," I said, and I placed her brother into her arms. I took an old pillow from the chair next to us and placed it in the space between the arm and seat of the chair. I handed her the bottle and guided it to his mouth. After a couple of tries we got the nipple where it was supposed to go and Travis sucked away.

The rest of the day blurred as I learned how to take care of them together. Travis was a mellow lump of lazy love, while Arlee walked and talked close on my heels like a fawn tracking its mother.

I had a little time in the afternoon, after I put Travis into the bassinet on the porch. Seeing me do this, Arlee pulled me into the living room, climbed up onto the sofa, and tugged at Grand's old afghan. I put it over her and she was asleep in no time.

I snuck toward the kitchen, but before I cleared the hall, someone pounded on the front door. Red rage made me want to strangle whoever might be there, but I managed to choke it back before I opened the door. It was good old Grace.

I blinked. She didn't.

"Yes?" I said, thinking to hurry things along.

"I wanted to see the baby," Grace said, "before I leave."

"You leaving?"

"That's what I just said."

"And you want to see Travis?"

"That his name?"

"Yes. Be quiet. They're both sleeping."

I turned, Grace followed, and we walked over to the bassinet. She looked down at Travis, and then she busted out laughing.

"What the hell was that?" I sputtered.

"Stella's gonna have a shit fit," she said. "Looks just like her old man, don't he?"

"That old man was my father," I said. "Show some goddamn respect, for chrissake. Why don't you and Stella both go and good riddance."

"Stella don't have nowhere else to go," Grace said. "I'm going because I don't like it here. People ain't friendly." And with that, she left.

"Where is your father?" I asked Arlee near suppertime as I sat in the kitchen feeding Travis. During the day, I hadn't thought much about

Bud's whereabouts, but now that the sun was warming the back of my head before heading for its nightly slumber, it occurred to me to wonder if he had gone back to Stoughton Falls without telling me.

Arlee ran to the window. "Daddy," she said. And Daddy walked through the door. Arlee ran to greet him.

He held her as he came through the door, and gave me a big grin. "Hello, Muthah!" he hollered. His eyes sparkled and swam.

"You been drinking?" I asked.

"Well, a couple of beers and a shot or two of whiskey," he said. "Ran into Bert and a couple of fellas at the Lobster Shack. Been catching up. Forgot the time."

"I guess you did."

"Well, pardon me for taking some time for myself. Figured Ma and Maureen was helping out here."

"No," I said. "Only person I've seen today is Grace."

"You whining?" he said, and smiled. "'Cause you sound like you're whining." He got down into my face and planted a sloppy kiss on my lips.

"Mama's whining," he said to Arlee. "Let's go see the water, and let Mama get over it." I watched them walk toward the wharf, wondering if her little hand was all that was holding him up. As I thought about following them, Maureen came out of the Warner house and joined them for a while, until a car I didn't recognize grumbled down the hill. Maureen waved, walked up the ramp, and hopped into the car. The driver, a girl I also didn't recognize, turned the car and rattled back up the hill. I smoothed back Travis's golden curls as he finished his bottle.

While I fixed supper, I wondered at the way Bud had said, *Mama's whining.* Almost like a sneer. It bothered me. He had never spoken to me that way. He had been drinking beer since high school, but he hadn't gotten ugly. Had the whiskey done that? Then, I reasoned, maybe the booze had just hit him wrong. Maybe it was his way of shaking off the butt end of a horrible winter. It had been hell on all of us. I tucked my resentment away and relished the fact that we were home.

We all deserved a little drop of kindness.

15

Bud fell asleep sitting up on the sofa after turning down supper. I fed the kids and worked around him.

"Daddy tie," Arlee said at one point. When she said it again, I came close to explaining the difference between Daddy tired and Daddy drunk. Patience and aggravation with my husband set my mood to cranky. I decided to cheer myself up by blessing Ida with Travis, Arlee, and myself. We walked down the hill as the sun sank below the treetops in the west.

"How's your first day back been?" Ida asked me as she took Travis from me and we sat down in the living room.

"Like I never left," I said. "Thanks for cleaning up and putting food into the fridge. Can't thank you enough for taking care of Arlee." My daughter clambered up onto the sofa and cuddled tight against me.

"She's glad to see you," Ida said. "She was a good girl, weren't you, honey?" Arlee snuggled closer to me. Ida said, "How'd you make out taking care of two babies?"

"Piece of cake, for today," I said. "Oh, Grace stopped by. She said Stella's staying. Has she fallen off the wagon yet?"

"Stella is trying her best to stay sober," Ida said. "I take her to church with me, every Sunday. I'm proud of her."

"Well, good," I said.

"It is."

Ida's face set. Time to change that subject.

"Maureen okay?" I asked.

"I let her go up to Long Reach for the night. She's made some nice friends."

"Aren't she and Evie friends?" I asked.

"They aren't like you and Dottie were," Ida said. "They're different."

"Dottie and I are about as different as we can get," I said. "And we get along fine."

"I'm happy with the friends that Maureen has now," Ida said. Her face set again. We were done with this topic too, evidently. Tiredness tugged at my bones.

Suddenly, I blurted out, "Sometimes, it's hard to talk to you. I feel like I say the wrong things, or I'm about to say the wrong things, or I'm thinking the wrong things."

Ida's eyes opened wide. "What do you mean, Florine? You can tell me anything."

"No, I can't. I live a hop, skip, and a jump away from hell's front porch, but I try. I try my best. Do you even like me?"

Ida smiled and said, "Of course I like you! I love you! I practically raised you, in a way. It's just that I believe it's important to live each day for Jesus, in any way you can."

"Well," I said, getting up, "I appreciate all you've done. I am what I am, and that's all there is to it. Grand always said that Jesus loved me, no matter what. I figure that gives me lots of room for messing up."

"Oh, honey," Ida said. "She was right. And that makes you one of Jesus's special ones. I wouldn't change a thing about you."

"Well, I would," I said. "I've had a day, Ida, and I'm going home now to put the kids to bed." *And to have a talk with your drunk son.* She stood up and I took Travis from her. "Say good night to your grandmother," I said to Arlee. Ida reached down to scoop her up, but my girl had had a day too, and she whined and pulled away. Ida kissed my cheek.

"I imagine as the days pass, you'll get your Point legs back," she said. "You had yourself a time for most of the winter. And you *can* talk to me, remember that."

No, I can't, I thought, but I hugged her and we trooped back up to Grand's house. We walked into the house as if Bud wasn't passed out nearby on the sofa. I turned out all of the lights and climbed the stairs so as not to wake Travis, who slept in my arms. I took Arlee to bed with me and read her a story. I put her into her little bed next to Travis's crib, went across the hall, and climbed into my lovely, warm bed.

Bud came upstairs about two hours later. He woke me up as he stumbled into the bathroom in the dark, snapped up the toilet seat, and peed for about five minutes. As the waterfall fell into the pool, Travis made waking sounds. Bud thumped the seat down and flushed the toilet, which roused Travis more.

He went into the kids' room and I heard his low voice trying to quiet Travis down. My baby boy did settle a little bit at his father's soft words, but just long enough to let Bud come across the hall, pull back the covers, and climb into bed.

"Love you," he said to my back and he kissed me somewhere near my ear before he stretched out on his side of the bed. Travis began to cry again. Finally, Bud turned over and said into my ear, "Florine? You awake? Travis is up."

"Bottle in the fridge," I said. "Diapers on the porch with the changing table." I snuggled deeper into the blankets as Bud took his son downstairs. Soon after that, Arlee wandered in and I brought her into our bed, where she took up any space I didn't claim. We woke up curled against each other. In the morning, I went into the kids' bedroom to see Bud coiled like a snail shell in Arlee's bed.

My kids and I began that day with bottles, cereal, and tea, when I could get a sip of it. Maureen came up just as we finished breakfast.

"Morning," she called from the hall. She walked into the kitchen and Arlee threw a fistful of Kix at her.

"That any way to say hello?" Maureen said to Arlee. "I've never thrown cereal at you." Arlee threw another piece of Kix and Maureen caught it and gulped it down. She said to me, "How are you doing?"

"We're good," I said. "Nice to be home. I thought you were up-town."

"Came back really early this morning," she said. "Can I take Arlee outside?"

"Fine with me," I said. Carrying Travis, I followed them out and looked down at the water. Gulls cracked rude jokes as they flew out to sea to play tag with the fishermen. My eyes tracked them down an endless sky busy running its race toward eternity.

Carlie had loved horizons. *"If you could walk through that line and come out the other side, you would be somewhere completely different. Wouldn't that be a gas?"* she had said, so many lifetimes ago. Travis cooed. "Whose sweet baby are you?" I said.

"Mine." My husband put his arms around my waist and rested his head against my shoulder. "And yours."

"You smell like yesterday's good time," I said. "Let's go inside."

He let go of me. "Ladies first," he said. I walked past him, to the kitchen, and then I turned to face him.

"I don't mind you having fun, but don't come home and start on me," I said. "And don't talk to me that way in front of the kids."

"Been a long winter, Florine. Could be I was melting the ice inside of me. Your being sick wasn't hard on just you."

"I didn't think it was," I said. "Do you think I planned it?" Travis squirmed as I tensed. I made myself relax and I studied Bud as he squinted against the brightness of the spring sun. His face sported a hangover along with what else? Regret? Resentment?

I said, "I know we owe money to the hospital. I know insurance didn't cover everything. But getting drunk on whiskey won't take care of any of that."

One side of Bud's mouth lifted. "Helped, for a while, yesterday."

"Not helping much, today, is it?"

Bud shook his head. "Nope," he said. "I should cut the lawn."

My nose touched Travis's head and I sucked in the scent of new baby as Bud left the house.

Maureen carried a sleepy Arlee back home at about noon. "We went to Ray's and picked up the mail," she said.

"Thanks," I said. "You want lunch?" Maureen said no and left. Arlee nodded off in her booster seat, leaving most of her sandwich for later. I covered her up on the sofa. Travis slept in the bassinet. Bud had finished the lawn and gone off somewhere. "Ain't leaving with the intention of tying one on, just so's you know," he had told me. "Going up to see Fred. I'll be back in a couple of hours."

I brewed myself a cup of tea, sat down at the kitchen table, and reached for the pile of mail. I flipped through bills, flyers, and one letter that had no return address. The small cream-colored envelope matched the one upstairs in my bureau. Same block writing on the front. Lewiston postmark. I sheared it open with a bread knife and pulled out a folded, white, lined piece of paper. The elegant cursive, slanting forward like the sail of a schooner taking on good wind, read:

C. I waited for you as long as I could. I asked you to meet me and you did not, although you had indicated that you would do so. Do not do that to me again.

"What the hell?" I said out loud. I held the lined paper up to the kitchen window and looked through it, as if some hidden words might appear. The paper had been torn above the words and below them, making a mystery out of whatever other writing it contained.

I crammed the piece of paper back into the envelope and tucked it into the junk drawer under the kitchen countertop. Who was "C"? Was this about Carlie? Had the first letter been for her? From who? Why was I getting them? Who was sending them? Why? What would Bud say?

I decided to sit on it for a little while.

My little girl woke up crying about a teeny scratch on her pinkie that had happened somewhere on her walk with Maureen. I fetched a Band-Aid, folded it around her finger, and gave it a big kiss. Bud got home on time and we carried on, two young parents and their two babies, supper, feedings, bath times, clean pajamas, a little picture book, and then bed.

Bud and I were both so tired we went to bed about an hour after the kids.

"Feels weird to lay here with the sun still up," Bud said.

"I know," I said. "I feel like I've been bad."

"Speaking of . . . I'm sorry about how I acted yesterday. I was an asshole."

"You were," I said, and then I changed the subject. "You sorry we're married?"

"Kind of dumb question is that? Why? You sorry?"

"That's a dumber question," I said. "No. Who the hell else would put up with me?"

"That's true. You're nothing but trouble," he said. I ran my hand over his thighs and showed him how much trouble I could be until dark flooded the room.

Sunday passed like a quiet prayer. I said nothing about the letter, barely even thought about it, in fact, my day and my arms were so filled with children.

Monday morning, Bud left for Stoughton Falls. I worked in the side garden all that morning, with Arlee's help, while Travis slept away the time in his carrier under the honeysuckle bushes. The breeze off the water begged us to come down to the shore, so after lunch, we wandered down that way. Ida took the baby, and Arlee and I continued on to the little beach. Arlee ran for the water as soon as I put her down, her sneakered feet slipping over the round stones, seaweed, and snails. I chased her and brought her back to the top of the beach, put her down, and let her run again before going after her. Finally, I slipped off my loafers, took off her sneakers, and we plopped our feet into the cold water.

Her small face opened like a blooming daffodil. I held her hand as she splashed in the salt water until her toes turned red. She whined when I whisked her out and dried her feet, but laughed when I kissed them all over.

We walked along, picking up deserted shells and little bits of seaweed she wanted to keep. Something red winked among the pebbles. I bent and picked up a jagged piece of red glass. Could this be a piece of Grand's red ruby heart? Most likely not. The heart had been solid. Being tumbled all over the sea bottom would have rubbed it smooth. I lifted the glass and looked through it, into a memory.

Carlie and I had once walked this beach, me picking up shells, wading in water that covered my feet. I saw me as Carlie might have seen me, a little girl wearing light-blue overalls. My curly hair was pulled back into a tiny knot. I saw Carlie's bloodred toenails. She hummed a song as we walked and said, "Careful," as I balanced on a crooked rock.

"Careful," I said to Arlee as *she* tried to balance on a crooked rock, possibly the same one I had balanced on. The connection of my mother and me, and me and my daughter, skewered time and confused me. I suddenly felt the need for a solid presence.

"It's time to go," I said to Arlee. She whimpered as I picked her up and hurried us off the beach. I passed Ida's house and headed toward the Buttses'. I was glad to see Madeline's car was in the driveway. She was as close as I could get to Dottie at the moment. She flung open the door before I could knock.

"Well, I hoped you'd come over," she crowed. "Hi, sweet cheeks!" she said to Arlee. Arlee smiled and Madeline took her in her arms.

"Come on in," she called to me over her shoulder.

Madeline swept paint tubes and a couple of canvases over to one side of her kitchen table, which, when I thought about it, had never been clear, and pulled out a chair for me. "Sit down," she said. "Want a cookie? Of course you do," she said to Arlee.

"Me too," I said as she pulled a homemade snickerdoodle out of the old beehive cookie jar.

"I can do that," Madeline said. "Where's your baby boy?"

"Ida has him for a couple of hours."

"Well, of course she does," Madeline said. I saw flashes of Evie in her dark hair and blue eyes. "Have some milk, munchkin," she said to Arlee, and she fetched it for her in a blue plastic cup. Madeline said to me, "How you making out over there? You glad to be back?"

"I am, kind of. No, I am glad."

"Kind of? Something wrong?"

"I missed it all winter. I'm glad to be in Grand's house. It's home."

"You like living in the trailer?"

"I like being back with Bud. The trailer's okay."

"So, how come you said you were only kind of glad to be here?"

"I don't think about Carlie so much when I'm there. Here, she pops up like a ghost."

"Oh, honey, I imagine she does! Wouldn't she be glad to see you and these beautiful babies, though? She'd want you to be happy. I'm sure of that."

"Yeah. But I'm getting tired of being reminded of her not being here."

"Well, of course. But no matter where you are, you got two things of your own to keep you on track for at least the next eighteen or so years."

A car door slammed. Tires spewed rocks and gravel as the car spun up the hill. Evie walked into the house, all swagger and smirks.

"Hey," she said.

"That Justin?" Madeline said.

"Was," Evie said. "Better get used to hearing a new name."

"Broke up with him?"

"Yup. Hi, sweetie pie!" Evie put her heart-shaped face up to Arlee's and rubbed turned-up noses with her, which made Arlee giggle.

"Can I have her? We can go play dolls," Evie said, holding out her arms. I passed Arlee over and Evie stuck her on one luscious hip and sashayed out of the room.

Madeline shook her head. "How could two kids be so friggin' different?" she muttered. "That one's going to be the death of me, for sure."

I didn't have much to say about that. I hadn't been such an angel.

"I mean"—Madeline lowered her voice—"she's a wild woman. Doesn't listen to a thing I say. I grounded her last week for sneaking out in the middle of the night. She just looked at me and said, 'I'm going out anyway.' Even Bert can't handle her. She's going to get knocked up by somebody if she don't watch out."

I clicked my tongue and shook my head. "I need to get Travis," I said. "Mind if I leave Arlee?"

"'Course," Madeline said. "It'll keep Evie out of trouble for five minutes or so."

But in the five minutes it took to pick up Travis, Evie fed Arlee half a bag of M&M's.

"She loved them," Evie told me as she brought her to the Buttses' front door.

"I'll bet," I said.

Evie widened her bluebird-colored eyes. "Did I do something bad?"

"Might keep her up. I'll let you know. Thanks for watching her."

Arlee ran across the road to the house and jumped up and down until I let her in. "Going to be a long night, Trav," I said to her brother.

And it was. Arlee tossed her spaghetti around and Travis fussed and didn't drink much formula. Arlee bounced from ceiling to floor. Travis was happy to go down. Arlee fiddle-farted around downstairs with me until ten o'clock, when her crabby self ran smack into a wall of restless sleep. I put her to bed and called Bud in Stoughton Falls.

"Don't give our kids candy near to bedtime," I said when he picked up the phone.

"Okay," he said. "Why?"

I told him, and then I went on with the news of the day.

He told me which cars were in the garage and what they needed done to them. "Car got towed in today. Old man drove up on a boulder in his driveway so he wouldn't hit his cat. Did a hell of a job to the car. Later, a lady comes in, swears she put a quart of oil in the tank when it was down. Engine almost seized up. Sure she did."

I didn't answer him.

"Florine? You okay?" Bud said.

"Bud, I got something on Saturday. One of those letters."

"What letters?" he said. "Wait. Another 'I love you forever' letter? What the hell?"

Before he got too wound up, I said, "Now, wait, let me read this." I opened the junk drawer and took out the letter. I read it to him.

"Holy shit," Bud said. "Who's 'C'? Where the hell did that come from?"

"I don't know. Carlie? It's different writing too. I don't know what to do with it."

"Give them both to Parker. This is bullshit."

"Why give them to Parker?"

"Well, it's weird. And maybe, just maybe now, it might have something to do with Carlie, and he would want to know. Or maybe someone's just trying to drive you crazy."

"I know," I said. "I know."

"Give 'em to Parker," Bud said. "That's all you can do."

We said our I-love-yous and talked about what we would do to each other if we were sharing the same bed and then we said our good-nights.

I hung up the phone, clicked off the downstairs lights, went out to the porch, and rocked back and forth for a long time.

16

Sheriff Parker Clemmons had given me his word that he would never give up looking for my mother. As far as I knew, he never had. I called him about the letters and he came by. He wasn't too pleased with me for handling the envelopes and notes.

"Probably not going to be able to get any prints from these," Parker growled, "what with you touching 'em."

"Sorry," I said. "Do you think someone might have sent these to Carlie?"

"Can't say. No names, no prints; postmarks, but no return addresses," Parker said. "I'll put them in the file. You let me know if something else like this happens again, right away." He smiled down at Arlee, who had been staring at him with her thumb in her mouth ever since he'd knocked at the front door. She didn't smile back.

"It's the uniform," Parker said. "Gets 'em every time." I walked him out.

"Bye," Arlee said as he drove away.

"Oh, now you're going to talk?" I said.

The screen door on my father's house slammed and I saw Stella walking toward us. Her black hair soaked up the sun, even as her white face pushed it away. She looked straight-line sober. "Hello," she said. "Two redheads standing in the spring sun. What a nice sight to see on this beautiful day." Arlee grabbed onto my leg.

"Hello," I said.

"Everything okay?"

"Yes."

"Well, I wondered, what with Parker stopping by."

"What can I do for you?" I asked.

"Well, I haven't seen the baby yet," she said.

"He's sleeping," I said.

"Heard you had quite a time carrying him."

"Wasn't a party, that's for sure."

"You're okay now?"

"Doing okay."

"I'm doing okay too," she said. "Better, now that Grace is gone."

"She said goodbye," I said.

"Surprised she did. She's not much for talking."

Arlee left my side and wandered into the side garden.

"Can't get over how much she looks like . . ." Stella said.

"I know," I said.

Travis began to cry. "Arlee, we need to go in," I called to my daughter. I said to Stella, "Now would be as good a time as any to see Travis." Lest she be carrying a weapon yet to be seen, I made her walk in front of me as we went through the door.

She stood in the kitchen as I picked up my son from the bassinet on the porch.

"Here he is," I said.

"Oh my god," she said, and her hand flew up to cover her mouth.

"I know," I said. "He looks like Daddy."

"Spitting image." Stella sniffed. She wiped tears from her eyes.

"You can touch him, if you want to," I said.

"Really?" she said. She put one shaky hand on his head and stroked the curly fuzz there. Travis looked her over, his blue eyes steady. "Hi, baby," she said, her smile young and naked. Travis's pale eyebrows rose and the corners of his mouth turned up.

"Oh!" Stella said. "What a sweetheart!"

"That's gas," I said. "He farted on my arm. He's too little to smile."

"No, it wasn't," Stella said. "It was a real smile."

"Suit yourself. He needs a change and we need to get supper ready."

"I won't keep you," Stella said. "Thanks for letting me see him." She let herself out.

I looked down at Arlee. "Did I almost just have a nice talk with Stella?" I asked her.

"Jeeza," Arlee said.

❧

It was only Tuesday, so I was surprised when Bud drove down from Stoughton Falls.

I hugged and kissed him and said, "To what do I owe this unexpected visit?"

"I missed the hell out of you," he said. "Cecil gave me Wednesday morning off. I'm going to work late tomorrow and Thursday."

As I fed him a late supper, I updated him on Parker's and Stella's separate visits and anything else that had gone on since Monday morning.

That night, we couldn't seem to keep our body parts separate. Travis only interrupted us once. In the morning, we looked like love-wrecked survivors. Bud's lips were puffy, and beard rash peppered my chin and cheeks.

At breakfast, in between kid chores, we locked eyes and smiled. Then he set to his over-easy eggs as if it were the most important meal he had ever eaten.

"Those eggs must be some good," I said. "You okay?"

He swallowed, put down his fork, looked at me, and said, "I don't think this is working out."

"What isn't working out?" I said.

"This. You and me . . ."

"What the hell do you mean?" I said, my voice razor thin.

"Calm down," Bud said. "Jesus, don't go off—"

"You can't say something like that and expect—"

"Settle down, for chrissake," Bud said. He stared me down. "You calm? Good. What I'm trying to say is I ain't happy not having you at home. I want you to come back to Stoughton Falls."

My heart tripped, then steadied. "Now?"

"No. I figure you stay through the Fourth of July, and then we go back. Christ, Florine, I miss you. The other night, I talked to myself in the bathroom mirror."

"Was it a nice conversation?"

"Compared to most of the people I talk to every day, yes, it was a damn good talk. But that ain't the point."

"This is The Point," I said. "My Point."

"Mine too," Bud said. "I was brought up right down the hill. Don't be a smartass."

That was like telling me not to breathe. I stared at Grand's old, square, red plastic clock on the kitchen wall. "I should dust that clock," I said.

"That it? That what you got to say?"

"That's a lot to spring on me at breakfast," I said. I got up, set Travis down in the bassinet, wet a clean washcloth, took it over to Arlee's high chair, and wiped banana goo from her cheeks.

"I know it's a lot," Bud said. "I wasn't going to say nothing, but I only been gone a week and Travis is that much bigger. Hell, Arlee looks a year older. I don't want to be someone that comes and goes."

"You told me we could stay here for the summer," I said. We looked at each other for a few seconds and then I turned and walked out onto the porch.

Bud's chair scraped as he stood up and walked over to me. He didn't touch me, but his voice went deep, melting my heart. "I know you don't want to leave," he said. "I know what I'm asking you to do. I know it's hard."

The summer sky was so blue it made my eyes smart. The tides promised to mark our days, to keep our place, whether we were there or not. But summertime was not back in a trailer on the side of the road. Hell, I thought. "After the Fourth of July," I said, not making an effort to hide my long, loud sigh. "We'll go with you then."

"Sounds good," Bud said. "I been cutting the lawn out in front of the trailer. Looks nice. Bet you could make it look some pretty with flowers. Maybe you can bring some of Grand's with you."

"Suppose I could," I said. "I'm going for a walk. Watch the kids for a while?" Without waiting for his reply, I kissed Arlee's head as I walked toward the front hall.

"I have to leave in about an hour," Bud called.

"I'll be back in time," I said.

I decided to take a seldom-used path through the park. To get to it, I skirted a pile of brush put there by the park rangers to block its faint presence. It was one I knew well, having taken it to and from Andy Barrington's cottage the winter we'd been together.

Just before I reached the edge of the woods that led to their place, I took a right onto a path as thin as a child's eyebrow that petered at a little clearing. Not much had changed in the year or two since I'd been there; the blueberry and juniper bushes were a tad taller, but the three flat rocks in the center of the clearing were still the perfect place to sit and think. I had gone there often after Carlie's disappearance, just to be alone and to talk to her in private. This time, though, I needed to take in what Bud had just sprung on me. I sat down, closed my eyes, and raised my face to the sun. A crow cawed as it passed close by. Something small rustled in the bushes. I whispered, "I don't want to go."

"Go where?" someone said, and I jumped to my feet in one leap.

Maureen stood in front of me, her light-brown eyes smiling.

"You scared the crap out of me," I said.

"Sorry," she said. "I didn't know you knew about this place. It's so pretty. I like talking to God here better than I do in church, but don't tell my mother. If I wait long enough, seems like Jesus and everyone else pops by."

"I guess," I said. "Who else?"

"Dad, mostly. I tell him the things I've always wanted to say to him. And sometimes, Grand comes by. She's funny. We have good talks."

"You remember Grand?"

"Of course. Sometimes I used to wish I could live with her."

"Would have been nice to have you for a sister," I said. "I've been coming here for a while, to talk to my mother."

Maureen frowned into the sun. "I don't remember her."

"You were five when she disappeared," I said. Maureen shifted her weight from one long leg to the other.

"Let's sit down," I said. "Pull up a rock."

She grinned. We sat down on the rocks and she snuggled against me. "I'm so glad you're married to Bud," she said.

"Me too," I said. *Mostly*, I added to myself.

"I knew you were the one he liked, all along. He liked Susan, but I could tell he liked you better."

"Well, he put on a good show of pretending he didn't."

Susan and Bud actually had been pretty serious, until I stuck myself between them. I hadn't played fair, but I wasn't sorry for that. I had Bud, and I was sure Susan was happy wherever she had ended up.

Maureen said, "Don't tell him I told you this, but when he was going out with Susan, he used to stand outside after she drove off for the night and look up at Grand's house till all the lights went out."

"Imagine that," I said. "What were you doing awake back then?"

"I don't sleep much," Maureen said.

"Come on up and give Travis his two a.m. bottle, in that case."

"I will if you want."

"I can manage. Anyway, we won't be here much longer."

"Why not?"

"Bud wants us to go back to Stoughton Falls. He misses us, he says."

"No!" Maureen jumped up. "You just got here. You can't go."

"We're staying through the Fourth of July," I said.

"Want me to tell him to go pound sand?"

I smiled. "I want to be with him, Maureen. I want to be here too, but for now, I'll go back with him. Maybe we'll be able to stay longer next summer. We might be down for the holidays."

Maureen sat back down and we went quiet for a minute, while she talked to Jesus or Sam or maybe Grand and I thought about what the heart makes clear. I had just told Maureen I wanted to be with Bud, and that was the bald truth. Suddenly, she said, "I'm worried about Glen."

"I know," I said. "I am too."

"I don't know why he wanted me to stop writing to him. I would think that a letter would cheer him up. I admire him. He's brave."

"He is," I agreed. "He's very brave."

Without warning, my babies gripped my heart and shook it. I said to Maureen, "I need to get back. Bud has to leave soon."

"I'll come too," she said. We pulled each other up and walked up the path to the crossroads. We looked right, toward the Barringtons'. I shivered. Maureen said in a near whisper, "The man in that house is creepy."

"Which man?" I whispered back.

"He's the dad of the guy you used to go out with. Andy's dad. I used to think that Andy was cute, but my mom prayed for you to stop seeing him, and Bud didn't like him much either."

"Why do you think that Edward is creepy?" I asked her as we turned left.

"Well, once . . . don't tell my mom, I was in the clearing and I heard someone coming up the path. I hid behind the juniper bushes. He got to the rocks and he knelt down and cried and yelled to himself for what seemed like forever. It was weird."

Edward came to the clearing? I shuddered. "He is creepy. Stay away from him."

"I can outrun him. He's an old guy."

"Don't get near enough so that you have to do that. Stay away from him. Promise?"

"I feel bad for saying that he was creepy. Jesus says there's good in everyone."

"I guess so, but just stay away from him. You can pray for him, you can hope for the best for him, but just stay away."

"Don't tell any of this to my mother," Maureen said.

"I won't," I said.

She put her arm around my shoulders. "Let's walk and talk again, okay?" she asked.

"Sure," I said. We began to hurry. I swore I heard Travis crying before I got to The Cheeks, but when I got home, he was sound asleep.

17

Bud left for Stoughton Falls again almost the minute I got back. Dottie showed up at The Point the next day and I was glad for her company. On Thursday afternoon, she and I took Arlee up to Ray's to pick up the mail.

Madeline had Travis. "Give me some time with that baby! I won't wreck him, I promise. After all, look how my girls turned out," she said, rolling her eyes. Evie hadn't come home the night before. "If she isn't dead somewhere," she told Dottie and me, "I'm going to kill her."

Dottie had something other than Evie on her mind. As we walked along, she said, "I've found out that even if I go pro, the bowling tour don't pay that well. I been adding it up. Unless I want to live in my car, I'll probably have to back my bowling up with an honest living, like bossing high school girls around a gym. Jesus, don't I hate the thought of doing that. I remember what pains in the asses we were to the poor suckers who tried to whip us into shape. Thankless job. And them kids won't care that I'm a champion bowler, so they won't be as impressed as they should be."

"Comes back around, I guess," I said.

"Does," Dottie said. She stooped down, bundled Arlee into her arms, and made a farting noise into the bend of her little white neck. Arlee screeched and giggled.

Dottie plunked Arlee down on the road and Arlee said, "Agin!"

"We're almost at the store," I said. "Dottie will do it some other time."

Dottie and I grabbed her hands and scooted her up over the front steps of the store.

"Hello, pumpkin!" Ray hollered when he saw her.

"Jeeza!" Arlee said.

"Great," I muttered to Dottie.

"He's been called worse, I bet," Dottie said.

Ray reached in back of him, took the mail from Grand's slot, and handed it to me. Her written name, *Florence Gilham*, in faded ink on yellowed paper, was still above the slot. I hadn't asked Ray to change it, and I never would.

I shuffled envelopes like gin rummy cards. One, two, and three. Bills, bills, and bills.

"I'm going to have to get a job too," I said to Dottie. "Can I come help you?"

"Might just as well," Dottie said. "Bring a whistle."

One small cream-colored envelope with my name and address in block letters on the front postmarked Long Reach. My heart sped up. "Shit," I said.

"What?" Dottie said.

Ray handed Arlee two lollipops. "One is good," I said.

"Two is better," he said.

"I'm not supposed to open this," I muttered.

"Why not?" Dottie said.

I turned to Ray and held up the envelope. "Where did this come from?" I asked him.

"The mailman," he said. "He stops in a truck every day and drops off the mail. Been doing it for years. Neither rain, sleet, nor snow stop him from his appointed rounds."

"Thanks for clearing that up," I snapped. "I thought maybe you shit it out and put it into the box."

He gave me a look. So did Dottie. And Arlee. Then Stella came into the store and we all looked at her.

"What?" she said. "What's happened now?"

"Hi, Stella," Dottie said. "How the hell are you?"

"Doing good, Dottie. Better than I have for a long time. How about you?"

Dottie walked over to Stella, and Ray walked over to me. "What the hell is up your butt?" he grumbled. "You pissed at me or the mailman?"

"Neither of you," I said. "I'm sorry." I took Arlee's sticky hand, brushed past Dottie and Stella, and went out the door.

"Daw come," Arlee said.

"She'll be along in a second," I said. "We have to go home."

At the house I showed the letter to Dottie. "I'm supposed to give this to Parker before I open it," I said. "In case there might be fingerprints."

"But it's addressed to you."

"It is, isn't it?"

"You and Ray and the mailman already messed up the envelope."

"We did, didn't we?"

"We could try and steam it open," Dottie said. "Can't harm nothing."

"I could take it out by the corners and pinch the paper along the sides so the middle doesn't get messed up."

"Could."

So we did. Dottie ran it along the teakettle steam and the flap let go. We turned the kettle off, sat down at the kitchen table, and looked at the now-opened letter.

"Well," Dottie said. "You going to read it?"

My fingers danced along the edges of the white paper folded inside its envelope cave as if it were on fire. "Different postmark. The first one was from Freeport," I said. "The second one was from Lewiston."

"That's weird."

I held the folded paper in front of me. My fingers trembled.

"Okay. Here goes," I said. Lined paper. Same flowing cursive as the second one.

Your games are not amusing and I don't like to look like
a fool. I would rather you tell me you do not want to
meet me or see me again. Please advise. I love you.

"Who the hell is this from?" I said. "Why the fuck am I getting
these letters? Who is sending them?"

My mind cast around for someone, anyone, and I suddenly remembered Patty, the funny, wild friend who had taken the trip with Carlie
the weekend she had vanished. Would she know something about the
letters? I wished I could show them to her, but she had left for New
Jersey right after Carlie had disappeared. I had never heard from her
again, even after I had written her a letter.

"I wonder what happened to Patty," I said to Dottie.

"Christ, you jump around. What does it look like in your head?"
She stood up. "I'm going to get Travis. I just heard some yelling. Evie
must be home. I'll be right back."

Dottie went out the door and I went to the phone and dialed Parker.
He showed up about an hour later, his cruiser in front of the house calling
attention to the fact that, yes, something was off yet again in Florine land.

"I just handled the edges of the paper," I told him.

Parker looked as if he didn't believe me. He picked up the envelope, took reading glasses from his front shirt pocket, and put them on.
"Long Reach postal mark," he said. As he read the short message, I
looked over his shoulder at it again. *Your games are not amusing and I*
don't like to look like a fool. I could agree with that. Then I looked
again. *Your games are not amusing and I don't like to look like a fool.*
Who talked like that? And then it hit me.

"Edward," I said. My skin crawled.

"Who?" Parker said.

"Edward Barrington."

"What about him?" Parker said.

"He talks like that. Amusing. Advise. We don't use fancy words
like that around here."

Parker's eyebrows bent into a serious-looking *V*. "Lot of folks use big words, Florine. Don't go trying to be some kind of detective. Watch out who you accuse of something you got no proof about. And if you want me to help you, stop opening them letters." His chair scraped as he got up.

He turned to go, and then he turned back. "We don't even know if these letters have anything to do with Carlie. 'C' doesn't tell us anything. And you know, Barrington ain't that bad a guy."

"Well, I know him in a different way," I said to him.

"Don't think something about someone because you don't like them," Parker said.

"All right, already," I said. "I get it."

After Parker left, Arlee bugged me to let her color, so I pulled a box of crayons and a coloring book from a kitchen drawer and we sat down at the table together. She was partial to blues and purples. I started her on a picture of a house just as Dottie walked back in with a sleeping Travis. She put him down in his bassinet on the porch and we went back into the kitchen and sat down. I filled her in on the latest exchange between Parker and me.

"Edward *does* use big words," I said. "He talked that way to Andy and me that time he came to take Andy back home with him. And he gives me goose bumps. Wouldn't hurt for Parker to check on it."

"Suppose not," Dottie said. "Not to change the subject, but Evie's in big trouble. Some guy dropped her off a little while ago. Older. Just dropped her and gunned it out of here. Smells like she went swimming in a keg."

"'Least she didn't drown."

"If she keeps up this happy bullshit, she might. Bert's about ready to drop her overboard with a rusty anchor wrapped around her legs."

"Well, let's hope she wises up," I said. "Like I did."

Dottie gave me a look.

"What?" I said.

She left shortly after that and I fed Travis and Arlee, after scrubbing big loops of violet crayon from the surface of the table. Next time, I would put newspapers down on the table's surface when Arlee colored, until she learned how to stay within the lines. Maybe she never would. That would be fine with me.

18

June faded away in its quiet green way, and Arlee turned two with a little cake, balloons, and everyone who loved her there to help her celebrate. The first week of July slipped into place. Bud took the week off and drove to The Point. I puttered as he did chores and helped Billy replace the old picket fence between the cliff and the house.

It was about twenty feet to the rocks below the ledge where Grand's house stood. When I had been little, Grand, who had a sixth sense about where I shouldn't be, would yell out the porch screen for me to "stay away from the cliff" whenever I wanted to slip through the gate to stand looking down. I had long outgrown the urge to toss down clams or mussels to see them break on the rocks, but now I had babies who would want to do the very same thing. Arlee was already mastering the art of running out of sight. I wouldn't have thought a kid could move so fast, but I was finding out how tricky she could be. So we decided to replace the fence.

When Billy showed up early on the morning of July 3, I noticed dark circles under his eyes. His smile was small and the light in his eyes dim.

"Hey, Florine," he said.

"Hey," I answered back. "You want some coffee?"

"Nope," he said. "Lots to do today. Bud ready?"

"He's upstairs getting himself pretty for you," I said. Billy ignored my joke.

"I'll get to it, then," he said. He spotted Arlee and his face brightened. "Suffer the little children," he whispered. He picked her up and she hugged him. His eyes shut tight as he held her, and I saw something sad pass over him. He put her down. "I'll get cracking," he said, and went outside.

Bud walked downstairs a few minutes later and I poured him a cup of coffee. As he drank it, I brought up something that had occurred to me in the middle of the night.

"What if another letter comes while we're back in Stoughton Falls?"

"Ray will forward it," he answered. "Or Dottie will let us know."

Dottie was staying in the house for the rest of the summer. I figured it was the least I could do for her. Life at the Butts house had gotten louder in the last couple of weeks, what with Madeline and Evie going at each other hammer and tongs.

"Too much hissing," Dottie told me. "Why the hell I came home, I don't know."

"To see me," I said.

"You're out of here," Dottie said. "I'd go too, except for my jeezly job at the park."

When I asked her if she wanted to stay at Grand's house, I thought for a scary minute that she was going to jump on me and give me a bear hug.

"Please keep it clean," I told her.

"Grand will make sure I do," she said. "I can just hear her saying, 'Dorothea, things don't stay clean by themselves.' She'll keep me in line."

The fence got finished around noontime and I fed Billy, Bud, and Arlee lunch. As I warmed a bottle for Travis, Stella called "Yoo-hoo" from the screen door.

"Come in," Bud called, and she rounded the hall and walked into the kitchen carrying a plate full of brownies. She ignored me and beamed at Billy and Bud. She said, "I saw you both working so hard in this sun, and I figured Florine wouldn't have time to make you something special. So I baked these."

"Thank you, Stella," Billy said.

Bud said, "You eaten lunch, Stella? You want something? Sit down."

Stella looked at me. I raised my eyebrows and shrugged and Stella took that as a yes. She sat down as I slapped together a ham and cheese sandwich for her.

"How you doing?" Billy asked her.

"I'm just fine, Pastor," she said. "How are you feeling?"

He nodded. "I'm okay," he said. "I'm here on this beautiful day, helping a friend, hugging babies, and eating the best ham and cheese sandwich I've ever had."

"The brownies aren't half bad either," Stella said, "if I do say so myself." She looked at me. "Where's that beautiful baby boy?"

Maybe it was because Billy was helping us out, and Stella had supplied brownies. Maybe generosity was the word of the day. *Maybe*, Grand said, *you could do something nice too*. I pulled Travis's bottle from its boiling pot and tested it for warmth and said to Stella, "This will be cool enough in a couple of minutes," I said. "You want to feed him?"

"I would love to feed him," Stella said, her voice filled with quiet surprise.

She took the foil off the brownies for Bud and Billy. They each grabbed two. Bud handed one to a wide-eyed Arlee, snatched her from her high chair, and they all headed out into the sunshine. I tested the milk for temperature, lowered Travis into Stella's arms, and handed her the bottle.

Stella crooned something to a contented Travis, who moved his pudgy hands in the air in a way that reminded me of kittens kneading on their mother's tummy.

"He's so beautiful," Stella whispered. "Is oo a pretty boy? Whose pwiddy boy is oo?"

The high pitch in her voice and her baby talk irritated me and I lost the urge to be kind. "Why did you bring the brownies over, really?" I asked.

She sighed. "To poison everyone," she said. When I didn't smile, she rolled her eyes. "Really, Florine, where does your sense of humor live? Is it even in the same zip code as the rest of us?" She looked back at Travis. "I wanted to see this widdle biddy boy. And to check on Billy."

"Why?" I asked. "You after him now?"

"Oh, for crying out loud. No. I wanted to see how his cancer treatments were going. That okay with you?"

My heart dropped to my stomach. "Billy has cancer?"

"Well, yes," Stella said. "I thought everyone knew it."

"I didn't know it."

Stella readjusted Travis in her arms. "Some kind of leukemia. He's had it for about a year. He just let the congregation know a week ago."

That explained things. I didn't congregate. Ida and Maureen must have known, yet, they had kept it to themselves. Why hadn't they told me? I looked out of the kitchen window and saw them walking up our way. Sadness for Billy washed over me.

He was good people, as Grand would have said. Billy had come to our house late one night when Daddy had been at his worst, during that hell-ridden time after Carlie had disappeared, before Stella showed up. I had been at my wits' end, what with missing my mother and fearing what Daddy might do to himself. When Billy had knocked at the door late that night, most likely because Grand had called and asked for his help, I let him in. On that dark night he and Daddy had fought the devil head-on and forced him into an uneasy truce. Compassion. That would be a big word Edward might use. Well, I knew it too. Billy had shown compassion that night and I would never forget it.

"It's too bad," Stella was saying. "Can't think of how to thank him for helping me through my awful days and nights. Brownies seemed to be as good an answer as any."

"I'm going into the garden," I said, bending and reaching for Travis. "We can finish his bottle out there." Stella got up from the chair and Travis and I followed her outside.

Billy sat on the grass beside Maureen. Ida and Bud sat next to each other, each leaning back in two of Grand's Adirondack chairs. I handed Travis and his bottle to Bud and sat down on the arm of his chair. He snuggled our son in his arms. Stella dragged a lawn chair up to complete our little ragged circle.

"Almost the Fourth," Billy said. "Razzle-dazzle on the beach this year?"

"Ray's got a few things up his sleeve," Bud said.

"I might come down and bless the works this year," Billy said.

"Someone will probably roast a pig," Ida said.

"I can bless the pig too," Billy said.

"And the potato salad?" Maureen said.

"If it has lots of mustard in it," Billy said.

We spun out conversation and the pauses in between as delicately as a spider web. No one mentioned cancer. We watched Arlee run across the lawn, the early afternoon sun twisting her fine hair into thin copper wires. Her little legs blurred against the summer grass. At one point she climbed up onto Billy's lap and hollered, "Biffy Jeezus!" Billy's eyes filled and he blinked to clear them. "I don't believe anyone has ever said anything so nice to me before," he said, and hugged her.

We sat there until the heat drove us further into our own days.

19

Arlee was sick to her stomach that night. I took her downstairs and put her on the sofa, where she threw up and wailed as I ran a cool washcloth over her face. I gave her watered-down ginger ale and crackers, and she finally went back to sleep. I dozed beside her in one of Grand's chairs.

Bud and Travis wandered down around two a.m. and Bud warmed a bottle for him. They sat down in the rocker near the sofa and we studied our kids, and then each other. He smiled first. "How did this happen?" he said.

"We forgot to have a plan," I said. Arlee stirred and muttered. I touched her little face. It was warm but not hot.

Bud said, "I like you like this. Your hair is all ratty and you got some greenish circles under your eyes. I want you bad right now."

"The growth on your face would trap a mouse," I said. "And speaking of ratty, your hair is sticking straight up."

"But you want me, right?"

"Nope."

Bud grinned. "I'd be hurt, but I know you're lying."

"Nope."

"You mad because we're leaving in a couple days?"

"I'm not too damned pleased about it."

"If I combed my hair, would you like me better?"

"I might," I said.

"If I shaved, would you give me all of your loving?"

"When Arlee stops puking, I'll get right on it."

His eyes lit themselves from somewhere inside, close to his heart. "What a woman," he said. He looked at Travis, who had fallen back from the nipple on the bottle and was sleeping, his little mouth slack. "Drunk again," Bud said, and shook his head.

"Burp him first," I reminded him. "At least one."

Bud put his sleeping boy over his shoulder and patted him on the back.

"Put some spunk into it," I said. "He won't break."

Bud patted him harder and leaned his dark head against Travis's curly blond one. "You sure I'm their father?" he said. "Not much of me in either of them."

"You'll have plenty of time to take in the parts that are you when we move back. Look at Arlee's hands and legs and feet. She's going to be long and thin, like you. Travis looks like Daddy, but when his little face shifts, I see you. His eyes are shaped like your eyes. He's got your nose, I think."

"See," Bud said. "That's what I'm missing. Little things, like noticing the particulars of who they are. And I like to watch you with them. I think to myself, You didn't do too bad for yourself, James Walter." One corner of his mouth lifted. "And then I think, And man, can that woman fuck."

"We got to stop with that word," I said. "Arlee will pick it right up."

"I suppose." Bud sighed. "But you can."

"You're a sweet man, Bud. All this tenderness makes me want to use my ratty hair to wipe the tears from my greenish-circled eyes."

"Better not do that, I might forget myself," Bud said, and yawned just as Travis let out a burp that would have been rude from someone who knew better.

Bud and Travis went back up to bed, while Arlee and I stayed down-stairs for another round of spitting up, crying, wiping, drinking, and sleeping. Somewhere around four a.m., she began to sweat and her body grew cool. I carried her upstairs, put her into a fresh pair of paja-mas, put her into her bed, then stumbled across the hall, fell into our bed, and toppled off a cliff into some sleep of my own. I didn't wake up until ten to find myself alone in bed, no husband and no children. I jumped up, my heart hammering.

I heard a girl laugh, and I looked out of the window to see Mau-reen whirling Arlee around in a circle. Their hair and the sun min-gled in a morning glow of browns and reds. Bud was down in his mother's yard messing around on the deck of the *Florine*. Travis, I assumed, was with Ida. I decided to take a bath. I soaked for a while and listened to firecrackers pop from across the harbor. That would continue all day and most of the night.

Once I got dressed, I walked down to Ida's yard and looked up into the boat. Bud looked down at me. "Lazybones," he said, and smiled.

"Thanks for letting me sleep. Where is our son?"

He moved his head toward Ida's house. I picked him up there and took him home to start making food for the Fourth of July festivities.

Although the residents in each of the four houses on The Point lived side by side, we tried to respect one another's privacy. Most days on The Point, everyone knocked on doors to announce themselves. But on holi-days, people wandered like loose chickens between houses. At one point during the late morning, Madeline Butts and Ida sat with me in my kitchen, passing around Travis. Madeline chugged down a Schlitz and Ida sipped strong black tea while I whipped up a potato salad for the pig roast. Loud music blared from the Buttses' house. Evie was grounded, again.

"I have to admit it," Madeline said. "I'm real worried about her. She's been raising hell and she thinks she won't have to pay for it. Maybe she won't, but I'm thinking it's going to catch up with her."

"She's not pregnant, is she?" Ida asked. I blinked at Ida's bluntness, but Madeline took it in stride.

"Not as far as I know. I hope not."

"Maybe you should have her checked."

"I suppose I could. I'm going to hold out for a while and hope she comes around."

"Do you trust her?" Ida said.

"Of course not, but that's beside the point."

"Might be the exact point," Ida said.

"She's using a line on you," I said. "Believe me. I know all the lines. No one trusted me, and they were right not to do it. It got bumpy along the way."

"What do you wish you'd done differently?" Ida said.

"Might not have quit school, but it felt right at the time. Now I wish I'd gotten my diploma. It would make it easier to find a job. Might have given me some idea of what I'd like to do."

"If Leeman had really tried to make you go back to school, would you have gone?" Ida asked.

"I wasn't listening to Daddy," I said. "I wouldn't listen to anybody."

Ida's face held the ghost of a smile. "And you listen to them now?"

"Now," I said, "I haven't got much time to listen, let alone do anything else."

"You've done all right," Madeline said. "You got another beer?"

I grabbed a sixteen-ouncer from the refrigerator, chunked it open, and handed it to her.

"I was twenty-four when I married Sam," Ida said. She looked at me. "Did you know that I was his second wife?"

I didn't know, and my face must have shown it.

"Pony Barnes," Madeline said. "So long ago, I forgot about her."

"Who was Pony Barnes?" I asked.

"Oh, she was a piece of work," Madeline said. "Wild woman. Fished with the men. Sam followed her around like a seagull looking for any treat she might toss his way."

"They got married," Ida said. "I'm not sure why."

"Her name was Pony?" I said.

Madeline peered at me over her beer. "Her name was Lucille. But the men said she liked to be ridden until she decided to buck someone off."

"Oh, Maddie," Ida said, and blushed.

"Well, she did," Madeline said. "Anyway, while she was married to

Sam, she met some other fella on one of the other boats and galloped off with him. Left Sam with a pile of bills and not much else."

"That's when he began to drink," Ida said. "We met in a bar, as a matter of fact."

"What?" I said, shocked. Ida, setting foot in a bar?

"Jesus hadn't made his appearance in my life, as yet," Ida said. "I'm thankful, every day, that he did. Anyway, Sam and I got to talking and I gave him a ride down here to the house. He tried to get me to come in, but I wasn't about to do that yet. We started going out, and we got married about a year later. I had Bud about eight months after that."

My mouth fell open.

"What?" said Ida. "He was conceived in love, like Arlee." She gave me a sly look. "I'm not such an old fart. And you're not the only little devil. I've had my fun," she said, which made us all laugh.

❦

Early that morning, Ray had driven his shaky-ass pickup down the hill and backed it down to the beach. Bert helped him dig out a pit, start and bank a fire, and prep the pig. It slow-cooked all day. During the afternoon, Bud left the *Florine* to help set up a couple of tables and some lawn chairs on the beach. Arlee took herself under the sofa for her nap and Travis caught a few fussy winks on the porch. Bud came up to the house around seven o'clock and I gave him a sandwich to tide him over.

"Pig'll be ready around eight," he said.

"Fireworks going off right after?" I said. "Can't imagine that the noise will set well with either of these guys. I'm hauling them off the beach before the fun starts."

"Far as I know," Bud said. "Ray's got a pile of shell rockets. They'll light up the sky for sure."

Ray's "special" fireworks were gotten every year from someone no one knew, from a place no one knew about. Glen had always loved looting his father's stash and setting them off. He and Bud loved lighting them off around all of our houses, scaring us and running away, laughing like fools.

Vietnam must be loaded with fireworks, I thought.

"Hey!" Maureen shouted at us from the screen door.

"It's open," I said.

"Want me to take Arlee?" she asked.

"Go Mo," Arlee said, crawling out from beneath the sofa and running to the door.

"See if she'll eat a little something," I said to Maureen.

"You can both help me pick up wood for the bonfire," Bud said, and off they all went.

I warmed a bottle for Travis as he shifted in his bassinet, and then carried him to the porch. We nestled into the rocker and I studied his perfect face, with its gold-dusted eyebrows and long, light lashes. His greedy mouth pulled every ounce from the bottle. "You're a handsome boy," I cooed. He looked at me and smiled around the nipple of the bottle. "Gas, hell. That was a real one," I said. He did it again. "Let's sit here forever," I said. "You and me." We rocked for about an hour, me falling in love with my son over and over again as the sun started its lazy summer journey toward night.

Carlie whispered a memory into my ear. I was eight years old. We were sitting on the wharf at dusk.

"*Listen,*" she said.

"*What? I don't hear anything,*" I said.

"*Today is a special day,*" Carlie said. "*The tide is changing and it's twilight all at the same time. Listen.*"

So I sat still. The water stopped, the birds went silent, and the sky held its breath. I froze, waiting with the world. And then the tide turned, the stars wheeled into place, and a fox barked.

"*We just made time stop,*" Carlie said.

Time doesn't stop, Carlie, I said to her now, cross that I had believed her, or anything she had ever said.

"You home?" Dottie hollered from the front hall, interrupting my memory.

"No," I said, and she tromped onto the porch and sat down beside me.

"You might think about putting on some lights. It's dark, case you haven't noticed," she said. "You coming to the beach?"

"Travis smiled for me."

"When?"

"Couple of minutes ago."

"Ain't that something."

Flames from the newly lit bonfire licked a hole in the sky.

"Let's go," Dottie said. "Smell that pig."

"Suck-yoo-lent," I said.

I never was much for hanging around, let alone hanging around with a sleepy baby boy in my arms. The minute I stepped onto the beach I wanted to leave and go back to the rocking chair, but I fought the urge and sat down in one of a line of lawn chairs, next to Ida. "Billy couldn't make it," she said. "Not feeling well." The bonfire mirrored the sadness in her dark eyes.

"That's too bad," I said. She reached for Travis.

"Get some food," she said, and I headed over to the table Ray had set up and loaded up a plate with my own potato salad, some chips, and pork. On the way back to the chair, something tapped on the door of my maternal instincts and I looked around.

"Where's Arlee?" I asked Bud as he tended the bonfire.

"With Maureen," he said.

"Where's Maureen?"

Bud straightened up and yelled her name. No answer.

I put the plate on the chair. "Maureen," I called. "Arlee?"

No response.

"They might be in the house," Ida said. "Check there."

"Saw them a few minutes ago," Bert said.

"I'm sure they're around," Madeline said.

I walked up the path to Ida's house and called out their names. No answer. The lights in the Buttses' house were off, so I passed it by and continued to Grand's house. No one. I headed up the hill, almost bumping into Stella as she headed down to the fire.

"You seen Maureen and Arlee?" I asked her.

"No," she said. "I haven't. They lost?"

"No," I said. "No, they're around somewhere."

"Want me to help . . ." Stella started to say, but I waved her off.

Calm down, I told myself. *Nothing's wrong.* But every nerve twitched. *Stop.*

A bubble of air stuck halfway down my throat and I struggled to take a decent breath. I stood for a few seconds, my hands on my knees. As I told myself to cool down, someone scuffed on the pebbles on the road. I straightened up to see Bud coming toward me. Before I could say anything, he put his arms around me and held me close. "Don't go all wacky," he said. "They're around."

"Where are they? Maureen? Arlee?" I yelled.

Bud let me go and peered up at Ray's store. "What's that?" he said. A cold, white light fizzed from the dark of the porch. A second light joined it, then a third. Sparklers.

A little girl laughed and I was gone before Bud could even move. "Arlee!" I shouted and hit the porch without touching the stairs. Maureen was crouched next to her. Their faces glowed as the sparklers spat silver light.

"Why didn't you answer me?" I yelled at Maureen. She jumped up. "I've been calling and calling to you." Arlee began to cry and I picked her up.

"I'm sorry, baby," I said, stroking her hair. "Mama didn't mean to scare you."

"Florine, it's okay," Bud said. Maureen started to cry.

"Jesus," a man's voice drawled from the dark of the porch. "Take five, for chrissake." Then he lit a sparkler. Glen's black eyes reflected two snappy stars in their pupils. "They been up here with me."

"Well, hell in a handbasket," Bud said. "Welcome home, soldier!"

"Glen!" I said, trying to regroup. "You're back! When did you get home?"

"Last night. Stayed at my mother's house in town. Watched the stupid-ass parade. Hitched a ride down." The sparkler in his hand fizzed itself out and we were all wrapped in darkness. Maureen sniffled, which made me feel awful.

"You home for good?" Bud asked.

"Most of me," Glen said. He lit another sparkler and turned to the right. Where his left ear had once been was now a ragged hole in his head. We all gasped.

"Blast took it straight off. They was calling me van Gogh over there. Hush your crying and come here," he said to Maureen, and she burrowed against his chest for a hug. "Florine's an old meanie," he said.

"Oh, for heaven's sake," I said. "Maureen, I got a thing about not knowing where someone is. It scares me not to know. I just need to know where you're going."

"Lighten up," Glen said. "Everything is all right, Florine."

"It is now," I snapped, hurt by Glen's apparent lack of understanding as to why I worried. "Come on, Arlee."

I began to walk down the stairs, intending to go down to the beach, gather up Travis, and take both my children home. Then I decided to tell Glen what I thought about his telling me to "lighten up." I turned back to tell him just where I thought he could stick his singsong, sneering tone.

BOOM!

Ray had set off something big. Glen shoved Maureen away and hit the porch deck, facedown. He covered his head. "Shit," he said, his voice muffled by the porch boards. "Fuck the fuckers."

20

So, Glen came home, minus an ear. He was also missing his old personality. On July 5, before Bud or Arlee was up, the sound of heavy footsteps thudding down the road took me to the kitchen window. As I peered through a thick fog, Glen came marching, one by one, toward the water. He caught me watching him and nodded without smiling as he headed toward the harbor. The fog swallowed him up before the sound of his footsteps faded away.

Bud thumped downstairs shortly after that. He had come home at about two a.m., stinking of beer and beach smoke. He walked into the kitchen and croaked a hello to me. I poured his coffee and, despite the steam rolling off the top of the mug, he swallowed it in three big gulps. "Damn," he said. "Too easy to party here. Probably be a lot better off up in Stoughton Falls."

After the previous night's shambles, I was almost ready to agree with him. Bud had coaxed Glen up off the porch deck, and had pointed out to him that these were fireworks, for chrissake, nothing more, and that there was food waiting to be eaten on the beach. Arlee and I had followed behind my husband and our shaky friend, while Maureen brought up the rear. I could tell by the distance between us that I had roughed up her feelings, but I wasn't ready to say something comforting. When I reached Grand's house, I ordered Bud to bring Travis home, which he did before leaving again.

Arlee and I watched Ray's fireworks from the porch as she sat on my
lap in the rocker. She must have sensed the rawness in my heart because
she stayed quiet, except for the oohs and aahs we made when fire-
sparked emerald, blue, red, and yellow flowers made their brief ta-das
before melting away into the night. Travis wasn't impressed. He whimpered and whined in his bassinet until they were through and I put
them both to bed.

"More coffee," Bud muttered. "I need more. Now."

"Arlee still sleeping?" I said as I poured him a cup.

"Yup."

"Glen's down at the *Florine*."

"Said he was going to get going early."

"When's she going in the water?"

"I don't know. Up to him."

"He going to be okay, you think?"

Arlee called from the top of the stairs, "Daddy?" He headed that
way, ignoring my question. I knew the answer anyway. It would take
a while, if ever, for Glen to get back to the friend we had known. Still,
he was one of us, no matter what.

I sat at the kitchen table and fed Travis as I listened to Bud and
Arlee wrestle over what she wanted to wear for the day.

We finished packing for Stoughton Falls over the next couple of days.
So many times I wanted to blurt out to Bud that he could go to hell, we
were staying, but after I played how that might go over a few times
through my head, I kept quiet. It was hard to get everything done
without giving myself over to the sight of the come-hither water beck-
oning me closer. At one point, I went down and walked the beach
alone, letting the little waves stroke the arches of my feet. *You'll be back*,
they whispered before the pebbles on the beach swallowed them up.

The last thing I did was to wash, dry, and put the red ruby glass
collection back in the polished cabinet. Memories of Grand floated

through my mind as I worked. I smelled her in the dish soap and in the lemon oil I used to buff up the shelves. But I hadn't traveled too far down memory lane when Dottie called, "Knock, knock," and let herself into the house.

"Looking good," she said.

"I don't want to go," I said.

"You'll be back."

"Won't be the same. Can't settle my heart in a place I'm always going to leave."

"'Course you can," Dottie said. "Click your heels three times and say, 'There's no place like home.'"

"Okay, Glinda."

Dottie snorted. "Never liked her. Couldn't figure out why she didn't tell Dorothy to click her heels *before* she left Munchkin Land. Would've saved 'em all a shitload of trouble. 'Least the wicked witch didn't pussyfoot around about what she was up to."

"I liked Glinda's dress, though," I said. "And that bubble she rode around in."

"I'd rather ride around on a broomstick, writing things in the sky. Not to change the subject, but what the hell is wrong with Glen?"

"Bud says he's not okay."

"Better figure it out," Dottie said. "Else I'll knock him sideways."

"I think he's already been knocked sideways and a few other ways," I said.

"Well, we'll see about that," Dottie said. We walked over to the kitchen window and looked down at Glen, Bud, and Bert standing around the *Florine*, talking. If I thought about it long enough, I could swear Daddy's ghost stood with them.

"Leeman will be happy she's going back out on the water," Dottie said.

"Dammit, stop reading my mind," I said.

"You have any cookies in that jar?" she asked.

"Fresh batch for you," I said. "Eat them slow. Last ones this summer."

The day before we left, I went down to Ida's house to pick up my kids, and I made my peace with Maureen. I found her and Arlee sitting on the living room floor, coloring in a book. Arlee scribbled thick blocks of lavender over the outline of a fairy. Maureen's fairy, on the page next to Arlee's, wore bright oranges, yellows, and reds, all within the lines. Neither looked up until I tapped on Maureen's back. "Come with me," I said. She trailed me through the kitchen and into the dooryard.

She shaded her eyes against the summer sun. "I'm sorry I made you worry," she said.

"I'm sorry I hurt your feelings," I said. "I get nutty when I can't find someone. It doesn't have to do with you. I've just had some bad luck in that department. You know how Dottie is the queen of bowling, and your mother is the queen of Jesus and Madeline might be the queen of painting and Evie is the queen of trouble? Well, I'm the queen of lost things."

"Because of your mother," Maureen said.

"Yes, and Grand, and Daddy," I said. "But anyways, I'm sorry. You've been so good with Arlee. And with me. With all of us."

"I'm going to miss her," Maureen said, "and you." Her face crumpled and tears leaked out of the corners of her eyes. "I love you all, so much."

"We love you too. Keep our secret place special for us while I'm gone," I said.

"I will," she said. She smiled her brother's crooked smile. "What am I the queen of?"

"Kindness," I said without missing a beat. "And legs. You have great legs." Maureen giggled and turned red.

I held out my arms and we hugged for a few seconds, and then we went back inside.

We left on Sunday night at about nine o'clock because Bud had to work on Monday. We'd planned to leave earlier, but goodbyes and supper, cooked by Ida, had kept us too late. As it was, we would be

reaching Stoughton Falls sometime around midnight. We put paja-
mas on Arlee and set her in the backseat. Travis slept in his car seat
beside her. Bud and I didn't talk until we reached Stoughton Falls. I
put the kids to bed and we opened windows and doors to make it less
stuffy. We went into our bedroom and I lay there, listening to cars
zipping to and from Portland.

Through closed eyes, I took a trip around Grand's side yard and its
gardens, stopping at the wall of orange day lilies, which had just
bloomed a few days earlier. Well, they would do it without me admiring them. I hoped that Dottie would take the time to say hello to them
in her comings and goings.

"Thank you," Bud whispered next to me. He took me in his arms
and we became each other's homes for a while.

21

It was good to wake up next to Bud every day. And I could focus more on the kids, get to know them better. For instance, I found out how much fun Arlee could be. Down at The Point, she had spent the best part of who she was with Maureen and Ida. I only got her back when she was tired and ready to show me her bad side. But during the long summer days at the trailer, she and I danced and sang to the radio in the backyard. She didn't care that I sounded like a crow with sawdust stuck in its craw.

Travis was sweet beyond words. He smiled and kicked and cooed for hours. Arlee and I loved singing to him. I whispered goofy things into his ear and called him "my sunny, funny boy."

The three of us went out into the front yard during the early afternoons when it was shady, or we had a picnic in the backyard. Bud bought an umbrella for the picnic table and a wading pool for the kids, and that's where we went when August sweated drops of hot sun onto the Earth.

We learned to trip trap over the bridges spanning the bad days, when Arlee couldn't figure out if she was coming or going. On those days, her moods were like the crayons she loved, indigos and lavenders. On those days, my colors had to be pale and neutral, grays and browns. Once in a while, hot orange-reds, yellows, and bright magentas surfaced and whirled around the both of us like mad sparks.

When that happened, I breathed and remembered Grand's patience with me.

One late afternoon, I knuckled down to the task of digging out a couple of flowerbeds while Bud and Travis watched a baseball game on TV. Arlee carried around a plastic watering can and talked to the grass. I planned to plant groups of tulip and daffodil bulbs and I hoped beach roses would grow. "They'll grow anywhere," Grand had once told me. "Rain, sun, sandy dirt, and they'll be happy."

Bud knocked on the picture window and when I looked up, he mouthed, "*Phone*." I scooped up Arlee. "Wahwah," she whined.

"Jeeza Arlee," I said, and she laughed as I carried her upside down into the trailer.

"It's Dottie," Bud said from his chair.

"Where's Travis?" I asked.

"Said he had to go see a man about a horse," he said.

I put Arlee down. "Could you get her ready for bed now?"

Bud groaned, but when Arlee clapped her hands at him and laughed, he melted. He carried her toward the bathroom.

"What?" I said. "Did I get more letters?"

"Nice," Dottie said. "What happened to hello? And no, I ain't seen any strange letters."

"That's a comfort. How's tricks?"

"Good," Dottie said. "Place is haunted, though."

"What do you mean?"

"Well, I sit down after supper, and someone tells me to get off my ass and do them friggin' dishes if I know what's good for me. Only she don't say friggin' and she don't say ass."

"I know that ghost," I said.

"Kind of weird being here without you."

"I miss it."

"I bet. Things okay up there?"

"Better than I thought they would be," I said. "I'm making a garden. Love having the kids to myself. Good seeing Bud every day. It's okay."

"Speaking of kids," Dottie said. "Guess who's pregnant?"

"You?"

"That'd have to be a virgin birth," she said. "Evie. Madeline's fit to be tied."

"What's going to happen?"

"Evie thinks she's going to quit school and raise it. Bert and Madeline tell her that's not going to happen. When this summer ends, she's going to have to get through school for a couple of months, no matter what. She ain't showing much, yet. But she says, 'Florine quit school and she's okay.'"

"Glad I could set such a nice example," I said.

"Yeah," Dottie said.

"What did Bert and Madeline say about that?"

"Took 'em back, for a few seconds. Then they said, 'Well, you just call her and ask her about quitting school. She'll tell you what's what.'"

"You think I'm the one to talk to her?"

"Hell, no. I told 'em not to get you into this. I said, 'She's got her own damn story.'"

"I do. I got my own damn story. When she due? Who's the father?"

"Mid-December. She's not saying."

"Not Glen?"

"No, Christ, no. I asked him. 'Why the fuck would you think that?' he said. Got real mad at me. 'How come everyone thinks it might be me? You all think I'm a fuck-up?' he said. Went on and on. Had to back up, he was spitting on me so much."

"How's he doing?" I said.

"Don't see him much. He's out on the boat from dawn to dark. Doesn't seem to bring much in. Just goes out. Walks up the road after dark. Never stops in. Don't talk to no one. Maureen made him some brownies the other day. Told her to stop doing that, for chrissake, he wasn't no charity case. Pissed off Ida."

"Oh, sweet Jesus, no," I said.

"Told him what she thought. Only person can maybe knock some sense into him."

"He living with Ray?"

"No, he's living in a tent off the path between The Cheeks and the state park."

"What? That's really weird."

"Yeah, well, that's where he's at these days."

"So, is there anything good going on?"

"Pastor Billy's feeling better. Came by the other day. Seemed surprised to see me answer the door. Made him some tea before he went down to Ida's for supper."

"You made tea?"

"I did. Turned on the stove, boiled water, stuck a bag in a cup, poured water over it."

"I'm proud of you, Dorothea. Makes me want to cry."

"Well, I got a life to run. And my sister is knocked up. Much as she's a pain in my ass, I got concerns."

"You do."

"Anyway, that's all the news from here. I'm leaving in a week."

"I know," I said. "We'll be down to tuck everything in for the winter some weekend."

"Say hi to Bud for me."

"I will. Talk to you before you go?"

"'Course."

After we hung up, I sat by the kitchen phone, listening to Bud sing a song to Arlee. It was a peaceful moment. I thought about Dottie's news. Glen living in a tent and being ugly to everyone, and Evie knocked up. We had all been expecting something like this with Evie, but Glen's withdrawal from everyone who loved him or who might help him broke my heart. I ached for the good-natured, goofy boy he had been growing up. Our scatterbrained, funny friend, the one who had tripped over his own clumsy heart too many times but had come up grinning, always. I missed him.

Bud clicked shut the door to Arlee's room and walked into the kitchen.

"Everything all right?" he asked me. I told him the news.

"Kind of glad I ain't there," he said.

I nodded. "For once, I am too."

22

How I managed to get through my teens without learning to drive baffles me. How I managed to get through my teens at all baffles me. But I never learned to drive out on a main road and I never got my license.

Grand never drove, and Daddy wouldn't let me do it anyway. He said that I was too young. And, truthfully, after the car accident I got into with Andy, I was afraid to ride in a car, let alone drive one. But after he moved in, Bud coaxed me into slipping behind the wheel and driving down dirt roads at night, to little beaches most people didn't know about. These puny strips of sand couldn't compare to the big state-park beaches like Mulgully and Popham, but they suited us fine. We walked them for hours under bulging moons and parked our butts on rocks along the beach shores, and we talked unless we didn't. Once in a while, if the moon was bright enough, Bud drove without the headlights on barely there roads leading through miles of bleached dunes and silver grass.

So, I knew the basics. Gas and brake pedals, lights, windshield wipers, and how to adjust the driver's seat. I knew how to go forward. Bud had always reversed us. When I got pregnant with Arlee, I stopped driving altogether, although once in a while, I thought forward to a time when I would be seated behind Petunia's wheel, tapping my pink-polished fingernails against the wheel to the beat of a favorite song, kids in the back, driving along to wherever life was taking us. Carlie, driving Petunia in just that way, was one of my favorite memories.

All that said, Bud completely surprised me when he signed me up for driver's education, which was taught just down the road in a Stoughton Falls Elementary School classroom. He loaded up the kids and me on the nights that it was held, dropped me at the door of the school, and drove home for the hour that class was in session. Then, he and the kids picked me up. I loved that little ritual. Arlee always clapped and smiled when she saw me, and her father's eyebrows wiggled as I swayed toward the car.

Mr. Dion taught ten of us the rules of the road. We watched grainy films and slide shows and studied our driver's manuals. After the inside classes ended, it was time to get behind the wheel and drive.

"I'm nervous," I said to Bud. "I don't know if I can get out on a real road and make sense of everything. And people go so fast. The crazy drivers that go by here don't think there's a speed limit. What if they catch up to me and crash into the ass end of my car?"

"What if they don't?" Bud said.

"Bud, if anything can happen to me, it will," I said.

"Got a point," Bud said. "But don't worry about it."

I did, of course, and something did happen.

Saturday mornings, Mr. Dion picked me up. Another student, an older woman named Olga Carlson, steered into our driveway and beeped. She was almost too old to drive, about sixty-eight, as she said. Her husband, George, was going blind, she told us, and so she, in spite of her great fear, needed to learn to drive a car, as they didn't want to rely on anyone else to be able to get around.

On that particular Saturday in September, I hopped into the backseat and waved goodbye to Arlee and Bud from where they stood watching us in the picture window. "Oh, isn't she precious?" Mrs. Carlson said, waving at my daughter, who rewarded her with a big smile. "Oh, my goodness, what a little sweetheart!" She launched into the charms of one of her granddaughters, who was just three months older than Arlee. Mrs. Carlson loved to talk. I suppose it was her way of flicking away her nerves. My way was to clam up and hold my breath. Mr. Dion, who took up all the space in the passenger seat in the front, snacked nonstop to take care of his own doubts about his student drivers.

Mr. Dion told Mrs. Carlson, "Put the car into reverse, please." She took a deep, shaky breath and scrunched her bony hand around the gearshift on the floor. She shifted into R and turned her head as far to the right as she could to see the road in back of her. She put her foot on the gas and, so slowly that the second hand on a clock could have passed her twice, she backed up.

"Don't forget, you've got your mirrors too," Mr. Dion said. This caused a complete stop on Mrs. Carlson's part, as she did what he asked.

"You don't have to stop. In fact, don't stop. Just check to see what's there," Mr. Dion said. "Those mirrors are there for a reason."

"Oh, right," Mrs. Carlson said. "George always says, 'Look over both your shoulders, not once, but twice, to make sure nothing's coming.'"

"George is a smart man," Mr. Dion said. "I bet he uses his mirrors too." He put a hand to the battered golf cap on his head and adjusted it against the grain of his close-cropped, salt-and-pepper hair. He reached into a potato-chip bag and brought out five or six chips. He made a sandwich out of them and bit into it, scattering crumbs and spit over the glove compartment and the dashboard on his side of the car.

Every Saturday, we drove along Route 100 to Portland. Mr. Dion gave orders for Mrs. Carlson to turn onto a side street just inside the Portland city limits, so she could practice parallel parking. "Oh, I get so nervous doing this," she said, every time we did it. So far, she hadn't been able to complete it. The only time she had come close, a car owner ran from his house and down his driveway and hollered at us to practice somewhere else; he didn't want to get his car dented again, goddammit. This flustered Mrs. Carlson, so that every time we practiced, her eyes skittered over the front doors of the houses around her. "Oh, I don't want to get yelled at," she said.

"You won't. Don't worry about it," Mr. Dion said. "Sometimes, people do get anxious, and when they do, we politely move on."

"We could get shot," I pointed out.

"That's not helpful, Mrs. Warner," Mr. Dion said.

But that Saturday, Mrs. Carlson parallel parked. With Mr. Dion's quiet assistance, Mrs. Carlson snaked her way behind a purple VW Bug that sported peace-sign stickers all over it, slid in slicker than shit next to the curb, and put the car into park.

"Oh, my goodness. Am I in?" she said. Mr. Dion opened the door.

"Perfect," he said.

"Good job," I said. Her face lit up like a lighthouse beacon. She looked at me in the rearview mirror and we smiled at each other.

Her good job was short-lived, however. We pulled out of the spot and drove to the end of the street, which joined up with Baxter Boulevard. I loved this part of Portland. The wide street curved around Back Cove, a large round tidal basin that took in water from Casco Bay at high tide and then let it all out, leaving cold mudflats during low tide. Big, beautiful homes sat on green lawns along the edges of the boulevard. High, clipped hedges hid some of them, but other homes faced toward the cove.

"Who lives in those houses?" I had asked Mr. Dion when we first saw them.

"Doctors," Mr. Dion said. "Lawyers. Judges. People with those kinds of jobs."

Traffic was heavy on Saturdays around the boulevard, as drivers streamed toward downtown Portland. It made me nervous to watch Mrs. Carlson, and I knew how she felt. Neither of us had a good sense of when we could join a line of moving cars.

"Now," Mr. Dion would say, but timid Mrs. Carlson usually missed her chance. It took two or three "nows" from Mr. Dion to get her to goose the gas and join the flow.

But on that Saturday, Mrs. Carlson had just conquered parallel parking. She reached the end of the street, saw the cars coming, figured she had time to pull out, and she did it, just as Mr. Dion shouted, "*Not now!*" She turned the wheel hard toward the curb and bumped it. A sharp pop harmonized with the vicious horn honk from the driver behind her. I lurched against the backseat as the car behind gunned it and passed us.

"Oh, no," Mrs. Carlson said.

"Jesus," Mr. Dion said, and climbed out onto the curb. He looked down at the right front tire and shook his head.

"Oh, look what I did," Mrs. Carlson said to me.

"It's just a flat tire," I said.

"Oh, I feel so stupid," she said. She started to cry. "I hate this. I hate that George can't drive. I can't do it. I can't."

"You can," I said. "Everyone gets a flat tire. I bet I'll get one before we're done."

"Oh, you drive good," she said. "You're young. You'll be driving for years."

"So will you," I said.

Mr. Dion opened the front passenger door and said, "You ladies get out while I change the tire. Be careful, Mrs. Carlson. Wait for the cars to go by."

"Oh, I'm so sorry," Mrs. Carlson wailed. Mr. Dion shut the door and I thought I heard him say, "Yeah, so am I," but I couldn't be sure. We stood on the grass by the curb while Mr. Dion fumbled around in the trunk for a jack and the spare tire. He looked at his watch, mumbled something about "no damn way to spend Saturday," and hauled out a set of golf clubs nestled in the folds of a well-worn brown leather bag.

"Oh, I've messed up your golf time," Mrs. Carlson said.

He sighed. "No, you haven't, Mrs. Carlson. I'm sorry for being so impatient."

He muttered under his breath as he worked, finishing in about fifteen minutes.

"You drive," he ordered me, and I climbed in behind the wheel and adjusted the seat and the mirrors. Mrs. Carlson sat quiet in the backseat. I looked at her in the rearview mirror. "You okay?" I asked her. She gave me a little smile and looked out of the window as I checked in back of me. All clear. I pulled out and we drove around the boulevard and ended up on State Street. This would take us up onto Congress Street, the spine of Portland. The first time I had done this, my armpits had dripped with sweat, but this time I liked inching along the big street. No one went too fast, and I got to look at the tall buildings on either side of me. I couldn't help sneaking peeks at people walking along, particularly red-haired women who might be my mother.

About halfway up Congress Street, it occurred to me that Mrs. Carlson hadn't said a word, which was unusual. She liked to comment on what was going on outside. A stoplight gave me the time to look back, and I saw that she was slumped against the window.

"Mrs. Carlson?" I called. She didn't move. "*Mrs. Carlson?*" I said, louder. No movement at all.

"Shit, what now?" Mr. Dion said, and turned to look at her as the light turned green. He reached over the back of the front seat and shook Mrs. Carlson's knee. No response. "Damn," he said.

"What do we do?" I asked. "Want me to pull over?"

"No. The hospital is up the street. Just let's get there."

What only took about five minutes seemed about an hour. Mr. Dion checked Mrs. Carlson's pulse. She had one, he said. I bumped along, red light to red light, until I reached the turn to Maine Medical Center, where, not so very long ago, I had been a guest in the maternity ward.

"Go to the emergency room. Follow the signs," Mr. Dion said, and I drove that way. We parked and Mr. Dion hurried into the building while I got out of the car and opened Mrs. Carlson's door. "Ummm," she mumbled.

"Mrs. Carlson?" I shouted. This reminded me too much of Grand's fatal stroke. "Cut it out, Mrs. Carlson," I pleaded. "Wake up." Her eyes fluttered and she looked up at me.

"What happened?" she asked.

The emergency room workers loaded Mrs. Carlson onto a gurney and hurried her inside. Mr. Dion parked the car and we walked into the waiting room. He looked at the paper he had on Mrs. Carlson—we all had one with next of kin listed, should we really fuck up and wind up hurting ourselves or other drivers—and roamed off to make some calls. I sat in a chair next to a little boy I guessed was about a year older than Arlee and his mother. The boy was hiding his head beneath her arm, but I saw dried blood on his green striped shirt. The mother and I exchanged sympathetic smiles.

"He's got a crayon up his nose," she explained. "I got most of it out, but it broke off and there's still a piece of it that I don't dare touch."

"What color?" I asked.

She smiled. "Burnt orange."

"My little girl would probably pick periwinkle or violet blue," I said.

We smiled again, and someone called a name. The mother said, "That's us. Let's go, Alessandro." They got up and walked toward a young woman clutching a clipboard.

She was around my age. Her long hair, pulled back into a ponytail, was dark red. Her eyes were brown. She wore a striped skirt and white blouse with a striped vest over it. She reminded me of someone.

When she smiled at the mother and her boy, I thought, Robin. Robin was my cousin. I had met her and her younger brother, Benjamin, once. They were the children of Carlie's brother, Robert.

To say Carlie was not close to her family would be an understatement. She didn't speak to them, and hadn't done so since before I was born. This bothered Daddy, who was lucky enough to have had Grand for a mother. His father, Franklin, who died when Daddy was young, was also kind. Carlie hadn't been so lucky.

Still, Daddy thought it might be good to have me know her family, so one Saturday when I was six, he packed Carlie and me into the pickup and we drove to her hometown in Massachusetts. I met Robin, who was four, and Benjamin, still a toddler. Carlie's mom, my grandmother, seemed happy to see us. Carlie's father didn't turn around when we came into the living room. He stayed in a chair watching television and smoking a cigarette. The long ash on the end of it drew me to him and when he had noticed me staring, he'd said, "What the hell are you looking at?" Along about then, Daddy came over, and Robin grabbed my hand and took me upstairs to her bedroom.

We understood each other right away. We giggled and played with her dolls and brushed each other's hair and I felt as close as I ever would to knowing what it felt like to have a sister. She would visit me, we decided, and we would have fun at The Point. Maybe she could stay for a long time.

All of that fell apart when Carlie got into a shouting match with her father. We left shortly after that and we never went back. I wrote to Robin. When I didn't hear from her, it quietly broke my heart. After a while, life happened and I pushed her to the back of my mind. But I had never forgotten her.

The young woman who looked like Robin came out from behind the curtain carrying her clipboard. She walked over to an old man sitting a few seats away and took his arm as if she knew him. And then I saw her nametag. The hair on the back of my neck stood up. She glanced at me and smiled. I stood up. "You're Robin?" I croaked.

She looked at me. "Yes?" she said.

"I'm Florine," I said. "I think I'm your cousin."

She frowned and studied my face. "My cousin?"

"Florine Gilham. Well, Warner now. My mother, Carlie, was your aunt."

Robin dropped the old man's arm. "Oh my god," she said.

A slow smile spread over my face.

"What? How? Where?" she said. "You're Florine?" She squinted, and maybe that helped her to see me as a child. She grinned. "You are! Wow! How great is that?"

The old man said, "I'm gonna puke," and Robin hustled him toward the patient rooms. But before they could get there, the old man upchucked on her shoes.

She looked at me and shrugged, helpless to move.

I fished an old shopping list and a pen out of my purse and hustled over to her, trying not to inhale the sharp smell of vomit. "What's your phone number?" I said. She told me. I wrote her number down. When our fingers touched, we smiled at each other.

I scurried back to Mr. Dion and Mrs. Carlson, who said she was all right, even though she was a little wobbly.

"I'll call you," I said to Robin as we walked out the door.

23

"Stop fidgeting," Bud said.

"I'm not," I said. I was, though. I couldn't stop moving. I moved the cheese plate around on the little dining-room table. I rearranged the plate of homemade bread.

"Bed, peas," Arlee said. I tore a corner off the top piece of bread on the pile for her, and rearranged it again. Travis grinned at me from his little swing in the living room. His fat toes scraped the floor. "Unh," he said. "Unh, unh."

"You tell her, pal," Bud said.

He sat on the sofa in the sun in front of the picture window, reading the Sunday-morning funnies. Arlee crawled up beside him and he read to her, moving his fingers from frame to frame. He sucked in the air and said, "That bread smells good."

I sighed. "Want a piece?"

"Wouldn't mind it."

"What's the magic word?" I said.

"Peas," Bud said.

I handed him a slice of bread.

"And how about some of that cheese, peas?" he said.

"Can you make me half a sandwich?" he asked. He elbowed Arlee, who giggled and said, "Peas?"

I grabbed the bread and cheese, stomped into the kitchen, grabbed mustard and mayonnaise and two knives, because god forbid the two should mingle on the knife, even though Bud liked them together on a sandwich. I slathered the bread, put the cheese on it, and folded the bread. Somehow, in the process of doing this, the glass jar of mustard fell to the floor and shattered, spattering my panty-hosed legs.

"She's here," Bud said.

"Of course she is," I said. "Screw it." I peeled the panty hose off, threw them into the trash, swiped the dishrag over the mustard on my legs, threw the rag back into the sink, and ran out of the house and down the driveway to the slender woman getting out of the navy-blue Toyota Corolla. She shut the door of the Corolla and we stood, taking each other in.

"I just got mustard all over my legs," I said, and she grinned. She came toward me, her arms outstretched, and then we hugged, crying and laughing and remembering that time, so far back, when we had looked at each other and known it was forever, no matter if we hadn't seen each other for almost twenty years.

"I couldn't believe it when I saw you in the hospital," I said.

"I hoped I would find you. I didn't know how or where, but I hoped we would meet up somehow," she said. "I'm in Portland to study nursing. When you said your name, I thought, there are not too many people named Florine. And then it struck me and I thought, oh my god, it's *my* Florine!"

Bud came out to meet us, holding Travis. Arlee trailed behind them.

"This is Bud, my husband," I said.

Bud's dark eyes shifted between us. "Definitely a resemblance," he said.

"It's so nice to meet you," Robin said. "And *you*," she said to Travis, who jounced his way into her arms. He charmed her until she laughed.

Arlee stood quiet by her father's side, holding his hand and staring at Robin, who squatted down to her level and said, "Do you like flowers?"

Arlee nodded.

I took the baby as Robin reached into her car and brought out a small African violet in a purple foil plant pot. "Do you think you can water it and make sure it gets some sun?"

Arlee nodded again.

"Well, then, it's yours," Robin said. Arlee let go of Bud's hand, took the flower, and cradled it to her. She grinned at me. "Jeeza fowa," she said.

"What did she say?" Robin said.

"'Jeeza' is Jesus," I said. "Ida, Bud's mother, told her that Jesus was in everything and everyone. So, Arlee thinks he's in the flower."

"I think I'll take the kids to the playground down the road," Bud said, shifting uncomfortably. "So you can talk."

"Oh, you don't have to go," Robin said.

"Yes, he does," I said. I kissed him and took the plant from Arlee, after promising to take care of it while she was gone. They all climbed into the Fairlane and drove away.

Sudden shyness washed over me. "Well," I said, "come in."

"Nice lawn," Robin said.

"Thanks. We don't always live here," I said. "I have to take you down to The Point."

"You know, Florine, I tried to find it, once, but I got all messed up and ended up sitting by the ocean in another spot so pretty I gave up and watched the sun set."

"Sit down," I said, motioning to the dining-room table.

"This is so cute," Robin said, taking a seat. "This trailer is adorable." She pointed out the way I had arranged little things throughout.

"Grand—Daddy's mother—had an eye for putting things in the right place," I said. "I guess she passed that on. She always said, 'A house doesn't need to be a clutter box.'"

Robin said, "Grandma Maxine did that too. Not one of my talents, I'm afraid."

"I only just met her that one time," I said. "She seemed sad, but nice. Is she okay?"

Robin's face fell. "She died when I was ten."

"Oh," I said. "I'm sorry to hear that. I wish I'd had a chance to know her."

"Grandma Maxine loved meeting you," Robin said. "She thought you were so pretty. She wanted to come and visit. She really did."

I smiled and said, "Okay, we're past the hellos, right?" Robin nodded.

"Was Carlie's father the mean son of a bitch Daddy told me he was?"

"He was cranky, but by the time I knew him, he had lung cancer and was probably dying. I didn't pay much attention to him, but Dad walked on eggshells around him. A couple of years ago, Dad told me the story of why Carlie left for good."

"Daddy told me too, when I was about seventeen. He said that Carlie got pregnant and her father was ashamed of her and wouldn't let her out of the house. She used to sneak out anyway, by going out her bedroom window. Said she would sneak to the lowest place along the roof and jump down."

Robin nodded. "That's what Dad said to me. He said one night she slipped and landed in the yard. Dad said the baby died. He said Carlie almost died too. After she got better, she stayed away from home more and more."

I nodded. "That's the same story."

"I can't blame her," Robin said. "Anyway, he died about a year after you came down."

"After he died, why didn't Grandma Maxine—and this is the first time I've ever said that—come to visit? Why didn't she tell you where we lived?"

"She had really awful rheumatoid arthritis. After Grandpa Dennis died, her body let go. That happens sometimes. The body stores up stress, and when the stress is gone, the body can react in negative ways. Not always, but sometimes. Anyway, she stayed sick five years after he died."

"But she could have given you the address. She knew where we lived."

"Well, she never let on that she did," Robin said.

"I don't know," I said, "maybe Carlie never mailed the letter."

"It's a mystery," Robin said. "But we've found each other now! The only time we ever saw her was that day. That was it. So, Grandma got sick, Dad had to take care of her, and Ben and I were just little kids. Grandma died, then Dad met Valerie and they got married. She moved in and we grew up. I graduated early, at seventeen, and came up here to college. Dad and Valerie sold the house and moved to California. That's my story, I guess. Not very exciting, but it's all mine. And now, here we are!"

"I can't believe you're here," I said, trying not to cry. "Finding you is almost like finding Carlie. You're a piece of both of us."

Robin knitted her mahogany eyebrows and said, "Did you ever find out anything about Carlie? I only knew she'd disappeared, and then Grandma got sick."

It took a while to fill her in. We ate lunch at some point, and then Bud was back, carrying a sleepy Arlee. I went out to the car and toted in a hungry Travis. Robin gave him a bottle. After she burped him, he fell asleep on her shoulder.

When she found out what Bud did for a living, she talked about her car and how it worked and didn't work. She asked him about his family and about how we had gotten together. She stayed until Arlee woke up from her nap and wanted supper.

"Love to have you eat with us," I said.

"Wish I could, but I have plans tonight," she said.

"I don't want to sound clingy or anything, but please come back," I said.

She hugged me tight. "I'll always come back," she said. She kissed me on the cheek and drove away. I stood in the driveway, rooted to the ground.

24

Just before Thanksgiving I got my license. I drove the Fairlane for the first time to The Point with my quieter-than-usual husband sitting shotgun. As the days had shortened, he had clammed up. All that space between conversations made me nervous.

"What's wrong?" I said from time to time.

"Nothing," he said.

"Is it my driving? Too slow? Too fast?"

"A little slow. Not fast. Doing good."

About ten minutes later, I said, "Why aren't you saying anything?"

"Nothing to say."

"Does it feel funny to be in the passenger seat?"

"A little bit."

"You want to change the radio to the country station? You like country."

"It's fine where it is. Can't beat Grand Funk."

"You're so quiet."

"I'm fine, Florine. I got something to say, I'll say it."

I sighed and imagined Dottie and now, Robin, sitting next to me. We would talk and laugh and our trips would fly by. "Oh!" I said.

"What?"

"Now that I have my license, I can take girls' weekends."

"What do you mean?"

"Like Carlie used to do. Travel up the coast with Robin and Dottie, or one of them. Stay overnight somewhere. Look at the sights. Eat something I don't cook."

After a short silence, Bud said, "I guess you could."

"Next summer, maybe."

"How you going to do that? Who'll take care of the kids?"

"Ida. You. You can do it for one weekend."

Silence. Bud switched off the radio. He said, "I'll have to think about it."

"I really don't need your permission," I said.

"Do if you want me to take care of the kids," he said.

"Wow," I said, "I didn't think it would be such a chore for you." I sniffed.

"Jesus, Florine, you get pissed if I have a few beers and come home late."

"That's because you add whiskey to that beer and you come home ugly."

"Oh, here we go," Bud said. "You're speeding up. Slow down."

"I'm a good mother and a good wife. I love it, but it would be nice to get away for a little bit. Now I have a cousin and a best friend to do things with. It would be a blast!"

"The Point is your vacation. You can have Robin down here."

"The Point is our home. A vacation is an away thing. You sound like Daddy. My parents had this argument all the time. Carlie wanted to go, Daddy wanted to stay."

"Slow down."

We both shut up and I concentrated on my driving. We didn't talk for the rest of the way. Arlee sang "Twinkle, Twinkle, Little Star" over and over, until I thought I'd lose my mind. We finally got to The Point at about eleven in the morning.

Before I had even stopped the car, Maureen ran up the hill. Had it only been a few months since I'd seen her? She looked less like a girl, more like a woman. I got out of the car and she hugged me tight.

"I missed you all, so much," she said, and reached into the backseat for Arlee.

Bud had Travis out of his seat by then. When Maureen had Arlee in her arms, she noticed Travis. Her eyes grew wide and she said, "Oh my god!" She put her hand over her mouth, in case her mother may have heard her use the lord's name outside of a prayer. She said, "He's so big!"

"He's a baby giant," I said. Travis snuggled his head into his father's neck. Maureen walked over to her brother and pecked his cheek. "Missed you, Bud," she said.

"My god, you're the same height," I said.

"I know," Maureen said. "When he used to tease me, I said he'd better watch out because someday I'd be as tall as him."

"You made it," Bud said. "You're going to pass me."

"Okay if I take her down to the house?" Maureen asked, shifting Arlee on her hip.

Before I said anything, Bud said to Maureen, "I'll go with you," and off they went.

"Well then," I said to myself, unlocking the front door, "Don't help. See if I care." I stood in the hall, listening to the cold and the quiet. The furnace was on just enough to keep the pipes from freezing. I turned the thermostat up and looked around. It was too clean for Dottie to have done it, so it had probably been Ida, who had also put some basics into the fridge. A pile of mail sat on the kitchen table. I went through it.

Among the recent bills and toss-outs were two cream-colored envelopes addressed to me in block printing, both with a Lewiston postmark. "Crap," I said. I didn't want to deal with this now, and I didn't want to call Parker on the day before Thanksgiving. I put the envelopes back on the table. The car needed to be unpacked and beds needed making. I rinsed out the teakettle, filled it, and clicked on the stove. Bud came into the kitchen. His eyes flickered, a sure sign he was mad at me.

"What is wrong with you?" I said.

"The thing is," he said, "you could have asked *me* to go somewhere with you."

"What?"

"I'm the one supports this family. You didn't even ask me, for chris-sake."

"Well, of course we can go somewhere alone, sometime. I didn't think I had to make that clear. But what would be wrong with doing something with the girls sometime?"

"It would have been nice for you to think of me first. Jesus, do you think of anyone else besides yourself?"

My jaw dropped. "Of course I do. I think of you all the time."

"Hell you do. Everything is all about you."

"Bud!" I said. I'd never seen him so mad. "No, it isn't. You're being crazy. Of course I want to go somewhere with you. I'm sorry."

"Bullshit!"

"What did you say?"

"Bullshit!"

"Why don't you come back when you're not so mean," I yelled.

"I might come back," he said. "Whether I do or not, stop being so friggin' selfish."

He walked down the hall and out the door, slamming it behind him. The kettle sang and I poured myself a cup of tea.

I sank into a kitchen chair, trying to make sense of what had just happened. Then I remembered there were things to be done.

Maybe he's right, I thought as I unpacked the car. I was friggin' selfish. I wondered if he had gotten such a good deal with me. Maybe he would have been better off with Susan, who had been a girl with goals. She would have had a plan for them. She would have had a job so he wouldn't have had to be the only breadwinner. They wouldn't have had kids so soon. Maybe he was thinking that too. Maybe he was done with me.

A door slammed and Madeline called up to me from her house, "Hey there. Happy Thanksgiving!" I wiped my eyes and smiled as she walked up the hill to me. She wrapped me in a warm Madeline hug.

"Happy Thanksgiving to you," I said.

"Dottie tell you I'm going to be a grandma?"

"Yes," I said. "How's Evie?"

"Happy as ever. Big."

"I have to unpack us," I said. "I'll be over soon. Dottie home?"

"She's gone uptown. Be down in a couple hours or so."

I lugged in the last bags and sat down on the sofa, twisted with worry. Bud walked in.

"You going to leave me?" I burst out.

He blinked. "Where the hell did that come from?"

"You said you might not come back."

He shrugged. "That was stupid."

"You were more pissed off than I've ever seen you."

"Well, sometimes the latest thing I'm mad at gets attached to something I was mad at before but didn't tell you, and it winds up sticking together."

"Well, how about you tell me what's going on before anything gets stuck to anything? And don't ever do that to the kids or you'll see how frigging selfish I can be."

"Got it," he said, and walked into the kitchen.

"I'm going for a walk," I called. "I'll be back in a while."

I took off for the state park. I intended to sit on the bench by the ledges and have a talk with the ocean. But someone was already there. As soon as I saw that, I turned, thinking to head for the clearing, but before I got far, a man's voice called, "Florine!"

I turned around. The man walking toward me had a little limp.

It was Andy Barrington.

25

The girl I had once been expected to greet an eager, restless boy with an electric smile and soft, beautiful eyes that had never been afraid to hold my gaze. But time had transformed both of us. I now stood in front of him as a mother and a wife. The boy I had known had changed too, leaving a thin, hesitant man in his place. Andy's dark eyes darted here and there, looking at me and then shifting away. A nervous smile quickened on his ragged face as the November wind tousled his dirty-blond hair, which was two or three inches shorter than it had been a few years back. The tips of his ears were red.

"You need a hat," I said.

He reached for me and, before I could think, I reached back and we held on to each other for about ten seconds. "It's so good to see you," he whispered. "Oh my god, it's so good to see you."

My nose took in stale cigarettes and old pot. He squeezed me tighter.

"It's good to see you too," I said.

"Oh my god," he said into my hair. His voice trembled.

"That's enough!" I laughed.

"Yes," he said. "Yes." He finally let me go, but his eyes continued to trip over my face. "You are just as beautiful as ever," he said. "Life agrees with you."

"Better than it did the last time we saw each other," I said. "Neither of us was in any shape to agree to anything."

"I know," Andy said. "Oh god. I run that night over in my head all the time. Fuck me. I could have killed you." His eyes filled with tears and I didn't know what to do. Our past and our accident all seemed so dreamlike. I decided to move things along.

"Well," I said, "we're okay, after all. It's nice to see you up and walking."

"Got the limp," he said. "Always will. Messed myself up good."

"We're here," I said. "And that counts for something. I'm a mama. And a wife."

"I heard," Andy said. "I'm so glad. My god, I'd forgotten how beautiful you are," he said again, in case I hadn't heard him before.

"I have a girl, Arlee, almost two and a half, and a boy, Travis, almost seven months."

Andy whistled. "Wow. You've been busy."

I changed the subject. "What are you doing here?"

"Oh, taking a break," he said. "The family is here for Thanksgiving."

"All of them?"

He laughed. "Mother is here. And Edward." He winced when he mentioned his father's name.

"Speaking of Edward, the last time we talked, you were in military school."

"I stayed about six months. They tried to march the limp out of me, and when they couldn't, Edward let me go somewhere else. I finished up high school with tutors and, somehow, Edward got me into UMass, but that didn't work out. So, I'm thinking about the next step."

"Oh," I said. "Dottie graduates from college this spring."

"No shit. I've seen the other guy. The big guy. Glen? I've run into him a few times, around here. We've shared a few tokes." He spat on the ground. "Fuckin' war," he muttered. "The one good thing that happened when we crashed was this limp. It kept me from being drafted."

We stood there, filling the silence with awkwardness. It seemed to be a day for silences. I thought about Bud and a strong longing to be with him made me want to turn and run. I started to tell Andy goodbye, but he had more to say.

"You got me through a hard time, Florine," he said. "No, don't shake your head. You did. Don't know what I would have done without you."

"We got each other through some hard times."

He wrapped his hands around my upper arms. "I mean that," he said, his voice soft.

I pulled away gently. "I have to go," I said. "Bud and the kids will want lunch."

"Can we get together sometime?"

"Oh, I don't know," I said.

"That means no," Andy said. He looked down at the ground. One cracked hiking boot scuffed the pine needles into a semicircle.

"But I'm glad to see you," I said, sounding too cheerful. "I'm happy you're okay."

His eyes filled with tears again and he wiped them away with his fists. He hugged me, once more, hard, until I almost wrenched myself away. Had he always been this needy? This desperate? Had I?

"You will always be special to me, Florine," he whispered. "I hope you know that. I will always love you. Always. And I hope you will forgive me."

"I do. We were both kind of crazy."

"No. I mean it. Please."

"Jesus, yes." I laughed. "I forgive you! Now, I have to get home."

"I will always love you," he said again.

"Andy, I will always love Bud," I said, finally. "Always. I hope with all my heart you find someone that makes you happy."

Andy shook his head. "Can't ever happen," he said. "Sold my soul a long time ago. Goodbye, sweet girl." He turned and shuffled out of sight, his head down and his hands crowding the pockets of his jeans.

I hurried away home.

❧

Bud was rocking on the porch when I got home. "Ma wants to know if we want to have supper with them," he said.

"Sounds good," I said. "Want to get the kids? They should come up here for a nap. They don't sleep as well down there."

"Do you mind going? I just as soon sit here," he said.

I bent down and pecked him on the lips. He sniffed. "You smell like . . ."

"I'll be right back," I said on my way out the door.

I met Glen coming up from the wharf.

"Hey," he said.

"Hey," I said. "How you doing?"

He shrugged. "Doing."

"Bud's at the house," I said.

He nodded. He walked by me and passed Grand's house. "Okay then," I muttered, and entered a warm kitchen filled with women and babies. I nestled in, cuddling my son's warm body against me and watching my daughter scamper around. We stayed for about an hour and then I took my babies home. Bud was napping in Grand's rocker as I put Travis into the bassinet. Arlee curled up under the coffee table in the living room. I stood in the kitchen, wondering how to spend this tiny pocket of spare time. Then I remembered the mail, and the letters. I sat down, picked up the envelopes, and sighed.

The rocker creaked as Bud got up and joined me at the table.

"You got more of them letters?" he said, yawning himself awake.

"I don't want to read them. But I don't not want to read them, if that makes sense."

"'Bout as good as anything else makes sense."

He picked one of them up by its corner, took from his pocket the small penknife he carried, and slit the top of the envelope. He opened it and placed the letter in front of me.

No date. No salutation. No closing.

> *I could gaze at you all day and all night long and never get tired of the view. But I cannot take this anymore. I loved you more than you love me. I know that. And so I say, goodbye, my love.*

"Jesus," Bud said. "Whoever it is needs to lighten up. '*Gaze*'? Christ."

"If you said 'gaze' to me, I'd split a gut," I said.

Bud opened the other letter and placed it in front of me.

> *I can't leave you. I love you. Please be patient with me.*
> *I'm sorry.*

"He should make up his mind," Bud said.

"We don't know that it's a he," I said. "I have to give these to Parker."

Bud shook his head. "Not today," he said. "Fuck it. Let's enjoy the holiday."

I took his hand and squeezed it. "I do love you," I said. I almost told him about seeing Andy, but I decided to stuff it. This, I thought, is how volcanoes erupt.

Arlee called my name from underneath the coffee table. Before I could get up to check on her, Bud grabbed my hand, hard. "Wait," he said.

"What?"

"*Perhaps*, I ain't perfect," he said. "But I could *gaze* at you for fucking ever. And, by the way, you ain't perfect either, *my love*." Our hands linked over the letters and smudged away whatever fingerprint evidence there might have been.

26

Robin cried when she saw The Point. "Oh my god, Florine," she said, "it's so beautiful here! You got to grow up here? What was wrong with our damn parents that they couldn't get it together so that we could visit?"

We flung our arms over each other's shoulders and looked from the top of the hill down to the harbor. "You should see it in the summer," I said.

She shook her head. "No, I love the colors in November best of all; the reds and browns, and yellows. November glows like the embers of a dying fire."

"You make that up?" I asked.

"Corny, huh? Well, I'm inspired."

Bud and I had discussed whether we should invite her for Thanksgiving. When I'd brought it up, he shrugged and said, "Why wouldn't you invite her?" as if we hadn't had a tense little talk about her new place in my life.

"You sure you're okay with it?" I'd said.

He'd rolled his eyes and said, "Of course I'm okay. Invite her, for chrissake."

"Because it seems to me that you got a little jealous when I said . . ."

"I know what I said," he'd grumbled. "Get her down here. Ma always has too much food anyways."

"I'll make sure she doesn't eat much," I'd said. "I'll keep an eye on it, smack her hand with a knife if she reaches for seconds."

"Especially the pie. She can't have any pumpkin pie."

She'd love to come, Robin had told me over the phone. "I'll bring a pumpkin pie." I'd smirked, thanked her, and told her I couldn't wait.

She arrived on Thanksgiving at about midmorning, tooling down the dirt road in her little Corolla. She would be staying in Bud's old room at Ida's house, but first, I showed her Grand's house. In particular, she loved the kitchen and the porch and rockers. She also loved Stella's house, which had been empty for about two weeks, according to Madeline. Robin and I walked up Daddy's driveway and viewed the house from all sides. I showed her The Cheeks at the back of the yard.

"It does look like the crack of someone's butt," Robin agreed. She turned back to the house. "I love this place. It's small and sweet."

"It was sweet," I said, "back in the day."

She smiled at me. "Maybe it will be, again. Good memories to come."

"Most people really love Grand's house when they see it," I said. "Sometimes they knock on the door and ask if it's for sale."

"Really?"

"Yeah. That's happened a few times. Happened when Grand was alive. She'd say, 'Well, probably about a million for the house, and a couple million more for the view. You come up with that, and we'll talk.' But she'd laugh when she said it, and she'd bring folks in for a look-see and sometimes they'd have tea. But I'm not Grand. Once, a young couple from Connecticut came by a couple months after Bud moved in. I just said, 'No, but have a nice vacation,' and waved them off."

"I guess they see what Aunt Carlie must have seen," Robin said. "Romance, beauty. It's like being in a book."

"Horror story, sometimes. Gets pretty cold and lonely in the winter, if you're not used to it. A few years back, and a couple of Points down, a wife murdered her husband in the middle of their first winter living there."

Robin shivered. "Well, it's beautiful," she said. "My dad would love it here."

I had never met my uncle Robert. He had not been at the house when we had visited that one time. I said, "Does Uncle Robert look like Carlie?"

Robin shook her head. "No. He looks like Maxine did: dark, thin, and tall. And quiet. No one is as quiet as Dad."

"Bud is spare with his words."

"Not like Dad."

"What did Uncle Robert think about Carlie?"

"I don't know, really. He's about ten years older than she was, so he was out of the house and married by the time she went through her trouble."

"Where's your mother?"

"She lives in Boston. She's a bartender. And she loves the life. Out at night, sleeps most of the day. She's on her third marriage. I don't hate her; I just don't know her. Once in a while we get together for a little visit."

"What about Ben?"

Robin smiled. "My little brother is a surfer dude. That's his job. Dad and Valerie let him be. I give him crap when we talk, but I don't care. What's it to me? It makes him happy, I guess. He's only seventeen."

"I had a baby when I was twenty," I said. "Carlie had a baby when she was nineteen. You're nineteen now. Isn't it time for you to jump on the bandwagon?"

"I'll catch up someday. In the meantime, I get to have people puke on my shoes, bleed all over me, and shit in my hands. Why would I give up the glamorous life of a single girl?"

"Sounds good to me, sometimes, but I wouldn't say that out loud. I love my kids past what I thought love could ever be."

"What would you do if you didn't have kids, though?" Robin asked.

"Well, I have them, and I love them, so this is just pretend."

"Of course."

I looked down at the frozen ground and thought for a little while.

"I guess I'd need to get my GED first. I quit school after Grand died. One more semester to go in high school and I quit. Stupid. I know that now."

"Well," Robin said, "you can get your GED, like you said. Then what?"

"When the kids are in school . . ."

"You can work on your GED while they're in bed, or Bud can watch them, or I'd be happy to help in any way I can, if you want."

Robin's voice had taken on a brisk tone that left no time for my half-formed thoughts. I wanted her to think that I was smart and together, even though I didn't believe it myself. Wiseass and bossy, yes, but together? "I need more time to think this through," I said. "I've been busy with diapers and bottles and stuff."

"Of course," Robin said. "You don't need to figure out your whole life plan right now." She shivered and I realized that I was cold too.

"We'll go for a longer walk, after dinner," I said. "Let's see if Ida needs some help."

❧

A big crowd gathered around the dining table in Ida's house for Thanksgiving dinner. Maureen, Robin, Bud and me and the kids, Ida. Ray made a special guest appearance. After dinner and cleanup, Robin and I took the kids up to Grand's house. They went down for afternoon naps and Ida and Maureen joined Robin and me for a vicious game of Hearts around the kitchen table.

Dottie wandered in at some point and livened things up.

"You got to be Robin," she said to my cousin. "About freaking time you showed up."

"I'm always late," Robin said.

"So's Florine," Dottie said. "'Least she's got kids to blame. What's your excuse?"

"I'm busy trying to beat your bowling score," Robin said.

That stopped Dottie and everyone else.

"You bowl?" I asked Robin. "Did you know that Dottie is . . ."

"Of course," Robin said. "She's famous. Anyone who bowls knows who she is."

"Not everyone," Dottie said. "Maybe a few people out there don't know."

"Don't be so modest," Robin said. She looked at me. "I knew who Dottie was before I knew you," she said. "I'm going to beat you someday," she said.

"Like to see you try," Dottie said. They shook hands.

"You're on," Robin said.

That settled, Dottie sat down and Ida left, taking a reluctant, wide-eyed Maureen with her. Bullshit flew around the room as Robin and Dottie talked about their adventures in bowling. The kids woke up and got restless, so I fed them a little supper. Shortly after that, Arlee got sleepy again and crawled under the kitchen table for a nap. I took Travis upstairs, bathed him, cuddled him, and sang him an off-key lullaby as we sat in the rocking chair. I loved holding my precious baby boy. I loved that the house was full of people. This, I thought, is how I want to live for the rest of my life. This is my goal—to have people in my home, having a good time. I can get a GED, I thought, and some kind of job, but this is what is most important to me.

I put Travis to bed and tiptoed downstairs in time to answer the soft knock on the door. Glen, and a very pregnant Evie, stood there. Both of them sported stupid smiles on their faces. Evie's blue eyes were bloodshot. So were Glen's black ones.

"Come in," I said. "Join the party."

"Happy Thanksgiving," Glen said, and wrapped me in a bear hug. The bones in my back cracked.

"Ooh," I said, "that felt good. Thanks."

"Robin, this is my pregnant sister, Evie," Dottie said. "That's Glen, our friend. It's not his baby. Only Evie knows for sure who the father might be."

Evie made a face at her sister.

Robin stood up and shook Glen's hand. "I've heard about you," she said.

He blushed and looked down. "Not all of it's true," he mumbled.

"It's all good," Robin said. "Hi," she said to Evie.

"Hi," Evie muttered.

Robin stared at her until Evie said, "What? I got stuffing between my teeth?"

"No, but you're stoned," Robin said. "And you're pregnant, and you have some puffiness in your face and hands. I don't mean to insult you. I'm a nurse."

"So?" Evie said. "Who made you the judge of me?" She said to Glen, "Let's go."

"Oh, don't go," Robin said. She stood up. "I'm just concerned. When are you due?"

"December fifteenth," Evie said. "Sagittarius, the Archer." She beamed as if this were great news.

Robin smiled. "December eighteenth. I'm a Sagittarius too," she said. "Optimistic, idealistic, and honest."

"Good for you," Evie said, readjusting her maternity blouse.

"Got any beer?" Glen asked.

"You know where it is," I said. He headed for the refrigerator.

"Where's Bud?" he asked.

"Watching football down to Ida's," I said.

He grunted. "I could go down there, I guess, with the men."

"Why?" Dottie said. "When you got us beauties to hang around with."

Glen laughed.

"What's so funny?" I asked.

"Well, nothing," he said. "Unless you're the one looking at you all."

"We may not be pretty," Dottie said. "But we're strong and we could take you down right now, if you don't behave."

"Except Evie," Robin said. "Probably not Evie."

"Shit, I could take you down too," Evie said.

Glen sat down in a kitchen chair. He leaned back, balancing it on its two rear legs.

"Down," I said. "Now. I mean it."

"He ain't a dog," Evie said.

I shot her a look that even she didn't dare cross. "Glen," I said.

He tipped back down, but when he straightened out his legs, his right, combat-booted, size-thirteen foot connected with Arlee's little left arm. When she screamed, we all jumped.

"Oh, damn," I said. "She's so quiet. I forgot." I ducked beneath the table to check on my girl, who was now sitting up, crying so hard that she wasn't making any noise. When she finally caught her breath, she let loose a storm of tears, snot, and noise. When I tried to touch her, she pulled away from me.

"Honey," I coaxed, "come on out. Mama needs to look at your arm."

"I'm sorry, Arlee," Glen said from somewhere above us. "Why didn't no one tell me she was there, for crying out loud? I'm sorry, baby." He got down on his hands and knees. Arlee scrambled away from him, toward the other side of the table. Dottie scooped her up and held her against her chest.

Glen got up and I crawled out from beneath the table, banging my head on the way. I bit my tongue to keep from yelling something rude.

"Ouch, man," Evie said. "Wow. This is turning into a real bad trip."

I went to my baby. "Let Mama see," I said. We surrounded her like some sort of witch's circle.

"Back up," Robin said quietly. We did. She took Arlee from Dottie while I swiped cards to the other side of the table. She sat her on the cleared spot.

"Is it broken?"

"Dammit," Glen said. He put his face into his hands. "I fuck everything up."

"Quit crying," Dottie said. "You didn't mean it."

Robin moved her quick fingers over Arlee's arm. "You're okay," she said.

"No, she's not," Glen said.

Arlee began to wail.

"I'm leaving," Evie said. "I'm not feeling so good." Out she went.

"Glen," Robin said, "if you don't make this a big deal, she'll calm down. If you can't calm down, you should leave until we figure out what's going on."

Glen turned and marched out of the house, banging the front door shut behind him.

Arlee had a big, fat bruise. I fetched ice and a towel and Robin applied it to her arm. We fed her a leftover summer grape Popsicle and she finally calmed down. Her eyes were swollen and the lids drooped. I picked her up and held her close.

"It'll hurt for a day or two," Robin said. "Ice it for fifteen minutes or so, three times a day. I'll be up in the morning to check on it."

"I can't believe I forgot she was there," I said. "What kind of mother am I?"

"A good one," Robin said. "We all forgot."

"Party's over," I said. "Time to settle down."

Robin walked down to Ida's house for the night and Dottie headed for her house. I gave Arlee a bath and put her into clean pajamas. Neither of us was ready for bed, so I carried her downstairs and out to the porch, where we rocked while I read her one of the storybooks that Robin had brought for her, about a peaceful bull named Ferdinand. I had just finished reading it when Bud came into the house and headed upstairs.

"Out here," I called. He tromped back through the kitchen and sat down in the rocker next to me. He held out his arms and Arlee crawled into them. He kissed her curls. "Daddy's girl is okay," he crooned. "Robin told me not to worry, that Arlee wasn't bad off. So of course I got worried. What happened? Can Daddy see your hurt?" Arlee held up her arm and Bud pulled off her pajama top to see it better. "Whoa," he said when he saw the spreading black-and-blue spot. *"What the hell?"* he mouthed to me.

"She's okay. Glen feels horrible."

"I suppose I should go to see him." Bud sighed. "This'll set him back a few years."

"Where is he?" I asked.

"Imagine he's gone to his tent," Bud said.

"Cold, isn't it?" I asked.

"Might be snow flurries."

"Bring him back here. Tell him he can sleep on the sofa."

Bud left and I put Arlee to bed. I pulled on a nightgown and piled myself under the quilts on our bed. Bud was gone longer than I thought he might be and I made myself stay awake, waiting for him to come back. I heard a car door slam at the Butts house. An engine started and I wondered who was going where. The car went up the hill. Another car door slammed and another engine started up. That car followed the first one.

I dozed off, only waking when Bud came into the bedroom.

"Well," he said, "Evie's gone to the hospital. In labor. I went out to the tent and Glen wasn't there. When I was coming back, I saw Madeline, Bert, and Evie headed up the hill. Dottie was behind 'em. She stopped and told me Evie's water had broken."

"Hope things go all right," I said.

"Me too," Bud said. He climbed into bed and snuggled close.

"So tired," I mumbled.

"Me too," he said. We spooned and fell asleep.

27

Evie had a hell of a time that night. Her blood pressure climbed to stroke levels and they had to fight to save her and the baby. In the end, both of them lived, and Archer Bertram Butts was born early the next morning.

Dottie called us at about eight o'clock. I'd never heard her sound so damn happy. "You should see him," she crowed. "Most beautiful baby in the world. Got dark hair. Long legs. Skinny feet. Big hands. I'm taking him places. I got to buy him some clothes. Get some toys. Teach him to play any sport he wants to play."

As I was congratulating Dottie, Robin walked up from Ida's house to join Bud, me, and the kids for breakfast. She sat down next to Arlee, who pointed to her own arm and said, "Boo-boo."

"I think it's better," Robin said.

Arlee frowned. "No," she said. "It hurts."

"Had a nice time talking to your mother and sister this morning, Bud," Robin said. "Ida talked a blue streak."

"Huh. That's good. She's quiet, usually," I said.

"Maybe it was easier to talk to someone she doesn't know well. Anyway, I love her quilts. She's an artist. She should be selling them."

"She don't like to do that," Bud said. "Says Jesus gave her the talent so she could give of herself to others.

"She told me that she wanted to be a nurse, once," Robin said. "Was ready to go to school, but life had something else in mind for her."

"Really? Did you know that, Bud?"

Bud wiped applesauce from Travis's mouth. "What?"

"That your mother wanted to be a nurse?"

"Nope. Never knew that."

During this whole exchange, Bud hadn't once looked at Robin and I thought that was rude. "Bud, Robin's talking to you," I said.

He gave me a look. "I know that," he said. He looked at Robin. "Nope," he said, "I never knew that." He looked back at me. "That better?"

No one said anything for a few seconds. Robin cleared her throat, pushed back her chair, stood up, and stretched. "You know," she said, "I think I'll skip breakfast. I'm still stuffed from yesterday. I want to head back to Portland."

"Stay!" I said. "You really have to go? Let me make you some toast, anyway."

"That's okay," she said. "I want to get back and settle in. We'll see each other soon."

"Glad you could come," I said.

"Are you kidding? My pleasure! What a wonderful place! And the company wasn't bad either."

When Robin said goodbye to Bud, he barely glanced up, just waved a spoonful of applesauce in her general direction and went back to feeding Travis. Arlee and I put on our jackets and walked Robin to her car.

I shivered. "I think there's some snow coming soon," I said.

"Is Bud okay with me?" Robin said. "He seems kind of distant."

"Don't take it personally," I said, although I was annoyed at him. "Bud's a mystery, kind of like a snail tucked into a clamshell and wrapped in seaweed. He'll warm up to you once he knows you."

"I don't want to wear out my welcome."

"No chance. You're always welcome. You'd better keep in touch," I said. I hugged her extra hard, breathing in the odors of clean shampoo and soap. "Knowing you're out there makes me feel better."

"Me too," Robin said. She kissed the boo-boo on Arlee's arm, climbed into her car, and started up the hill. As we watched her drive off, Arlee used her hurt arm to wave.

"Guess you'll live," I said to her. "Want to go for a walk?"

She nodded.

I told Bud where we were going, grabbed mittens and hats for Arlee and me, tucked a loaf of homemade wheat bread under one arm, and we were on our way.

As we walked slowly along the path leading to the state park, I peered through the pines and spruce on the right, looking for the place Bud had told me led to Glen's campsite. It wasn't easy to find, but finally, I spied a barely there trail snaking its way beneath thick branches. "Do you want to visit Glen?" I asked Arlee. She grabbed her hurt arm. "Ow," she said.

We ducked underneath a thick pine bough and followed the trail. Not too far along, I smelled smoke. "Glen's home," I said to Arlee. We continued for about fifty yards and stopped. I hollered, "Glen?" No answer. "Glen?" I called. "It's Florine and Arlee."

"Come ahead," he said. We ducked and wove through brush until we spied his tent, which was covered over with nets and camouflage. Arlee stopped and said, "No, Mama."

I crouched down until we were eye level. "Let's say hello," I whispered.

She touched her arm again.

"He didn't mean to do that, honey. He felt really bad. Let's make him feel better."

Arlee frowned. She walked past me up to where Glen sat on a campstool, showed him her arm, and said, "Kiss it."

Glen gave it a big smacker. "All better?" he said.

She nodded. He went into the tent and brought out another campstool. He put it down, looked at me, and pointed to it. I sat.

Arlee said, "Dis?" and pointed at a lantern swinging from a broken branch. The point of the branch had been driven into the ground. After

Glen told her that it gave him light, she wandered around the whole campsite, pointing to everything. He patiently told her everything she wanted to know and then she crawled into the tent. He followed her. I heard him say, "I got some colored pencils and some paper. Think you can draw me a picture?" I didn't hear Arlee's answer, but Glen joined me outside. "I got her started," he said.

We sat for a few seconds in silence. *"Itsy-bitsy spidah up the wadda spout,"* floated out from the innards of the tent.

"I love that little girl," Glen said.

"I know. She's lucky to have you in her life."

"I wouldn't do nothing to hurt her. Nothing."

"I know."

"No, you don't," Glen said, and he began to cry.

I put my arm on his back but he shook it off.

"Down is the wain and washa spidah out."

"What's wrong?" I asked him.

"You couldn't understand," he said, and then he said, "I can't make sense of nothing. It's like I don't belong anywhere anymore."

"What do you mean?" I said. "You belong here. You've always—"

"No. That's not what I mean," he said. "I don't belong in this world."

A shiver ran up my spine. *"Out cayma sun and dye up alla wain."*

"What are you talking about?" I said.

He used the flats of his palms to wipe the tears off his cheeks. "I can't even explain it, I'm so goddamn dumb."

Our breath mingled in the November cold. I pulled my mittens from my jacket pocket and slipped them over my hands. "Arlee," I called, "are your hands cold?"

"No," she said.

I said, "Glen, you're not dumb. You're the only one who thinks so. I'm listening. I want to know what you think."

"I wish I could talk to all of you, but none of you would get it."

"Well, maybe not, but try me."

Glen opened his mouth, closed it, shook his head. He shook his head again. "It's hard," he said.

"I would imagine," I said. "Maybe talking about it will make you feel better."

"Okay," he said, and he took a deep breath. "Over there," he said, "was like being in hell. We all felt like we'd been put there for something we'd done, but we didn't know what it was. Bugs the size of mackerel. Hotter than a steam iron, and Jesus, didn't it rain. I got moldy in places I didn't know could grow mold. We went through swamps up to our necks, looking for little bony yellow people that wanted to deer gut us all.

"That's what the devil looks like, Florine, them little people, all after you, only some of them wasn't, but it was hard to tell if they was or not. I shot people, Florine. I don't know how many. Sometimes I couldn't know if I got the right ones, or if I had the wrong ones. They lived in these villages and sometimes they smiled at you, but then they threw grenades when you turned your back. I killed women. I know I did." He stopped, clenched his fists, rubbed them over his face. He rocked back and forth on the little stool.

"You don't have to say anything else," I whispered.

He shook his head. "Fuck it all," he said.

Trying to make him feel better, I said, "I wish I had a flask of whiskey and cocoa for you. Remember when Grand was dying in the hospital, and you brought me some? It helped. It did. I wish I had some for you right now."

"Nothing will help," Glen said. "I got a feeling I'm done for."

"Don't talk like that," I said.

"Thing is, Florine, I went to the army 'cause I didn't want to work with Ray. Ray didn't make me do it. I did it because I didn't know what I wanted to do. High school was over. Football was over. I'm too stupid to go to college. So I signed up. I love my country, but I wasn't doing it for that reason. *I just couldn't think of nothin' else to do.* How numb is that, for chrissake?

"I mean we wasn't saving Americans, exactly, was we? We're a long ways from Vietnam. Can't see us being overrun by the bastards anytime soon. So there wasn't much danger in that. Wasn't saving the world. We was fighting the 'Communist Threat,' they said, but we was more likely to rot to death. Or get shot or blasted into eternity.

"How would you feel if you was walking along with Dottie and someone shot her? No more Dottie, just her lying dead, blood everywhere. No more bowling. No more best friend. And just seconds ago, she was telling you a joke and you both was laughing. Do you know what it's like to see a person's soul leave their body, Florine?"

"I'm pretty sure I saw Grand's soul leave," I said.

"Sudden, I mean," Glen said. "Soul goes somewhere else and you just got a dead person that you liked a bunch and someone else probably loved lying on the ground, and it ain't pretty. And you didn't even get so much as a scratch. Feels like they took the bullet for you without you even having a say about it."

My insides twisted for him having to see that. At the same time, I wanted to jump up and run. I wished Arlee would come out of the tent and ask to go home. But she didn't. She mumbled and sang to herself as she colored.

I straightened up on the stool and blew out a breath.

"You don't have to stay," Glen said gently.

I reached over, grabbed one of his big hands, squeezed it, let it go, and sat back. "Go on," I said. "It's not pretty to listen to, but go on."

He said, "It got so that any letters from home didn't mean nothing, because they didn't have nothing to do with what was going on. It was like torture, Florine. All them cheerful words and news from a place that wasn't real anymore. I hated mail call. I hated getting something from someone who might as well have been living on the moon. 'S why I told Maureen to stop writing. I'd look at her words and I couldn't even make sense out of 'em. What the hell was she talking about? *I pray for you every night. I think of you every day and hope that you are okay.*' Of course I Christly wasn't okay!"

"She felt bad when you asked her to stop writing."

Glen nodded. "I know she did. But you just don't know what it was like. Some guys just walked off into the jungle and didn't come back.

"And then, them damn protestors. Now, I can see why they think it might be wrong to be over there. Like I said, it was hard for us to figure it out and we was there." Tears ran down his cheeks, unchecked. "I got piss thrown at me in the airport in Boston," he said.

"Holy shit, Glen."

His chin trembled. "Some girl did it. She was pretty and she smiled at me like she knew me, so I went over to her. She was holding a drink and when I got close enough, she threw it in my face. It was hot piss," Glen said. "I still smell it if I close my eyes. They hauled her off, but by then, it was done. They blame us, Florine. They blame the soldiers. They don't know nothing. They don't know nothing."

Glen stopped talking and hung his head.

I was out of words.

He said, "So, I'm sitting here, trying to figure out what I should do, Florine, because I don't belong in this world. I could go back to hell, I suppose. I don't know. I feel so fucking stupid. I feel so lost."

I grabbed at a feeble straw. "What about Evie?" I asked. "Maybe you and Evie . . ."

Glen snorted. "Evie's hard as nails. If I was to get together with someone, it'd be someone soft. All I can say is it's a good thing there's good people in that baby's life."

"Well, maybe someone else will come along . . ."

He shook his head. "Not counting on anyone showing up for me. I wouldn't know what to do. I don't deserve someone else anyways. Something always goes wrong. I might bring it on myself. I don't know. I get scared I ain't good enough. Or they come on too strong and that pisses me off. So, no, I ain't finding anyone soon. I'm too fucked-up to even think about that. I feel bad enough as it is."

"What are you going to do?" I asked.

"I'll stick around for now," he said. He jerked his thumb toward Arlee. "Got these babies to love. It's good being out on the water again. Nothing or nobody out there to spit on me, piss or shit on me, or shoot at me, or stare at me like I have some god-awful disease. Just the gulls to rag at me."

Arlee crawled out of the tent and handed me a drawing. Most of the paper was covered in orange, pink, and yellow lines. But one black line met itself in a crooked circle in the middle of the other lines.

"What's that?" I asked her.

"Boo-boo," she said.

She handed her drawing to Glen and gave him a hug and a kiss and made him kiss her arm again. I got up from the stool, leaned down, and kissed him on his forehead.

"Why don't you stay in Grand's house for the winter," I said. "It'll get cold out here."

Glen nodded. "I'll think about it," he said. "Thank you."

Arlee and I left him there and hurried back to our warm house.

28

Robin's instinct about Bud had been right. He wasn't partial to her. When she called me, he shook his head and made faces.

"Why do you do that?" I asked. "It's rude. It's also not your conversation, so it's none of your business."

"You should hear yourself. Your voice gets all high and goofy. You don't sound like yourself," he said.

"I feel more like myself when I talk to her than I do with anyone but Dottie or you," I snapped. "She's my family. What's your problem?"

He shrugged. "No problem. It's just that she takes up time."

"What does that mean?"

"We got no time as it is, what with the kids. When she calls, she's taking time we didn't have in the first place."

"That doesn't make sense."

"I know what I mean," he said. "That's enough for me." And then, silence, Bud-style.

I hated it when we argued in the trailer, especially during the cold weather, when there was nowhere else to go. Hurt feelings ricocheted off the back of the kitchen wall, hit the rear wall near the bedrooms, glanced off the roof, and bounced back.

I could only hope, with time, he would warm up to Robin. I began to call her when he wasn't home. If she didn't have classes, or wasn't

working at the hospital, I invited her over for coffee or tea to visit with
the kids and me for an hour or two.

"What are you doing for Christmas?" she asked me during one visit.

"Bud wants to stay here," I said. "He wants it to be small, just us, this
year."

"Well," Robin said, "if I had little kids, I'd like to have that time
together too."

"Not that I wouldn't like you to spend the day with us . . ."

"No, I have plans anyway," Robin said, but I could read her face
pretty well, and I didn't think that she did. I hated leaving her out.

Dottie called me one day and asked if she could stay overnight on
the sofa at the trailer. "I got to drive to Falmouth. The junior high
needs a gym teacher. I might have the job if they like me." Falmouth
was just up the road from Stoughton Falls.

Bud lit up when I told him Dottie was coming.

"Okay, why are you excited about Dottie and not Robin?" I asked.

"Dottie's Dottie," Bud said.

"Robin's Robin," I replied.

"Yeah, but we already know Dottie."

"So, you're not going to like people we don't already know?"

"'Course not."

"Sounds that way."

"You can read it any ways you want to."

I threw up my hands. He laughed but didn't clear up anything.

Dottie and I talked it over the night she came by. "He don't want
someone new taking you away from him," she said. We were sitting on
my bed after putting the kids to sleep. Dottie said, "Sees her, watches
you and sees how happy you are when you're with her, like she's a new
toy or something, and he gets jealous."

"I never figured he'd get jealous that easy," I said.

"You didn't see him when you was dating Andy," Dottie said.

"He didn't have the right," I said. "He had Susan. What the hell?"

"Well, he doesn't have her now, does he?" Dottie said.

"And I sure as hell don't have Andy." I debated telling Dottie about my encounter with him, but I changed the subject. "How's Archer?" I asked.

Every time his name came up, Dottie's face flowered. "I'll see him plenty, even if I get this job," she said. "I'll be down there weekends and vacations, and whenever I get the chance," she said. "I ain't going to leave him alone for too long."

"How's Evie doing with him?"

Dottie frowned. "She's Evie. She's who she was before she had him. Sticks him on her boob, then gets rid of him as fast as it takes her to get to the mirror to check out her makeup and see if she's lost more weight. Madeline's been trying to make her eat so her milk will be better. Evie doesn't want to eat. Says she's fat."

"Who cares?" I said. "Doesn't she have bigger things to worry about?"

"Mmmm. She's going back to Long Reach High School after Christmas vacation," Dottie said. "She passed in all the homework they sent to her and got A's on the tests. For someone so smart, she's wicked stupid. Madeline will watch Archer during the day. I'll watch him anytime I can."

"Maybe you'll have your own little Archer someday," I said.

"I might," Dottie said. "I'll figure that out if it ever comes up."

Toward Christmas, Robin called and offered to babysit the kids for a Saturday so Bud and I could shop.

"Really?" Bud said, after I'd hung up the phone. "She'd do that?"

"Of course she would," I said. "She's a great person."

"Well," Bud muttered, "it's nice of her."

The Saturday before Christmas, Robin came over midmorning, and Bud and I took off for Portland.

"When was the last time we had a date?" I asked as he drove the Fairlane around Baxter Boulevard.

"Never, I think," Bud said. We'd gone to movies during our first year together, but then Arlee had showed up, and Travis after that.

He parked the car in a lot that charged us too much money for his liking, and he grumbled a little. We huddled into our coats and scarves and held hands on the busy city streets. We went into a few stores to pick out things for Arlee and a couple of small gifts for Travis. He would be more interested in paper and boxes anyway.

When we'd had enough of the crowds, Bud and I ducked into a little place on Congress Street for lunch. We sat in a booth that looked out onto the street, so we could watch people walk by.

Bud chowed down on a cheeseburger. I bit little chunks out of my cheese and tomato sandwich.

My Carlie radar kicked in when my eyes locked with a little red-headed woman bouncing on the balls of her feet as she moved down the sidewalk. This woman was not Carlie, but I liked the cheerful way she walked, head up, arms filled with packages. She caught me looking at her through the window, and before I could look away, she smiled. I smiled back, even as something inside me tinkled and broke, like a Christmas-tree ornament.

I put down my sandwich.

"You not eating that?" Bud asked.

"I can take it home."

"What's wrong?"

"Nothing. Take your time," I said. But after a few minutes, I said, "I'm tired. Not having the kids makes me want to take a nap. You'd think I'd have some energy, but no. I want to sleep. Crazy, right?"

Before Bud could answer, our waitress came over. She took my sandwich, wrapped it up, and gave it to me in a brown paper bag. Bud finished his cheeseburger. We paid, left, and walked up the street toward the parking lot. Little bits of sleet pinged against our faces. Wind traveling up a city canyon stung my eyes. We paid the man in the parking lot and Bud drove us back through Portland.

"I want more," Bud said when the city limits were behind us.

"What?" I said. "More what? Did you want dessert?"

Bud shook his head. "No. I want you to listen to me and not go wacky. I mean that I want to do more than we're doing. I don't want to just live in a trailer in Stoughton Falls. I want to travel places, work in different places. I want to see things."

"Okay. What things?"

"Famous things. The Golden Gate Bridge. See the Grand Canyon sometime. Go to Florida. Be nice to live somewhere warm for the winter."

"We can take vacations. Let's wait a couple of years, till the kids are bigger, so they can remember what they see."

We were quiet for a minute or two. Then Bud said, "And sometimes I might want to go places by myself."

"Didn't we have a big fight for me wanting to go somewhere by myself with my girlfriends? Are you saying this because of that?"

"No, but it got me to thinking. I might like to take a trip alone sometime. I make the money. I can put a little bit away each week for myself."

It hurt me that he had pointed out that he was the breadwinner, but something else bothered me even more. "You couldn't stand us being away from you a couple of months ago," I said. "I wanted to stay at The Point, but I packed up and moved back with you. And now you want some time alone. I don't get you."

"I don't mean, right away," Bud said. "But I've always dreamed of seeing other places, by myself. Like an explorer. Not because I don't love you. It's like you said, you and me will go places together. But sometimes, I'll want to go alone."

I stared out the windshield at the light snow. After a minute, I remembered to breathe.

"You okay with all this?" Bud said.

"Let's not talk for a while," I said.

"Jesus," Bud muttered, and goosed the gas. The car skidded on the snow.

"Don't do that," I cried. "Don't fucking do that."

We made it home without any more swerving. Or talking.

Robin was sitting on the floor with Arlee and Travis when we walked through the door. "Hey," she said with a smile. I bent to pick up Travis.

Bud nodded at Robin, took off his coat, and headed for the bathroom.

"Did you have a good time?" Robin asked me. I forced myself to smile.

"Yeah," I said. "Santa will be coming to the Warner house this year for sure."

"That's good," she said.

I headed for the kitchen, son in arms, daughter clutching at my coat. "You hungry?" I asked Robin.

"No," she said. "We ate peanut butter sandwiches just a little while ago. And Oreos."

"I see that," I said, wiping dark goo from Travis's mouth with a wash-cloth.

Bud came out of the bathroom and walked into our bedroom.

Robin reached for Travis as I shucked myself out of my coat. I tossed it over my daughter's head, making her giggle.

"Oh," Robin said. "Someone called here. Parker?"

"Parker Clemmons?" I asked. "What did he want?"

"Said to call him as soon as you could." At my look, Robin said, "What?"

"Could be something. Could be nothing," I said. "Want to stay on the sofa? It's starting to storm out there."

"Thanks. No. If I leave now, I'll be able to get a parking spot near my apartment."

She passed Travis to me and we gave each other a clumsy hug with him giggling between us. "Thank you, Robin," I whispered. "Merry Christmas."

She was about to go out the door when I remembered her present, a dark-brown fisherman's sweater that I had knitted for her. The yarn matched the color of her eyes.

"Here," I said to Robin. "Merry Christmas."

"You didn't have to do that!" she exclaimed. "You're my present this year."

"Can't wear me," I said. "Or wrap me. Don't open until Christmas."

"Thanks," she said. "When you get a minute, look in the pan cupboard."

After she left, I sat down on the sofa, gathered my kids in my arms, and hugged them for as long as they would let me, trying to live this moment before whatever Parker had to say changed who we were, yet again. We stayed there until Arlee took her blanket and slid under the dining-room table for her nap. I set Travis in his crib and stroked his hair until his eyes closed. I shut his door and tried to quiet my heart. I crossed the hall and went into our bedroom. Bud's hands were folded over his chest. He looked dead.

"Parker called while we were out," I said. He sat up. Not dead, after all.

"What did he want?" he asked.

"Not sure," I said. "Will you come sit with me while I call him?"

He followed me into the kitchen. I lifted the phone off its base and dialed the number Robin had copied down in her neat handwriting.

"Hi. This is Florine," I said, when Parker picked up.

"Remember them letters you got?" he said.

"Of course I do. We got a couple more, actually," I said. "I was going to . . ."

"Someone brought in a bundle of their own."

"What?" I said. "*Who?*"

The blood pumping through my ears was so loud I almost didn't catch the name.

29

I had never met Andy Barrington's mother, Barbara. I had never even seen a picture of the woman. When Glen, Bud, Dottie, and I had accidentally set the Barringtons' porch on fire during the firecracker raid, we had destroyed a beautiful rosebush she had planted, but she hadn't shown up for our Big Apology. A few years later, when Andy and I got together and we talked about our parents, I gathered that, while Edward was the type to fetch his son home and call the sheriff, his mother, Barbara, let him do what he wanted. At one point, Andy told me that his mother, whom he described as airy and timid, had left Edward because of Edward's drinking. But who knew how much of it was true. Andy twisted things.

Dottie's encounter with her had been the first I'd heard of her in years. Now she had stumbled into Parker's office to deliver a bundle of letters to him, high on something else other than life, according to Parker, makeup running down her face, winter hat cockeyed on her head. "Take these," she had said to him. "I found them. I finally found them. I knew he couldn't keep it in his pants, even here. Despicable. A bounder."

"What's a bounder?" I asked as Bud and I sat in front of Parker's desk in his office. The kids were with Ida and Maureen. It looked as if we would be spending Christmas at The Point with family after all, which was fine with me.

"Them people know words we don't even know exist," Parker said.

I had identified my mother's handwriting on the opened envelopes. About thirty letters, most of them going back years before I had been born to her and to Daddy. All of them addressed to Edward Barrington. I held them to my nose and breathed in musty dust. I was dying to know what was inside, but at the same time, I wanted nothing to do with them.

"I guess you was right," Parker said.

"Oh, really? About what?" I said.

"Barrington. Well, at least about me talking to him."

"You contact him yet?" Bud asked.

"He's coming in after Christmas with his lawyer," he said. "Told him he'd better. The good police officers in Boston know he's a person of interest. He's being watched."

"Why aren't you arresting him *now*?" I said. "He killed Carlie."

"We don't know that at all," Parker said. "Don't jump the fence, Florine. We still don't know much about who wrote them letters you got. They didn't have no signature, remember. We don't know if Barrington is involved with them or not."

Bud shook his head. "What if he don't show up?"

"He will," Parker said.

"What day? What time?" I said.

"December twenty-seventh," Parker said. "Morning, sometime."

"What if he admits it? What then?"

"That's a step down the road," Parker said.

"He'll just deny everything," I said. Bud helped me to my feet.

Parker reached for the letters. "Got to keep those for now. You can have 'em later to read. You might want to know what they said."

My hands shook as I handed the letters to Parker. "I don't want to fucking look at them ever again," I said. I turned to Bud. "It's Christmas," I said, "let's go see the kids."

I stuffed everything connected with letters, the Barringtons, and Carlie in a seldom-used part of my mind and I focused on the light that my kids, with their joy and energy, brought to the season. Playing with them, feeding, scolding, comforting, cuddling, and loving them left little time to think about what my mother might or might not have done with Edward Barrington. Every time one of those ugly visions tried to gain a foothold in my head, a small hand or a little voice swept it away.

It was good to be with everyone we loved.

We were staying with Ida this trip. I had thought that maybe we could share Grand's house with Glen. But after we arrived, I went to see how he was making out. I knocked on the door, and when he didn't answer, I pushed the old house key into the lock, turned it, and walked inside, not because I was nosy but because I wanted to make sure that he was all right. I called his name, but got no answer. I walked down the hall and looked to the left, toward the kitchen. It was a mess; dirty dishes piled up in the sink and scattered over the table. The floor hadn't been swept for ages.

But what Glen had done to the living room shocked me. He had pushed furniture against the walls and had put up his tent in the middle of the floor. The air stank with the sweetish odor of marijuana and the staleness of old beer.

Goddamn it, Glen, I thought. How dare he bring drugs into Grand's house? How goddamn dare he? Then I felt Grand's big, soft, ghostly hand on my shoulder. *He's got to come back to himself, if he can*, she said to me. *He's down deep.* If she was okay with this, I decided I would try to be okay with it too. It was hard to leave the house without at least cleaning it, but I did. I shut and locked the door and walked down to Ida's house.

The bedrooms down there were tiny. For the sake of convenience, Arlee and I shared Maureen's room, while Bud slept in his old room in a twin bed beside Travis's crib. Maureen and I whispered to each other in the dark after Arlee dropped off to sleep.

"I'm glad you're here," she said.

"Me too," I whispered back.

"It's funny to hear other people breathing in my room. It's nice."

"Your brother snores," I said. "I hear that every night."

"Dad used to snore so loud that Madeline Butts came down from their house one summer night and pounded on our door. When Ma answered, Madeline told her to turn her husband over or stuff something in his mouth, before she killed him."

I laughed. "Never heard that one."

"After that, Ma made sure he didn't get too far into it before she poked him, or did whatever she did to make him stop."

"Well, I hope Bud doesn't get that loud," I said. A sharp *snork* came from the other side of the wall and we both giggled.

❧

Christmas dawned with Maureen shaking me awake at five thirty a.m.

"What the hell?" I mumbled, turning over toward the wall.

"We have to get up," Maureen whispered. "We have to see what Santa brought."

"The kids are still asleep," I said. "That's their present to me. Go back to sleep."

But then, Travis let out a peep and I stumbled up and staggered into Bud's room. I swayed in the dark for a few seconds before I crept to the crib and listened to his breathing. Even. Deep. I touched his blond curls.

"While you're here," Bud whispered, "I got a present for you."

"Did Santa bring it?" I asked him.

"Santa had nothing to do with it," Bud said. I peeled off my night-gown and joined him in his little bed, where we gift wrapped each other for a while.

"Merry Christmas," Bud whispered when we were through.

"Well, I got what I wanted," I said.

Travis made a real noise and I unwound myself from my husband, slipped my nightgown over my head, and went to my son.

Bud's other present to me was a box with a key inside of it, much like the one I had given to him on our wedding night.

"You're giving Petunia back to me?" I asked him.

"Nope," he said. "I'm giving you the Fairlane."

"That's nice," I said. "What are you going to drive?"

"I'm fixing up a 1967 Ford F-100 pickup," he said. "Got a good deal on it."

"How good?"

Bud smiled. "Good."

"Thanks, honey," I said. It would be good to have a set of wheels for myself. And I had a mechanic with a drive shaft that wouldn't quit living with me. Anything that might go wrong could be fixed.

30

Christmas passed in a flurry of paper and boxes. The kids and I spent the next day playing inside and outside. We all went to bed early that night, but I didn't sleep. The morning of December 27, 1973, was hell for me. I knew Edward Barrington was in Parker's office. I pictured him sitting in a chair across from Parker, a little smile on his face, relaxed and cool. Maybe he was speaking in that soft whisper that could coil itself into a shout and strike down a person without warning.

He was someone I hardly knew, yet knew more than enough about.

A memory: The time he had talked down to us after the failed firecracker raid. So cold, yet his eyes burned. When he had said something to me, Carlie had answered him in my defense. He had snapped back at her. I could still feel her delicate hands gripping my shoulders. Had she feared him too?

Another memory. I was thirteen. It was late June. I had gone for a walk, alone, in the state park and run into him. He had been drunk. It had taken a few seconds for him to focus on me. "It's you," he had said. He acted like he wanted to kiss me. In light of what we knew now, I realized he probably mistook me for Carlie.

A final memory—the clearest and most awful memory I had of him. Andy, shaking, gripping my hand in the living room of the Barrington cottage on a freezing winter night as Edward's voice tore his spirit in two right in front of me. Andy and I leaving the cottage and Edward following us, slipping on the icy back steps. Edward, lying unconscious on the ground. It didn't take a lot of memory to still feel his warm, sticky blood on my hands.

What had he done to my mother?

Bud stayed with me until noon, when he went up to the house to visit Glen. He sent Dottie and little Archer down to be with me.

"He looks like his mother," I said. Dark curls, blue eyes. Red lips. Unmarked skin, clear eyes, sweet brows, soft hands and fingers. Archer bobbed his head against Dottie's chest, looking for lunch. "Nothing there for you, bub," she said as she fished a bottle of milk from her parka pocket.

"Where's Evie?" I asked.

"Who the hell knows," Dottie said. "Pump and run." She stuck the warm bottle between Archer's wet lips and he sucked milk down like a pro. "He's some good at this," Dottie said with pride in her voice.

Arlee wandered into the kitchen, followed by Maureen, who made a fool of herself over Archer. Ida brought Travis from the living room and he gave Dottie a goofy grin. I made Arlee a peanut butter and jelly sandwich. I mashed a banana for Travis and let him muck himself up with it. He batted his eyes when we laughed.

"That's new," I said.

A knock at the door interrupted our laughter. Ida stood up, and her expression immediately changed.

Edward Barrington was looking through the window in the front door.

"Shit," I said. I stood up and took in the face of the man who had possibly killed my mother. I had last seen him about five years earlier, and this was not the face I remembered. Lines crisscrossed his wide forehead like fishermen's nets. Deep creases guarded both sides of his downturned mouth. What was left of his blond hair was combed back off his forehead. His eyes were red, as if he'd been crying.

"Call Parker," I said. "Take the babies out of the house and call

Parker." Chairs scraped back as people gathered kids. All except for Arlee, who pressed herself against my legs. "Go with Grammy Ida," I said, but she didn't move. Edward looked down at her, then back up at me.

I put my hand on her head and pushed her behind me. "What do you want?" I shouted at Edward through the storm door window. "Go the fuck away. We're calling Parker, right now."

Edward held up his gloved hands. "I mean no harm," he yelled back. Moisture from his mouth fogged up the glass.

"I don't care, you bastard," I hollered. "You have no right to be near me or my family." Arlee squirmed her way to the side of my leg. "Bad?" she asked.

"Go," I said to her, again. "Please."

"No," she said.

Edward looked down, and too late, I realized the door was unlocked. He turned the knob and I sprang forward and pushed myself against it as it opened. "Go away," I shouted. "Get out of here."

"Florine, calm down," he said. "I just want to talk to you for a few minutes. That's all I want. I promise."

"No. You have nothing to say to me." And then it occurred to me that Parker hadn't slapped him in jail. Why wasn't he headed to prison? Had he seen Parker at all?

As if he'd read my mind, Edward said, "I've talked to Parker."

"Bullshit," I yelled, and pushed with all my strength against the door. Edward stepped back and I slammed the door and locked it.

"I loved her," he yelled. "Yes, I'm a bastard, but I could never hurt Caroline."

Caroline. Not Carlie, but her full name.

Edward said, "I wanted to tell you that. And," he said, "I wanted to tell you that, no matter how hard I tried to make her love me, she loved your father."

"Shut up," I said. Tears flooded my eyes. "You're a liar."

"It's true," he said. "I wanted you to know that."

"Fuck you," I said. Someone touched my shoulder and I jumped.

Ida murmured, "We don't say that in this house, Florine. Let the man in. I'm tired of hearing you both shout through the door. And you're scaring Arlee."

"No. Are you crazy?"

Ida said, "This is my house. Hear what the man has to say. And keep your temper. Jesus will protect us."

Hell he will, I thought.

"Maureen and Dottie, this may not be a conversation fit for the kids. Please take them up to your house, Dottie, if you would," Ida said. Maureen, holding a solemn Travis in her arms, bent down and spoke softly to an upset Arlee. "Go, honey," I said to Arlee. "I'll come get you soon." Arlee took Maureen's hand and they followed Dottie and Archer out the back door. Ida walked to the front door and opened it. "Hello, Mr. Barrington," she said. "Won't you come in?"

Edward stood on the doorstep and looked at me. I backed up and stood in the living-room doorway, both hands gripping the door frame. A glance out a back window showed me Maureen, Dottie, and the kids walking through the dusting of snow up the hill.

"Would you like some tea?" Ida asked.

Edward looked at her. "That would be nice, Mrs. Warner. Yes."

"Milk? Sugar?"

"A dash of milk, please."

"Sit down," Ida said to him. She pointed to the kitchen table and he lowered himself into the chair where, just minutes before, Dottie had fed Archer.

I didn't know what to do with my arms, so I hugged myself with them.

"Florine," Ida said, "would you like a cup of tea?"

"No," I said.

"Why don't you sit down, dear," Ida said.

"I'm fine, here," I said.

"All right," Ida said. "Did you have a nice Christmas, Mr. Barrington?"

What the fuck was she doing?

Edward played along. "Yes, I did, Mrs. Warner. And you?"

"Oh, wonderful. It's so nice having children in the house during the holidays."

"Yes," Edward said. "It's been a long time, but I imagine it would be."

"Oh for Christ—heaven's sake, *Mr. Barrington*," I cried, "say what you have to say and get out."

"Not until he's had some tea," Ida said. She gave me a look, which I ignored.

"Well," Edward began, and then Bud burst through the door with Glen on his heels.

"Where is the bastard?" Bud said.

"Fuck do you want?" Glen said, plunking himself down across from Edward. He leaned his bulk toward him, and Edward pushed his chair away from him.

"James Walter," Ida said. "Manners. And, Glen, if you use that language, you'll have to leave."

Glen muttered, "Sorry."

Dottie walked back in and looked around. "Well," she said, "the gang's all here. Isn't that cozy?"

Ida poured a little milk into Edward's teacup.

"Ida," I said, as calmly as I could, "this man may have murdered my mother."

"I didn't," Edward said. "I told you through the door, I could never have hurt her. I loved her."

"You had no right to do that," I said.

"After a while, no, not legally," Edward said. "Of course not. She loved your father. But that didn't stop me from loving her."

Ida set his tea down in front of him.

"Thank you," Edward said. We all watched him stir his tea, take the teabag out and squeeze it, and put it on the teabag holder Ida had placed in front of him. He took a sip of tea, put his cup down, and looked at me.

"I can see why you might think I would hurt Caroline," he said.

230   Morgan Callan Rogers

"You've seen my temper, unfortunately. But I—and she, I'm sure—never would have chosen for you to find out about us. Or what was once 'us.' There was no 'us' after she met Leeman in terms of, well, in terms of . . ." He waved his hand around, finally snatching the word "that" out of the air.

"You're a liar," I said.

He smiled, and I saw that one of his top front teeth had gone bad. "I am many, many things, Florine, but I am not a liar. I do have secrets, but if they happen to come to light, which this one has done, I will not deign to be untruthful."

"Will you just talk normal?" Dottie grumbled.

"I believe he means that he would not stoop to telling a lie," Ida said.

"Yes, exactly," Edward said. "That's what I mean. Anyway," he said, "let me go back into the past, back to when I met Caroline."

I shook my head, but Ida took my arm and said, "Let him tell the story, Florine. Let him be done with it and then he'll leave."

He paused, and took a deep breath. "I met Caroline in Boston," he said. "She was seventeen years old, but she was pretending to be older. I was twenty-one years old and I wasn't pretending anything. We met in a park, actually. I was taking a break from my studies. I was an English major at Boston University. It was fall. Come to think of it, it was just after her birthday, October thirteenth. Am I correct?" He looked at me.

I hated that he knew when her birthday was. I didn't nod. I didn't shake my head.

He went on. "At any rate, I was walking through the park. It was cloudy, but there was a flame sitting on a bench to my right. The flame was Caroline's hair. She'd let it go wild. It was long and tumbled down her shoulders like a river of fire. It perked me up, seeing all that marvelous hair, so I stopped in front of the bench. She was slouched down, hands in the pockets of her coat. It's amazing what one remembers. The coat was navy blue and she had on a red plaid skirt. If she'd taken off the coat, I would have seen a school uniform."

Edward smiled at me. "'What do you want?' is what she first said to me.

"I said, 'I wanted to let you know that your hair is beautiful and that it has made my dismal day much brighter.' She said to me, 'And just who in the hell are you?' I fell in love, immediately."

"Why do you think I care about this shit?" I said. "My mother has been missing for ten years. If you knew her so well, why haven't you said something before?"

"Say what? That we were friends? That we'd known each other for years? That I loved her?" For the first time during the visit, I caught a bit of his temper.

"Why not?" Bud spoke up.

"Well, why, actually?" Edward said. "I don't know what happened to her any more than you do." He placed the teacup onto its saucer with a tiny clink.

"You had those letters from her. They might have given us a clue," I said.

"Those letters were personal. They were old, for the most part, and wouldn't have helped anyone find her."

"Turns out they were evidence," Bud said. "Or at least your wife thought so."

Edward glared at him.

"Don't look at him like that," I said. He turned his glare on me.

"And by the way," I said, "someone has been sending me scraps of letters that you, most likely, sent to Carlie. Would that have been your wife too? I'm sure Parker talked to you about those."

"Yes," Edward said. "He showed me some cut-up letters. They were, in fact, bits and pieces of correspondence between me and Caroline and they are nobody's business. Whoever sent them to you is a mystery to me."

"You were pissed off in a couple of them," I said.

"I was. I was losing the woman I loved. Those letters were desperate and angry and I'm ashamed of them. I had lost her already, and I should have left it at that."

"Why should we care about you and my mother?" I said. "All I care about is my father and who they were together. Compared to him, you're nothing but a piece of—"

"Florine," Ida said.

"This has nothing to do with you," I snapped at her. "This is between him and me. I didn't even want to let him in."

Ida crossed her skinny arms over her chest. The cross hanging from her neck glinted gold against her pale skin.

"Florine," Edward said, quietly, "I want to clear things up between us. I imagine you have some questions, and rightfully so. Let me finish up, if just to give you some closure on our story."

"How many times do I have to tell you? I don't care about your fucking story," I said, blinking back tears.

"You've made her cry," Glen said. "I didn't like you before, and I don't like you even more now."

Edward looked at Glen. "My intention is not to make Florine cry, but to reassure her that her mother was loved, and that her mother loved one man. That man was not me."

Ida said, "Mr. Barrington, please finish your story. While you're welcome here, I think that brevity may be your best bet right now."

"Snap it up, so we can get rid of you," Dottie said.

"Of course," Edward said. "Long story short. We struck up a conversation that continued at a coffee shop close by. At that point in her life, Caroline did not like to go home. Or to school, but at least school was not home."

He paused and looked up at me. "Do you know about her earlier life? Do you know about her . . . trouble at home?"

I nodded. "Of course I do."

"Then you know how hard it was to live there. So, she went to school, sometimes, and then she spent the afternoons and evenings with me, studying or having coffee or tea or what-have-you. While she hated school, she loved to learn, and we had many long discussions about poetry and literature. I encouraged her to finish school and go to college. I loved being with her. She was funny and bright, young, but old at the same time. She had all the makings of a muse. My poetic muse."

Before anyone could ask him what the hell that was, Ida spoke up. "A muse is an inspiration," she said. "Mr. Barrington is saying that Carlie inspired him."

"I thought I was going to write poetry and novels," Edward said. "I thought a great many things, then, and it was the best time of my life, although I didn't know it. Soon enough, as it got colder, Caroline began to stay with me in my room, nights, and we became lovers. But then, school ended in May. She went off to wait tables in Cambridge, and I came here, to Maine, to be with my family.

"I missed Caroline and, at first, I wrote to her all the time. Love letters. Yes, some of those letters are filled with things that happened that don't and needn't concern you, Florine. Your mother had a life prior to you and to Leeman, and I was a part of that life. I don't regret it, and I don't believe you have a right to deny me our time together."

"Don't tell me what rights I have," I said.

He sighed. "Our letters began to drop off in early August. I got caught up in what was going on here, and I'm sure she must have been busy in Boston. And then, I met my wife-to-be. She was a cousin to friends of ours, a couple of cottages down. She, like me, was an English major, at Vassar, and she was writing a novel. Barbara had come for a few weeks, and we . . . well, we got together.

"When summer ended, I told Barbara that I had made a mistake, that I loved someone else. She took it hard, but she let me go. I returned to Boston and to Caroline and forgot about Barbara entirely. What a year that was! We were drunk on one another, and on language and poetry and love."

"Hurry up," I said. "This is making me sick."

"My apologies, Florine. As I said, this is not my inten—"

"*Just get it over with*," I shouted. Bud got up from the table, came over to me, and put his arm around me. "It's crap," he whispered. "It's a story that got done a long time ago."

Edward overheard Bud's deep-voiced whisper. "Some things are never done," he said, and sighed. "I graduated from college the next May, and Caroline did make it through high school, although she didn't apply to any colleges as I'd hoped she would. I know now that making it from day to day for her was a victory of sorts, that thinking ahead for someone surviving from hour to hour is almost impossible, and that she was younger than both of us pretended. And, although I tried to fight it, I began to think about how life might be, married to an uneducated girl not within my social class. Yes, I thought about marriage. I loved her. But I never took her to meet my family. And for that, I'm ashamed. I thought, I suppose, that I was too good for her. But it turns out that she was out of my league. It has been the greatest regret of my life." Edward's face went all sad and droopy and, I think, if we had let him, he'd have paused to feel bad about his choices. But when Bud cleared his throat, he continued.

"Caroline didn't tell me of her plans to drive up to Maine and work at the Lobster Shack. She'd learned about it through her friend Patty, whom I later got to know. Patty, it turns out, was familiar with the area through someone who knew someone who owned the Lobster Shack. She obtained a summer job through those connections and convinced Caroline to drive up and join her. I had no idea that she was coming, but in the end, it didn't matter. She stopped at Ray's, met your father, and never did look me up. Barbara and I stopped at the Lobster Shack for dinner one night, and there she was, all fire, but for someone else.

"Of course, I wanted her more than ever. But she would have none of it. At least, not in terms of us getting together the way we had been. We did meet to talk a few times, near my house, in the woods, just to catch up."

"I know where it is," I said.

Edward looked startled. "You do?"

"Of course," I said. "The three rocks. The clearing. And bullshit, you just talked."

He blinked and a smidgen of fear darted across his face. He picked up the teacup again, and his face resumed its cool, superior expression. "We just talked, Florine," he said. "We loved to discuss books, music, and life. Later, we discussed you and Andrew. I found out in late July that Barbara was pregnant. She delivered Andrew in late December. Caroline delivered you the next May. You and Andrew met in the state park once, when you were toddlers. You threw a pinecone at Andrew, and he cried."

Glen snorted. "Right," he said. "No surprise there."

"We only met a few times. But I won't forget those little minutes. She had one rule. We were never to talk about her marriage to Leeman. I was not to bring him up. She was the guard at his gate and, if looks could kill, she would have speared me through and through the few times I mentioned him. I wish I . . . Well, I wish a great many things, but wishing about the past doesn't make sense."

Edward put down his teacup and stood up slowly. "To end this, I don't know what happened to her, but the sun dimmed considerably when I found out that she was missing. As time passed, I had the park position a bench down by the water, and had the plaque placed upon it. For the rest of my life, I will always regret not being a part of her life. I should have married her. I am also sorry that I hurt Barbara, who is more fragile than I even guessed. I wish she hadn't turned Caroline's letters in to Parker. He says I may not get them back. I can't have time back either, or Caroline back, and I can't undo the mistakes I've made."

He looked at me. "You'll find, Florine, as you age, that you'll make mistakes," he said. "I hope you'll find the compassion to understand that we were young and that we loved each other. Know that your mother was loved. And know, finally, that she loved you more than life itself."

Edward turned to Ida and put out his hand. She put out her own hand and they shook. "Thank you, Mrs. Warner, for your hospitality," he said. He turned to me. "I've somehow managed to alienate you, first with Andrew, now with my relationship with your mother. I don't want your forgiveness. I don't want anything. I just wanted to clear things up." He nodded and turned away.

"You say that you wouldn't have hurt my mother for the world," I said. "You used the word. 'Hurt.' Do you know that someone hurt her?"

He turned back, the thick line of a big frown dividing his pale forehead in half. "What are you asking me?" he said.

"You heard me."

His eyes went darker, if that was possible. When he took a step toward me, Bud tugged at my shoulder to pull me back. But I stood my ground. "You know that someone hurt her?" I asked, again.

"I don't," he said, not breaking our stare. "As I said, I don't know what happened. But I've imagined what might have happened, and I've come to the conclusion that it must have been tragic. She would never, ever have left you behind."

He turned away again and opened the door, but then he stopped, shut it again, and said to me, "Please forgive me, but I am wondering if you would indulge me with an answer to a question I've wondered about for a number of years."

"What?" I snapped.

"Thank you," he said. "On the night you and Andrew were in the car accident—that night we almost lost you both . . ."

"It was your fault . . ." I began, but he held up his hand.

"I am not absolving myself of blame," he said. "But the question I have is in regards to the time before that, when I slipped on the step."

"What about it?"

"Just this: What happened?"

"I'm sure Andy has told you."

"Yes, he has."

"Then why—"

"Because I don't remember it, of course, and that frustrates me. I want to hear the details, if you recall them."

"Okay." I sighed. "You came to the cottage to get Andy to take him back to Massachusetts with you. You told him that the sheriff had been called, and he would be coming up in a few minutes. Andy told you he was going with me, and we went out the door. You came after us. You slipped, cracked your head on the step, and went out. I didn't know if you were dead or not. I touched the back of your head. You were bleeding. I told Andy we needed to get help. He said we would call a doctor later, so we got into your car and we left. We didn't get a chance to call a doctor. We got into an accident."

"You told Andy you needed to get help for me? You didn't tell Andy that you both needed to leave, right then?"

"Andy was in no shape to think at that point. You scared the crap out of him."

Edward looked at me for a few seconds, and then he gave me a small, sad smile. "Thank you for telling me your side of the story," he said. He let himself out and closed the door quietly behind him.

Bud dropped his hand from my shoulder but put it back again when I slumped.

"My legs won't work," I said. He guided me to the kitchen table, where I sat down.

"There," Ida said, "we've heard the man out." She picked up his teacup and carried it toward the kitchen sink.

"Something tells me he ain't telling the truth," Glen said. "The army did teach me something about how people stand and look. Something ain't right."

Ida put the teacup into the sink, turned around, and shivered. I saw that what she had just done had not been easy for her. "I never want that kind of negativity in here, ever again. It's as if the devil just blew through here," she said.

"He has that effect," I said.

When someone knocked at the door, we all jumped. When we saw that it was Parker, Ida let him in.

"Just talked to Edward at the office," Parker said to me.

"So did we," I said.

"He come down here, did he?"

"Yes," Ida said.

"Well," he said to me, "I'm sorry, but I ain't got nothing to hold him on. Can't arrest someone for having letters."

"He knows something," I said.

Parker frowned. "Florine . . ."

And then, as she sometimes did, Ida surprised me. She said, "He bears watching."

31

The day after Edward's visit, I asked Glen if he would mind if I came by to clean Grand's house. Glen shrugged and said of course not, it was my house, for chrissake, he'd get right out of my way. He and Bud rode up to Long Reach to get into some kind of trouble up there. Arlee and Travis stayed with their grandmother and their aunt.

I skirted past Glen's tent and started upstairs, giving the bedrooms a quick once-over, as he hadn't touched either room, it appeared. As I dusted Arlee's room, my foot knocked against something under the bed. I crouched down and fished out Arlee's cigar box treasure chest. My eyes roved over her little collection of dried and wrinkled flowers and clovers, feathers, pebbles, and shells. "So sweet," I said, tenderness washing over me for a second. I swept and dusted under the bed, and then slid the box back.

I cleaned the bathroom while breathing as little as possible. I wondered whether to inform Glen that when the toilet bowl turned brown, it was time to clean it. The ring around the inside of the tub was caked on. It took me some time and a lot of words I was glad no one could hear me say to scrub it away. I would leave him a note, I decided, because if I didn't, come summertime I would have five months of yuck to sandblast off.

Downstairs, I worked my way around the living room, leaving

Glen's tent and the stuff around it as alone as I could, until the closed flap on the front of the tent was too much temptation for me. What was inside, I wondered? Finally, I threw the flap up, unzipped the nylon mesh liner, and skittered inside.

The light from the living room filtered through the tan cloth, and I tried not to gag at the smell of stale farts and sweaty socks. After I got used to it, I looked around. Glen had taken a baby stepstool that usually lived in the kitchen and put a kerosene lamp on top of it, beside his sleeping bag.

Magazines scattered near the little makeshift table featured busty women on their covers, promising a lonely and fucked-up ex-soldier living in a tent inside the house of a friend cheap and harmless company. I was about to pick one up and compare my own pitiful boobs to what I might find inside when the front door opened and someone came in. "Shit," I said, and I threw the magazine onto Glen's sleeping bag, where it flopped open to the pinup in the middle. The blonde pictured there had spread her legs and her private parts, and she grinned up at me as if she was happy to be doing it. I didn't dare to move. I wished for whoever was inside the house to go away, but nope. The nylon on a winter jacket zizzed against itself as someone took heavy steps down the hall. My heart looped around itself as I held my breath. Glen had staked out his privacy by closing both the net and the flap. I had had no right to trespass.

As I tried to figure out how I would explain what I was doing in the tent, the sound of the footsteps plodded closer, and I saw big boots and corduroy pants. Dottie leaned down and said, "What the hell are you doing?" Then she saw the pinup. She twisted her head to get a better view. "She doing what I think she's doing?" she said.

"Yep," I said. Dottie ducked inside and sat down on Glen's sleeping bag. She picked up the magazine and turned it this way and that. She shrugged and put it down. "I seen better," she said, and gave me a sly grin.

"What?" I said. "What the hell do you mean?"

"I like girls," she said. "Happy New Year."

"What?" I said, again. "What the hell do you mean?"

"You remember that talk we had with Grand, about Germaine?"

I did. Glen's mother, Germaine, lived with her girlfriend, Sarah, up in Long Reach. Glen had gone through some bad teasing about it in high school. Dottie and I had decided to shock Grand one night at supper by asking her if she knew what a lesbo was, but Grand had turned it back on us. "Is what Germaine likes hurting you?" she had asked us. When we'd said no, she'd added, "That's good, because I say it's none of your business."

Dottie's brown eyes twinkled. "Had to tell you. Haven't told no one else."

"I won't either then. How long you known?" I asked her.

"Well, probably for always, but for not too long," Dottie said. "Been meeting all kinds of interesting people."

"I'll bet," I said. For the first time in our lives, I didn't quite know what to say. I wondered all kinds of things, such as, had she thought in certain ways about me while we were growing up?

"You ain't my type. Too skinny," Dottie said, as if she was reading my mind.

"What's wrong with that?" I snapped. Then I said, "I got to think about this."

"What's to think about?"

"Well, I've always pictured us living here with our husbands and children, raising them up, like Ida and Madeline."

"I can still have kids," Dottie said. "Way things are going, I might have to raise Archer. Wouldn't mind that a bit."

"He could do a lot worse," I agreed. "You happy?"

Dottie shrugged. "Same, I guess," she said. She sniffed the air and changed the subject. "Smells bad enough in here to gag a maggot," she said. "Let's exit, stage left." We closed the pages on the spread-eagled blonde and tossed the magazine on the floor of the tent with the others. Dottie straightened the sleeping bag and we backed out and zipped and closed the flaps, hoping to leave it as it had been before we'd snuck inside.

"I don't get why he needs a tent inside," Dottie said.

"Maybe it's like Arlee's fuzzy blanket. It's comforting."

"Could be."

"You want to help me with the red ruby dishes?"

She and I washed and dried every piece out of the cabinet, lemon-oiled the cabinet, washed the glass that fronted the cabinet, and set the dishes back inside. While we did that, we talked about Edward's visit.

"Thing is, no matter what he does or says, he gives me the creeps," Dottie said. "He could be wearing wings and playing a harp and I'd still think he was a slimeball."

"I'm wondering if he was even supposed to come down at all, after he talked to Parker. What was the point? Why did he bother?" I said. "And he said, 'I didn't hurt Caroline.' Who says she was hurt?"

"Ida had her radar up too," Dottie said. "Parker paid attention to that."

"I know," I said. "He believes her but he thinks I'm crazy."

"You are."

"I know that. But what I think counts. I'm Carlie's daughter, for crying out loud."

"He probably thinks you're too close to it all."

"I am. Of course I am. But I want it done with," I said. "The letters stirred things up, but I've got this life now. I want my family to come first, always, and I can't do that because my damn mother keeps popping up. You know what I mean. I want Carlie to come home, one way or another."

"That'd be good," Dottie said.

We worked for a while, and then I said, "So, you have a girlfriend in mind?"

Dottie laughed. "No, not yet. I ain't in no hurry to get tied down."

A couple of minutes later, Glen and Bud burst in, reeking of beer, liquor, and cigarette smoke.

"Got a cool bar up to Long Reach called the Harbor Light," Bud said. "Had a couple. Don't freak out now, Florine. I know how much you hate it when I have fun."

Glen let out a burp that replaced most of the air in the house.

"Jesus, bring it up later and we'll vote on it," Dottie said to him.

"Okay with me," Glen said, and he and Bud laughed like hell.

"We're leaving," I said. "Glen, clean the toilet and tub once in a while, would you?"

"Yes, sir. I'm on it, sir," Glen said, and saluted.

"She gets like that," Bud said to Glen. "Kind of bitchy and bossy." He grinned at me.

"I'll see you down the hill," I said to him. "Whenever you feel like showing up."

As Dottie and I left the house, Glen and Bud busted up laughing.

"Bud's kind of nasty when he's drunk," Dottie said.

"Whiskey and him don't get along as far as I'm concerned," I said. "Whiskey and beer and him don't get along worse. Hope this doesn't get to be a habit."

32

The next morning I found myself back in Grand's house again. She always kept a sock with spare cash behind a brick in back of the stove, and I had followed her lead. Financially, things were a little tight with us, and it was time to raid the sock. I hated to do it, but we needed it. So, I walked up the hill from Ida's house and knocked on my door, again thinking how foolish it was to have to do that.

Glen let me in, dressed in camouflage pants and a white T-shirt. He was carrying the coffee mug Bud usually used.

"Want some tea? I feel funny asking you that," he said, and grinned.

"I would love for someone else to make me a cup of tea," I said.

We walked into the kitchen and he put the kettle on. "Want some eggs?" he asked. "I can fry some up in no time."

"I ate," I said. "I came to withdraw some cash from behind the brick." Glen frowned. "The what?"

"Grand's stash," I said. I reached behind the stove and pulled out the loose brick, reached inside the dark space it had left, and pulled out the old sock.

"Well, I'll be damned," Glen said. "I had no idea it was there."

"Old trick that Grand caught onto, way back," I said. "Her family had a habit of hiding money. When her father died, he left her and her mother with no money, so they thought. Turned out that he'd cut a hole in his mattress and stuffed it full of bills. Grand found it when she was playing under the bed."

"Think we should have a scavenger hunt to see if there's money anywhere else?" Glen asked.

"No, she would have told me," I said.

"Bud mentioned things was a little stretched," Glen said.

"He told you that?" I said. The teakettle whistled and I automatically reached for it and switched off the stove.

"You sit down, let me get the tea," Glen said, skipping over my question. "Tell you what, go into the tent and I'll bring it to you."

The kitchen table would have worked for me, but if the tent worked better for Glen, why not? The flap was up and I ducked inside. No sign of his girlie magazines, and the funk had faded, somewhat. I listened to him whistle as he brewed my tea.

"You take milk?"

"Yep. And a little sugar."

"Coming right up." In a few seconds, his whistle grew louder and I scooted over to make room for him. He ducked through the flap, handed me my tea, and sat down on the sleeping bag in almost the same place Dottie had hunkered down the day before during her confessional about being a lesbian.

"Sorry about the magazines," Glen said. "I probably should have hidden them when I knew you was coming up to clean."

I blushed. "Sorry I invaded your privacy," I said. "Dottie and I couldn't resist coming in. It's cozy. I guess I can see why you put it up in here."

"Thought you might think I was crazier than I already am," Glen said.

"I couldn't possibly think you were any more crazy," I said, and smiled. "You feeling better?"

"It comes and goes," he said. "I'm calmed down. Nights are the worst."

"You figure out what you want to do yet?"

He shook his head. "No fucking idea," he said.

"Maybe you shouldn't worry about it," I said.

"Well, spring's bound to come, and I can't live here when you come back down. I can go back out to the woods for the summer. That wouldn't be so bad. Come back here in the winter."

"You could do that for the rest of your life," I said. "But we'll be coming back, at some point, to The Point to live all year round."

"Bud says that probably won't happen," Glen said. He sipped steam off the top of his coffee while what Bud had said sunk into me. We had never said that to each other.

I tried not to sound mad as I said to Glen, "I guess you and Bud got things all figured out. Sounds like he's got a plan. Guess we'll talk about it someday."

Glen shook his head. "Well, him and me, we talk sometimes, like you and Dottie do."

"What else does he say?" I asked. I slurped tea from Grand's old, thick diner mug and took comfort in its plainness, in its devotion to duty.

"I can't tell you," Glen said. "Nothing you don't already know, probably."

"He tell you he's going to go traveling by himself when he gets the chance? That he's leaving me and the kids behind to do it?"

"He said he'd like to take some trips, yes."

"Does he want to get rid of me and the kids?" I asked, frustration making my question sharp. "He want to go back to Susan? He wish we'd never gotten married?"

"Jesus, Florine, of course not. He's just restless. And he's nervous about money. He ain't sure about working at Cecil's, but he don't want to come back down here. Says he would feel like a loser, if he did. He's scared of letting you down. He says he thinks you're too much woman for him sometimes."

"Oh, for chrissake," I yelled. "That's the stupidest fucking thing I've ever heard."

Glen looked down at his coffee. "Yes, ma'am," he said.

"Is that why he's drinking whiskey? Because I'm too much woman?"

"I ain't saying anything else," Glen said, looking out of the tent flap toward the kitchen, wondering, maybe, how he could get out without getting hurt.

"Because the whiskey, you know, it doesn't set right in Bud," I said.

"I agree," Glen said. "I don't like the way his eyes get when he downs a shot or two."

"You got to stop him from doing that," I said.

"He's a big boy," Glen said. I watched his face shift as he tried to change the subject. Suddenly his face brightened. "I got a date tomorrow night, in Long Reach," he said.

"You do?" I said. "Who? Do we know her?"

"Nope. She's new in town. Works at the shipyard."

Long Reach existed because the waters along its shores, the Kennebec River, were deep and wide. The shipyard had produced some of the best destroyers ever built for the navy. Daddy had never worked there, but almost everyone in town was either employed there or had a relative who was a ship fitter.

"Where'd you meet her?"

"Harbor Light, the other night. She come right up to Bud and me whilst we was sitting there. Friendly."

"That's comforting to know," I said. "That makes me feel good."

On he went, bumbling into quicksand, Glen-fashion. "Well, she looked at Bud first. But he just flashed his wedding ring and pointed at me."

"Good for me, I guess," I said. "I don't want to have to fight her for my husband."

"No, you don't have to do that. She and I are going to the movies."

"I hope you have fun," I said.

"Me too," Glen said. His face darkened. "You know, I think I told you, it ain't ever worked out for me. Me and girls, well, something always happens."

"You had lots of girlfriends in high school," I pointed out. "Dottie and I stopped remembering their names, there were so many of them."

"Yeah, but, I don't know," Glen said. He ran his thumb around the rim of his coffee mug. "Things go wrong," he said. "I want to tell them to go to hell when they get too close to me."

"How come?"

"I don't know. I guess I think they might wind up thinking I'm not who they want me to be. That I ain't good enough for them."

"Well, Glen, that's bullshit," I said. "Of course you're good enough for them. Any woman would be lucky to have you in her life."

To my surprise, he teared up. "Someone told me once that I wasn't much," he said. "That no one would put up with me because I'm stupid and the only thing I had going for me was my dick. Excuse me, but that's what she said. I think of that when I'm with other girls; that I'm too stupid to be anything but a fuck machine. And when someone gets all gooey-eyed, what she said just takes over my head and I get scared they're going to find out how numb I am and then they'll leave." He struck the sleeping bag with his fist.

"Well, fuck that girl," I said. "You talked to Bud about it?"

Glen shook his head. "You're the only person knows that. Don't tell Dottie."

"I won't," I said. "But you know she was an asshole, don't you?"

"I'm beginning to think she was a ballbuster, but what she said still messes up my head, along with everything else. She was smart. She was older than me. She was . . ." Glen stopped talking.

"Do I know her?" I asked.

"Nope," he said, and with that he crawled out of the tent, stood up, and walked into the kitchen. I followed him. We put our mugs into the sink and I took the money-filled sock from the kitchen table.

"Happy New Year," I said. "Clean the bathroom. Have a fun date and don't worry about what some asshole said once. You're a good guy. You're amazing." I hugged him hard, left the house, and headed down the hill.

33

Our little family left for Stoughton Falls on December 29. Then 1974 blew in, toasting itself with a spiteful blizzard. It also was kind enough to hand out, for free, nasty colds to both kids, and it gave an extra one to Bud.

Travis was the one who broke my heart. His nose was completely filled, and he hated the rubber bulb thing that I stuck up his nostrils to clear them out. He cried and hacked and coughed so bad that one night I found myself in the bathroom, running the shower at full steam, on the advice of the kids' doctor. The next day I took him in to see her.

"Yep, croup," Dr. Rollins said. "Going around."

"Scary," I said.

"Yep," she said. "He'll be okay, though, believe it or not."

"You come sit with him and tell me that," I said, growling with grumpiness.

"Believe me," she said, "I've spent time sitting by worse things. I could give you a list, but that would be a waste of time. Besides, he's with the best people he could possibly be with to see him through this. Am I right?"

When she put it that way, what could I say but yes?

After a week of dancing from bedroom to bathroom to living room and back with medicines and tissues, the three of them began to come back to themselves, even as snow continued to shimmy down from the silky silver skies.

"It's January everywhere," I said to Bud at breakfast one morning.

"Zat bad?" Arlee asked.

"No," Bud said. "Just freakin' long."

And it was. If summer made a mockery of our memories of winter, winter made mincemeat of summer's memories. Once the kids were better, I bundled us all up and lugged us outside. I stuck Travis on a slat-sided sled and dragged him around the back and front yards while Arlee trailed us at her own little pace. She stopped to eat snow, or to leap facedown into it, shrieking with laughter, which made Travis lose his mind with giggles. Their antics knocked January back on its ass for brief periods.

Dull routine shrouded our days. We grew stir-crazy and bored. Bud and I handled it in our own ways. By the time he got home from work, it was dark. He ate supper and played with the kids for a while before he sat down in front of the news with a shot of whiskey and two to four beers. The shot of whiskey made me wary, but I left him to his territory until seven thirty or so, when both kids went to bed. Then, armed with knitting bag and needles, I would claim my space in front of the television in Grand's rocker, which we had lugged up after Christmas. As I knitted, I took comfort in the fact that sitting in that rocker felt as if she were hugging me.

Once in a while, I would attempt a conversation to push us out of our winter-forced doldrums. They usually went something like this:

Me: "You okay?"

Bud: "What do you mean?"

Me: "You're awful quiet."

Bud: "It's friggin' dark. All I can do to stay awake."

Me: "I know all that. I'm making sure you're okay."

Bud: "I appreciate that. I guess when I got something to say, I'll say it."

My concern for his state of mind grew, particularly when he began to add a little whiskey to his coffee thermos in the morning. The first time I caught him doing it, I think he thought I was in Arlee's bedroom, but I was standing in the hall, holding her while she tried to wake up, watching him fill a shot glass and pour it in with his coffee.

"Do you really need that?" I said, walking up to him.

He jumped. "Puts a little heat in the day," he said. "Warms me up." He stared at me, daring me to say something, so I obliged.

"Do all the guys in the garage drink?" I said.

"I don't ask 'em. They don't tell me."

"You're working on cars that weigh a ton," I said. "You're working with gasoline and oil and stuff that catches on fire. That's dangerous work. You've gotten along without any help from booze before this. Why now?"

Arlee squirmed and I put her down.

"It's a shot of whiskey, Florine," Bud said. "A pick-me-up. I don't even taste it in the coffee. It don't affect my work at all."

Before I could say anything else, he closed up the thermos and put it into the lunch bag I had packed for him. He gave me a peck on the cheek. "Love you," he said, and went out the door.

"Love you," I murmured. He backed his truck out onto Route 100 and drove toward the garage. "Dammit," I whispered.

"No, Mama," Arlee said, from the sofa.

My life brightened when Robin called in mid-January.

"I just got back from California," she told me. "Dad bought me a ticket. How was Christmas?"

I filled her in.

"Must be frustrating as hell," she said. "You get snippets of info, then nothing."

"It's been that way for over ten years," I said. "I'm used to it."

"But you know, clues keep coming to you," she said. "Letters, people. They're turning up."

"So?"

"Maybe Carlie is pushing things along. Maybe she wants to come home in whatever way she can. Maybe the universe is telling you something."

"That's weird."

"Might be. But how is it stranger than anything else that has happened?"

"It isn't."

I wanted to tell her about Bud's drinking, but a sense of loyalty to him stopped me.

"Love to see you soon," she said.

"Me too. We'll figure something out."

Figuring out time to get together with Robin became a challenge, as a knotted string of storms raged well into February. She surprised me when she showed up, unannounced, on a rare, clear Saturday. I pulled in behind her little car after buying the weekly groceries. I hoped she and Bud were getting along. I honked for help, but no one came out. "The hell with you all," I said as I opened the Fairlane's trunk. Bud came out to rescue me as I stood wondering how many trips it would take to get the six bags into the house.

"How long has Robin been here?" I asked.

"About a half hour," Bud said. "Thought she'd drop by, see if you wanted to get out for a while."

The set of his mouth as he hefted three grocery bags told me he wasn't pleased about the prospect.

"You want to go out, instead?" I said. "Or we all can take the kids down the road to the park in town. They've plowed it out."

"Why don't I go out?" he said. "Might go into Stoughton Falls for a while, have a beer at the Wayside Bar and Grill. Sounds good to me. Sound good to you?"

"Not really," I said.

He shrugged and I followed him into the house. Robin sat on the floor rolling a ball to the kids. She was wearing the sweater I'd made her for Christmas. She grinned. "I *love* this," she said.

"It looks great," I said, conscious of how hard Bud was setting the grocery bags on the counter.

"I'm going," he said abruptly. He pecked me on the cheek. "You girls have a good time." And he was out the door, backing out of the driveway in a spray of loose gravel. He burned rubber until he was out of sight. I sighed and put the groceries away while Robin continued to play with the kids.

Quick as I could, I said, "Let's get out of here." We dressed the kids and packed them into the car. I drove us into Stoughton Falls, past a diner, a hardware store, and a sweet library. I parked in a lot close to that library. We lifted the kids from the car and put them down on a plowed pathway that led through the town's park while Robin got the sled from the trunk. Soon we were moving along, me pulling Travis while Arlee ran ahead and jumped into snowbanks.

"The sweater is beautiful," Robin said. "No one has ever made me a sweater. Florine, it's amazing. You could sell these for some good money!"

"Once in a while I do," I said.

"You could strike up a deal with some craft stores."

"You think?"

"I think," Robin said.

Arlee grabbed her hand and they jumped into a virgin patch of snow. I pulled Travis from the sled and we watched them, our breath mingling. The sun burned the fog from my brain, and a touch of happiness crystallized into a pearl of pure joy.

Robin and Arlee waded back to the path. Arlee climbed onto the sled. I put Travis in front of her.

"I'll pull them for a while," Robin said. "Not to keep hammering at you but, no kidding, Florine, you could make and sell these. Valerie asked me if I could ask you if you'd make one for her. And for my father, for his birthday. They'll pay good money."

"Well, get me sizes," I said.

"Valerie works in a clothing shop and she said she could carry one or two to see how they sell."

"Wow!" I said. If someone in California was willing to carry my sweaters, maybe people living in other states might like to too. I'd have to knit like a bastard, but I worked fast, as Grand had taught me.

"Did you happen to find the present I left for you?" Robin asked.

I stopped walking. "Shit—I mean shoot—no! I totally forgot. I got the phone call from Parker and off we went. Crap! I'm so sorry."

"You can open it when we get back," she said, which made me want to hurry, so we dragged the kids back to the car, stuffed them into their seats, and drove through the small town. We all staggered into the trailer red-faced, cold, and happy, dripping melted snow throughout the trailer.

Robin helped Arlee shuck her coat and boots and began to undo Travis's snowsuit.

"Where is it?" I asked.

"The angel-food-cake pan near the back of the cupboard," Robin said. I fished out a small square package wrapped in red-and-gold-striped Christmas wrap. Robin had curled the same color ribbon over the top. I admired it quickly, and then tore open the wrapping.

The plain white box revealed a layer of soft cotton. I lifted it and gasped. It was a gold bracelet with a red stone. "Oh my god," I said.

"Mama, no," Arlee said. I ignored her.

"It was our grandmother Maxine's," Robin said. "She left me all of her jewelry. She didn't have much, but what she had was nice. I wanted you to have a piece for yourself. The heart is made of ruby."

"You have no idea what this means," I said. Tears ran down my cheeks. I sat down at the kitchen table and wiped them away.

I said to Robin, "I don't think I told you, but you know Grand's red ruby glass cabinet? The one in the corner of the living room? There used to be a red ruby heart that sat in the center of the middle cabinet. I took that heart one day when I was really upset and I threw it off the ledges at the end of the state park."

"Why were you upset?" Robin asked. She sat down across from me at the table. Arlee clambered into my lap and Travis crawled over to her. She picked him up and then settled back to listen.

"It was New Year's Day. Grand always cleaned the glass on that day and I usually helped her. I wasn't living with her then; I was still living with Daddy. Carlie had been gone for a little over four months. I had stayed overnight at Dottie's house for a New Year's Eve party. I was walking up to Grand's to help her with the glass when Stella Drowns walked out of Daddy's house. She'd slept with him. Oh my god, Robin, I was so mad. I went into Grand's house and I yelled about Stella and Grand tried to calm me down. I grabbed the heart and I was going to wash it, but Grand said I should settle down first. I got mad at that and I stormed out, without a coat, by the way, and ran to the ledges. I threw the heart into the ocean and asked for my mother back in exchange for the heart. It was insane, I know, but I was crazed."

"Hungee, Mama," Arlee whined.

"In a minute," I said to her.

"Wow," Robin said. "I wish I'd been there for you. I would have kicked Stella's butt for you."

"Well, you're here now, and you've given me back the heart, in a way. It's a piece of Carlie."

Robin grinned. "The universe, again, working in strange ways."

I slipped the bracelet onto my arm and admired it. It was made of thin gold that twined itself around tiny prongs cupping a precious stone. I touched the ruby and held my finger on its surface until it grew warm and my finger throbbed with the pulse of it.

Arlee said, "Eat now, Mama."

Robin cleaned the kitchen as I put the kids down for naps. We sat down at the table again with cups of tea. I stared at the stone in the bracelet, trying to see into the center of the heart.

Robin took in a deep breath. "I'm moving to California," she said. I looked up, startled. "What? Why? When?"

"In June, when school lets out. I'm torn, but I like the weather, and I like being close to my family."

"Not to be selfish, but I was getting used to having you here."

"I'll be back. And you and Bud and the kids can visit. We can go to Disneyland, and to the beach. And you can meet your uncle for the first time. He can't wait to meet you!"

I gave her a little smile, hoping it covered the sudden lump in my throat.

"You okay?" she asked, and I said of course. We went back to chatting about what we would do while she was still here. She would help me with my GED. We would visit Portland and look for places that might sell beautiful, homemade sweaters. We still had some days together, we told each other, and we would make the most of them. But in my mind, she was already gone.

After she left, the blues settled in and I mooned around the trailer, cleaning up the mud and water from our earlier visit to the park.

The kids and I ate supper without Bud, who never called to let us know he'd be late. I sat through a boring television show after I put them down for the night. I switched it off at nine thirty and sat on the sofa, twisting the golden bracelet with the red ruby center around my arm, trying not to worry.

About an hour later, his pickup's lights pinpointed the icy particulars of our gravel driveway.

34

Bud lurched from the driver's seat, started for the house, realized he'd left his headlights on, and wove his way back. Finally, he stumbled through the door, shut it, saw me, and stopped. "You still up?"

"No," I said. "I'm a ghost, standing here, watching her sloshed husband come through the door."

"You do look faint," Bud said. He laughed. "Christ, all's you need now is a rolling pin," he said.

"They're down to The Point," I said.

"The Point, The Point, the precious Point," Bud said in a singsong voice. "I'm starved. We got anything to eat? We should, you bought groceries."

"Yes," I said. "Get it yourself. I don't want to talk to you. You're in your mean son-of-a-bitch mood. I'm going to bed."

"Wait a minute, dammit. Sit down for a minute."

"Why should I?"

He said, "Look, you've been wanting to know what's up with me? Well, I'm ready to talk. So, sit down. Wait, I got to piss like a racehorse. What does that mean, anyway?" He chuckled as he swayed on an invisible tightrope down the hall to the bathroom.

As he passed me, my nose took in the burn of whiskey, along with the stink, the gloom, and the stale smoke that buries itself in the clothing of barflies. I walked to the front door, opened it, and sucked down fresh, cold air. I shut the door, closed my eyes, and waited for a comforting word from Grand. *To have and to hold*, she said. *Thanks*, I said. *I got that*. I sat down at the dining room table.

Bud banged his way out of the bathroom. He looked at me and frowned, his fuzzy brain ticking away. Finally, it occurred to him. "You going to make me a sandwich?"

"Make your own fucking sandwich," I said.

"Oooh, oooh," he said, and giggled. "Make my own fucking sandwich. Okay then." He snickered his way into the kitchen, where he hauled out meat, cheese, bread, mayonnaise, and mustard. He clanked around as if we had no sleeping kids.

"Quiet down," I said.

"Can't help it," he said. "Stuff makes noise."

When he was finished, he cut the sandwich crosswise from end to end instead of across the middle, which was the way I always did it. "See," he said, holding the two halves up. "I like it cut this way. You always cut it the other way."

"I don't know as we've ever discussed it," I said. "And frankly, so what?"

Bud sat down at the table. "So, this is why I don't like Robin." He bit into the sandwich. Bread stuck to the roof of his mouth and he smacked as he ate. Why the hell did I fall in love with you? I wondered.

"Why don't you like her?" I asked.

"Because, she reminds me of Susan."

"Why does Robin remind you of Susan?"

A piece of cheese fell from his sandwich and landed on the page of a coloring book. The unicorn on the page sported a turquoise mane, courtesy of Arlee and her shades-of-blue crayon army.

Bud grinned. "Aw, isn't that some pretty," he said. "We got good babies. We got that, at least."

"I hope we have more than that," I said.

Bud slammed his sandwich onto the table. "Jesus Christ, Florine, it ain't that I'm not happy. I ain't, but you're not the problem. Problem is, I'm twenty-three years old and I got a wife and two kids. And that might be all I ever have."

"If that's all you ever have, you're a lucky man," I said.

"I know," he said. "But here's the thing. Susan, well, she wanted me to make something out of myself. Instead, we got together, you got pregnant . . ."

"With a little help from you," I said.

"Yeah. I was there. I remember," he said. "Anyway, Robin reminds me of Susan: Going to college. Having a career. Someone who's making something of themselves. She reminds me that I'm not." He leaned over the table toward me and I studied the red veins in his eyes. "You know what Robin asked me before you got home today?"

"No," I said. "I have no idea."

"She says, 'If you could do anything you wanted, what would you do?'"

"What did you say?"

"I asked her what the hell was wrong with what I was doing now."

"And she said what?"

"She said, 'Oh, don't get me wrong. What you do now is fine. I just wonder about people and what they'd do, if they could.'"

"Well, what would you do?"

"Fuck if I know!" he shouted, and I shushed him. "That's the thing. Goddamn her, why did she have to bring that up? She got me to thinking, anyways. Why *can't* we do what we want, Florine? I'm scared all I'll ever be is a shit mechanic in a shit garage working for shit money."

"Well, when the kids are in school, I'll have my GED and maybe . . ."

"My god, that's years from now!" Bud cried. "In the meantime, heigh-ho, heigh-ho, it's off to fucking work I go and you stay home, doing whatever you do all day."

I gave him a look that he knew enough to respect, even in his drunken state. "I do my share," I growled, "and more. Be patient, and for the love of all that's holy, lay off the goddamn whiskey."

He started to say something.

"Listen to me," I said. "Arlee goes to school in two years, and Travis goes to school in four years. I will start working on my GED now. Robin got me to thinking today too. Maybe I can sell sweaters and other knit goods. I can bake. I can do lots of things. I'm good at math. Maybe I can do something in a store, or be a bookkeeper. In the meantime, we can work on what it is you really want to do. Give it time. We have time."

Bud stared at me for about half a minute. Then he stuffed the rest of his sandwich into his mouth and forced it down his throat. He said, "I'm tired. Tomorrow's Sunday. I get to sleep this shit off and watch television all day." He got up and kissed me on top of my head. "Night," he said.

Off he went, leaving me to clean up the mess he'd left behind.

35

I couldn't even shake Bud awake the next morning. The kids and I did our thing without many tears or too much drama for a couple of hours before Arlee decided to wake Daddy up to come and play with us. The sorry-assed version of Bud that appeared in the hallway made me laugh.

"Not funny," Bud said.

"You're right. It's not," I agreed.

The kids and I went outside while Bud drank his coffee. During the night, as we had slept, warm air had blown in, producing a late thaw that put the snow on the run. As we watched, a giant icicle toppled forward onto the front lawn. After a while, I took Travis inside to sit with his father while Arlee and I made snowmen. In all, we made ten of them, all different sizes, standing all over the lawn. We went inside at about noon to find Bud feeding Travis lunch at the table.

I made peanut butter and Marshmallow Fluff sandwiches for the rest of us. I cut Bud's sandwich the way I had always done it. When I set it in front of him, I said, "Is there anything else I can do for you? I hope it's up to your standards."

"Why the sarcastic tone?" he asked.

"You don't remember?"

He shook his head. "I don't know what the hell you're talking about."

"Evidently, I haven't been cutting your sandwiches the right way for all the time we've known each other. Last night was the first night you'd ever said anything about it."

"Christ," Bud said, and ran his hand over his face. "Who cares?"

"That's what I said. But you cared about it, last night," I said.

"I'm sorry. I can't remember anything I said. Can we just forget about it?"

"No. You said some things last night that make me wonder about what you want in your life. If you're not happy, maybe we can try to fix it. If not, well, we can't, I guess."

"What's that mean?"

"I don't know, yet. But you married me. You didn't choose Susan. You knew, or at least I thought you knew, the differences between us. Now, I'm not sure you ever left what you had before. Sounded to me, last night, as if you wished you were doing something different. You didn't seem to think that my suggestions were good enough. And you were drunk on your ass. You figure out what you want, let me know so I can make plans. You keep drinking, and the kids and I will leave you."

The look on Bud's face went from confusion to denial to regret. He looked down at his sandwich, then at Arlee, who had taken apart her sandwich and was dragging her index finger through the Fluff on the bread, and at Travis, who was nodding off in his high chair. Neither of us had raised our voices, and I didn't intend to do that.

"Arlee, eat the sandwich," I said. "Don't play with it." I looked at Bud and said, "And you, don't play with *me*." I left the table and went into the bathroom, where I sat on the john for about ten minutes, trying to calm down and wondering if we had enough Windex to clean the bathroom mirror. It was spotted with toothpaste, and it probably always would be. "What's the frigging point," I said. I left the bathroom and went across the hall to clean the bedroom.

Bud shuffled up the hall and leaned against the door frame. "I love you," he said.

"I love you too," I said. "But you're an asshole."

"Not all the time. Not most of the time."

"More and more of the time."

The phone rang. "Want me to get it?" Bud asked.

"No," I said. As I brushed by him, he took my arm and turned me. His lips touched mine for a second. "I'm sorry," he whispered. "I'll stop drinking. I promise."

"You should be." I hurried to the end of the trailer to pick up the phone.

"Hi, Florine," Ida said. "How are you all doing?"

"Oh, peachy, Ida," I said. "How are you guys? Arlee misses you."

"We miss her and Travis," Ida said. "I'm calling for a couple of reasons. First, before you hear it from anyone else, Pastor Billy is staying here with us for a couple of weeks. He's in Bud's old room."

"What? Why?"

"Well, he's been going through those cancer treatments for a while. I've been keeping a close eye on him, every Sunday. He's just been looking worse and worse, and finally, last Sunday, he stopped halfway through his sermon and told the congregation that he had to sit down. Before I could move, Maureen jumped up and helped him out. And then, Florine, I could hardly believe it, she went up to the pulpit and she led us in hymns for about ten minutes, and finished up with prayers! I was so proud of her. She did all of this on her own. She's just turned sixteen years old!"

I smiled. "Grand would be proud of her," I said, thinking about the grin that would have crossed her sweet, worn face. "She's a keeper for sure."

"Yes," Ida said. "Well, anyway, Billy was so weak after the service he could barely stand up. A few of us were going to take him up to Long Reach, to the hospital, but he didn't want that. He wanted us to drive him back to Spruce Point, to his house. 'No,' Maureen said, 'you're coming home with us. You're staying in Bud's room, until you feel better. Right, Ma?' I thought, Well, why not? and so I said yes. Billy objected some, but Maureen was not going to give an inch, so we brought him back here with us."

"How's he doing?"

"Well, he sleeps most of the time," Ida said. "I know from living with Sam's cancer that rest is what he needs. When he's awake, Maureen sits with him and they talk about the Bible and such. And, until they can find another pastor to take his place for a while, Maureen is helping him to find other people to lead the Sunday service. She works on his sermons with him. I just may have a preacher in the making in the family!"

As Ida went on, her not-a-chance-in-hell-of-ever-being-a-preacher son bumbled around in back of me, perfuming the air with the sharp remnants of last night's liquor. "I can't believe it either," I said, "but Maureen's always been headed toward the light, as Grand would say."

"She has, hasn't she," Ida said happily. We went on to talk about the kids and how everything was going. It was hard not to tell her the truth. Maybe she would have understood, but it may have brought Sam and his sad journey to the forefront, and right then she was so happy about Maureen.

"How's Glen?" I asked her, digging for a change of subject. "Have you seen him?"

"Oh, that's the other thing," she said. "He's moved out of the house. Cleared all of his stuff out a few days ago and lit out for who knows where. I went and checked the house. He cleaned it as best he could, being Glen. I'll give it a good go-over before you all come down. Do you know when that might be?"

"Well, it might be earlier than you think," I said. "I don't want you to worry about cleaning the place. The kids and I might come down for a few days soon. It would be a nice change from the trailer."

"Be great to see you," Ida said. "We'd love to see the kids! I might have to come up there to see you, instead of having them down to the house, just until Billy's stronger."

"That's fine," I said. "I understand that. Do you have any idea where Glen went?"

"I don't," Ida said. "I haven't had a chance to ask Ray."

Poor Glen. Another lost soul out driving around in the butt crack of winter. Maybe Bud knew where he had gone. I hoped that Bud could find himself too, before he wandered too far away.

That night, while Bud dozed in front of the television, I put Travis and Arlee onto her bed and let them play for a few minutes before I read to them. Travis stared into space before his eyelids closed, while Arlee and I went on for at least another story. Afterward, I carried Travis to his room and his crib, settled him, and tucked Arlee into her bed. I walked into our bedroom and turned on the radio, which set on a small shelf above our bed. I picked up my knitting needles, both filled with loops of yarn the color of Travis's eyes. I stretched out on my bed and watched a sweater grow before my eyes. My mind turned toward Grand. She had set me down beside her in a rocker on the porch to teach me how to knit scarves. I was impatient and I treated it as a contest.

"Done," I would yell, and she would say, "Well, let me look at it." She always found places where I'd slipped a stitch or suddenly knitted looser or tighter. "Do it again," she'd say as she ripped out my work. "Make sure your work is steady." Eventually, I learned and, although I liked to see the results, she had been right. It was more important to make sure the work was well done.

Thinking of Grand took me to The Point. *The precious Point.* I sighed.

"What's going on?" Bud said from the doorway.

"I was thinking about The Point, The Point, the precious Point," I said.

Bud ignored me. "What did Ma want?"

I told him about Billy and about Maureen's becoming a substitute minister.

He smiled. "Where she came from, I don't know. Probably the best of Ma and Dad." He looked at me. "He did have a good side, you know. He wasn't just a drunk."

"No one is just a drunk. No one is just anything."

"That's right. And just because I drink once in a while doesn't make me a drunk."

I slipped a stitch and fixed it.

"Is that all you think I am?" Bud continued. "A drunk?"

"Is a dumb girl who didn't finish high school and got knocked up all you think I am?"

"What the hell?" Bud said. "Don't take what I might have said last night to heart. I got the right girl. I'm smart enough to know that. Jesus, give me some credit."

"You should hear yourself when you're bombed. You'd think you were a dink too."

"I think I'm a dink every day," he said.

"I don't think that," I said. "Unless you've been into the sauce. And if you think you're a dink every day, I'm sorry for you for thinking that."

"Well," Bud said, "you should be inside of me."

"I've got enough shit to deal with."

My knitting needles clacked. Bud inhaled and exhaled. The refrigerator engine snapped on, droned for a few minutes, and then turned itself off.

"Well," he said. "I'll come to bed soon."

My needles flashed as I picked up the pace.

36

After our conversation, Bud kept to only one beer after work. No whiskey. At least that I could tell.

Arlee and I grew our snowman village and we began to get fancy. I mixed together food coloring and we gave them blue or brown or green eyes and red lips. We wet brushes and painted on different-colored hair. We dotted buttons down their fronts, or sloshed on skirts or pants. They had the usual carrot noses, with slices of oranges for the ears. The ears didn't last long because the birds loved them, but that was okay. I knitted matching headbands for each one. We built about forty snowmen, women, and children.

Someone passing by on Route 100 must have noticed them, because one day, a photographer showed up from the *Stoughton Falls Weekly Reader* newspaper, and took a picture of us with our snow people. I cut out the article with its caption and sent another one to Ida and Maureen. It was a peaceful couple of weeks.

And then, Glen showed up.

It was about midnight on a Friday night. When we heard tires pop bits of gravel in our driveway, Bud slipped over my body and pulled on a pair of jeans. My heart skipping double-time, I followed him down the hall in my T-shirt and panties. "What's going on?" I whispered.

The twin suns of headlights pierced the closed drapes over the picture window. I moved to stand beside my husband, but he hissed, "Stay here." He crept to the front door and stood to the side of it. The lights went off and I shivered and waited in the darkness of the living room. "Bud?" I whispered.

"Quiet," he said. A truck door slammed. The sound of footsteps crunched toward the house.

Bud switched on the front-stoop light and the footsteps stopped. "Jesus, my eyes," someone whined, and Bud and I breathed a single sigh of relief.

Bud opened the door. "Get in here," he said.

Glen lumbered up the steps and entered the trailer, pulling damp March air along with him. He reached back and shut the door behind him.

"Took me a while to find this place. Wasn't sure this was it till I saw the Fairlane. How the hell are you guys?"

"Good," I said, glancing at the clock on the stove. "For midnight."

"Oh, is it?" Glen said. "Shit. I'm sorry. I don't sleep good, so I don't bother counting the hours. Anyway, I was up this way, and . . ."

"Come in," I said.

He did, and just as he did, I remembered what I was wearing. "I'll be right back," I said. "Bud, put the coffee on. Glen, boots and coats go in the laundry room."

As I changed into jeans and a sweatshirt, I found myself thankful that his wanderings had brought him to our door, no matter the time. Grand would say the best way a lost soul can find itself is by seeking out the comfort and company of loved ones.

I went back out into the living room. Glen was sprawled out in Grand's rocker.

I leaned down and gave him a peck on his cheek and headed for the refrigerator. I pulled out sandwich fixin's. "I'm so glad to see you both," Glen said, letting out a big sigh.

Bud, who had been leaning against the breakfast bar in the kitchen, rubbed his eyes and grinned. "Glad to see you, too, brother," he said.

I made a stack of sandwiches and put a pot of coffee on the dining-room table. We sat down and watched Glen inhale the food.

"Why did you move out of the house?" I asked. "It's still cold. You could have stayed there for another couple of months."

"I got restless," Glen said. "Guess it's from Nam. Up and at 'em. Thanks for letting me stay for as long as I did."

"Where you living now?" I asked.

"Oh," Glen said. "You can't see it, but I bought me a new pickup. Got a cover on the back. Been bunking down in there. Fixed it up so it's plenty warm. I been all over the place. I drive for a ways. Set up a little camp at night, and then go to bed. Do the same the next day. Been up to Crow's Nest Harbor and beyond."

Crow's Nest Harbor was one of the most beautiful places I had ever seen, but it would always remind me of Carlie's walking off into thin air.

"Went up to the tip of the county," Glen said.

"Which county?" Bud said.

Glen snorted. "Only county that counts. Aroostook," he said. "On my way down to Kittery in a day or so. Then, I guess I go across and zigzag my way up again. Big state. Lots of moose too. You and me should get some licenses," he said to Bud. "Lots of meat in one of them bastards. Should go up to Rangeley. Go to Katahdin. Moose-head Lake. Mooselookmeguntic."

I laughed at that name. "Moose lick ma what?"

"We might do that," Bud said to Glen, rubbing his hand over his face. "Could be a good time."

"When's the last time you went hunting?" I asked Bud.

"Too long back," Bud said. "Only got one deer so far in my life. Want at least a couple more under my belt before I die."

He and Glen started talking about the joys of killing Bambi and Bullwinkle, a line of talk that left me cold, so I left the table at about two thirty a.m. I stretched out on our bed with my clothes still on and nodded off.

When I woke up, late-morning light was squeezing its way through the bedroom curtains, and Arlee sat beside me, combing my hair with a toothbrush.

"Good Mama," she crooned.

I wound my right index finger through one of her fat, red ringlets and pulled on it. It sprang back to its place on her head. "Boing," I said, and she giggled.

Out in the living room, Travis was laughing so hard I had to smile.

"Gen," Arlee said. "Come see." She pulled on my arm.

"Okay," I said. "I'm up." When I walked out into the living room, both Bud and Glen greeted me with way-too-cheerful hellos.

I looked at the clock. "It's noon," I said. "How'd I sleep so late?"

"You was tired," Glen said. "That'd be my guess."

"Kids had lunch?" I asked.

"Not yet," Bud said. "We was going to get it, but we didn't."

I walked over to the kitchen. "We all want lunch, is that right?" I asked.

"Wouldn't mind it a bit, if you wouldn't," Glen said.

Mind it or not, I fed those with teeth some sandwiches, and mixed up cottage cheese and baby pears for my teething baby boy. I tried not to focus on the pile of beer cans on the dining-room table, but I couldn't help it. I wondered where drinking this early would lead Bud. I wondered how the day would go with Glen there to egg him on.

It didn't take long to find out.

"It's Bud and Glen like I've never seen them," I said to Dottie, my hand cupped over the mouth of the phone. I had called her at her college dorm, in desperation.

"How's that?" Dottie asked. "I thought we'd seen every damn way they could be."

"This is them, sitting around drinking beer and laughing their stupid asses off," I said. "We might have seen that, but what's different is they're leaving me out. I might as well be invisible."

"What are the kids doing?"

"Travis is in his baby walker."

"He's walking now?"

"Almost. Arlee's climbing up and over Glen and Bud at the table and then she's jumping down and doing it again."

"Sounds like a good time to me," Dottie said.

"I've told them to watch her, but I'm afraid she's going to slip and fall."

"It's your job to worry, I guess."

"You sure you can't drive four hours and join us?"

"Nope. Going to try to bowl a string or two with Addie."

"Who's she?"

"Oh, someone I met."

"Does she have a last name?"

"Not yet. Got to earn it first."

The hollow sounds of scattering empty beer cans got my attention, and I turned around in time to see Bud bend down to pick Arlee up off the floor.

"Gotta go," I said, and hung up. "What happened?" I asked.

"She's fine, just scared," Bud said. "Hit her head a little, that's all." Arlee screamed and held out her arms for me. I took her in, kissed her, calmed her down, wet a washcloth with cold water, and held it against her forehead.

Bud kissed her head and touched her curls. "You're okay," he said.

"We'll see how big the lump on her head gets before we decide that," I snapped.

"What now, Ma?" he said. "She's okay. Let's all just relax."

"That was an accident waiting to happen," I said. "You should—"

"*Okay.* Okay. Jesus, Florine, she's not dead."

Bud kissed the top of Arlee's head, went to the refrigerator, and pulled out more beer.

"Does it breed in there?" I asked, and he snorted. I took Arlee into my bedroom and held a bag of frozen peas to her head. I rocked her back and forth for about a half hour, until her eyelids and her neck drooped. I went back into the living room, fetched Travis, and settled him into his crib.

After I put them down, I decided to be a good sport and join Bud and Glen for a beer. I walked into the living room, grabbed my knitting bag, made a cup of tea, and joined them at the table. I spied the used shot glasses and the half-empty bottle of Jack Daniel's sitting in front of Glen. Shit, I thought. This isn't good.

Glen said to me, "That army of snowmen outside is wicked cool."

"Did you see the picture of Arlee and me on the refrigerator?" I said. When he shook his head, I jumped up and fetched it.

"That's some special," Glen said. "Guess you're famous now, around these parts."

"We had fun," I said. "Each one of them is named, too."

"Mind if I build one?" Glen said. "Add my two cents' worth?"

"Not at all," I said. "The snow is still sticky. I expect they'll all melt soon, but go ahead and do it."

"I don't want to go outside," Bud said. "I'm happy here."

"Well," Glen said, "be nice to get up off our asses, wouldn't it? Get out of Florine's way."

"She's all right," Bud said, deciding how I felt for me. "What's she got to do anyway? Kids are in bed."

"I imagine she could come up with something," Glen said, winking at me.

"I could," I said. "I could clean up this mess on the table. Get the table ready for the next mess. Go play outside."

Glen got up and went into the laundry room to put on his clothes.

Bud's eyes were glassy with booze. He smirked as he got up. "Sorry we're such a goddamn bother," he said. "Sorry you have to clean up our mess."

"Me too," I snapped. "I'm sorry you're drunk."

He turned around and glared at me. "I ain't fuckin' drunk, goddammit," he said. "Jesus, let me have some fun."

I glared back at him until Glen started out the door. "You coming?" he said to Bud.

"Yep," Bud said, and he followed Glen out the door without putting on his coat and hat. The day wasn't freezing, but still, in his condition he wouldn't know how cold he was until he was past needing a coat. But I didn't want to tackle that topic. I decided to let it go for a few minutes.

Travis made a small sound and I went into his bedroom. I found him deep in a dream place where twitching and moaning were part of the language. I walked into Arlee's room. I smoothed back her curls and noted that the lump on her forehead had gone down.

I went back into the dining area and gathered beer cans, shot glasses, and debris from the sandwiches and snacks. I looked out of the picture window on the way over to the sink. They were rolling a big ball of snow down at the end of the yard, toward the road. As I watched, Bud slipped and fell. Glen laughed and Bud made a snow angel before he jumped up to help Glen push the ball to their destination.

I cleaned the kitchen, which took about ten minutes. When I looked out the window again, the ball had been abandoned. Glen and Bud were ducking behind the snow people and throwing snowballs at each other. They were laughing like fools, until Glen nailed Bud in the side of the head as Bud was making a break for it. Bud grabbed the side of his head and kicked at Betsy, one of Arlee's little snow girls. She went flying in all directions. "Oh shit," I said, and ran outside into the yard.

"Bud, what are you doing?" I yelled. "Don't wreck those. Arlee will be heartbroken."

"'Don't wreck those,'" Bud whined in a singsong voice, imitating me.

"I mean it, Bud," I said. "Those are her friends. She thinks they're real."

Bud looked down at the ground and kicked at the snow. Then, he bent down, balled up a snowball, and heaved it at me. He hit me in the shoulder.

"Hey," Glen said. "Hey, Bud, now . . ."

The snowball contained ice and it hurt when it struck me. But I was damned if I was going to let him know that. I bent down and made my own snowball, and I threw it as hard as I could at him. It got him in the arm.

He scooped up a large amount of snow. I stood my ground as he packed it. "I don't care if you hit me with that thing," I said. "But don't you dare wreck Arlee's snow people." He threw the ball with such force I didn't have time to duck. It hit me in the face and I tasted warm blood in my mouth. As I stood holding my hand to my mouth, he bent down and made several snowballs. He gathered them up and heaved them, one by one, at me. My eyes stung with tears at the anger in his face. "Stop," I said, trying not to cry. "Bud. Stop."

"STOP!" Glen shouted.

We all stood as frozen as the snow people in the front yard. When I heard Arlee crying, I turned and walked back into the trailer. As I passed the picture window, I saw Glen standing in front of Bud, yelling something into his face. Whatever it was made Bud mad. He turned away and kicked down a little snow boy. I didn't look to see what happened next.

I went into the bathroom, took a cold washcloth, wiped my face, and held it to my puffed-up lip.

"Mama," Arlee called, and I went to her.

"Pee," she whimpered. Sure enough, her panties were damp and the bedsheet was soaked and stuck to the rubber lining that protected the mattress.

"Well, let's take care of all that," I said. I took her into the bathroom and cleaned her up. Travis woke up with a series of grunts.

I changed him and took them both into the living room. I tried to distract Arlee from looking outside, but I had to stop and stare, myself. Bud had kicked down at least ten of the snow people. Their food-colored carcasses lay scattered over the yard. Bud and Glen were standing by Glen's truck, beers in hands, scuffing at the ice on the driveway. Neither one was talking.

"Mama!" Arlee shouted. "The people are gone!"

"I know," I said. "Some of them fell over."

She stood at the window, her hands pressed against the glass. Bud looked up and saw the expression on his daughter's face and he hung his head. But not before he saw the look on my face.

He stared at me until I broke eye contact with him. "Let's go for a ride," I said to Arlee.

"Can we go to the toy store?" Arlee asked.

"We'll see," I said.

I was dressing Travis when Bud and Glen came into the trailer. Arlee ran out to meet them. A chair scraped back as someone sat down at the dining-room table. When I turned to take Travis out of his room, I found the doorway blocked by Bud. He wove a little bit as he stood there.

"Let me by," I said. He looked at my lip. He reached out to touch it, but I pulled away.

"I'm sorry," he said.

"Let me by now," I said, and he moved. I wrestled the kids into their winter gear. "Move your fucking truck," I said to Glen, and he hurried out to do just that.

"Florine . . ." Bud said behind me. He touched my shoulder and I whirled around.

"Don't," I said, and I went out the door with the two kids in tow.

37

I didn't really have a plan. Arlee's plea to head for the toy store, which meant Elephant Mart, was as good a destination as any. It was close by, which suited me, because soon it would be suppertime and we would have to head back.

I pulled into the parking lot and found a space near the store. "Toys," Arlee crowed from the backseat. Travis cooed.

I got out and grabbed a deserted shopping cart a couple of spaces away from the car. I plunked Arlee's pudgy brother into the basket, put Arlee in the front, and we headed inside to bright lights and aisles of dirty, wet boot tracks. My ears picked up the tinny music being piped from the ceiling.

"Toys," Arlee said, and pointed.

"Let me pick up a few things first," I said.

"No," Arlee said, but then she leaned against the front of the cart and spread her arms like a bird. "Fying," she said.

"Hold on before you fall out," I said.

A slender, petite blond woman passed us, saw my children, and smiled. "So cute," she said.

"Thanks," I said.

I had no particular destination; I just wanted to avoid the toy aisle for a few minutes. I found myself pushing my cart down an aisle containing paper goods. I grabbed towels, toilet paper, and tissues, although I had enough at the trailer. I also picked up floor cleaner, furniture polish, and dish detergent.

"Toys, Mama," Arlee said. "Toys."

Travis grabbed the front of my jacket with his little fist.

"Toys," Arlee said.

"Know any more words?" I asked her as I loosed myself from Travis's grip.

"Now," she said.

"Not quite yet," I said, starting up an aisle stocked with auto supplies. That reminded me of Bud. My lip throbbed as I wondered what Glen and he were doing at that very moment.

Then Arlee grabbed onto the front of the cart, stamped up and down, and shouted out into the store, "I want toys!" as loud as could be. She switched on the tears. "Toys," she sobbed.

"Not going to work," I said, as I turned that way. "You need to stop crying." But she kept on and my temper rose. We passed by steel trash cans for sale and I thought about stuffing her into one of them. But too many witnesses were rolling by us, probably thinking, *My child would never behave like that.*

The blond woman who had passed us earlier came up the aisle toward us. Arlee held out her arms and shouted, "Want to go." The blond woman stopped and stared at her, then at me. Before she could say anything, I said, "Ignore her. The devil shit on a rock and the sun hatched her," and we moved on.

Arlee dropped to the bottom of the cart, trying to cry herself to death to make her point. Travis turned around to check her out. "It's okay, sweet man," I said. "She's just mad."

I stopped the cart. "Stand up," I said to Arlee.

"No."

"We will go to the toy aisle," I said, "but I want to talk to you, first. Stand up."

I fished a barely used tissue out of my jacket pocket, picked her up, and put her onto the floor. I wiped her eyes and nose.

"Look at Travis," I said.

"Why?" she sniffled.

Travis grinned at the both of us. "Whoo, whoo, whoo," he said.

"Is he a baby?"

"Yes."

"Is he crying?"

"No."

"Are you a baby?"

"No."

"Then why are you crying?"

"Want a toy," she said.

"We all want something," I said, and thought, A sober husband would be nice. Out loud, I said to Arlee, "You don't see me crying every time I want something, do you?"

"No," she said. "Toy."

"We'll pick out one toy. How many is one?"

She held up her little pointer finger.

"If you cry and scream again, we're leaving the store with no toy."

"One toy," she said. I put her back into the front of the cart.

"When we get to the toy aisle, you get a toy. How many toys?"

"One."

In the end, she didn't try any funny business. She stuck to our bargain: a little ragdoll she hugged to her chest. I bought Travis the doll's twin. We checked out and drove back toward the trailer in the quickening dark, me thinking about how I didn't want to face my asshole husband and our troubled friend. I didn't want to deal with what Bud had done or why he had done it, or how I felt about it. I was tired of worrying about when he would drink next, and what that would mean. I wanted to go home. My real home.

Glen's truck was gone when I pulled into the driveway. He and Bud were nowhere to be found. I made the kids supper and sat with them while they ate it. We spent what was left of the day together on the sofa. Arlee held on to her doll. Travis just wanted to snuggle. I read books to them and both of them went down early.

I stood in my bedroom, thinking about what it would take to get us to The Point in the morning. I began to pack, slipping into and out of the kids' rooms, listening to their even breathing as I gathered their things. I put the packed suitcases into the laundry room. We would leave early in the morning, I decided, while Bud slept it off. I went to bed at eleven p.m. and toppled over a steep cliff into sleep. Travis woke me up at six a.m. Bud and Glen hadn't returned.

"Damn them," I said. Worry kicked in. I called the State Police at about nine a.m. No, ma'am, no accidents, whoever answered the phone said. No one hurt or killed. No reports from hospitals. If they don't show up soon, give us another call.

Glen called about an hour later. "Morning, Florine," he said. "Hope we didn't get you all worried. We got to drinking at Snoozy's Bar down to the waterfront in Portland. That closed up and we sat outside in the truck, talking. Must have fallen asleep."

"Where's Bud?" I said.

"Not feeling too good. We're going to find coffee, and then head back to the trailer. I'm sorry, Florine. I really am. We was assholes yesterday."

"Put Bud on the phone."

"He's not so—"

"On the phone. Now," I said.

Mutterings for about ten seconds, and then, "What?" Bud said in a cracked voice.

"What the hell do you think you're doing? Who the hell are you?" I said. I didn't wait for an answer. "The kids and I are heading to The Point." Tears rolled down my cheeks. "Get some help," I said. "You talk about Sam. You're just like him. I don't want our kids to go through that." And then I hung up, wiped my eyes, blew my nose, packed the kids in the car, and headed out.

"Where's Daddy?" Arlee asked.

"Daddy's staying here," I said. "He has work to do."

38

Halfway down to The Point, it started to sleet and I slowed way down. Twice, I got out of the car and scraped ice off the windshield. The kids sat through it all, quiet as mice, peering at the scenery with large, puzzled eyes.

What have I done? I thought as I crept along. My heart beat fast, in time to the overworked windshield wipers. I've just left my husband, I thought. Me. For once, I'm doing the leaving. Bud, who told me he would never leave me, didn't leave me. I left. I just did something I told myself I'd never do.

We slipped and slid down the hill to Grand's house, but I managed to stop the car just outside the door. "Home?" Arlee asked.

"Home," I said. My hands hurt from squeezing the steering wheel. My whole body, which I had kept ramrod straight during the ride, turned to a quaking pudding when I got out of the car. It was late morning. The sun pushed aside a curtain of ashen clouds and shot bright beams into the thick water in the harbor. I wanted nothing more than to settle into a good cry, but Arlee called, "Mama," and I turned and tended to the kids.

I opened the front door. A stale trace of Glen lingered in the air, but the living-room furniture was back in place. Arlee ran into the kitchen. "Food, Mama. Time to eat." I turned on the heat and followed her into a clean kitchen. It was clear that Ida had been there, even though I had told her not to worry. I put Travis down in the hall as I dashed outside, opened the trunk, and tossed suitcases, boxes, and bags onto the floor. He amused himself by climbing over my growing pile of stuff. I unloaded the box with food into the refrigerator and cupboards and then fed the kids. Arlee smiled at me over a peanut butter sandwich. "Home," she said again.

"Yes," I agreed. I took a deep breath.

"Gammy and MoMo?" she asked.

"Let me call them first," I said. I didn't know if Billy was still resting there. I dialed Ida and she picked up on the first ring.

"You down for a visit?" she said, instead of hello.

"Yeah," I said. "I have a little girl who would love to come down. Is Billy still here?"

"No," Ida said. "He's better and stronger. He left a couple of days ago."

"So Arlee can walk down?"

"I don't think she'll have to," Ida said, and laughed. "Maureen is on her way up." The sound of feet thudding on the hard ground was the next thing I heard, then Maureen busted through the front door.

"I'll talk to you later," I said to Ida.

Maureen bolted toward me and squeezed me in a long-armed hug. "I'm so glad you're here!" she said, and then she twirled Arlee in a circle over her head while Travis stared at them, his eyes round as full moons. Maureen lowered Arlee to the floor and went over to him. "He's wondering who this crazy person is," she said. But the kindness and joy in her face made him smile. He ducked his head, looked at her out of the corners of his eyes, and smiled.

"Oh my god, he's flirting," I said. "His first crush!" Maureen held out her hands and he reached for her. She picked him up. "Holy heck," she said. "He's heavier than ever!"

"He's a truck," I said. "How are you doing? Hear you've been preaching."

"Oh, my, yes," Maureen said. Her face lit up. "Well, Billy's been telling me what I should say, and other people are helping out. It's been great because Billy doesn't have to worry. I've even gotten a few 'amens' from the congregation."

"Wow," I said. "Good for you. I don't think anyone's ever given me an amen. Maybe Grand, but she wasn't praising the lord. She was praying for my sinner's soul."

"Well, amen is amen," Maureen said. She put Travis back into his chair and fluffed up his curls. Arlee grabbed her hand and pulled her toward the door. "You coming down later?" Maureen called as they rounded the corner.

"Oh yeah," I said. "More than likely." The door shut behind the girls and I watched them walk down the hill together, Maureen making sure they skipped the icy spots.

The phone rang and I knew who it was before I picked it up.

"You got there safe?" Bud said.

"We're here. Arlee just went down to Ida's house."

Pause on both ends.

"I'm coming down. We got to talk."

"We've talked," I said. "You got to decide what you want."

"What the hell does that mean?" Bud said.

"You don't even know what you're doing when you're drinking," I said, "and you can't remember it afterwards."

"For chrissake, Florine."

"No, you for chrissake, Florine." My temper shot up. "You wrecked something your daughter made and loved. I loved it too. We had so much fun doing that together. You took out whatever the hell is wrong with you on me and more importantly, on her, and I won't have that."

I stopped to let the heartbeat throbbing in my ears slow down. I looked out at the harbor to calm myself. Thick swells rolled like wheels toward the ocean. How I wanted to be that cold and clueless.

Bud broke the silence. "Yeah, well, I have to go."

"That's all you got to say?" I said.

"I don't even know what to say, Florine. I'm tired. Kiss the kids for me and tell them I love them." He hung up.

I squeezed my eyelids shut, willing the tears behind them to go away, but when I opened my eyes, down they came. I smeared them off my cheeks.

Travis whimpered in his chair. "I'm sorry, sweetie," I said. I turned to pick him up and jumped back about six feet. Ida was standing in the kitchen doorway. She held up her hand. "Sorry I scared you," she said. "I knocked, but you were on the phone, so I let myself in. I came to say hello and to see Travis."

I tried to smile. Travis held up his chubby arms to her. She grunted as she hauled him from the chair. "You've been eating well," she said, bouncing him in her arms. She looked at me. "That was Bud on the phone?"

"Yeah," I said.

"You had a fight and you left him and came here?"

"Wasn't just a fight," I said. "He's been drinking and he destroyed something Arlee had made. I don't want the kids around him when he's like that. So, I came home."

Ida frowned and kissed Travis's curls. She walked over to his bouncy chair and set him down. He stood on his toes, crowed, and pushed his feet and the chair forward.

"Is this how you're going to handle disagreements between you?" Ida said.

"This isn't just a disagreement," I said.

"Well, you've left your husband because something he's doing doesn't suit you. Is this what you're planning to do every time something comes up?"

"No," I said. "But I'm not raising my kids around a drunk. He was raised that way and it sounds like it was awful."

After a little pause, Ida said, "Sam had drinking problems. But he was a good man who loved us. He had flaws, but I have flaws too. So do you. So does Bud. It doesn't mean you pack up and run away, leave him when he needs you most."

"I'm not leaving him," I said. "He needs more help than I can give him."

"He needs his wife and children."

"He doesn't know what he needs," I said. "Until he figures it out, we're staying here. He knows where we are. I'll do anything I have to do to make sure the kids are safe and happy."

Ida shook her head. "You're wrong, Florine," she said. "You'll regret this."

"No, I won't," I said. "But it will kill me if our marriage doesn't work out."

"Well, running off won't help its chances."

"Oh, Ida," I said, suddenly so tired that I wanted to melt into the floor and sleep for a very long time. "Please don't . . . I don't know. Just please understand."

"I don't," she said. She turned back to Travis. "But I'm glad to see you, pumpkin." She plucked him from his chair. "Do you mind if I take him down to the house?"

"He's going to nap in a little while," I said. "I'll bring him down when he wakes up."

"Why don't I plan on having you all down for supper?"

"Okay, if you don't judge me over the potatoes."

"We're not having potatoes." She handed Travis over and left without a goodbye.

❧

Supper was both a comfort and a curse. The kids were the stars of the show, and they knew it. Any thoughts Ida might have had about what I had done was twined in among strands of spaghetti and hidden within the delicious meatballs and tomato sauce. Maureen begged for an overnight with Arlee, so I left her and walked up the hill with my little boy clinging to me like a snail to a rock. I tucked him into his crib and went into our bedroom. I sat down on Bud's side of the bed and smoothed my hands over and over against the bumps on the white chenille bedspread. I got up and looked out the window, over at Daddy's house. It was dark. Stella was still gone, I guessed, but her whereabouts weren't that important.

I crept downstairs and rocked on the porch for a long time, knowing that Grand wouldn't have judged me the way that Ida had. And if Ida thought it had been easy for me to do this, she was wrong. I wished with all my heart for Bud to drive down that hill, sober, loving, and satisfied with his life. We would hold each other close, get up in the morning, and go on.

The night hid moving water beneath its belt of dim stars. Time was passing. Time would tell.

39

Bud and I talked on the phone every night that week. Those talks had a definite pattern to them.

Bud: How could you leave me? I'm a good father, Florine. I'm a good husband, or I try to be. And I love you all more than anything in the world.

Me: We love you too. And you're a good father and husband, when you're sober. But when you drink, you become someone else, someone ugly. Someone I don't want to know and someone that I'm afraid of because I don't know what you're going to do next.

Bud: I can't be that bad.

Me: Yes, you are. When you drink, you're a prick.

Bud: Well, you're not a saint either.

Me: Never said I was. At least I'm a sober prick.

And so on. On Tuesday, he was drunk when he called me. On Wednesday, he sounded almost normal. On Thursday night, he told me he would be down on Friday night after work. I judged him to be about half and half when he told me that, so I didn't quite know what to expect.

I didn't sleep much that night. An owl hooted over by The Cheeks and I thought about cowering, helpless things. I dreamed that Carlie and Stella were friends. "That's where you went," I said to Stella in my dream. "We've been fooling you all along," she said. "We have," Carlie said, and giggled.

I woke up, went into Arlee's room, lifted her quietly from her bed, and put her in with me. Her calm breathing helped me drift off. I woke up to the weak light of a late-March dawn. I looked over at Arlee and found her looking at me. She grinned and pounced and we wrestled before we started our day.

I fretted all day Friday and kept to myself, except for a morning trip with the kids up to Ray's to buy something for dinner. Ray looked tired, but he was happy to take Travis for me while I shopped around. They had quite a conversation.

"I need a vacation," Ray said to Travis. "But got no one to run the store. You want to do it?"

Travis laughed and clapped his hands.

"He can't," I said. "I keep him busy. He does the housework."

"Wouldn't surprise me," Ray said.

"Hey now."

"You seen Glen, lately?"

"Oh, yeah," I said. "He visited us last Saturday in Stoughton Falls. He seemed okay. Said he's been traveling through the state."

Ray shook his head. "He ain't okay, not by a long shot."

I took Travis back while Ray rang me out.

"I ain't joking about needing a vacation," Ray said. "Be nice to go to Florida. See my sister."

"Well," I said, "someone would take over for you for a couple of weeks, I bet."

"How about you do it?"

I snorted. "I look like I've got time to do it?"

"Ida would take care of the kids."

"Why don't you ask her or Madeline? They're home all day."

"Madeline can't add to save her ass, and Ida would be ringing up Jesus along with the groceries. Not that Jesus is bad, for chrissake. Don't get me wrong."

"Well," I said, "I'll be going back to Stoughton Falls soon anyway."

Ray sighed. "You hear of anyone can add and say hello to whoever comes in without bringing God into it, you let me know, okay?"

"I'll try," I said. "Where's Stella? She's a pain in the ass, but when she worked here, she made a good sandwich now and then. Maybe she'd work for you again. Give her something to do."

"Oh, she's got a new man," Ray said.

"*What?*" I said. "I thought she was going to die loving Daddy forever."

"Forever is a long time for Stella," Ray said. "Long time for anyone."

"Who's the lucky guy?"

"Some flatlander from New Hampshire. How she met him, I don't know. She's been living in the mountains with him. Seems like a nice guy. They been down a couple of times to check on the house. Not sure why it's empty. She could rent it."

"Who knows why she does or doesn't do anything," I muttered.

"Stella ain't that bad, Florine," Ray said.

"Right," I said. "Well, we have to get going. Hope you find someone to work."

The rest of the day was filled with chasing kids, feeding kids, putting kids down for naps, getting them up, keeping them out of trouble, and pacing back and forth until four p.m. I thought about Ray's offer, a lot. I pictured myself ringing up customers, having little chats and cracking jokes, directing new customers and tourists toward the delicious bread I would bake, or toward my knitted goods.

But over all of that, I listened for Bud's truck. I was in the kitchen serving up some of Ida's leftover spaghetti to the kids when I heard it chug to a stop in front of the house.

I leaned against the sink as he walked through the door. We locked eyes when he paused at the doorway to the kitchen until Arlee ran to him and grabbed his legs and he lifted her up and squeezed her tight. He walked over to Travis and kissed the top of his head. His hand lingered on his curls. When he looked at me again, his dark eyes a burnt-out blend of hurt, confusion, and love, I burst into tears and he came to me and held me. I held him right back, our bodies telling us things no phone calls ever could.

We spent suppertime as a family, Bud telling us about his week at work, talking to Arlee, playing with Travis, looking at me, and me watching him. I told him about Stella's new man.

"No shit," he said, and then covered his mouth as Arlee looked up at him.

"Bad word," she said.

"Seen Ma?" Bud asked.

"Not much," I said.

"She called me at the trailer."

"Of course she did," I said. "I would be surprised if she hadn't."

Hurt flashed through his eyes again, and he lowered them as he bent to finish his supper.

He put the kids to bed for me while I waited downstairs in a rocker on the porch. It felt almost like a first date with someone I didn't know well. Why, I thought, am I so nervous? This is my man. This is the man I love. My heartbeat picked up when I heard him cross the downstairs floors to join me. He sat down next to me and took my hand. We watched the afterglow of the winter's day fade away.

"How many times do you s'pose we've done this?" he said.

"Forever, it seems like," I said.

"I used to watch you rocking on the porch, after Grand died. I wanted to sit with you then."

"You had Susan."

"I did," he said.

"Why did you have her and not me?"

"Didn't want to get messed up in your shit. So much stuff was going on with you."

"Bud, we can make a life, together," I said. "You don't have to be a shit mechanic in a shit job . . ."

He let go of my hand. "What the hell are you talking about? You think what I do is shit?"

"Okay, here we go," I said. "Those were your words. I didn't say them. You did."

"When?" he said. "When the hell did I say them and why would I say them?"

"This is what happens when you're drunk."

"You're making this up," he said. "Why are you doing this?"

"I'm not making it up, Bud."

He got up.

"Don't leave," I said. "We have to talk about this."

He shook his head. "I can't believe I'd say something like that." He walked into the kitchen and opened the refrigerator. I knew he was looking for a beer. When he didn't find it, he shut the door, walked back onto the porch, and looked out the window again.

"So, I said I had a shit job?"

"Yes," I said. "You said you wished you'd done more with your life, like Susan had wanted you to do. You said that Robin reminded you of Susan."

"I did?"

"Yes," I said. "Do you want to do something else besides work on cars?"

"I've thought about it," he said.

"What?"

"I don't know. Susan thought I should get a business degree, but that don't do much for me. I like working on cars, I guess, until I think of something else."

"I saw Ray today," I said. "He was looking for someone to run the store for a couple of weeks so he could go on vacation."

Bud snorted. "You see me running a store?"

"Not you," I said. "Me. I thought about it all day. I could do it. Maybe not right now, but in the future. Robin and I talked about me selling my sweaters. I could take 'em up to Ray's, maybe. Get started selling them here on The Point."

"I don't know," Bud said. "What about Stoughton Falls? That's where my job is."

"I know," I said.

"Maybe you could get a job up there, in town."

"Maybe," I said, in a tone that lacked enthusiasm. Living in Stoughton Falls had worn pretty thin. "We haven't done so well up there," I said to Bud.

Before he could answer, Travis whined and I left to go see what was up. He was sitting up in his crib, his diaper soaked through into the sheets. While I changed him, I heard Bud go outside. I heard the truck door open, then shut, and then I heard Bud walk back through the house and go back to the porch.

I took Travis down and I handed him to Bud, who took him with something like a sigh of relief. "Empty hands are the devil's playground," he whispered to his son as they rocked back and forth.

We put Travis into his newly sheeted bed at around midnight. Back in our room, in our bed, Bud filled his hands with me, and then he filled me with himself, and we moved together with no space for questions or for fear.

40

Bud stayed sober for the whole weekend. He left Monday morning, feeling good, he said. No problem, he said. My heart broke as I waved him away up the hill.

On Wednesday night, Maureen shared supper with the kids and me. While I did dishes, she entertained them both. I puttered around, doing little chores. I finally got around to taking them upstairs to bed and I expected her to be gone when I came back downstairs again. But she had made herself a cup of cocoa and was sitting at the table.

"Whew," I sighed, sitting down across from her. "Thanks for the help."

"I love them so much," she said. "They make me laugh." She leaned in toward me, as if she were about to reveal a big secret. "Ma doesn't laugh much," she said, as if Ida might hear her. "It's pretty serious at home. But when the kids come down, she lightens up and I remember that part of her from when I was little."

"Life takes a toll," I said, thinking about Ida having to deal with Sam's battle. That would have taken her humor down a notch. My trials with Bud had changed my view of things. My insides sagged with the weight of the battle we faced. My thoughts must have shown on my face, because Maureen said, "Florine, I think Bud and you will be okay. He isn't our father."

"Drinking is drinking," I said. "Booze makes people do crazy things."

"It does. But Bud sees the world different than our Dad."

"How so?"

Maureen's face lit up. "Oh, Bud is so curious and interested in everything. His room used to be filled with posters of places to go. We would close our eyes and stick pins in a map of the world. Then we'd look those places up in the encyclopedia. He made model cars and airplanes, and he liked puzzles and games. He liked to build stuff, like birdhouses and boats. He likes to be busy. He loves to learn."

I knew some of the things about Bud that Maureen was telling me. Bud was curious. He loved tinkering and adventure. But this version of Bud seemed to have disappeared. The man I lived with now sat in front of the television and drank. Had being with me and the babies worn him down that much?

"How does that make him different from Sam, though?" I asked.

Maureen's hazel eyes darkened with sadness and memories. "Dad was older than your father. Florine, your father was so handsome!"

I nodded. "He was. Travis looks like him."

"He does. Anyway, Dad was older. He was tired most of the time. The fishing just beat him up. You know what makes me sad?"

"What?"

"I don't know what his dreams were. I asked Ma once, and she said he was a man who needed routine, a paycheck, and a family. Those were his dreams."

"Do you think we're holding Bud back?"

"No! No, I don't!" Maureen said. "He loves you more than anything. But . . ." She sat up straight and pressed her hands together as she thought about her next words. Then her eyes widened and she said, "You know what? I think he's afraid he's going to turn into Sam. I think he thinks that he has to stay away from here to keep that from happening. He hasn't figured out yet that it's not where he lives, it's his fear of being like Dad that's holding him back."

That made such sense to me a chill tickled my spine. "No wonder Ida is excited about you becoming a pastor," I said. "You'll make a good one."

"I love helping people," she said, her eyes shining. "I love that more than anything but Jesus. Anyway, I think Bud will figure it out."

"Well," I said, "you might just have hit on something."

The phone rang, and Maureen jumped up, hugged me, and left.

I picked up the phone and said, "Hello?"

Heavy breathing and television noise filled my ears.

"Hello?" I said. More breathing and noise.

"How come you haven't called me?" Bud finally said, his words tripping over each other. "You with someone else?"

My heart caved in. He was past dealing with.

"Yes," I said. "I was with Maureen. She stayed for supper and she just left."

"That's bullshit," Bud said. "You're with someone else."

"How has your day gone?" I asked, trying to change the subject.

"It didn't go good."

"That's too bad."

"You don't mean that," he said.

I stretched the loopy phone cord over to the kitchen table so I could sit down.

"What happened today that made it bad?" I asked.

He proceeded to tell me, using language that made even me fidget. A story about a customer and a car and a shouting match about a repair job he had done about two months earlier. My insides squirmed for the both of us, for the love we had for each other, and for this poison liquid shit storm that fouled up those feelings. Finally, he stopped raving and I guessed it was my job to say something.

"Guy sounds like an asshole," I said.

"It wasn't a guy. Didn't you listen? It was a woman. A dumb bitch that wouldn't know a transmission from a radiator."

"She sounds like an asshole," I said.

"Yeah, well," Bud said. "I got to piss. I'll call you later."

"I'm going to bed," I said. "We'll talk tomorrow."

"You trying to get rid of me?"

"You said you had to pee."

"Right. But you're trying to get rid of me."

"I'm tired," I said. "Been a long day for me too."

"Well, everyone's tired. You're tired. I'm tired. We're all fucking tired. You can take some time to talk to me."

"I can," I said, wanting to hang up more than anything I'd wanted to do in a long time. "Do what you have to do, and then come back."

Bud dropped the phone and I heard him shuffle down the hall to the bathroom. After a while, the toilet flushed and I tensed for the next round. I heard him walk back to the phone. He picked it up, said, "What the hell? Why's the fucking phone off the hook?" and hung up.

I got up very early the next morning, before our kids were up, and dialed our number at the trailer. The phone rang ten times before he picked up.

"Do you know what time it is?" he growled. "Who the hell is this?"

"Me," I said. "You hung up on me last night."

"Jesus, Florine."

"Two words that shouldn't be used in the same sentence, most likely," I said. "You did hang up on me. Last night, when you called, we talked for a while and you went off to the bathroom and then you came back and hung up the phone."

"What?" he said. "I did that? Goddamn." He didn't say anything for about thirty seconds. And then he croaked in a shaky voice, "I can't remember calling you."

"You did," I said. I told him about the rude customer and the car.

"I don't remember talking about that," he said.

Arlee called my name from the top of the stairs.

"I have to go," I said. "I love you, Bud. We'll talk tonight."

"Holy shit," he said, and hung up.

I thought about Maureen's revelation. It all made sense, but so what? The reasons why Bud drank wouldn't necessarily stop him from careening down the road to destruction. I could only hope he got a clue before that happened.

41

After that phone call, Bud sobered up for about a month. When he wasn't with us on the weekends, we talked on the phone for an hour a night during the week, even when there wasn't much to say. Sometimes, I sat and knitted, and listened to the television set while he watched it. "You still there?" he'd say, and I'd answer, "Yes."

Fridays after work, as soon as he could put the car into gear and step on the gas, he hustled down to The Point. We held tight to the time we had together. I learned to think in terms of minutes when he was with us, instead of dreading what might happen. We had the kids, so the present took up a lot of our time, which was good. But on Monday mornings, after I saw him off to Stoughton Falls, my fears for him crowded back in on me.

Winter looped back again. Snow and sleet snarled and snapped at April's attempts at spring. To avoid being completely cooped up, the kids and I spent time with Madeline and Archer, or with Ida.

Because we were stuck in the house so much, Arlee developed a talent for getting into precious things. One day, when my back was turned, I heard a crash in the living room. I ran from the kitchen to find her standing in front of the red ruby glass cabinet, eyes large as two suns. "Jesus, I'm sorry," she said. I almost laughed because it was the first full sentence she had ever said. But it didn't seem funny when I looked down and saw the sugar bowl that matched its red creamer lying broken into more pieces than I could count.

Patience, Grand said. *It's glass, Florine.* I took a deep breath. "Mama told you not to touch the cabinet."

"I know," Arlee said. Her lower lip trembled. Mine did too as I swept up part of Grand's legacy and dumped it into the trash.

That night, after the kids were in bed, I wrapped every piece of glass in newspaper and packed it all in a couple of sturdy boxes. When Bud came down on Friday night, we moved the boxes into the crawl space in the attic. Bert and Bud moved the empty glass cabinet upstairs to our room. It crowded us, but at least the kids wouldn't fall into it. I moved Travis's playpen into the space it left in the living room.

During the last two weeks of April, hard rains finally killed off winter. Those rains kept us inside some more. Although I adored my children, I ran out of ideas on how to entertain them, and the things they loved to do became tiresome for me. I was in real danger of dying of boredom.

"You can only play the same game for so long," Madeline sympathized, over at her house one day. "Dottie used to drive me crazy. Couldn't play by herself at all. Had to have company. Didn't like books. Wouldn't sit still. Hated dolls. Didn't like to color. Always on the move, always into something. Evie was much better, back then, anyways. She entertained herself pretty well."

"Dottie and I must have played together," I said.

"You were a funny little bug," she said. "You loved to twirl around and run. Dottie tried to boss you around, but after a certain point, you didn't take any shit. You'd smack her. She'd smack you back and then you both would bawl and run to Mama. Carlie and I laughed so hard at the two of you."

"What was Carlie like back then?" I asked.

"She was fun. She was only twenty-two or three, about the same age as you are now, so she was a few years younger than us, and full of piss and vinegar. She raced around and chased you two everywhere. She'd roll around on the grass like a kid. I loved to watch her. We got to be friends, but she always kept her distance from everyone but Leeman and your grandmother."

"What about Bud?" I asked.

"Oh, he was so serious," Madeline said. "He played trucks in his driveway with Glen, when Germaine brought him down. And once in a while, the four of us mothers got together and we sat and watched you all. That was a good time. Sitting there in the sun, not knowing what would happen to each of us and not caring."

"Well," I said, "we can sit on the lawn when spring decides to drop in for good." Madeline smiled, even as sadness clouded her blue eyes. Evie had moved out, gone to Portland with some friends. Told them all at home that she needed time to "figure things out." "What's to figure?" Madeline had asked me. "She's got a baby here. She should give him a chance. She'll regret it if she don't."

Back in the present she said, "It'd be nice to set on the lawn and watch the kids play. I wish Evie knew what she was missing. Every time Archer does something new, I write it down. I'm keeping a little diary for her, just in case she comes to her senses."

"Archer has you and Bert and Dottie," I said.

"Dottie's wild for him, and Bert thinks he walks on water. He's the boy Bert never had," Madeline said. "When Evie does come home, she plays with him, looks after him, but no more than anyone else. She holds back, like she doesn't want to love him. But I know my girl. She does have a heart."

Not everyone, I thought, is cut out for raising babies. But I didn't say that to Madeline. Not while she still hoped that Evie would come around. Much as I loved my own babies, there were days when I thought that everything had happened too fast. Still, would I change a thing? Not friggin' likely.

Bud drove down on Friday night and we spent a hectic two days with the kids, both of whom always went over the edge when Daddy came home. But this weekend seemed worse. He hollered at Arlee once, and when she burst into tears, he went off and cried.

He was tired. He'd had a fight with Cecil just before leaving for The Point about pay, hours, and everything else that went with his job. He wanted to be with us, but he needed to rest. I could see all this by the way his eyes darted around, looking for a way out. Early

Monday morning, he kissed me deep, held me, told me he loved me, and then got into the truck, threw it into gear, and left us behind.

He didn't call me Monday night at our usual time. At about nine p.m., I was wild with worry. At ten p.m. I decided to drive up to Stoughton Falls. I called Maureen to come and stay with the kids. As I hung up, the phone rang.

"Hey, cuz," Robin said.

"Hey," I said.

"Listen, Florine, not to worry, but Bud was brought into the ER."

I stopped breathing for a few seconds.

"Florine?"

"Is he okay? Is he hurt bad?"

"Not really, luckily. He's badly bruised and scraped up, but nothing is life threatening."

"What happened?"

"He was walking along the road in the dark, about a mile from your trailer, and someone hit him. He was thrown a ways, but he's a lot better than he could have been."

"What the hell was he—"

"He was drunk, Florine," Robin said. "He's half in and half out of it right now, but he'll be fully conscious tomorrow morning. Odds are he'll feel like a car hit him."

"I'll drive up," I said.

"Oh, honey, it's late," Robin said. "Wait until morning. I'll let you—"

"No," I said. "I'm coming to the hospital, as soon as I can get there."

"Right," Robin said. "I'd do the same thing. Please be careful."

Maureen found me throwing things into an overnight bag.

"What's wrong?" she said when she saw my face.

"Bud's in the hospital in Portland," I said. "But he's going to be okay."

"We should tell Ma," Maureen said.

"Yes," I said. "I guess we have to do that. Call her, please."

I wanted to be out of there before Ida showed up, but she was there almost before I finished saying "Call her." I gave both of them the details as I stood stiff with worry in the kitchen, holding two bags filled with god-knows-what in my hands.

Ida put her cold hands on either side of my face. "Be careful," she said. "Call when you get there."

"I will," I said, trying not to cry.

"No tears," she said. "You can't see to drive that way."

Before I left, I walked upstairs to plant kisses on the smooth cheeks of my babies. I closed my eyes and listened, and I wondered this: Is there anything so soft and strong as the sound of children breathing in their sleep? Calmed and torn, I left the house, got into the car, and headed for Portland.

Almost three hours later, I followed Robin down a shiny corridor. We turned right, then left, and we reached Bud's room. I walked past a curtained bed with a machine clicking, to Bud's section. A blanket of cuts, nasty scrapes, and violet bruises covered his face. He was sound asleep.

Robin put her hand on my shoulder and I let her hold me up for a few seconds.

"You need coffee?" she asked.

"Tea," I said. When she came back I broke my wedding vow to Bud to honor our secrets. I spoke about his struggles with alcohol, about his doubts, and about his fidgety nature. I told her how much I loved him and how I worried about him. I talked to her until someone paged her and she had to go.

I called Ida, who answered the phone so fast that I figured she must have been sitting on it. After I filled her in and we hung up, the hours ticked by and I wished I'd packed my knitting.

Bud opened his eyes at about five a.m. Confusion created lines in his face and for a second, I knew what he would look like when he got old, if he was lucky enough to get that far. I pushed the call button for help as he tried to move.

"Am I dead?" he moaned. I grabbed a little pink plastic puke bowl while a nurse turned him onto his side so that he could hurl his sore guts out.

42

I drove him back to the trailer the next afternoon. We didn't talk much. He slept, mostly, drugged by pain medication and exhaustion. That night, he stumbled out to the living room and collapsed onto the sofa. "Hell," he said. "I guess I fucked up this time."

"You almost died this time," I said. "And where's your wedding ring?"

He looked at his hand. "I don't know," he said. "Back at the hospital?"

"Are you asking me?"

"I don't know. I was hoping you'd know."

"Not my job to keep track of it."

"Florine, don't be mad. I'm not doing that good, in case you haven't noticed."

I just stared at him until he looked down at his lap and frowned. "I don't know where it is," he said softly. He looked at me. "I'm sorry. Sometimes I take it off. It might be at the garage, in the office."

"I'll check tomorrow," I said.

"Tomorrow? I can do it. I'm going to work."

"Bud, you're a mess. You're dizzy and you're hurt."

"I can work."

"You probably could, but I called Cecil and told him you'd had an accident. Told him you needed a few days to get back to normal."

"Jesus, what'd you say?"

"I didn't tell him you were drunk and you're lucky to be alive, and you've completely fucked up the nice couple that hit you by accident."

He stared at the television. "Can we watch something besides Tony Orlando?"

I got up and went into the kitchen. "You can watch your ass, for all I care."

"That's not nice, Florine," he said.

I whirled around and marched back to him. "Bud, you almost died last night. You almost died. Why? Because you were stupid and drunk. At this point, I don't care if I'm nice or not. I can't live my life or raise my kids worrying about your sorry ass or your self-pity. I don't have the energy for it. Even as short as a day ago, I was trying to figure out what would make you happy and make you stop drinking. Now I don't care. It's up to you, not me. You need to decide what makes you happy, and whether you want to live or die. The kids and I are moving on."

Dead silence as I dumped tomato soup into a pan and put it on the stove to heat. I wanted to throw the can at him or to run into the bedroom and slam the door, but I forced myself to stay in the kitchen, acting as if what had just come out of my mouth hadn't surprised the hell out of me. I stirred soup as Tony Orlando sang "Tie a Yellow Ribbon 'Round the Old Oak Tree."

"So . . ." Bud said. "You leaving me?"

"I'm leaving tomorrow to go to The Point. If you want to come, fine."

"I don't want the kids to see me like this."

"Then you shouldn't have been so damn numb."

"All right! I fucked up, big-time. I'll go home with you, tomorrow. Jesus."

"You don't have the right to get mad at me."

"What do I have the right to do?"

"Answer your own questions."

"I'll come home, but I still don't want the kids to see me."

"You can stay at Ida's house."

"Fuck I will."

"Fuck you will," I said. "You need quiet and sleep. At least for a couple of days."

"What's Ma going to say?"

"She's none too pleased."

"She knows?"

"'Course she knows. Who do you think is watching Arlee and Travis?"

"Damn," he said. "Can I have crackers with the soup?"

Early the next morning I drove us down to The Point. Puffy clouds in the light-blue sky soaked up pink rays from the rising sun. A hint of green played hide-and-seek in windrows of dead winter grass. It was a nice time of day to be traveling.

"Travis will be a year old in less than two weeks," I said. "Can you believe it?"

Bud didn't answer me for a few minutes. Then he said, almost too soft for me to hear him, "Was I ever this strong for you? Was I ever good for you?"

My heart broke at his words and I blinked back tears, because, as Ida had said, "You can't see to drive that way."

"Oh, Bud, all the time," I said. "Those times you've done things for me that you didn't want to do, but you did them anyway, because it was me. Those times you came and sat in Petunia with me because the damn car reminded me of Carlie. That time after my car accident, when I stayed at Daddy's house and you found me in the mud in his driveway trying to get over to Grand's house. You helped me get all set up to stay there. That time you drove me up to Crow's Nest Harbor on a school day so we could see the place where Carlie disappeared. That time you came out to the boat after Daddy died and took me back to The Point. When you took care of me when I was so sick. All those times. How strong is *that*?"

He put his hand on my knee, and then lifted it away and looked at his naked ring finger. "I can't even remember what I did with my ring," he said. "What if I can't beat this thing? What if I turn into some drunk that falls down and pisses his pants? What if I don't even know my own name?"

"That won't happen."

"How do you know? Christ, look at me."

"It's up to you, Bud."

As we drove down to Ida's house, I glanced to the left and saw cars parked at Daddy's. "Stella must be here," I said to Bud.

Arlee walked out of Ida's house and smiled up at the car.

"Oh shit," Bud said, sliding down in the seat.

"You are hiding from your almost three-year-old," I said. "What does that tell you?"

Arlee burst into tears when she saw Bud and she hid her face in my thighs. I bent down and looked at her, eye to eye. "Daddy got hurt, but he's all right. He probably needs a hug from you right now."

"I'm okay, honey," Bud said. "I have lots of boo-boos, but they're getting better."

Arlee touched the stitches on his left cheek. "How?" she asked.

"I went into the road and a car hit me by accident," Bud said.

"Don't go in the road," Arlee said.

Bud hung his head. "I know. I did a dumb thing," he said. "If you hug me, I'll feel better."

Arlee gave him a hug.

"Sofa's ready for you, Bud," Ida said from behind us. "Or bed."

"I want to go with Daddy," Arlee said to me.

"Sofa," Bud said. "Time for meds?" he asked me, hope in his eyes.

I left Arlee and Bud on the sofa at Ida's house, and I lugged my butterball boy up the hill. "You need to go on a diet," I told him.

As I fed him lunch, someone knocked at the door. "It's open," I called.

"Hello," Stella said as she walked into the kitchen.

"Wow," I said. "Look at you!" She looked amazing. She had to be fifty-three or fifty-four, as she had graduated high school with Daddy, and she looked great. Her wild black hair had been cut and styled so the curls framed her pale face. Her eyes shone a clear, soft gray. She had put on weight, and it looked good on her.

She smiled. "Well, thanks," she said.

"Heard you have a new man."

She blushed. "I do, Florine. Wasn't looking for anyone. Didn't want anyone, and then Bernard came into my life. I met him in Long Reach, believe it or not."

"That's good. Daddy wouldn't want you moping around."

"I'll always miss him, more than I can say, Florine. I'll always love him. There's no way I can't and there are days that all I do is see his face and hear his voice. But Bernard is a widower, and he understands what I go through along those lines."

"You and Bernard moving into the house?" I asked.

"Oh, no. That's what I came to talk to you about," she said.

For heaven's sake, Florine, ask the woman to sit down, Grand whispered.

"Have a seat," I said. "Want some tea?"

"No, thank you," Stella said. She sat down beside Travis, who reached out and grabbed her hair in his fist.

"That's his newest thing," I said. "Hope he's smoother than that when he starts going out with the ladies." I untangled his hand from her hair. "You hungry?" I asked.

"Oh, no," she said. She sighed. "Florine, I need to say something that's hard to say, but I hope you'll think about it."

"Seems we always have hard things to say," I said. "Nothing new there. Hit me."

Stella shook her head and smiled. "You know," she said, "you're more like your father than you probably will ever know."

I blinked back tears. "Yeah, well, tell me."

Stella took a deep breath. "Okay. Here's the thing. Bernard comes from New Hampshire, and he has a house on Lake Winnipesaukee. It's a beautiful home, and he wants me to live with him. He wants to marry me, Florine."

"I noticed that rock on your hand," I said. "I put two and two together."

"Yes. Well. The thing is, I won't be coming back here again. There are too many memories and too many reminders of a life I'm not living anymore. I want to spend what time Bernard and I have traveling and living on the lake."

"So, you're selling the house?" I said. "Damn."

Before everything in my childhood had gone to hell, that house had been my home. Now strangers would live there, and chances were, they would overpay for the view. That would trigger property assessments, which would increase the value of all the houses on The Point and raise taxes to a place where none of us would be able to afford to live there anymore. Damn.

Stella said, "I want to sell it, yes. I want to sell it to you for a dollar."

She shocked me stupid for about thirty seconds. I finally squeaked out, "*What?*"

"I want to sell it to you, for a dollar, and I'll take care of any expenses that go along with that."

"What? Why? *What?*"

"I know I could get a lot of money for it, but it would change the face of this place, and I want to leave it like I found it. I know you'll take care of it."

"What's the catch?"

"No catch," Stella said. "It's really your house anyway."

With all of our history, all of our fights, jealousies, resentments, vandalism, and assaults, our awkward truces, and everything else we'd put each other through, this was the strangest twist yet.

Stella reached over the table and placed her bejeweled, milk-colored hand with its perfect, red-polished fingernails on my bigger, rougher hand with its broken nails. "Look," she said, "Grand would approve of this. She'd say it's practical and that it makes perfect sense."

I nodded. "She would," I said.

"Well, then, think about it. I'm here, with Grace, for a couple of days while we figure out what to take and what to leave—or if you don't want anything in the house, we can move it all. Talk it over with

Bud. You've got some time. I'm not deciding anything until I hear from you."

Suddenly overwhelmed with something that felt suspiciously like gratitude, I decided to tell her something I'd kept from her since Daddy's death. "Daddy's not buried on the hill," I said. "We took him out to sea the night of his funeral."

Stella smiled. "I know," she said. "Billy told me, after a while. I still put flowers there every year." She got up, bent down, and kissed Travis's curls. She held out her hand to me and we shook on our upcoming deal. I saw her out and watched her walk back to the house.

My house.

43

Friday night, Bud hobbled up from Ida's at about midnight.
He woke me up out of a sound sleep with a gentle shake and
a whispered, "Florine."

I stared up at what I could see of his face in the murky dark.
"What's wrong?" I said. He pulled back the covers.

"Bud, I don't want to—"

"Come down to the porch. I want to talk to you," he said.

"Talk to me here."

"I don't want to whisper," he said.

I followed him downstairs even as sleep pulled me backward. We
walked through the living room, hall, and kitchen and ended up on the
porch in side-by-side rocking chairs. "Do you want some tea?" he asked.

"No, I want to go back to bed."

"What I have to say won't take long," he said.

"Okay, what?" I said. I yawned.

He drew in a ragged breath and let it out. "I called Billy today and he's
getting me into an AA meeting. I'm going, Florine. I can't lose you and
the kids. I know you want to live here and that's fine. I want to live with
you. I can figure something else out. If you want to work at Ray's, you can
work at Ray's. You can do whatever you want to do. Just don't leave me."

His eyes glittered in the small light cast by the half-moon hanging
high overhead.

I wanted to throw my arms around him and say yes, yes, yes, but instead, I said, "Go to the AA meeting. Let's take our time. I want to live with you too. You know the conditions."

"I know," he said. "You're being a hardass, and I guess you got a right to be. I guess that's one reason I love you. You got my word that what's been happening is going to stop. I promise."

"I don't care about your promises. I care about you being sober."

We rocked back and forth for a minute or so.

"You sending me back to Ida's?" Bud said.

"I am tonight," I said.

He stopped rocking and looked at me. "Okay," he said.

We kissed good night at the door and I watched him hobble down the path. It was all I could do not to call him back to me. Instead, I forced myself inside and walked upstairs.

"Mama?" Arlee called.

I walked into her room. Travis was sound asleep. "What is it?" I asked my daughter.

"I want Daddy," she said.

"He'll be home soon," I told her. We walked across the hall and cuddled for the rest of the night.

Ida let herself into the house early on Saturday morning. She stood and watched me try to cram sneakers onto Arlee's restless feet.

"I can do it," Arlee said, so I let her put them onto the wrong feet and tangle the laces before I untangled them and put them on the right feet. I double-knotted them, as my mother had done for me.

"I heard Bud leave last night," Ida said.

"Then I guess you heard him come back too," I said.

"I did," she said. "He's still in bed. The sleep will do him good."

Arlee pointed to her feet and said to Ida, "I did this myself."

Ida smiled. "You have a wonderful imagination," she said to Arlee.

"Do you want some tea?" I said.

"Love some," Ida said, and we went into the kitchen. I put on the kettle for her.

Travis, who had been crawling around his toys on the floor, followed his grandmother into the kitchen. When Ida sat down at the table, he pulled himself up. She set him on her lap. "Billy's coming down this morning to talk to Bud about things," she said.

I said, "Bud told me he called him yesterday. Said Billy was going to get him into an AA meeting."

Ida looked at me. "I called Billy a few days ago. Billy said Bud needed to take the first step. I'm happy he's done it."

I nodded. "How is Billy?"

"He's much better," Ida said. "Back to performing services."

"You took good care of him. He's lucky to have had you do that."

"Maureen helped. I think she has a crush on him. She's been moody since he left."

I'll bet, I thought. The phone rang. It was Robin, asking if she could come down to visit. She asked how Bud was doing. He was doing much better, I told her, and I would love to have her visit.

I hung up the phone and joined Ida, again. She said, "My son is lucky to be alive."

"Damn lucky."

"It's hard to know what to do. Obviously he can't handle hard liquor the way his father couldn't handle hard liquor. Sam blacked out too sometimes. Didn't remember what he had done or said."

"I know what to do, Ida. I expect Bud to shape up."

She nodded. "Of course you do. He's lucky to have a strong woman in his life."

"Two strong women," I said.

Ida looked down at Travis. He grinned at her and pulled her nose.

"Can I get a cup of coffee?" Bud said from the kitchen doorway.

"Daddy!" Arlee shouted, and ran to show him the sneakers she had tied.

Robin, Arlee, and I took a walk later that day, up over The Cheeks—soon to be *My* Cheeks—and up the path that led to the park. Little hunks of snow humped up here and there, but we kicked it aside and kept walking.

"You excited about California?" I asked Robin.

"For now, I guess it's where I want to be. It's nice to be near Dad, and I love Valerie."

"You might miss the seasons."

"I might."

"You might need somewhere to stay when you come to visit."

Robin smiled. "I might," she said.

"I might have a place for you."

"No offense, but your house is about filled up."

"I'm talking about Daddy's house."

"What do you mean?"

I told her, and we grabbed hands and jumped up and down.

"Me too," Arlee said, and we all jumped up and down. Then we walked on.

"You know, you should rent it out. You'll need the income. It shouldn't be empty," Robin said.

"I haven't even told Bud," I said. "We'll have to talk about what to do with it."

"You should have told him before you told me."

"I couldn't wait anymore. I only found out yesterday and I'm rolling it around in my head."

I wanted to show Robin my secret place, and so we skirted the brush and took the path that led to the Barringtons'. A large crow flew toward us. The closer it came, the lower it flew, until Robin and I ducked. The satiny brush of a black wing touched my cheek as the bird rose again.

"What the hell?" I said.

"Jesus crow," said Arlee.

"That was weird," Robin said. "In Ireland, crows represent war and death on the battlefield."

"That's gloomy," I said. "And we're not in Ireland."

"We're Irish. Your mother is Irish."

"I want to go, Mama," Arlee said.

"Me too," I agreed, and the three of us trotted back to the main path and walked to the bench. We watched the water flow for a few minutes, but we couldn't shake the creepy feeling surrounding the low-flying crow, so we headed back toward the house.

When we reached The Cheeks, Robin and I jumped down. As I reached up to help Arlee, we heard two women screeching at each other from Daddy's house.

"Don't you dare!" (Stella's voice.)

"Ain't yours to dare me." (Grace.)

"Grace, those are mine."

"No, they ain't. They never was."

"I want to get rid of them."

"Not yours to get rid of."

"What do you care? Please, give them to me."

"She should know."

"She doesn't need to know. She's got enough problems."

"I'm giving them to her."

Thumps in the house, then a yell, as if someone had been hurt. The front door opened and the screen door whined, and then slammed. Slammed again. "*No!*" Stella hollered. "Give those to me."

"Let's see what's going on," I said, and Robin, Arlee, and I ran around the house to the sight of the two sisters tug-of-warring at a wad of paper.

"Hey," I yelled, "cut it out." Stella and Grace stopped and looked at me. Another door slammed as Bud crossed the road from our house. Billy, who had evidently come to visit Bud while Robin and I had been walking, followed him.

"What the hell is going on?" Bud said.

Grace ignored him. "I got some letters from someone to your mother," she said to me.

"They're nothing," Stella said. "I was going to burn them."

"Whatever they are, they belong to Florine. Hand them over," Bud said. With his busted-up face and battered body, no one sane would have argued with him. The trouble was, neither sister wanted to be the first to let go, so Bud grabbed the letters from between them. A couple of them fluttered to the ground and Stella snatched them up. Bud held out his hand.

"They're nothing, really, Bud," she said.

"Yes, they are," I said. "What are they?"

Stella sighed. "Oh, Florine," she said.

"What are they, Stella?" I yelled.

"Oh, they're stupid, really. They're letters to Carlie from Edward Barrington. If she'd wanted you to have them, I'm sure she would have given them to you."

"Maybe she would have if she hadn't disappeared, Stella. Give Bud the letters."

"Florine, stay calm," Billy said. I glared at him.

"Mama," Arlee whimpered, and I lowered my voice.

"Are those the letters someone has been sending me?" I asked.

"Oh, honey," Stella said. Her face crumpled and she sat down on the front steps. "Why does it matter now?" But she handed them over to Bud.

"Thank you, Stella," Billy said. Bud scowled at all of us and said, "I'm going back across the road." He limped away, Billy talking to him as they walked.

I said to Stella, "Anything having to do with Carlie will always matter. Always."

"I sent you some," Grace said.

I stared into her plain face. "What?" I said.

"I sent you some," she said.

"You sent them? Why the hell did you do that?" I said.

Grace shrugged. "You been so mean to Stella."

"What?" Stella and I said at the same time.

I walked toward Grace. "What's between Stella and me has nothing to do with you." Blood does boil. I know it does, because mine was about to blow out of the top of my head.

Grace said, "You're an awful person. Treated your father so bad he died early. You walk around this place like you own it, but this is Stella's house and you made her feel so bad . . ."

Stella said, "Grace . . ." just as I slapped her across the face with my right hand, and then my left one. Arlee screamed, "Mama!" as Grace, who evidently had been a boxer at some time in her mysterious life, smacked me in the left eye, hard, and I went down.

Then Bud was somehow there again with Billy, who backed the Drowns sisters into the house while Bud helped me up and hustled Robin, a shrieking Arlee, and me into Grand's house.

44

Robin went for the freezer and cracked open a couple of trays of ice cubes. She rinsed out a clean dishcloth and tied some cubes inside of it. "Here," she said. "Hold this against your eye."

I did what she said and bent down to Arlee's level. My little girl was shaking.

"Mama's okay," I said. "I shouldn't have hit Grace." Arlee wrapped her legs around my waist. I picked her up and we both sat down on a kitchen chair.

"Anyplace else hurt?" Robin asked.

"My hands sting," I said.

"Fuck were you thinking?" Bud growled.

"Grace sent her the letters," Robin started to explain.

"I'm not asking you, Robin," Bud said. "I'm asking my wife."

"Grace sent those letters," I repeated.

"Nut job," Bud said. "Nut freakin' job." His eyes crackled with anger. "Look," he said, "only you would pick a fight with the craziest woman on Earth. And I'm so damn sick of all of this. We got to figure this out. You want me to move on and quit drinking? Okay, then, you get this shit settled, so we can both just stop fiddle-farting around with 'where the hell is Carlie?' Christ on a crutch, this needs to go away."

"Daddy's mad," Arlee observed from my lap.

"I don't blame him," I said. "He's right."

"You think I'm right?" Bud said.

"Yes," I said.

"Well, Hal-the fucking-lujah." He threw his arms into the air, and then flinched.

"Bud, how are you feeling?" Robin asked. "I drove down to see how you were."

"Like I've been hit by a car, but otherwise good."

"If you don't mind, I'd like to look at your scrapes and cuts before I leave."

Bud nodded. "Thanks," he said. "Thanks for everything."

The front door opened and closed. Billy walked into the kitchen with Stella and Grace in tow. The hair on the back of my neck stood up. "Are you kidding me?" I said to Billy.

Billy held his hand up. "Be charitable," he said.

"Why should I? They—"

"Because Grand would want you to," Billy said.

Dammit, I thought. Yes, she would.

"I want to explain," Stella said.

Robin said, "Well, we were just saying that we'd all like to get this settled, so why don't you two sit down at the table."

"Just talk. Then go," I said. I said to Arlee, "Mama's going to talk to Stella and Grace. Think you can go in the other room and color for a little while? Maybe you can make Robin a nice picture?"

Arlee stomped over to Grace and hit her leg. "Leave Mama alone," she said.

"Say you're sorry to Grace," Bud said, picking her up. "You should never hit anyone, and you shouldn't swear."

"Mama did."

"That was bad for Mama to do," I said. "Say you're sorry to Grace."

"You first," Arlee said to me. Billy ducked his head to hide a smile.

I frowned at Grace and said, "I'm saying I'm sorry because it's the right thing to do."

"Least you're doing it," Grace said, and I fought to keep myself in the chair.

"Now, Arlee," I said, taking a deep breath, "tell Grace you're sorry."

"Sorry," she said to Grace.

"Okay then," Robin said. "Can we all sit down?"

We all sat.

"Everyone set?" Billy asked.

"Let's get this over with," Bud said.

"I'll be quick," Stella said. "I found these letters upstairs in the house, tucked away in back of an eave, when Leeman and I were turning it into a sewing room." She looked up at me. "I didn't want to show them to Leeman. It would have broken his heart." She touched the pile of letters. "I only read one. I don't know what the rest of them said because I didn't open them. But the one I looked at was full of . . . well, things that . . ."

"I'm not going to read them," I said. "I'll turn them over to Parker. He already has her letters to him. I didn't read those either. Why didn't you burn them if you didn't want Daddy to know about them? Why didn't you throw them out?"

"Oh, I was going to do it," Stella said. "But someone held me back." She looked at me. "Your mother haunts that house," she said. "Everywhere I turn, it seems like she stands just outside the corner of my eye. I swear, sometimes, I can smell her perfume. I've tried to paint her out, redo the house to confuse her, anything to get rid of her, but of course I never will because she always sat first in Leeman's heart. After Leeman died, she didn't go away. And she's still there. It was her that told me to keep the letters. Somehow, Grace got a hold of them and thought she'd do something stupid and wrong."

"Wasn't wrong," Grace said.

"It was," Stella said, sharp as sleet. "It was very wrong. You had no right to do it. And I want you to apologize to Florine, Grace."

"I did it because she—"

"I don't care what you think she did, Grace," Stella said, raising her voice. "Say you're sorry."

Grace pressed her lips together.

"Say you're sorry."

A tear rolled down her stony cheek. "I'm sorry," Grace whispered, and she got up and left the house. I saw her walk across the road from the kitchen window, her head down, her arms at her sides.

"I can't figure her out," I said.

Stella sighed. "I know. No one can. She's the oldest out of four of us sisters. She jumped off a cliff on a dare near our house when we were small. She's lucky she lived, but she hurt her brain. My sisters and I take turns taking her in."

"We never talked about your family," I said.

"We never talked about a lot of things," Stella said. "I regret that. I really do. Anyway, we all love Grace, but we've all had to apologize for her actions at one time or another. Grace can function—she drives and so on—but she doesn't have the personality to be able to work for long without offending someone. She's very blunt."

"No kidding," I said.

"She's overly protective and we have to be careful what we say when we're around her. She's also nosy and she watches too many detective stories on television. She found the letters during one of her stays with me. I told her they were private, but she knows we have a history. I guess she thought she'd shake you up by sending the letters to you."

"What about the postmarks? There were different postmarks," I said. "From where?"

"Lewiston. Freeport. Long Reach."

"Frances lives in Lewiston. Judy lives in Freeport."

"That explains it," I said.

"I'm sorry," Stella said again. "I'm always sorry around you for something."

"It'll be dull around here without you," I said. Stella looked up and we shared a smile.

"You too," she said. "Then you want the house? Have you talked it over with Bud?"

"I haven't had a chance," I said. I looked at him. "Stella wants to sell us the house . . ."

Bud snorted. "We can't afford it."

"For a dollar."

He looked at Stella. "What?" he said. "*What?*"

"That's what I said," I said. "She's getting married to someone who lives in New Hampshire. She wants us to have the house."

Bud thought about that for a few seconds. "Buy it," he said. A twinge of pain crossed his face.

"You need to rest," Robin said.

"I know, but I can't get up," Bud said. "You're all killing me."

Robin scraped back her chair and went over to him. I stood up as he did. He let Robin take his elbow. The stair risers creaked as they took it slowly.

Stella stood up. "It's settled then. I'll have movers take away the stuff and the house will be cleared out and you won't have to bother with it."

"Just take what you want," I said. "I'll deal with the rest later."

"Good," Stella said.

Forgive, Grand said. I sighed. "Why don't we forgive each other before you go?"

Stella said, "I would love that. Should we shake hands?"

"That's okay," I said. We smiled at each other and she left.

Billy said, "That was a good thing you did. Now you can go forward."

"Grand made me do it," I grumbled. "Thank you for talking to Bud," I said. "I hope it takes."

"I hope so too," Billy said. "He knows what he's got in his life, and he's determined to keep it. He knows you mean what you say. He loves you. You're one of a kind."

I blushed and looked down at the pile of unopened letters. The risers creaked again as Robin came back downstairs.

"What are you going to do with these, really?" Robin said.

"I'm going to give them to Parker, just like I said."

"I don't think we've met," Billy said to Robin.

"I'm Florine's cousin, Robin Collins," she said.

"I'm Billy Krum. Baptist preacher, lobsterman, carpenter, cancer survivor, world-class sinner, poker player, and, let's see, anything else?"

"An angel," Arlee yelled. She ran to him and he snapped her up.

"No angel," he said to her. "Not by a long shot, pumpkin."

"Come on upstairs, Billy," Bud called from the upstairs landing.

"On my way," Billy said.

"Tea?" I asked. "Coffee?"

"No thanks," Billy said. "Nice to meet you, Robin," he said, and he headed upstairs.

Robin looked at me. "A lot just happened," she said.

"Yeah. A lot always happens," I said.

Arlee said, "I want ice cream." Travis woke up and whined for me. I headed upstairs to get him.

45

Parker came by and picked up the letters and said he'd get around to reading them when he could. A messy case involving warring lobstermen was taking up a lot of his time, he said. I said, I'm busy anyway and got back to my life. Stella and Grace left the house the day after our little showdown. Robin went back to Portland to finish her school year. Bud went back to Stoughton Falls to work after a week off.

"You going to be okay?" I asked as we stood by the pickup on the morning he left.

"I'm going to a meeting tonight and every frigging night this week. Billy got me all set up. I'll call you when I get back to the trailer."

"Please, please call me if you need me," I said.

"I need you all the time," he said, putting his forehead against mine.

"I love you," I said. "Remember, call me."

He called me for three nights straight. "This is hard," he said.

I decided to join him on Thursday. I left the kids with Ida and Maureen and drove to Stoughton Falls. I had supper waiting when he got home from his meeting. He was thoughtful and quiet, and told me that he had found a sponsor he could talk to when he needed to dull his cravings. Billy had called him every night that week, just as I had, to check on him. We made love for the first time in a while. We were careful with each other, tender. Afterward, we held each other until daylight.

I scoured the trailer for his wedding ring on Friday morning before I left for The Point, but I couldn't find it. He had already looked through the truck and the shop and had come up with nothing. He felt bad about losing it, and I missed seeing the bright band of gold circling his rough, grease-stained ring finger. We decided that in June, on our wedding anniversary, we would buy him a new one.

Per our usual routine, he joined us for the weekend, and then drove back to Stoughton Falls on Monday morning. One Monday night, though, he surprised us by showing up back to The Point. "Daddy's here," I said to the kids, and Arlee ran, while Travis crawled, to the door. Bud came in and I heard him talking to them, giving them kisses and hugs, and then he walked through the kitchen, brushed right by me, and picked up the phone.

"Hello, honey, how are you?" I said. He waved at me.

"Billy? This is Bud," he said. "Yeah, you busy? . . . That'd be good."

He hung up the phone and walked over to me. He kissed me, hard, and then let me go.

"What's going on?" I asked.

"Well," he said, "I got fired."

"Why?"

"Evidently I carry gloom and doom around all day," Bud said. "Cecil said the customers been complaining that I'm not real friendly to 'em. He said I got too much going on in my personal life to pay attention to my work. I says, 'Is my work bad?' He says, 'No, but your attitude is. I'm going to have to let you go.' So he did. Well, I'm yours, honey. I'm meeting Billy at the Lobster Shack. Want anything?"

The Lobster Shack. Every time someone brought up the name, thoughts of Carlie thundered through the halls of my memory. I remembered the times I had hung out there while she worked. How I loved to watch her and Patty have fun and flirt with customers. Those two had been such a team.

"No," I said. "Good luck."

I tried to feel bad about him getting fired, but I was overjoyed. Maybe, I thought, this will work out. Maybe Bud will be able to handle living here. The Point will be our sun and we'll revolve around it; go out into the world and come back here, for always.

Maureen joined the kids and me for a mac-and-cheese supper. I didn't tell her about Bud's job. I did tell her Arlee had called Billy an angel and she smiled. "He's not," she said. "But he might be closer to God than the rest of us." Her smile stretched to a grin. "At least, I think so."

Bud walked back into the kitchen about halfway through supper.

"Dish up a plate," I said.

"Ate," he said. He sat down. "Well, Billy's got me working with a carpentry crew. And he wants me to sand, caulk, and paint his boat too. Get it ready to go out. Wants me to be his stern man on the *Blind Faith* for the summer." He filled Maureen in. "Guess you can tell Ma," he said to her. "It'll save me a trip."

"Billy can use the help," Maureen asked. "I could help too, if he needs it."

"We're all set. We got it planned out for the summer. You stick to the Bible and Sunday school."

Maureen's fork clattered onto her plate. "I can do anything I want to do, James Walter. I don't have to just 'stick' to anything. Don't you tell me what I should be doing."

"Calm down," Bud said. "Billy needs you at church. He said so, while we was talking about what needs to be done. He says you're his right-hand girl. He says he feels like he's part of the family, what with the way you took care of him last winter."

"Oh," Maureen said. "Well, that's all right then." She helped me with the dishes and left. I put the kids to bed and joined Bud on the sofa.

Bud said, "You know what I've been thinking? Everything in life is a deck of cards. You got your kings, aces, queens, jacks, jokers, and numbers that stand for the rest of us."

"What made you think of that?"

"I don't know. It's as good an explanation as anything."

"What number am I?"

"I'd say you're an eight."

"Why?"

Bud smiled. "It's curvy on the top and curvy on the bottom," he said. He leaned over and kissed me. Then, he said, "We got to move out of the trailer." That turned me on so much I unzipped his fly, right then and there. Afterward, with television light from *The Six Million Dollar Man* reflecting off my bare butt, we decided where and when to move things from the trailer.

~

At seven on Tuesday morning, I found myself standing in front of Daddy's empty house. I took a deep breath, unlocked the front door, and entered the kitchen, where my childhood hit me like a ton of bricks.

Stella and Grace had left most of the furniture, along with dishes, linens, and day-to-day items I could choose to keep or to throw away. I walked into my old bedroom and remembered the night I escaped through my window to go explode firecrackers at the Barringtons' with Dottie, Bud, and Glen. I walked into the bathroom and could almost hear Daddy puking up his guts every morning after trying to drink away his grief for his absent Carlie. The kitchen, where he and Carlie had waltzed to "Love Me Tender." Here was the living room, where I had fallen asleep on the sofa night after night after Carlie had gone, while Daddy drank himself down to hell. Daddy's workshop, which I had swept up before Stella had first come to dinner. I walked upstairs to the two tiny rooms that once had served as storage. Stella had turned them into sweet spaces that would make fine little bedrooms.

Something thumped somewhere in the house and I held my breath. "Are you still here?" I asked. No answer, but something warm moved through me, from the bottoms of my feet to the top of my head. Whatever it was, it left me crying a soft rain of tears. They wet the dust in my soul and sank into my heart, and I knew that my old house and I would get along just fine.

46

May 1, Travis's first birthday, was clear and warm. While he took his nap before his little party, I threw together a spaghetti sauce and let it simmer while Arlee and I went outside to the side garden to check daffodil and tulip bulbs.

A car headed past the house and parked in the Buttses' driveway. My smile showed up before Dorothea Butts even got her car door open. Arlee dashed across the road before I could say no, me on her tail.

"Hi there, you two!" Dottie called. Arlee flew at her and Dottie caught her up in her arms. "When the hell did you get so tall?" she asked.

"You remember it's Travis's birthday?" I asked.

"'Course I do. Couldn't forget that one. You home for good?"

I smiled. "Looks like it. Come over when you get settled."

Madeline stepped outside, carrying Archer. He shrieked for joy when he saw Dottie. She headed straight for him, with Arlee following right on her heels.

"Send her home when you get tired of her," I called.

"Will do," Dottie said, and they all went inside.

At five p.m., Billy, Ray, Ida, Maureen, Bert, Madeline, Dottie, and Archer and our family filled the house with spaghetti, cake crumbs, melted ice cream, and party hats that Dottie had dug out of somewhere.

Travis didn't have a clue that the whole thing was about him, but he ate it up anyway.

It was over fast, presents strewn everywhere throughout the house, people stepping over babies and toys and boxes and ribbon to bring me their dishes from wherever they had found to sit. Ray brought me a soupy ice cream and cake plate. "Thanks," he said. "You get a chance, you come up to see me."

"I come up there too much already," I said. "Maybe we should start dating."

"I'm too young for you," he said. "I told you before, I need someone to work at the store. Part-time, I know you got the kids, but I need help. Think you might be interested?"

"I am," I said. "And I have some ideas I want to talk to you about."

"Well, we'll see," Ray said. "Anyways, let me know soon, will you? Don't play hard to get and make me wait."

&

"I think I'd like playing store," I said to Dottie later, as we rocked on the porch.

"You would," Dottie said. "You can add, you like to keep things neat, you can make sandwiches, you're a wiseass, and you don't put up with bullshit. Kind of what Ray does every day."

"How much he going to pay you?" Bud asked from his chair.

"Haven't got a clue," I said. "Just asked me to come up and talk to him."

"Make sure he pays you decent money. We could use it," he said.

"Did you finish up the strawberry ice cream?" Dottie asked him.

"Scraped it clean."

"Bastard," said Dottie. "S'pose I'll have to have some more butter-scotch."

"That's gone too."

"Cake? Is there some cake left?"

"That was gone before everyone left," Bud said. "Got to be quicker than that."

"I wonder," I said, "if we could sell other things at the store."

"Like what?" Dottie asked. "I'm heating up the leftover spaghetti."

"A lot of us make stuff. Ida does the quilts, I knit, and Madeline paints. What if we were to make space for crafts and things like that?"

"Where would you put that stuff?" Bud asked. "Store's cramped as it is."

"Maybe upstairs. We could put it in one of the rooms, or something. And, maybe, we can put in an oven so I can bake bread up there. Imagine how nice that would smell when you walked in?"

"When you going to have time to do that?" Bud said. "You're only working part-time, and you got to watch the store."

"Not all at once," I said. "Over time."

"Kids, me, house, store," Bud said. "Not enough of you to go around."

"Maybe not," I said, "but like you just said, we can use the money. And at Christmastime, we can sell wreaths up there."

"Got any cheese left?" Dottie called from the kitchen.

❧

A few days later, I went up to Ray's with some of my ideas listed on a sheet of paper.

He took them from me and pursed his lips. He didn't say anything for a long time. Finally, I said, "Well? What do you think?"

He looked at me over the top of his glasses. "I think you been thinking about this backwards," he said. "All I want is for someone to work behind the register and to make sandwiches; to run the place when I want a friggin' day off. Let's start there, if that's okay with you. And though I'm sure time will prove me wrong, I'd be your boss. To start with, you'd be working for me."

"Well, you got me all excited about this," I said.

"One thing at a time, is what I'm saying," Ray said. "And there's one catch."

"What?"

"You got to get that thing people who quit high school and live to regret it get."

"A GED. I got it covered. I'm looking into it. Gonna work on it this summer."

"Well, I guess I can break you in while you get that GD."

"GED. Right," I said.

"So, when can you start?"

We worked out a few hours a couple of days a week, to begin with. I had to talk to Ida first, since she or Maureen would be taking care of the kids. I really had to get cracking on the GED. My mind spun like a waterspout as I walked down the hill to home. A breeze leapt up from the harbor as if hounds were chasing it. It kissed my cheeks and flung strands of my hair into my face.

I moved to the side of the road when I heard a car engine behind me. A Volkswagen bus passed me and Evie waved at me from the passenger's side. Painted on the back of the faded yellow bus were the words PEACE and LOVE. It stopped in front of the Butts house and Evie jumped down and ran inside. A thin red-haired haired man followed after her. Soon, loud voices came from the house. "Doesn't sound good," I muttered to myself as I went into the house and helped Bud bundle up the kids for a visit to Popham Beach. While we were inside, the bus farted its way back up the hill.

"Evie don't tend to stay long, does she?" Bud said, and we headed out. We took the last parking space near old Fort Popham and spent a couple of hours walking that glorious beach, along with half of Long Reach. Shiny seals messed around in the briny water where the Kennebec River blended with the Atlantic Ocean. The kids threw wet driftwood into the waves and ran like hell from the incoming surf. We ate lunch on a bleached log and looked out over the Atlantic, soothed by the vastness of it. When the kids got cranky we stuffed them into the pickup and followed the line of cars back up the road. At home, we put Arlee and Travis down for naps and went outside to sit in the side yard. We hadn't even lowered our butts into the chair seats when Glen's truck skidded to a stop in front of our house. He strode into the yard, a big grin on his face. "How's it hangin'?" he said, just like the old Glen might have done before Vietnam.

"Fine and loose," Bud said. "How's it hangin' with you?"

"Tight and nasty," Glen said.

"Should I be here?" I asked. Glen pulled me from my chair and wrapped me in a bear hug. "You thirsty?" I asked him.

"Wouldn't mind a beer or two," he said.

I looked at Bud. He looked back at me.

Glen caught the look. "Or coffee, maybe? Been a long drive."

I was inside when I heard Dottie and Glen shout hellos at each other. Shortly after that, she barged into the house.

"Shhh," I said. "Kids are sleeping."

"Sorry," she whispered. "Hey, did you notice Glen's kind of normal? He on drugs?"

"Well, if he is, I hope he stays on them," I said. "What's the latest with Evie?"

"Oh, Christ," Dottie said. "She's decided she wants to live with Albert—that's the guy she's been with—in Portland. She wants to take Archer along with them. Albert's in some band and Evie says he'll support her and Archer."

"Is Albert Archer's father?"

"Hell, no. He's the latest loser to go gaga over Evie. Madeline said that no, that wasn't going to happen. Told her that it was better for Archer staying with us, and if Evie wanted to fight it, she was going to file a runaway report and Evie would have to come home until she was eighteen."

"I imagine that went over big."

"Oh, wicked big. Evie said we could all fuck ourselves, that she was Archer's mother and that she was going to take him back, that she'd be back with the sheriff to pick him up. Madeline said, 'Over my dead body.' Evie flounced out the door in a cloud of smoke. Albert took off after her. 'Peace,' he says to us. 'Peace.' Peace, her ass, I say.

Madeline won't let Archer out of her sight. She and Bert are trying to figure out whether to get the cops to bring Evie back home, or let it lie until Evie comes around."

"That likely?"

"Nope. Anyways, right now she's with someone who don't appear to have the brains God gave an ant, but at least she's warm and dry."

"Coffee?"

"We ain't drinkin' anymore?" Dottie said. "On account of Bud?"

"Don't want to do it in front of him."

"Okay with me," Dottie said. "By the way, I broke up with that Addie. She only liked me because I'm a famous bowler."

"A ten-pin groupie?"

"Yep. I got 'em."

We carried coffee and store-bought cookies out to the boys. I sat down next to Bud. I took his hand for a minute before squeezing it and letting it go. I grabbed the grass under my feet with my toes and tugged spring up and into my heart.

"I feel better than I have in a long time," Glen said.

"You look pretty good," I said. "What changed?"

"Well, I'm on drugs," Glen said.

"What'd I tell you," Dottie said to me.

Glen gave her a look. "Yes, I'm on drugs. They help with whatever's wrong with my head. I might not ever get back to normal, but it's a start."

"When the hell were you normal?" Dottie asked.

Glen smiled and shrugged. "Traveling around this state changed up my head. Christ, I went everywhere. Might be a Maine Guide. I'd like to do that, I think, take people places to go hunting, or fishing or hiking, or whatever else they do. Talked to a few rangers and a couple of wardens. They told me how to go about it. Might move up north. Not that many people, just thousands of miles of woods."

"You got a girl yet?" Dottie asked.

"No," Glen said. "You want the job?"

Dottie and I laughed.

"What's so funny? I'm a fine catch. I'm only a little crazy and I got a great—"

"Truck," Bud said.

I looked at Dottie, and she nodded. "Tell 'em," she said.

"Dottie plays for the other team," I said.

She rolled her eyes. "Bowls. I bowl for the other team."

"What the hell does that mean?" Glen asked.

"I'm a lesbo," Dottie said.

Bud and Glen looked at each other. Glen held out a hand as Bud fished out his wallet and slapped a twenty into his palm.

"What's going on?" I asked.

"Glen said she was a lesbo about five years ago. I didn't think she was," Bud said.

"But, Dottie, the offer to be my girl still stands," Glen said. "Might solve everything."

"What do you mean?" I said.

"You gay?" Dottie asked.

Glen blushed. "No," he said. "Never mind. Congratulations for being a lesbo, Dottie."

"Thanks," she said. "And congratulations to you for having a big truck."

Bud stood up, stretched, and looked toward his mother's yard, where the *Florine* was berthed. "Speaking of being your girl," he said to Glen, "what you doing with her?"

"Oh, I'm going out this summer," Glen said. "Going up north next winter, though. You want, you come up with me for some time."

Bud looked at me. I shrugged. "I'm not your keeper," I said.

"Hell you're not," Bud said, but smiled when he said it.

"And you're not mine," I said.

"Nope," he said.

That weekend, we cleaned and moved out of the trailer in Stoughton Falls. The four of us, Glen, Dottie, Bud, and I, made short work of it. I left the grass a little long, and I did feel bad about not putting together the garden I had dreamed up, but it was the only thing I felt bad about. I would not miss anything else about it.

Bud and I celebrated my birthday up in Long Reach, where we went to an Italian restaurant and saw a movie at the same theater Daddy and I had gone to shortly after Carlie had gone. That night so many years before, restless and stunned, we hadn't stayed for the whole movie. We had gone back to the truck, where Daddy had said to me, *"Florine, the only thing we can do is take it day to day. You got school and I got work. We got to get on with both of them. You with me?"* We had done that, he and I, longing for an absent woman we both loved more than each other. He had gone on to the arms of someone else, and I had, with the grace of Grand, Jesus, and everyone else on The Point, tripped and fallen into marriage and motherhood.

But this night with Bud didn't hold painful memories. I sat through a whole movie holding the hand of the man I would love for the rest of my life.

Life was going well. Our friends were happy, Bud was working hard on staying sober, and we were thinking about our future. Our children slept in their beds, watched over by a loving grandmother and a sweet aunt.

And then, ten days later, my mother came home.

47

Arlee spent the early part of Tuesday morning, May 28, being pissed off at me because I wouldn't let her wear the purple velvet dress that Robin had bought for her in California. She had sized it one up for Arlee, so that she would be able to fit into it for the upcoming Christmas. That morning, I made the mistake of trying it on her to see if it fit. Not only did it fit, she would outgrow it before Christmas.

"We'll find someplace special to wear it when the weather gets colder," I promised her, and I hung it back up in her closet.

"Why?" she asked.

"It's hot, and it's not a play dress," I said.

"Why?" she asked.

"Because you can't," I said, and walked away with her brother in my arms. "Mean Mama," followed me all the way down the stairs. "Yeah, yeah, yeah," I mumbled. "Yeah, yeah, yeah."

I set Travis on the kitchen floor while I turned around to put the kettle on for a midmorning cup of tea but a sudden retching sound turned me around in a hurry. He sat covered in vomit. "Oh, honey," I said, "what the hell is that?"

He began to cry and I picked him up, holding him away from me as I carried him up to the bathroom. The telephone rang.

"Not a good time," I said to the phone.

I bathed Travis, dressed him in clean clothes, and hoped he wouldn't puke again. He whined and I cuddled him close.

I peeked into Arlee's bedroom. There she stood, in front of the mirror, admiring her little madam self, still wearing her purple velvet dress. "Are you kidding me?" I hollered. "I told you no!"

"Don't care," she hollered back.

Travis whimpered and I lowered my voice.

"Take it off," I said to Arlee.

"No."

The phone rang again.

"Change it," I said. I carried Travis downstairs and grabbed the receiver. "Hello," I said. "Warners' nuthouse." I waited for a laugh but got a pause instead.

It was Parker Clemmons. "You busy right now?" he asked.

"Hah!" I laughed. "Yes, but I am every day. Why?"

"I'd like to come talk to you," he said.

"Oh—you read Edward's letters," I said. "I didn't touch them. They—"

"Florine," he said. The quiet tenderness in his voice made my insides go hollow.

"What is it?"

"Is Bud with you?"

"He's at Billy's. What's the matter?"

"You might want to have him come home."

"Why?"

"I'm on my way over to talk to you. I have some news."

"Why can't you tell me now?"

"I want to tell you in person," he said.

"Did . . . Did . . . Carlie?"

"I want to talk to you and explain what's happened. We've been through a lot, you and I, and I want to talk to you proper."

"Okay," I said, and I hung up. Travis put his hands on my face and patted my cheeks. I buried my head against him and took deep, deep breaths while my heart hammered in my ears.

Bud came home and brought along Billy, Ida, and Glen, who had been painting the hull of the *Florine*. Glen had knocked on the Buttses' door on the way up and gathered up Dottie. It was a warm spring day, but I shook with cold. Ida put her arm around me. We gathered in the kitchen. "Sit down," she said. We all took chairs at the table. Bud sat next to me and Dottie took my other side, Glen next to her. Billy leaned against the wall behind the table. Bud took my hand and gave it a gentle squeeze. Billy said, "Let's have a prayer."

Healing phrases with "faith" and "forgiveness" in them bounced like buckshot throughout Billy's words, but I didn't hear most of what he had to say until "amen" came in strong at the end.

The room went quiet except for the blocks that Travis was banging together on the porch floor. Ida asked, "Do you want me to take the kids down to the house?"

I shook my head, but Bud said, "If you could, Ma, that might be best. We'll let you know what's going on when we know."

"Travis may have some kind of bug," I said, motherhood kicking in on automatic. "Arlee needs to change her dress before it gets dirty."

"No," Arlee said. I looked up, startled to find my little girl downstairs and standing in front of Billy. His hands rested on top of her head.

"You look some pretty," Dottie said to her.

"Don't encourage her," I said.

"I a princess," Arlee said.

"Come with Grammy, princess," Ida said to her. She grunted as she picked up Travis. "Good lord," she said, "Grammy isn't going to be able to do this much longer."

"I'll help," Dottie said. She took Travis from his grateful grandmother and they went out the door.

"I should make coffee," I said to the three men in my kitchen. "You'll have some coffee, won't you? Think Parker might like some?

It is getting later in the morning, so maybe everyone has had enough coffee for the day. He's going to tell me she's dead. I know he is. She's dead."

Bud caught me before I crumpled onto the floor and steered me back to the kitchen chair. I sat and covered my face with trembling hands. The front door opened and shut and Dottie came back in and sat down next to me. She rubbed my back with her big hand.

"Where's the Kleenex?" Bud asked. I pointed to the porch, near the bassinet that Travis had outgrown. As he got up to get it, someone knocked at the door. Billy answered. I pulled myself together as Bud handed me a tissue and sat down.

Parker stood in the kitchen doorway, his hat in his hand.

"Tell me straightaway, please," I said.

"Carlie's dead, Florine," Parker said. "I'm sorry."

My heart snapped and I squeezed my eyes shut. Bud and Dottie grabbed my hands.

"When did she die?" I asked Parker through the storm in my head.

"In 1963, in Crow's Nest Harbor. She's been dead since before Patty reported her missing."

I swallowed something sour. "How did she die?" I asked.

"Her neck was broken," Parker said. "She didn't feel a thing."

I went numb. "Who did it?" I asked.

"We have a suspect in custody," Parker said.

"Edward Barrington?"

"We have a suspect. Let me take you through this step by step."

"I have to go to the bathroom first," I said, and bolted upstairs. If anyone heard me upchucking everything I'd ever eaten going back through the past almost eleven years, no one ever let on. When I was done, I brushed my teeth, slapped water on my face, walked back downstairs, and sat down again. Dottie plunked a cup of hot tea in front of me and I put my hands around the mug. The warmth seeped into my palms.

"Okay," I said to Parker. "Tell us what happened."

"Did you read them letters Stella and her sister gave to you? Them letters from Edward to Carlie?"

"No. I didn't want to know what that suckass had to say to my mother."

"Well, I matched most of 'em up with the ones that Barrington's wife dropped off last winter.

"Carlie's letters to him are kind of like I remember her. Funny, light, pretty clever, about stuff she had going on in her life. She wrote about how much she missed him and told him she loved him. Up until she met Leeman, that is. The last letter she sent to him, in July 1950, she said that she loved Leeman and she hoped that Edward would be happy.

"Now, Barrington's letters are a different story. From the get-go, his letters are filled with how much he loves her and how he can't live without her. Later on, he talks more and more about what he's going to do to her when he sees her. Stuff that made even me blush, and I've heard it all. One letter says 'I Love You' for twenty pages. That letter was written in August 1950, when Carlie was eighteen and Barrington was twenty-two or three or thereabouts."

"Carlie and Daddy were together by that time," I said.

"Didn't seem to faze him. He was married and had a son on the way, but he wrote the twenty-page I Love You letter after his wedding. He also wrote Carlie a nasty letter, after he found out about Leeman. Says that she won't be happy with him, that he's just a fisherman. That she'll get bored and come back to him, and he was going to wait for that, no matter how long it took.

"His letters didn't stop with the letter telling her she'd be sorry she met Leeman. He kept on sending letters to her. Twisted stuff, like how he was better at sex than Leeman, and how he could make her happy that way. About how much money he had compared to Leeman. About how he'd seen you at The Point at Ray's with Dottie. Said he gave you both lollipops. The date on that letter tells me you and Dottie was about five."

Dottie and I squeezed each other's hands at the same time.

"Other stuff too. Says he watched Leeman and her in bed one night."

"Oh my god. Why didn't she turn him in?" I cried.

"Because she never read them letters. You saw how the envelopes were sealed shut. She didn't know he'd given you and Dottie candy, or he was pretty much stalking her."

"Then why did she keep them at all?" Bud asked.

"I can't say," Parker said.

"Maybe she knew something might happen to her," Dottie said.

"That's conjecture," Parker said. "May help build a case, but evidence seals them. She never read the letters, and she didn't turn them in, so I can't say why she kept them."

"Who killed her?" I said, hating those words. "That's all I want to know."

"We have a suspect . . ."

"You said that. Who the hell killed my mother?"

"Florine, take a deep breath," Billy said. "Parker will tell you."

"Thank you, Pastor," Parker said. "I don't know as you noticed, Florine, but none of them letters—except for the ones that Grace Drowns sent to you in different envelopes—has a postmark or a stamp. Barrington didn't want them going through the mail, so I wondered how he might have gotten them to Carlie. He could have left them in her car while she was at work, I suppose. Or he could have stopped by the Shack and made sure she got them that way.

"I went to the Shack when Carlie first disappeared and talked to everyone there. They was confused and scared, but they didn't know nothing. Cindi and Diane both said that, as far as they knew, Carlie always went home after her shifts. Edward didn't come up, because no one thought he might be involved. And of course Patty swore up and down she didn't know nothing.

"After I read the letters, I went back and I talked to Cindi about Barrington, about two weeks ago. She's the only one still there that knew all the players.

"She told me that Barrington's been coming to the Shack since he's been legal to drink. Spent a lot of time there over the years. Sits at the bar by himself. Cindi said that he came in when Carlie was working, and he came in when she wasn't there. Said Carlie acted the same around him as her other customers, friendly and nice. He talked to Patty a lot, Cindi said. Said she never thought much about it. Patty liked anyone who gave her good tips, and Edward was loaded.

"So, then I got to thinking about Patty," Parker said. "I asked Cindi if she knew where I could find her. Cindi gave me the address where she sent her last paycheck and I looked it up. Turns out her sister lives there, with Patty, who has emphysema and needs an oxygen tank. I asked Patty if she'd mind talking to me. Took a while, but finally she agreed. So, last week, I went to New Jersey to talk to her."

Parker shook his head. "I was shocked when I saw her. She's forty-two years old or thereabouts, but she looks to be about thirty years older. She couldn't even get up. She had to stop and catch her breath a lot when we was talking.

"She had a lot to say. She told me that she wanted to get it off her chest, that it might help her to breathe better. I asked her about the letters. She told me that Barrington used to slip the letters to her, along with a ten-dollar bill. She would sneak them into Carlie's car sometime during the shifts she and Carlie shared. She said that Barrington wouldn't do it because he had a reputation to protect and was afraid of being caught."

"Why would she do that?" I asked. "She and Carlie were friends."

"She liked the money," Parker said. "And she said she didn't see the harm. She admitted that she liked to stir things up. But when I asked her, she said she never told Barrington when she and Carlie were going to be in Crow's Nest Harbor. Patty figured out he was a creep when he showed up in the Harbor the first time."

"He could have asked anyone else at the restaurant where they'd gone without them becoming suspicious," Bud said.

Parker nodded. "That's probably what he did. Out of the nine years they went up to the Harbor, he showed up for five of them. They'd be walking through town and there he'd be. They'd go to a restaurant, and he'd waltz in and sit at the bar and watch them. Neither Patty nor Carlie wanted him around, but Patty told me they agreed that they'd be damned if they were going to let him ruin their good time and their special place, so they put up with him. They even made a game out of finding ways to avoid him.

"The summer Carlie disappeared, Patty told me that she came up with the idea that Carlie should bleach her hair blond and wear Patty's clothes, while she dyed her hair red and wore Carlie's clothes. They did it partly for laughs, and partly to confuse Barrington, should he show up."

"Why did they go to all that trouble?" I asked. "Why didn't Patty just come forward and tell someone she thought Edward was weird? For that matter, why didn't Carlie?"

"I don't know why Carlie didn't," Parker said. "Maybe she didn't think he was a threat. Maybe she thought she could work it out on her own. Maybe she didn't want the attention. But I know why Patty never came forward," Parker said. "She had her own issues. And Barrington found out what they were."

"What do you mean, her own issues?"

"Well, she liked to play around with young boys."

"What do you mean?" I said, not understanding.

"Oh my god," Glen groaned. I turned to him, surprised.

"What's wrong with you?" Dottie asked.

Glen put his face into his hands. "Oh my god," he said again.

"She messed around with you?" Parker said, softly, to his nephew.

As we all stared at Glen, I recalled the words he had said to me that day we'd talked in his tent in Grand's living room: *"What she said still messes up my head, along with everything else. She was smart. She was older than me. She was . . ."*

"Patty?" I said. "You were talking about Patty?"

It took him a while to answer, and during that time, I ran everything

I had thought about Patty through my head. Funny, sassy, flirty Patty. I had adored her and wanted to be like her. This was the same woman who had made my friend feel like shit? Had done things to him? Things that were wrong?

Glen took his hands away from his face and sat up straight. Dottie handed him a Kleenex and he blew his nose. "She did it to me," he said. "I was one of those boys."

"What she did was against the law," Parker said to his nephew. "Do you feel like talking about what happened?"

Glen wiped tears from his cheeks. "If it helps Florine, I will," he said.

"Take a deep breath," Billy said.

Glen did just that, and then he said, "I was ten. I used to ride my bike to the Shack. Ray'd give me money and tell me to go bug someone else for a while, so I'd pedal up the road for French fries and a Coke. One day, Patty was leaving the Shack to walk back to the cabin she lived in, and she asked if I wanted some homemade cookies. So, I followed her. When she brought the cookies out, she wasn't wearing nothing. I'd never seen a real naked woman before. She asked if I wanted to touch her boobies.

"I didn't know that we was doing something bad," he said. His face darkened to crimson. "She told me we wasn't hurting nobody, and she thought I was special. Later, she got mean. She'd touch me down there and laugh and tell me what a loser I was, that no one would ever love me. Then she told me to get lost, and if I said anything, she'd tell the police. She said, 'You know what rape is? I'll scream rape if you say a word.'"

We all sat in silence as Glen stared out at the sunny day, letting his tears run unchecked. No one had known. No one had even suspected. I thought about when Carlie had died. No one had known or suspected that either. My heart ached with the unfairness of it all. Bud squeezed my hand again.

Dottie got up and walked over to Glen. Dottie, who brushed off anything that got too sappy with her smart remarks. Dottie, who surprised all of us by bending over Glen's chair and wrapping her arms around him from the back to comfort him. She stood that way for a minute, and then she sat down again.

Bud cleared his throat. "I don't mean to make less of this than it is," he said to Parker. "And I can't believe the bitch did that to Glen. If I'd known, I would have strangled her with my bare hands. But what does that have to do with Carlie?"

Parker said, "Glen, I don't know as it will make you feel less alone, but you weren't the only boy Patty 'liked.' When I talked to her, she mentioned Andy Barrington."

Far off, from somewhere inside my head, an ocean began to roll forward.

Parker said, "He used to visit her 'for cookies' too. But when I talked to Patty last week, she said she had told him to bug off earlier that summer because he was getting rough with her. Said he was strong for his size. Told him she'd call me if she caught him hanging around. He stayed away for a while. But he knocked on her door the night before she and Carlie left for Crow's Nest Harbor that last night. She wouldn't let him in. Threatened him with me again, and he left. But somehow, he found out where they were going and he hitchhiked up. His family didn't know he had gone. No one watched the kid, really. They mostly noticed when he got in the way."

And then Andy's words floated through my memory: "*I was deflowered by a—uh—woman of experience, in New York City. Taught me to touch her where it mattered most.*" That woman, not from New York, but from New Jersey, had been Patty. I barely heard what Parker said next.

"Andy hung around their motel until he saw the person he thought was Patty walk into town. He stayed far enough away so that he couldn't really see her face. Just followed her by the color of her hair and her clothes. She came back along the cliff walk after that, and he followed her along the path."

Suddenly Parker stopped talking and laid a hand on my hand. "Florine," he said, "you all right?"

"Jesus, you're so pale," Bud said.

"Put your head down between your legs," Dottie said.

Bud got up and pulled my chair back. Dottie gently pushed my head down until it rested on my knees. My back whined, but the pain brought me back to myself. Hands patted my back, stroked my neck. I sat up.

Andy's desperate voice sounded in my head: *"I hope you will forgive me. . . . I mean it. . . . Sold my soul a long time ago."*

I had loved him. And he had killed my mother. And he knew what he had done every time he touched me or told me he loved me.

A voice that didn't sound like mine whispered, "How did he kill her?"

Parker held my eyes. "He thought he would jump her, scare her a little. Remember, he thought that she was Patty. Carlie was so shocked when he grabbed her that she fought him and during the struggle, Andy broke her neck."

I put my hands into my hair, grabbed it, and pulled. A wail burst from my throat: part grief, part rage. Bud and Dottie said soothing things that made no sense, but the sound of their voices eventually calmed me down.

Bud said to Parker, "What happened after that? What did he do with her?"

"Andy put her body into some thick bushes off the path and left for home. Edward Barrington *was* up there that day too, but he didn't see Carlie, or Patty, so he headed back to his place just after dark. He caught Andy hitchhiking by the side of the road. He was in rough shape. Barrington hammered at him until Andy told him what had happened. Edward could have gone to the police, but he didn't do it. He told me he didn't want Andy arrested. Didn't want the Barrington name dragged into it.

"Edward drove them back to where Andy had hidden Carlie's body. Somehow, they got her to the car without being seen and they drove south. They buried her near their cottage the next day."

"Where?" I said. Parker told me.

I cupped my face in my hands. In my place, my secret place, over by the pines on the other side of the clearing. My mother had been that close to me, for all that time.

"Her body is in Augusta," Parker said. "We needed to autopsy the body to be sure it was her first before we could tell you."

"I want to see her," I said.

"You think that's such a good idea?" Bud asked gently.

"I want to see her," I repeated, hitting the table with my fist. "She's my mother. I've been waiting for a long, long time for her to come home."

I didn't ask about what was going to happen to Andy or Edward. I didn't want either of those bastards to have the last word. My mother's body had been found and I could bring her home. That was what mattered.

Arlee's voice, singing a song I couldn't quite catch the words to, arched over us, high and sweet, from way down in Ida's yard.

"I bet she hasn't changed her dress," I said. I stood up. "I don't want her to get it dirty." I left the house. Arlee was down by the *Florine*, slapping a paintbrush onto the sanded hull. The ruined dress was covered with a shade the color of midnight.

"Hi, Mama," she said.

Ida ran out of the house. "Oh, my goodness," she said. "She was watching television not thirty seconds ago. I'm so sorry."

"That's okay," I said.

Ida saw me, then. "Oh, dear god," she said. "Is . . ."

I nodded. "I don't want to talk right now," I said.

Ida nodded. "I'll say a prayer," she murmured.

"Thank you," I said. She touched my arm and went inside.

Arlee pointed to a second paintbrush. "Help me, Mama," she said. I dipped it into the can and we painted the boat, together.

48

O f course, I still had questions, and after a sleepless night spent on the porch with my son in my arms, my husband snoring beside me in the next rocker, and Arlee asleep on the sofa, I called Parker again. Bud and I went to his office for this meeting. My body ached with sorrow, but I was calm.

"I'm confused," I said. "How did you find out that Andy had done it?"

Parker said, "After I got all those letters and I read them, I called Barrington. Told him I wanted to talk to him again. He wasn't as eager to do it as he had been before, but he said he would come up to the office. Andy was at the cottage with him. I keep an eye on Andy anyway. Deals drugs, but he's not the big pin. I was hoping he'd lead me to his supplier, but he's got bigger fish to fry now. Anyway, while Barrington was talking to me, Andy walked in. Said he was tired of the bullshit. Said he had killed Carlie, but that it was an accident. Edward tried to shut him up, but Andy told him to fuck off, that they should have done this long ago. I talked to Andy and he told me how things had happened. Then, I talked to Edward, and he finally broke down and admitted it. Said he hadn't wanted to turn his son in, no matter how things had happened."

"What about the purse?" I asked. "Carlie's purse was found by that pond near Blueberry Harbor. Why was it there?" The only clue to

Carlie's whereabouts had been the finding of her purse by a pond near Blueberry Harbor, one hour south of Crow's Nest Harbor, three and a half years after she had disappeared. Nothing further had ever come of it, but I had always wondered about it.

"Barrington said he got to drinking and had a lamebrain idea—his words, not mine—that if he moved it there and buried it, it would somehow break things up. Said he drove up the coast to the pond near Blueberry Harbor because it was the first place he saw that was off the road. It didn't hold any special meaning for him. Don't make sense, I know, but that's what he did."

"What happens to them now?" Bud asked.

"Well, Andy was a minor when he did it. Got to figure out the particulars of that. We'll let the law work it out. The crime took place in Crow's Nest Harbor, so what happens will happen up there. The Barringtons have called their lawyer."

"What happens to Patty?" I asked.

Parker frowned. "Nothing. Patty overdosed on painkillers. She's dead. I got the call when I was at your house yesterday."

We all paused, and then Bud said, "Probably best. It appears she fucked up a lot of people."

Parker pursed his lips but didn't say anything. I noticed how tired he looked. He said to me, "You sit tight and we'll see what happens with the Barrington boys. Although the chances of you sitting tight are slim to none, I imagine." He smiled at me.

We all stood up and I gave Parker a hug. I said, "You said you'd do it, and you did it. Thank you."

He coughed and said, "You're welcome."

Bud and I drove home in his pickup, holding hands across the front seat. When we got back to the house, Robin was there.

"How did you know?" I asked, holding her to me. "I didn't have time to call."

"Bud called me and I came right away," she said.

We sat at the kitchen table over coffee and tea while I blubbered

out my grief and confusion. "I loved Andy," I said. "How could he be
with me without . . . feeling anything? How could he act like nothing
had happened? What was in his head?"

"People compartmentalize things," Robin said. "They put traumas
in dark closets way back in their heads and they nail the door shut. The
problem is, they leak out somehow. Didn't you tell me once that he did
tons of drugs and never met a school he couldn't flunk out of? And he
had his father holding it over him too."

"He was scared shitless of Edward," I said.

"We should all be scared shitless of Edward," Robin said. "From
everything you've said about him, that guy has no heart. Or conscience. He's a textbook sociopath."

Travis, who had been napping in his crib upstairs, yelled, "Bup. Bup."

I said, "I'll get him." I climbed the stairs toward him, my heart
lifting at the thought of seeing my baby boy. My girl, who had ruined
her dress and salvaged my heart at the same time the day before, had
gone to work at the state park with Dottie for the morning. Ida would
care for her later that day, while Dottie, Bud, Robin, and I headed up
to Long Reach and the funeral home.

In the days to come, we would know more about Edward and
Andy's plights, and newspapers would pick up Carlie's story again
until they moved on to something else.

But at that moment, I filled my arms with my wriggling son.

"I forgot to ask you," Robin said as the four of us headed up to Long
Reach, "when we figure out when the memorial service is, would it be
okay if my family rented your dad's house for a couple of weeks? It
would be Dad, Ben, Valerie, and me."

The thought of having my mother's family, my family, being close
to us, and soon, perked up my heart and I said, of course, and welcome. "I'll have to get it ready," I said.

"Well," Robin said, "if you agree, I'd like to stay there until they get here, and then I can pack up my apartment and fly home with them. Maybe I can help you work on it."

"Sounds good," Bud said. "Keep Florine out of mischief."

"I'll give you a hand too," Dottie said.

"Okay," I said to Dottie. "You make the cookies and bring them with you."

"I ain't making nothing," she said. "But I'll help eat whatever's there."

The funeral director, Mr. Desmond, had a nice smile. He asked us to wait in the hall for a few minutes. He walked away, his shiny shoes making no sound on the thick rugs that led to somewhere in the back.

This was the same place we had come to when Sam had died. In the daytime, it looked different. Rich colors seeped through the rooms. Everything in the hallway was dark red. The carpets, the little flowers on the wallpaper, the runner coming down the dark, polished stairway. A clock ticked somewhere. The sound of a television or a radio barely reached my ears.

"They live here, you know," Dottie said. "You imagine?"

"Well," Robin pointed out. "Someone has to live here. Who would take care of the dead people? Who would receive them and stay with them?"

I grabbed her hand as Mr. Desmond walked back down the hall.

"Are you all going in?" Mr. Desmond said.

"No," I said. "Just me."

"You sure?" Bud and Robin said at the same time.

I nodded. Mr. Desmond took my arm. "She's in the sun room," he said quietly as we walked. "She's was buried in the ground for a long time," he said. "Please understand that. Time takes its toll on the body."

"I just want to be with her for a couple of minutes," I said, and then, through no thought on my part, I bent over double and began to howl. My heart chose that very moment to cleanse itself of years of worry, grief, hurt, and anger. Hurried footsteps thumped up the carpet to Mr. Desmond and me. Bud knelt beside me, took a clean white handkerchief out of his pocket, and wiped my face with it. After a couple of minutes, with his help, I stood upright again on shaky legs. "You don't have to do this," Bud said. "It will be okay with Carlie, I'm sure."

Mr. Desmond added, "It might be best if you remember her as she was."

I took a deep, shuddering breath. "Let's go," I said. I dug my fingernails into Bud's arm as we finished our walk up the hall.

When we reached the doorway, I blinked. I had wanted to view her body before having what remained of her cremated, but I had expected to view that body in a simple pine box. Instead, a rich mahogany casket lay on a maroon velvet platform in the middle of the bright sun porch, surrounded by bouquets of spring flowers.

I gasped. "What . . ."

"The casket is borrowed for the morning," Mr. Desmond said gently. "And the flowers are from your uncle—her brother, and his family. I thought it might be more pleasant for you to see her in the light, and to be able to look outside. After your viewing, we will proceed with the cremation, per your request."

"Thank you," I whispered.

"We have covered her body with a blanket," Mr. Desmond said. "If you would like the blanket removed, I can do that."

"No," I said. "I just want to see that it's her and that's she's somewhere that's not just in my head."

We walked forward and I dug my fingernails into Bud's hand. A crumbling skull rested on a blue velvet pillow. Thin bits of colorless hair still clung to it. A small gap between her two front teeth brought back her smile.

I shook as I let go of Bud's hand. "Can I be alone?" I asked.

"Of course," Mr. Desmond said.

"I'll be right outside the door," Bud said.

After they left, I stood until I stopped trembling. I took a deep breath, and let it out in tears that drenched what remained of Carlie's face. "I missed you, so much," I said. The light outside gave Carlie's skull an odd ivory sheen. I reached out my hand and touched it. It was cold and hard, not like my Carlie at all. But the bright spark that had occupied my mother lived on in the face of my daughter.

Cheery birdcalls came from outside, and I looked out into the backyard. Fat robins hopped on the lawn. A blue jay bossed its way among bright, light, young leaves. I lifted my hand from Carlie's skull.

Soft footsteps behind me stopped as Bud put an arm around me. We stood silent.

Bud cleared his throat. "You know, them bastards didn't win."

"What do you mean?" I said, wiping my face.

"Well, they may have buried her body and not told anyone about it until they got caught, but they'll have to live with it until they die. Carlie will be here a long time after they will. When they buried her, right away she became part of everything around her. She'll be here long after they rot in hell."

Tears trickled into my mouth and I tasted salt. "She's gone," I said. "But she's home. Welcome home, Carlie."

I leaned into the coffin and kissed her skull. Then my husband took my hand and we walked down the hallway.

49

We gathered on the little beach at the end of The Point at dusk on the second Sunday in June. Me, Bud, the kids, Ida and Maureen, Madeline, Bert, Dottie, Archer, my uncle Robert and his wife, Valerie, and my cousins, Robin and Ben. Ray and Glen were there and Parker and Tillie Clemmons stood off to the side together. Even Cindi, from the Lobster Shack, showed up per my invitation.

Torches stuck into the gravel and sand turned our faces into the flickering, bright-orange glow offered up by the insides of jack-o'-lanterns.

Glen knelt down by a big rocket containing a mix of firecracker powder and Carlie's ashes, and waited for our signal.

Billy and Maureen stood together facing us.

Maureen began to sing "Amazing Grace," and I swore that even the ever-flowing tide in the harbor paused to hear those beautiful sounds. Billy stood beside her, swaying, his eyes closed, listening to her sing. Something told me that in a few years, if all went well, they would be together.

As Maureen finished, an owl from somewhere across the harbor cracked open the twilight hush. "*Who?*" it demanded. "*Who?*" We laughed. I leaned against Bud and watched Arlee follow Travis as he wove an unsure, stubborn path through the little stones on the beach. He might fall, but he would pick himself right back up and go on. That was his way. And she would always watch him, because that was her way.

Billy said, "I have only a very few words to say, because Carlie, like her daughter, didn't like sermons. She relied on what her heart told her, and she had a good heart. My father and I went into the Lobster Shack once, after we'd been fishing, and she was running around waiting on people, carrying plates, smiling, twirling around to dodge anyone who got in her way. I was about fifteen and I couldn't take my eyes off her. She was like the light itself, flitting around the room. She was a woman who danced through life. And I admired that. What happened to stop that dance will never diminish the woman she was, nor should it. She was a beautiful soul who served the lord as a wife, a mother, a friend, a sister, and an aunt. She was a free spirit, and that spirit lives on in Florine and in her children. Carlie never came to church, but I'm sure that Jesus was with her always. How could he not be, when she was so much fun? There is no doubt in my mind that they knew each other well.

"I'll finish up with a couple of lines from Revelations: *'He will wipe away every tear from their eyes, and death shall be no more, neither shall there be mourning, nor crying, nor pain anymore, for the former things have passed away.'*

"I would also like to add a few lines from a poem by William Butler Yeats, an Irish poet, because as her brother, Robert, whom we are blessed to have here with us today, has reminded us, Carlie would have loved these lines. The poem is called 'The Fiddler of Dooney,' and these are the two last verses:

> *For the good are always the merry,*
> *Save by an evil chance,*
> *And the merry love the fiddle*
> *And the merry love to dance;*
>
> *And when the folk there spy me,*
> *They will all come up to me,*
> *With, 'Here is the fiddler of Dooney!'*
> *And dance like a wave of the sea."*

I listened to the hushed water in the harbor whisper against the shore, and just as I almost caught what it was saying, my uncle Robert took my hand into his own sturdy one. He was tall and shy, unlike his sister, and dark, with curly hair. I saw her in the freckles on his face and in the laughter in his eyes. Arlee, who was hanging on to his leg, adored him, her aunt Valerie, and her cousin Ben.

Travis tugged at me to be picked up. I let go of Robert's hand and hoisted him into my arms. Bud pulled me closer.

Glen, still kneeling by the rocket, cleared his throat, and I nodded to him. He struck a match, lit the fuse, and we all stepped as far back as we could go without falling into the beach-rose bushes. Sparks traveled up the length of the fuse and the rocket took off, streaking into the dark purple of the summer night. It exploded into a swirl of brilliant colors and scattered Carlie's ashes all over creation.

50

Evie Butts came to see me one morning shortly after Carlie's memorial service. She strolled into the house without knocking while I was feeding the kids breakfast.

"Thought I'd come say hello," she said. "I'm living at home now."

"You moved back?" I said. "What about Albert?"

"Right. Albert. He's gone. I'm here, for now," she said.

She looked worn down. She would always be one of the prettiest girls in the room, but something old clung to her face, though she was only seventeen years old. She sat down at the kitchen table, folded her hands, and watched Travis munch down cornflakes.

"He's big, isn't he, for his age?" she asked.

"Daddy was a big guy," I said. "Travis will be as big as he was, if not bigger."

"Want to play dolls?" Arlee asked Evie.

"Not right now," Evie said.

"I color good," Arlee said. "Want to see?"

"Sure," Evie said.

Arlee ran upstairs. "Be careful," I called.

Evie raked her fingers through her dark curls.

"I love your hair," I said to her.

"It's a pain in the ass," Evie said. "I wish it was straight, like Cher's."

"I loved my mother's hair. It was bright red, like Arlee's. Mine is kind of butterscotch with a little bit of pink in it. It's just strange."

"I'm sorry about your mother," Evie said. "I'm sorry she's dead."

"Thanks," I said.

"You been through some things," Evie said.

"So have you."

"I guess. How did you know what to do to make it all right?"

"What do you mean?"

Evie twisted her hands around each other. They were small compared to Dottie's fists. "Well, you got a guy and you got pretty babies and a nice house."

I laughed. "You think I planned this? No way. It all happened on the way to somewhere else."

"Where was somewhere else?"

"I don't have a clue. Just somewhere. I was going to show everybody."

"What?"

"Hell if I know. I was mad at everybody."

"I am too. They all drive me crazy."

"They do. But sometimes it's good crazy."

"I don't know how it's going to turn out for me. I got this kid I don't know what to do with. Somehow, I got to figure out how to raise him."

"You have help."

"Yes. But I don't know as I love him like I'm supposed to. Did you love your kids from the start?"

"Yes, I did," I said. "And I love them more every day. They drive me nuts, but I'd kill anyone who tried to hurt them."

"When I had Archer, I just looked at him and waited to feel something, but I didn't. It freaked me out. I felt bad about that. And now, every time I look at him, I remember that, and it still freaks me out."

"You had a hard time having him," I said. "That probably had something to do with it. With Arlee, I felt a flood of love. But I had a C-section with Travis, and I felt fuzzy for a while. Every time feels different, I imagine."

Evie picked at her fingernails. "Seems like I do stuff all wrong and it don't even matter to me that I'm doing it wrong. I just"—she shrugged—"do it."

"I used to be like that. I didn't care what I did. I didn't care that I didn't care."

"Me too, but I don't want to do that anymore. I don't want to be like that."

Arlee carried three coloring books over to Evie and plunked them on the table in front of her. "Crayons," she said. She ran back upstairs to her room.

"If you stick around, you'll get to know Archer," I said. "Madeline, Bert, and Dottie know him better, because they've been raising him."

"I don't know. I guess I'll see if that works," Evie said.

Travis threw a wet cornflake and hit her in the face. "Hah!" he crowed.

"Ewww," Evie said, and Travis laughed.

Evie's mouth quirked a little bit. "Ewww," she said again.

Travis laughed harder. She smiled more.

He threw more cornflakes, she said, "Ewww," and they laughed until Arlee came downstairs carrying her little treasure box in her arms.

"I thought you were going to bring down some crayons," I said.

"Evie," Arlee said, ignoring me, "want to see inside?"

"Okay," Evie said. "Hit me."

Arlee looked confused. "No."

"It's something people say," Evie said. "I would love to see what's inside that box."

Arlee opened it up and pulled out her shells and flowers and a new blue jay's feather I hadn't seen. While Evie was admiring them, Arlee pulled something else out and held it behind her back.

"Guess," she said to Evie.

"I don't know," Evie said. "Give me a hint."

"A hole in it," Arlee said.

"Is it a doughnut?"

Arlee rolled her eyes. "No."

"Give me another hint."

"Yellow."

Evie shook her head. "Is it an egg yolk?"

"An egg yolk?" I said. "Really?"

Evie shrugged. "I don't know. Tell me."

Arlee brought her closed fist around to the front and opened it slowly.

It was Bud's wedding ring.

"Oh," I said. "Daddy would love to see that. He's been missing it."

Arlee closed her fist around it. "Mine."

"Sometimes people drop things by mistake, Arlee. When I married Daddy, I gave him that ring. It's his, forever. Like you are. His, forever."

"Maybe you can make a trade for something else," Evie said.

"Okay. Ice cream," Arlee said.

"Sounds good to me," Evie said. "I have to go soon."

"Stay for a while," I said. "Have a cup of tea."

"I drink coffee," Evie said.

"I have that too."

"Okay," Evie said. "Then I need to go home to see Archer."

"Bring him by, anytime," I said, heading for the stove. "The door's always open."

Epilogue

Bud and I went out on the *Florine*, today. Glen captained her, as he bought her a few years ago. I asked him once why he hadn't changed her name.

He told me, "She's tough, she treats you right if you do the same to her, she's reliable, she's got heart, and she's got great lines. Can't think of any other name that would suit her."

Since we were taking the day off, I made sure to leave the store in good hands. Arlee was at the register and Madeline was in charge of the gallery, crafts, and gift area. Arlee grumbled about working. I'm sure she would rather have been up in Long Reach with her gang of three best friends. She's twelve, the same age I was when I lost Carlie. She's as tall as I am now, and a handful.

"You get the child you deserve," Ida told me once, but she winked as she said it.

Travis was gardening when we left. He's been crazy about it since he stuck his first shovel into the dirt. Much of The Point is covered with flowerbeds and shrubs, bushes, and trees. He's only ten years old, but he works with gardeners from the surrounding areas to help care for other gardens, including the one owned by the people who bought the Barrington place.

It's been nine years since the summer we found out who killed my mother. Edward Barrington died of a heart attack before he and Andy came to trial. Andy was charged with second-degree manslaughter and served four years, which was way too short a time in my estimation. I talked with Billy about the unfairness of that. "He has to live with his crime for the rest of his life," Billy said. "It will affect everything he does. He'll never get away from that fact. You need to forgive him so you won't hold it in your heart forever. That's how you'll get even."

I've said the words several times. Someday, maybe, I'll be able to mean them.

Tourists come to Grand's General Store because, evidently, it makes "destination" lists in magazines. After they stop in, they walk down the hill through flower-lined paths Travis has created to protect our privacy. They wind up on the wharf and buy fresh lobsters, crabmeat, and clams at Leeman's Little Lobster Shack from whoever is around. Billy, Bert, and Bud built it together about three years ago. On their way up the hill, tourists pause again to take in the beauty of the gardens tumbling down to the sea, and of the houses still standing sturdy in their stubborn way.

"This is such a beautiful place," they always tell me. "Just beautiful."

I always smile and agree, knowing that if they ever showed up in January, they would sing a different tune.

Ray sold Madeline Butts and me the store just two years ago. She and I run the place. Ray and Ida retired to Florida. I was surprised, first by their almost invisible romance, and then because Ida was so eager to leave and become a snowbird.

"God's everywhere," she said. "Warm weather is a wonderful thing." Ray just goes along with whatever she says. He traded his wisecracks for a wise woman. Ida makes and sends quilts up to the store. Many of them have won prizes and she has quite a reputation.

The gallery was Madeline's idea. Billy and Bud gutted the upstairs and put large windows in to catch and reflect the light. Madeline hangs her paintings upstairs, along with art from artists living in the surrounding community. My knitting is upstairs, along with hand-dyed weavings and pottery created by an aging commune of hippies down the road. We're always looking for new work. We both have to approve it, although I let Madeline have the final say. She knows art better than I ever could. Bread and knitting. That's all I have time for besides Bud and the kids.

It's enough. Bud and I had a couple of years where we both ran hither and yon trying to catch up with ourselves, but it evened out in the end. Bud has remained sober, and I'm so proud of him for that. I love him more every day. We've been on a few vacations—once to Hawaii, twice to Florida, and once to California to visit Robin and her husband, and to see my uncle Robert and aunt Valerie. We are planning more vacations, most of them together, but once in a while apart.

Today, at about noon, Bud and I boarded the *Florine*, along with Glen and his girlfriend, Mooney, a dark-haired, dark-eyed woman of few words but many smiles. He found her up north, is all he'll say, and she obviously adores him.

Dottie was late, because Archer's baseball game went into extra innings. Dottie and Archer come down to The Point as much as they can. They live in Falmouth, where Dottie is the athletic director for the school system there. She's still single and she still bowls better than most people. She has many fans. Dottie's never officially adopted Archer, but he spends most of his time with her and he goes to school in Falmouth while she works. He's spoiled as hell, but happy nevertheless.

Evie seems okay with this arrangement. She's still a wild girl and sings in a rock band based out of Long Reach. She and Archer are more like brother and sister than mother and son. Evie still lives with her parents, when she's not living with someone else.

"What can I do?" Madeline says. "I keep her room ready."

We all hope she settles down, but that isn't up to us. All we can do is love her.

When Dottie finally showed up, we chugged out of the harbor on a fine, sunny day in July weather that reminded me of another fine July day so many years ago.

On that day, my father died of broken heart on the deck of the *Florine*. Today, the waves tried to sass the *Florine*, tried to boss her around, but she rolled with every swell like the determined lady she is. She took us out to Beaver Island, which is remote and private. Bud and Billy have done carpentry work out there, and the owner has given them permission to picnic, swim, whatever, if no one is home.

Glen anchored the boat off the beach and the five of us jumped or dove off her and swam to shore, where we stretched out on the little beach and got sunburned. We told stories, old stories about people we know or knew, stories about crazy things we did and about how those things shaped us. We talked about our kids. Glen and Mooney made an announcement. They're going to be parents, they told us, and we all got up and whooped and hollered for joy for them.

We hiked to a spot on the island that overlooks a granite rock left behind by the glacier that shaped Maine millions of years ago. Someone hung a rope swing there and we took turns swinging out over the water, letting go, and living in a moment of terror before letting the water welcome us in.

We boarded the *Florine* about two hours later and ate our lunches on deck. We did some more talking, but all of us are older than we used to be, and a little more tired. I was feeling the pull of the store. Bud was probably thinking about a cabinet he's making in Daddy's workshop for a summer visitor across the harbor. Glen and Mooney sat close together, already changed by what was coming. Dottie's thoughts are never far from Archer. So, stunned by the sun and by time passing, we headed back.

It was late afternoon when we arrived back to The Point. We walked up from the wharf and past Ida's old house, now occupied by Billy and Maureen Krum. We were quiet as we passed. Billy is going through a rough patch with his cancer, and we all hope the best for them. Maureen is a full-blown minister now. She is the official voice of the church up the road.

A young couple with two small kids are renting Daddy's house for the summer. I love the noise of the screen door slamming and the lights streaming from the windows long after dark. It was a sad house for so long. Maggie, the wife, tells me she sometimes senses a presence. I smile, but I say nothing. I know the ghost inside is friendly, and she loves people. She always did.

Bud surprised me tonight. After supper, Arlee, Travis, and Archer headed off for adventures in the night, like the ones we used to have, only hopefully not as dangerous or destructive. Instead of sitting down in front of the television as we usually do, Bud suggested we go outside. We sat side by side in the Adirondack chairs and looked up at the underbelly of the falling night.

"Damn fine day," Bud said.

I nodded and smiled, cracking the dried seawater on my face. My hair was caked with salt and my body itched with sunburn. If anyone were to ask me the best feeling in the world, I would answer: this one. The one when I've been out in the sun on a summer day, and I'm content to not stray too far from the second I'm living in.

"Dance with me," Bud said.

I love him for many reasons, not the least of which is he can still surprise me.

"You don't like to dance," I said. "When have we danced, except at our wedding?"

"We're going to dance now, if you can get off your ass," he said.

"I can do that," I said. "Come and get me."

He got up from the chair and held out his hands. He pulled me onto the side lawn and I put my arms around his neck. He held me close and we danced in the dark on a lush lawn fragrant with lilies and roses, watched from above by a vast collection of stars, and by whatever souls might be passing by, headed for their own idea of heaven.

Acknowledgments

I owe this one to Karl Krueger in large part. You are the best. New England booksellers are blessed to have you as their fierce and enthusiastic advocate. I also thank Rachel Bressler and Clare Ferraro, who believed in this book as well as in *Red Ruby Heart in a Cold Blue Sea*. To Kate Napolitano, my wonderful editor, I am so very grateful to you. You've been a joy to work with. Gail Hochman, my indomitable agent, and Marianne Merola, literary agent extraordinaire, have supported my work from the beginning and have taken me to places I never imagined I would go in my wildest dreams. And, believe me, I've had some wild dreams.

To the Bearlodge Writers group in Sundance, Wyoming: What would I have done without all of you? You held me together, you made me laugh, and you made me feel like I could have been a cowgirl. There is no higher compliment than that. Pat, Jeannie, Katie, Andi, Connie, Carol, Jim, Jytte, Maureen, Amanda, Kathryn, Kathy, Brittany, and everyone else involved with the group, so many good times at table. Love also to Manning, Dale, Meg, John, Angie, and Michael. I miss you all. I will be back.

This is a book about the joys and struggles of a relationship and sticking together through all of it, good and bad. I thanked some of my women friends for their amazing support during the time I was writing

Red Ruby Heart in a Cold Blue Sea. For this round of acknowledgments, I want to say how grateful I am to know the partners who have been there for my favorite people through thick and thin. Paul Brown, Allen Gaul, Christopher Horton, and John Paige, you all set such loving standards. My brother, Mick Rogers, and my brother-in-law, Derek Leopin, also shine as fathers and spouses. John Beebe and Joe Lombardo, you are fine, fine men. David "Beaver" Bourget, you truly were The Point's red ruby heart in a cold blue sea. We will hold you dear, forever.

To the kids I like to think I helped raise in some small way: Thanks for the lessons in patience, humor, astonishment, and love. Molly, Casey, Krista, Danica, Jaime, Tommy, Brian, Michael, Rachel, Emily, Anna, Alessandro, Ray, Shannon, Mary, Celeste, Michael, James, Jeremy, Tim, Emma, Willa, Ian, David, and Bonnie—I'm so proud of you. You all humble me. Some of you are beginning your lives as parents and it is such a joy to watch the circle continue, unbroken. To the B-man—you are a hoot. Can't wait for your next chapters.

My parents, Warren (Smudge) Rogers and Frances Callan Rogers, were high-school sweethearts. They married in December 1950 and celebrated their sixty-sixth anniversary at the time this book was being published. In their quiet way, they managed to raise four children who turned out "pretty decent" as my Dad would put it. During a dance at a wedding, a deejay asked them how they had managed to stay married for so long. "Just be good to each other," my father said. Good advice.

Readers, thank you for embracing Florine and Bud's world and for cheering them on. Love who you love with everything you have and just be good to each other.